MARKED BY Sin

SHANNA SWENSON

Every Sin begins with a Secret.

Marked by Sin
Shanna Swenson

Marked by Sin is an original work of fiction. Names, characters, places, organizations and incidents either are the product of the author's imagination or are used fictitiously. Any resemblance to actual persons, living or dead, events, businesses, companies, or locales is entirely coincidental.

Copyright © 2020 by Shanna Swenson

Paperback ISBN: 978-1-7329626-9-9

www.shannaswenson.com

Editing by: Jennifer Soucy
Cover Design by: Cara Wade
Formatting by: Shanna Swenson

FOREWORD

Marked by Sin is book 4 in the Sin and Secrets collection. These books are intended to be read in order, starting with *Delivered in Sin*: Book 1 by Nicole Rodrigues.

It is *highly* recommended that you read the prequel novella, *RISE*, as it is a precursor to the events in this book.

This dark romance is intended for a **mature**, adult audience (18+). This novel contains scenes and topics that may be triggers for some, including (but not limited to) sexual assault, abuse, murder, bondage, and kidnapping.

READER DISCRETION IS ADVISED.

To all those who suffer in silence...
This one is for you!

INTRODUCTION
EDEN

TEN YEARS AGO...

"Ok, don't freak... just hear me out, ok?" I say to my sisters as my eyes take in the destruction of the strip club that was my Hell on earth, *The Devil's Playground*. A brilliant idea just came to me, one that takes my mind off the horrors I just witnessed firsthand and will need serious therapy for, I'm sure. Now my mind is running a million miles a minute at the possibilities, or maybe it's just the adrenaline still coursing through my veins. "We should take all this money and open our *own* club."

There's *so* much money, Marco had said. And now it's ours. Oh, the possibilities...

The Devil who raped, tormented, and punished me on a daily basis is finally gone, as well as my beloved Marco. I'm shocked, saddened, and relieved all at once, but I have to focus now on myself and my sisters. We aren't safe, not yet.

"What?" The shock in Magnolia's tone is evident. "Eden, we just...how... Why would you wanna do that?"

"It doesn't have to be anything like Vince's place. It can be...different." So different. Because as fucked up as it sounds, I've been a masked stripper so long that I don't think I can really "be" anything else. If I don't have this, what do I have? Of course I'm going to college to work on my undergrad, then eventually to get my Masters in Library Science, but that will take time.

"Different how?" Lia asks, looking at Addison and Everleigh; they look like I've slapped them.

"However we want." I shrug. "It'll be ours. Ours to run, as equal owners. A place where we can have our freedom, a safe haven for little birdies like we were." Yes, a safe haven for girls who've been used and abused like me and Lia, a venue for single mothers to make money to raise their children, a stepping stone for women who need a reliable paycheck...

Not to mention, a perfect place for you to hide, Eden, my subconscious says; my alter-ego who's found her voice amid the death of a stage performer's shell. Roxie, I call her.

Nothing makes me feel more alive than being on that stage, dancing my heart out. Men never touched me, anyway. Vince didn't allow it. I was *his* little dove, caged, safe until the music stopped. Which makes this an even better idea...

"We don't have to strip if we don't wanna," Lia blurts out. I can see the wheels turning in her head. "And we don't have to...we don't have to do *anything* with any of the men if we don't wanna, either."

I slowly nod. "Exactly." The once powerless girls can now have all the power. "It would be completely up to us what we do and who we do it with or not at all. *We* control everything. *No one* can *make us* do anything ever again."

PROLOGUE
EDEN

I sigh as I get out of my monster of a truck that morning. It's been ten years. Ten long, bittersweet years without him.

Marco.

My rock.

My first love.

My dark knight.

The emptiness I felt following his death still hasn't left me, and hits me especially hard today, the anniversary of that awful day. The day he sacrificed himself for me. The day he destroyed my enemy. The day we burned down *The Devil's Playground*. The day the caged birdies flew free from their bonds.

The vivid memories of that night come barreling into me this morning as I remember the pit that swallowed me whole, the vortex of emotion once I realized what Marco planned to do to free me. What he'd meant when he said Cordelia had to die, for it was him who had to die beside her in order to save me from the Devil himself.

Even then...we still weren't safe—*aren't* safe! It was a false sense of security because there are still people we're hiding from, which is why we founded RISE in the first place.

I can't help the smile that crosses my lips as I look up at the four-sided brick building that has been my escape these last many years—my library, Walters Regional Library, where I work as the library manager.

My sisters and I have only grown closer as time marches on, we've been through so much and seeing them all happy with men that love them as much as we sisters love each other makes all the suffering and heartache seem worth it.

Almost as if reading my thoughts, my phone buzzes with text messages.

Lia: *I love you, I'm here if you wanna talk.*

Ev: *Stay strong, you bad-ass phoenix.*

Then my phone rings and I answer it, smiling as I see that Addy's calling me.

I answer with, "Hey, lady."

"You doing ok today, sis?" Addison's soft voice asks me.

"I'm hanging in there."

"I know today's gonna be a tough one for you. You working?"

"Yeah, you?" I thought about taking the day off, but what else would I do? Wallow in a pint of Ben & Jerry's while watching *The Notebook*? Been there, done that. Not today.

"Me too. We have a meeting I'm not looking forward to."

"Man, I'm sorry."

"Don't be. At least I have a good view. Hot boss and all." She giggles.

I can't help but grin. Her "hot boss" is Ethan Freeman, who also happens to be her boyfriend. "Well, don't work too hard, girl. Thanks for checking in on me. I'll see you later tonight." I hang up the phone.

Crap! I see Samantha Zeller, AKA up-and-coming fantasy author Sam D. Zeller, standing at the door to the library. "Oh, jeez, I apologize."

I forgot today is her talk here and I'm running unusually late this Thursday morning.

"No worries," she states as I move to the door and unlock it.

I hurry to flip the lights on and throw my bag surreptitiously on the counter, then turn to her and extend my hand.

"It's a pleasure to finally meet you, Ms. Zeller. I'm Eden Riser. I'm a big fan of yours."

"Oh, really?" Samantha asks, surprised. "I'm flattered, truly. Thanks so much for having me here today."

She's lovely, brown hair and blue eyes, clad in a gray dress suit with a cream silk blouse and red pumps.

"Of course. The library loves to support its local authors." I give her a big smile and she returns it.

"Well, it means a lot to an indie like myself. Every avenue helps."

"Where do you want these, Sam?" comes a rough voice, and as I look up to the face behind it, I freeze.

Callan Manning stands there, his big, tattooed biceps holding an overflowing box of books. He's as gorgeous as he was the last time I saw him, the night of the charity ball I went to with Addy and Ethan—and Cal as my date. In person, he's larger than life, as entrancing as he is on every book cover I've ever seen him—and his Instagram page that I stalk like a fat kid drooling over cake. His brown hair is close cut, spiked with some gel, his jaw is thickly bearded and his tight navy polo and denim jeans fit like a glove. But it's his sparkling blue eyes that hold me captive. My heart is hammering in my chest, and I feel my jaw drop as they suddenly take me in.

That night comes rushing back to me. God, it's been over a year ago but I remember it like it was yesterday. Dancing, dining, and laughing with him. Him holding me close, the feel of that solid body firm against my own. Gah, I felt like Cinderella and he was a perfect gentleman, walking me back to Addison's—and, unknowingly, my own—apartment complex and kissing the back of my hand. That night I was "Roxanne," some random, masked companion. Simply an alluring arm toy for a man like him. He'd not asked to take me "home," and I hadn't invited him to for a few reasons: one being my fear of intimacy; but the main being that I didn't wanna burst that perfect bubble I was floating in that night, even if I'm positive Ethan demanded Cal behave himself, come hell or high water.

"Hey there," Cal says, and I'm completely speechless. I know I'm totally fangirling right now, but I can't help myself. I'm still completely smitten with this gorgeous stud of a man, who despite his image on Sam's cover, surprises me with his presence here today.

"Ms. Riser," Samantha says and turns towards me.

"Oh, umm..." *Shit, get a grip on yourself, Eden.* "Right this way."

I turn, tearing my eyes from Callan's enticing tall, broad frame.

I hear his heavy footfalls behind me as I lead him down the hallway and open another door with a key, walking in and throwing on the switch as I blushingly show him a table and podium that's set up for the talk.

"Right here, Mr. Manning."

He smirks, unsurprised that I know who he is—as if I couldn't.

"Call me Cal," he says and extends his hand after he's set the box down, making it look feather light.

"Eden." I take his hand gently, feeling my heart leap into my throat as his big palm interlocks with mine. Funny, it did the same thing the night of the ball.

"Wow, that's a beautiful name."

"Thank you." *And you're a beautiful man.*

"Cal," I hear Samantha say, coming through the door. I drop Callan's hand like it's a hot plate and look at Samantha. "I see you've met my brother," she says to me with a smile. "Cal, I'm gonna go grab Caleb and Sally."

Callan nods at her and gives me another crooked smile. I swear to God my panties are soaked now. I've forgotten that he's a walking, talking orgasm. "So, you recognized my biceps." His voice drops, laced with superiority, and *Poof!* My bubble bursts just as quickly as it encased me.

Now I remember why I hate men—all conniving, manipulative men—with a passion as heated as a hot July day here in Atlanta, Georgia. My smile fades and my logical, sarcastic self takes over; my invisible mask suddenly covers my face, hiding me well.

"I recognized your eyes," I retort and turn on my heel. "If you'll excuse me, I need to get the library ready for the morning. Feel free to set up as you wish, and let me know if you need anything."

"Sorry, didn't realize you were a lesbian," he mumbles under his breath.

"Excuse me?" I whip around, my brows furrowed.

"You heard me," he smarts.

"I'm not even going to *dignify* that with an answer."

"Ok, whatever."

I roll my eyes. "Are you always so incorrigible?"

"I don't even know what that word means." He leans back against the table and props his hips there, looking far too comfortable in his skin, despite that he's just confessed he's not the most intelligent man in the world—not that he has to be, with a face and body like that.

"Sounds like you need to spend more time in the library then, Mr. Manning," I sass.

"Sounds like *you* need to spend more time under a real man." He raises a brow, and I close my eyes in annoyance and walk off.

After clocking in, I toss my new brown leather Michael Kors purse into its usual hiding spot, then turn on the computers, still steaming from his comments. I hear the automatic doors open and look up to see the cutest little boy, along with Samantha and an elderly woman, coming toward me in a power wheelchair. He favors Callan, and immediately I wonder if this child is his. He gives me a bright beaming smile, and I melt right in my chair. I stand and return it, speaking first. "Well, hello there, handsome."

He lets out a small wail, in an attempt to communicate, that sweet smile returning and my heart feels like it might just explode with emotion for this precious, physically disabled child with an innocence as endearing as his smile.

"This is my son, Caleb," Samantha states as they stop in front of the counter.

"Hi, Caleb. I'm Eden. It's good to meet you. Are you a big fan of books?" I ask.

"Oh, he *loves* books. Especially when we do the voices," says the white-haired lady who comes to a stop behind him. She gives me a warm smile. "I'm Sally."

"Eden. Welcome to Walters Regional Library. Please, come in and get cozy."

Sally's smile widens, and I'm at ease with these people...until I hear Callan's voice.

"Sis, where the hell do you want this banner set up?"

"Callan, *language!* You aren't a child. I shouldn't have to tell you these things," Samantha grumbles and walks toward the conference room.

I shake my head. *What an imbecile*. I should have known!

Callan Manning is the face of Samantha's book covers and —who am I kidding—the body, too. Her latest book is a gorgeous fantasy novel entitled *Made for Glory* with Callan, face covered by a spartan-type helmet, his huge biceps thrusting a massive sword into the mud, clad in only a cloth that drapes around his hips to cover his man-parts. His eyes pierce one's soul as the blue orbs stare back at you. A vibrant lightning bolt strikes in the background.

I've stared at this cover far too many times, entranced by those eyes, and overcome with lust for that big, muscled body of his. To say I'm obsessed is an understatement. I check his social media pages every single day, multiple times a day. It's pathetic, I know, but after the pure hell my uncle put me through on a daily basis for years, I'm fucked up. Possibly beyond all repair. Although men are now my play-things and I want nothing more than to control them—and I *do* in my club —I still enjoy the male physique and lust after it. And a face, eyes, and body like Callan Manning's are easy to get overcome by.

I try to shake my disappointment away; I had this image in my head of how great he was in person. I mean, he *was* great in person—last time I met him. I couldn't have asked for a more charming prince charming but this guy... Well, needless to say, that sparkling image is gone, and my stomach burns sourly with annoyance, disillusionment, and pain. He's just like every other man I've ever known since Marco; he's not special at all.

Sounds like I need to send out an invitation to my club so I can break him down at the knees. Hmm... Roxie's *exactly* what a man like Callan Manning needs.

Callan

Damn, the librarian is a smoking hot fox. Tall, curves that go on for days, and plump, red lips that I imagine wrapped around my big johnson.

I give her a wink as I place Sam's books back into the box, then lick my lips as she pushes her glasses back up her nose. I entertain a fantasy of fucking her right here on this desk with *only* those sexy red frames on. It would be so easy to spread those long legs and jerk that clip from her hair. Man, if I'm not sporting a boner in a library. There's something so taboo about that.

Sheesh, get a grip, Manning, I tell myself, but there's something so familiar about her. I feel like I know her. I've seen her before... That voice, I know I've heard its pitch somewhere prior to today.

I ponder as I haul the final box back to my truck, then turn to head back inside to see what else my sister needs help with, only to stop as she and the librarian are exiting the front doors.

"Thank you so much, Ms. Riser. It was truly a pleasure."

"Just Eden, please. The pleasure is all mine, I assure you, Samantha."

Eden. Wow, that name is so sexy, like her. I grin as she shakes Sam's hand.

Caleb and Sally went on back home after about an hour. He got his books and was good to go, plus Sally had promised Caleb ice cream, so he was eager for that.

I take a bag from Sam and pull it to my shoulder, watching the librarian lock up for the day. I can't believe we closed it down, but Sam had lots of visitors; despite that it was a success, I can see she's exhausted.

"I look forward to seeing you soon," Eden says.

"Likewise. I'll be in touch." Sam waves and approaches me.

"Good to meet you, Eden," I say and give her a nod. Her lips pucker and her brow raises, but I get no verbal response. *Good going, ass-wipe, she hates you.*

Then I stop dead in my tracks as I watch her walking to my right, to a brand-new, jacked-up, blacked-out GMC Sierra. No fucking way that's hers... Is it?

"Uh, Eden?" I ask because I just can't help myself. I gotta know... "That your truck?"

The devilish smirk on her gorgeous face is a stark contrast to her heavenly name. "Sure is."

Well, stuff my ass and call me a turkey! I'll be damned. I know I'm gaping, but I'm utterly stupefied, and as this sexy dame hops up on the nerf bar and opens the truck door, I'm drooling all over myself.

"That is one sexy as *fuck* vehicle, m'lady."

She has the nerve to grin and winks as she says, "Eat your heart out, stud."

By God, I think I just met the woman I want to marry.

1
CALLAN

I called up Ethan Freeman two nights after Sam's event at the library. He's my old buddy from high school. It's been a good *year* since we've hung out; the last few times I've been back in town, something's come up and we've not been able to do so. I was glad when he answered on the third ring with, "Fuckin' Manning, how the hell are you, brother?"

"Good, good. What you up to?"

We laughed and caught up quickly. He, once again, avoided my questions regarding the mysterious Roxanne, whom I've asked about several times since our night at the ball. Eth just says, "Oh, she's fine," "I don't know what she's up to," or changes the subject altogether. Apparently, she's dropped off the face of the planet—or Ethan is trying to hide her identity which is cool, I guess. I just know that we had a great night together, and I wouldn't mind taking her out just the two of us.

"Planning a proposal soon," he admitted with a deep inhale. He was dead serious too.

I can't believe the asshole is talking engagement. I'm the last bachelor around, it would seem. At thirty-three, I've seen all our pals on Facebook with wedding photos and kids and, I won't lie, I'm a little jealous. I mean—don't get me wrong—this bachelor has enjoyed the *hell* out of being single and in the prime of his life. I'm a freaking model, for God's sake. I have pussy coming at me twenty-four-fucking-seven, and I'm not complaining. But there's a part of me that wants to know what having a wife and children feels like.

Then again, I've watched the shitshow that was Samantha and Drew crumble to pieces, so there's the other part of me that's glad I don't have divorce to add to the ink on my chest and arms.

After all, there are perks to being single, and the golden ticket I received to the elite club, *RISE*, is one of them. I'm not certain what I did to earn a spot in the swanky gentleman's club that caught the attention of Forbes *30 Under 30*, but whoever Madam Roxie is has given me a front-row seat to her performance and requested my presence there. I mean, it *would* be good publicity. I'm sure my PR guy, Mick, would have a field day knowing I went there. He's always looking for ways to get my image out in the world and hanging at one of the finest strip clubs in the nation certainly can't hurt.

So Ethan and I meet up for dinner at Chops in Buckhead. He's brought his pal, Landry Laurent. Apparently, Landry's wife, Magnolia, along with Ethan's soon-to-be fiancée, Addison, are having a girl's night so Eth brought him along. The more the merrier, I say.

We're shooting the shit, well into dinner, when I begin telling them about this club I've gotten an enticing invitation to, thinking if I do, one of them might tag along.

Landry gives me a smirk and looks back at Ethan, brows raised.

"You're still a member of *RISE*, aren't ya, Lando?" Ethan asks with a chuckle before sipping his beer.

"Yes. Yes, I am." Landry grins big.

"You guys wanna come with me?" I ask with a shrug, hoping I won't have to go to a strip joint alone. I don't wanna look like *that* guy.

I see Landry smirk again, and Ethan almost chokes on his beer.

"I'd love to. Let me just go call the wifey and let her know not to expect me for a while." Landry winks and excuses himself.

I'm wondering how that conversation will go—surely he's not telling his wife that he's going to a strip club! I can't imagine any married woman really being ok with that. I look back to Eth, who gives me a frown, and I'm kinda bummed he won't be joining in on the fun. Once again, I'm rather grateful I don't have a "ball and chain" I have to ask permission from to do guy stuff.

Ethan regretfully declines with, "Nah, I can't tonight, man. Got other plans I gotta see to." He gives me a knowing smile and then I remember why I was actually flirting with the idea of wanting a wife—yeah, a steady sex-life. There is that.

Can't have it both ways though, I guess. I tell Eth he's missing out.

"I know, I know. But you and Landry go. You boys will have a blast."

MY EYES SLOWLY ADJUST TO THE DARKNESS THAT ENVELOPES THE large stage, four separate jetties with four separate poles. I see two curvy silhouettes against the blood-red backdrop curtain. They start walking out slowly then move toward the individual poles in the center. "Now performing for you live, two of the founding madams of *RISE*. Welcome to the stage, Madam Roxie and Madam Siren."

I smile as spotlights fall over the madam called Roxie, as she is referred to, and madam be damned, I understand now why. She's scantily clad in lingerie, mask, and tiara befitting a queen; the sheer piece of lace hugging her voluptuous body is as vibrant as the cherry-red Ferrari sitting in my garage back home, a gold wig sits atop her head and a matching black and gold mask covers the upper portion of her face. She's athletic with curves that go on for days, a tall, voluptuous body that I would love to run my hands over. Her skin is olive-toned and her eyes are a unique red-brown color, almost cat-like behind that black and gold mask. She cracks a whip in my direction then takes a stance at her pole, wrapping a muscular leg around it.

Well, hell-fucking-oh, Madam Roxie.

She eye-fucks me as the music starts, lowering herself down the pole and licking it seductively before she goes to town, her body moving in perfect rhythm to the song. She and the other madam move in a stunning performance that's well choreographed, wrapping their bodies around the poles and swaying their hips in the most provocative ways. Their toned bodies roll and seduce. It's the most incredible thing I've ever seen. I clap as the song ends, and they give a bow.

I watch, mesmerized as Madam Roxie moves back to her pole, turns and wraps her legs around it, then bends her toned torso back at me. My eyes fall to her melon-like breasts, regretfully concealed by the red lace. The round mounds spill forth, barely contained, and I pray they emerge from their hiding spots so I can indulge in this erotic fantasy suddenly encompassing my mind.

It's like we are the only ones here, and I find myself drawn to this mysterious enchantress, like a moth to a flame. She gives me a wicked grin and crooks her finger at me, motioning me over. Fuck, that smile looks so damn familiar... I look around to Landry, suddenly remembering I'm not alone here in this club, and see that he, too, has been pulled into the spell of the girl in front of him. Damn, is this witchcraft? We are spellbound by these *madams* and damned if I ever want to come back to reality.

I look back at the sassy vixen before me, who's now upright, moving off the stage, and approaching me. *Fuck me*, she's close, closer than before. I feel my dick jerk in my pants, hungry for a taste of the fire hidden behind that smile. It's been a while since I've had my cock stand at attention with just one look, and I suddenly realize I've never been so turned on by a stripper in my life before.

I almost moan as she reaches me and seizes my collar, jerking me towards her tall frame. She's like a damn Amazon woman! I smile, realizing a muscular woman like this was built for a pounding, a pounding I'd love to give her, feeling those powerful thighs wrapped around my waist as I take her against a wall.

"Ever been dominated before, big guy?" she asks in a voice dripping sex and cracks the leather whip at her side.

I raise a brow. "I'm usually the one doing the dominating, your highness," I quip and look her over, my eyes falling down her ample breasts, the cleavage in between, and lower.

"Don't knock it 'til you try it, Manning." She recognizes me; of course she does. Hell, she's the one who invited me, right? Nah, she probably has her own PR team too. I am a public figure, a model, mostly for book covers, but I've been on other products too so I'm sure her team simply reached out to mine. Perhaps they want new faces here.

The challenge in her eyes is unmistakable, but I'm not a man who yields—not to anything or anyone, not even this gorgeous masked dancer whose sex appeal is stirring my body in the most unexpected ways. "I've put stronger men than you to their knees." She smirks.

I'll just bet she has. I inhale her scent, the most alluring fucking thing I've ever smelled. As fun as having her would be, being with a dominatrix isn't really my thing...or it wasn't before I came in here.

I've been needing this type of break from reality, and I'm sure my sister, Samantha, and my nephew, Caleb, need a break from me too. I've come to stay with them since her idiot bastard of a husband up and left them a couple of months ago. My nephew needs constant care—the little dude has cerebral palsy—and my only sister was on the verge of a breakdown when Drew left her for his secretary. It's been tough, and our parents aren't any help, so what other choice did I have?

"So, do you, uh, do you have a private room you use to 'whip' your men into submission?" I can't help but laugh at the word submission because I have no intentions of letting this woman have her way with me. In fact, I'll be having mine with her if there will be any "having" done tonight.

The masked stripper looks me over again, her lips puckering, contemplating what she wants to do with me. Finally, she gives a subtle nod, a small bow of her head, and tugs on my collar once again. She's fierce and feisty, and I can't wait to have her begging and whimpering beneath me. I'm so turned on that my cock bobs in my khakis as she leads me to the back.

She gives a big, burly bald man a nod.

"Everything alright, Madam Roxie?" he asks, giving me an eye.

"Fine, Bruno. Just givin' Mr. Manning here a *private* tour."

The man named Bruno nods, and Roxie pulls a key from her top—where the hell it was hidden is a mystery to me. She begins unlocking a door that has a sign over it, labeled "Roxie's Garden."

Once I'm through the red door, she closes it behind me and steps back, her eyes are darker now as if she's not comfortable being alone with me. But I'm in the tigress's lair right now, and I'm slightly confused for a moment as she crosses her arms over her chest. She's evaluating me, sizing me up, and it's almost unnerving.

"What's the matter, Madam? I thought I was the canary to your cat?" I smart.

"Clearly, you've never bowed to a queen before." Her sultry smile is back, and I laugh aloud.

"Yeah, that'll be the day," I chide and look around the room.

It's blinged out in diamond wallpaper with gold embellishments and earthy tones. There's leather straps on racks and even crops and floggers. Not quite the "garden" I was expecting. Damn, I've stepped into Harriet Potter's Chamber of Horrors.

"I intimidate you," she states, moving toward me and biting into her lip as she grips my collar. Jesus, this lady is ridiculous. She's like Christian Grey's long-lost sister or some shit.

"No, darlin', I'm not intimidated. I simply wanna fuck those full lips. Then take you from behind as I spank that succulent ass of yours." There's no way she's gonna be the one spanking *my* ass. To hell with that!

I bite my lip just thinking about how hot fucking her will be.

She gulps, clearly taken aback, and turns from me toward the bed that I now see has more leather straps attached to the four posts. They're for tying someone down. Damn! This woman doesn't play.

She cracks the whip so close to me that I literally jump. "Fuck, lady. Easy with that thing!" I state loudly.

"This is the part where you get on your knees and beg me for mercy, Mr. Manning." The dark humor on her face is back.

"Ha. It's you who'll be begging for mercy, sweetheart. Mercy because I'm gonna make you come on my big dick, over and over, again and again and again."

"It doesn't work that way in here," she says with a tisk.

"Well, I'm a bit of a rule breaker myself." I shrug and give her a grin. "Let's break 'em together, sexy lady."

"No," she scoffs and cracks that fucking whip at me again.

"I'm about to take that fucking whip and throw it across the damn room," I growl.

She does it again, and I frown. She's dead fucking serious.

"Look, Roxie, I'm not really into this kinda thing, to be honest."

"Then perhaps you should've stayed out there." She approaches me with those burning red-brown eyes, and I swear I'm so turned on. What the hell is this lady doing to me? "Be a good boy, Callan, and do as I say, or you'll be punished. Take your shirt off."

"Now we're talking," I answer and begin to do as she says. She watches me and licks her lips as I pull my shirt over my head and toss it on her bed. "Now what, Madam Roxie?"

She bites her lip in pleasure and looks me over. I can feel my cock stiffening as her eyes fall over my chest, my chiseled abs, and down to the fly of my pants which juts out at her. "Now, your slacks."

"Wait just a damn minute here..." I scold with no conviction. "I paid to see *you* get naked, not the other way around."

Her smile is diabolical. "You haven't paid for *anything* yet."

I remedy that and pull out my wallet from my back pocket. I take out two one-hundred dollar bills and move toward the bed, throwing them down. "Better?" I ask and take a step forward, but she takes a cautious step back and motions to a chair.

I take a seat and watch her stalk toward me. She's gorgeous, so scantily clad in that lacy teddy, and all I can think about is running my tongue over every inch of her gorgeous skin, tasting her, fucking her.

"So, you don't want to obey me, huh?"

"I'm a bit of a bad boy, I guess you could say," I smirk again as she comes over and stops right in front of me, settling between my legs. Her closeness sets my body on fire. I wanna grab her hips and pull her down onto my lap and let her see what she's gotten herself into, let her feel the hard-on she's induced.

"You're *my* boy now," she coos and cups my cheek with the hand that isn't holding the whip.

"Mmm, and what does the madam intend to do with me?" I lick my lips in anticipation.

I almost regret asking because her eyes sparkle with deviance. She leans forward, her nose touching mine. "Let's put it this way, Cal. I'm gonna make you regret disobeying me."

I shiver. Pain isn't really my thing. But maybe there are safe words or whatever for this kinda stuff. "How about you dance for me? I mean, this *is* a strip club and all."

"Yes. Yes, it is, isn't it? Where are my manners?" She throws the whip aside, and I breathe out a big sigh of relief.

She then begins an erotic lap dance, the best one I've ever had, as her curvy body rolls over mine. I groan as she lowers her teddy down her shoulders and I'm rewarded with the sight of her large breasts with their brown tips. She presses them into my bare chest, teasing me with her peaked nipples. I long to touch her but know that I shouldn't push it. She moves her body down mine, licking my nipples, and leaving me arching my hips against her bottom as she turns. I'm as hard as a rock and so close to begging her to remove that piece of lingerie and letting me slide myself into her.

When she turns back around, I lean forward and cup her full breast, grabbing the soft mound in my hand, and pull it to my mouth. I suck her nipple and feel her shudder as my tongue swipes it back and forth. I pull back after a moment, starting to do the same to the other one, but I see her frowning down at me as if I've misbehaved.

"You shouldn't be touching me," she murmurs.

"I thought the rules changed in here," I add with a shrug. "Besides, I wanna make you feel good. Don't you want me to make you feel good?"

Her face changes and she pulls back, her hands resting on my thighs. "Well, what about *you*? You need to feel good too, don't you, big guy?" she asks.

Her fingers play at the button of my jeans, and I come close to whimpering. God, how I want her to make me feel good. When she pulls the zipper down, her hands move to my left wrist, and I feel leather straps being tied around my skin. "Roxie, I won't touch you. I just—"

"I make the rules in here, stud," she almost growls, and I realize I'm in for it.

I give a nervous chuckle. "Uh, maybe we should go over like the uh, safe words…"

"Safe words?" Her brow arches like she doesn't know what I'm talking about. Clever girl. She tilts her head and puckers those big lips, and I wanna jump out of this chair and show her who's boss. She must see my face change because she quickly moves to restrain my right arm. Damn. I really am in for it. She moves over to the bed and picks up the money I laid there. I hear a deep throaty laugh and she turns to me, planting a perfectly manicured hand on her curvy hip. "Is this an insult?"

"Insult?" I haven't been to a ton of strip clubs, despite that

I'm a published model, and the times I *have* been, I didn't go to any private rooms. I had a few VIP dances where the girls practically dry-humped me in a curtained room but this, this is a whole other level. And I'm starting to wonder if I've made a giant mistake. I'm kinda good at that...

"My rate *starts* at $1,000."

"$1,000 for a dance and a blowjob?" Is she serious?

"Is that what you thought you were getting?" I don't like that face she's making.

I'm at a loss for words here. What have I gotten myself into?

"I don't have a thousand dollars in cash, sorry. Carrying around that kind of money isn't wise in Atlanta."

"We'll just put it on your tab," she smirks. "But trust me, this is gonna be worth your while. Every. Single. Moment of it."

I gulp, and although her tone makes me think otherwise, my body agrees with her as my cock jumps in my unzipped pants once again.

She must see this for she smiles and moves back toward me. "I see you agree. So, we'll continue."

I moan as her fingers run over my naked chest, cool from the air conditioning blowing overhead, despite that my blood is on fire from her touch. Her fingertips are unhurried as they trace the curve of my jaw, neck, collarbone, indention of my pecs and abs, over my navel, and down to my pubic hair where she's pulled my boxers down. "Lift your bottom so I can take these off." She motions to my khakis and I nod, wishing to eradicate every barrier so that my bare flesh can touch hers. When I'm completely naked, she moves over to a stereo system and turns a sexy, thumping song on then turns her back to me, her plump ass barely covered by the lacy lingerie. I admire her athletic and curvy body, the strength it takes of her core to be able to dance on the pole she did not long ago. I bet she has abs as rock hard as mine are, and I long to see her fully naked.

She begins to move her hips along with the music, bending over and giving me a view that makes my lust sky-rocket as I can almost see where my cock will soon be nestled. I moan aloud as my hard-on becomes full throttle and begins to throb almost painfully for release. But her torturous ways have just started. Her dance is erotic, perfectly calculated, and so fucking sexy as she turns and moves her hands over her curves, thrusting her pelvis and pulling the thin piece of lace so achingly slowly down her body that I want to scream.

Finally, when she's clad only in that mask and red, high, *fuck-me-hard-Callan* heels, I drink in her voluptuous frame. She's as gorgeous as I imagined, despite the dim lighting in here, and her abs are chiseled. She's strong as fuck, and it turns me on even more. A woman that my tall, big frame can tangle with. I fucking love it.

"Come here, gorgeous," I whisper.

She smiles seductively and saunters, unhurried, my way. When she's just inches from me, she begins to touch me again then to my delight, she straddles me and sits on my lap, her bottom mere centimeters from my erect member. Her hands fall to my thighs, and she moves her bare breasts over my chest and her hips against me, my cock hitting her plump ass. Fuck, I want to be inside her so badly. $1,000 psshh, what's $1,000? I'll pay double that for this experience, whatever it takes to have this sinful seductress tonight.

She does this for a time, dry-humping my pubic bone, letting my dick curve and tap her backside as she does so, and I grind as hard back against her as I can, aching desperately for further contact. The leather straps wear into my wrists as I crave to touch her, to feel the contrast of her soft skin and muscles on my palms.

I lean my face toward her, to kiss her, and she giggles and pulls her head back. "No kissing. Not in here."

My first reaction is, *Why the fuck not?* I guess I can kinda understand. But, damn, kissing is one of my favorite things to do, and with lips like hers, I bet she knows how to do it and well.

"Well, then perhaps you can kiss my cock," I offer, my brows arching in hope.

Her devious smile returns, and I wonder if I've made a mistake with this request, thinking maybe she'll tie my shaft down next, dominatrix that she is.

"I bet you'd like that, wouldn't you?"

"Yes, ma'am. I'd like that very much." Again, I'm answered with a wicked smile. Fuck. I just want to take her, end this torture, and hear her screaming my name as I fuck her brains out.

She shifts and moves off me, leaving me bereft as she comes down in front of me, her hands resting on my thighs once more. My torment has only begun as she tickles me with her red fingernails, running them up and down my inner thighs, so close to my shaft and testicles. God, I'm so damn hard, I wanna cry out for her to suck me. Finally, when my breath starts to come out in pants, she grips my member in her hand and squeezes.

"Oh, fuck," I whimper as her fist moves down to the base of my cock, twists, and moves back up to the tip. "Yes, baby. God that feels so good."

"You haven't felt *good* yet." She giggles again.

Her other hand moves to my scrotum, and she tickles my balls very gently. Again, I'm thrust into a private hellish pleasure I've never known before. This woman knows how to build up an orgasm, and I know that when I finally blow my load, it's gonna be exquisite.

Between her fist milking my shaft and her hand on my balls, I'm becoming putty in her hands. If her eyes are any indication, they reflect that. She's getting off on making me her bitch, and as disturbing as this should be to me, it turns me on all the more.

"Oh, Roxie, baby. I want your mouth on my cock, please?"

She grins once more but much to my surprise, her head moves in. "You want me to suck your dick, Cal?" I can feel her breath fall over my stiff member and my head falls back, the anticipation of having her mouth and tongue on me is complete damn torment.

"Yes, baby, please? I wanna feel those gorgeous lips around me." I hate begging. I'm not a beggar but damned if this foxy woman hasn't made me one.

She must know this for the next thing out of her mouth is, "Beg me." She smirks and with a long, pink tongue slowly licks the pre-cum off the head of my cock.

Fuck me. This lady really knows how to push the envelope. "Roxie, darlin', I—"

"You want me to suck you off or not? If not, I have many other clients that will—"

"No," I nearly shout. The thoughts of her doing this to anyone else makes my blood boil, and the realization of that shocks me beyond belief. I just met this woman. How does she have such power over me? "Please, baby, suck my cock? Get me off. I wanna come all over those beautiful tits." My voice is almost desperate as I feel my climax coming ever closer with her stroking fist.

That damn diabolical smile returns, and I swear I've met the devil himself tonight. But my pleasure intensifies as her full lips fall to the head of my cock, and I groan out loud, my hips arching up off the chair. I watch as her eyes never leave mine and her mouth slowly takes me in all the way to the base.

"Oh, fuck me," I cry, my head falling back in the most exquisite torment I've ever felt. This woman is something else. I feel her hand move up then back down my shaft and look back down, seeing my cock disappear down her throat and reappear once again as she sucks on the head and her other hand cups my balls. "Oh, yeah Rox. God, that feels *so* fucking incredible. Please don't stop."

She giggles, even as her mouth is full of all nine inches of my rock-hard member. My release builds as her speed and suction increase. I swear I'm touching an equivalent of heaven being in this sinful torture chamber of hers. Just when I think my climax is coming, she begins to slow.

"No, Roxie, baby, please don't stop."

"Are you begging me?" she alludes. Those flaming red-brown eyes burn into mine.

Fuck! Yes! Dammit! Yes!! "Please? Please make me come?" I'm so damn close. My balls are tingling, and I know I'm about to shoot my load.

She plants her lips back on the head of me and works her fist harder, twisting and pulling, and I lose myself to her magic. I roar as I tumble over the edge and pump my hips. I look down to see that I'm ejaculating all over her gorgeous breasts, watching it drip down her nipples. It's so damn hot, I swear I could come again at just the sight alone. I moan as my orgasm slowly fades and she sucks the head of my cock back into her mouth. I whimper and pump against her again and again, and finally, I stop moving as I'm spent.

"Fuck, Madam Roxie, you've not only blown me, you've blown my damn mind, sexy lady."

She smiles in victory. "Best money you've spent in a while, I take it."

I realize I'm out a grand for a freakin' blow job, despite that it's the best damn blow job I've ever had, but I nod in earnest.

She moves away towards a separate room that I assume to be a bathroom, and when she comes back in, she has a new piece of lingerie on. "Bruno will see you out. Enjoy your evening, Mr. Manning. Thank you for your patronage."

I have no time to retort before she's moving out the exit door.

Fucking hell... I shake my head, even though deep down, I know I'll be back. For if that's how she gives head, I can only imagine how she fucks.

Yup, dammit to Hell, I'll be back.

EDEN

LATER THAT NIGHT, LIA AND I ARE BACK IN MY PENTHOUSE apartment just a block from the club, having a night like we four once used to have after we closed RISE down for the night.

Addy and Everleigh have joined us, for old time's sake, and brought Aliana, who is now sleeping, as I sip a glass of wine and stroke the sweet little angel's hair.

"Ohhhhh, you have that romance novel tone to your voice," I say as Lia reminisces about how she and Landry ended up together and how amazing tonight was with him, all impromptu like it was when he called her to tell her he and Callan were coming to RISE.

"Oh stop," she giggles. "What about *you*? Speaking of romance novels, don't think I missed your big, burly man-crush drooling in front of your stage. Another willing victim to Madam Roxie's sadistic ways?" she taunts.

"You know it," I say with a wink. "Big, burly *idiot* is more like it, but he was fun to...play with."

And he absolutely was. I can't wait to pleasure myself later tonight as I remember exactly what his face looked like as he blew his giant load on my tits. God, he was so fucking hot. Every muscular inch of him.

"Can't have it all," Addy smirks. "Good looks, big muscles, *and* brains."

"What a fucking disappointment," I quip.

"Oh, E," Ev says, her big pregnant belly hitting mine as she pulls me into her arms. "Someday your prince will come, honey. And when he does, he's gonna sweep you off your feet."

"Sounds like *all* y'all have been reading one too many romance novels." I smirk in disgust at the lot of them.

They've gotten their happily ever afters, dammit. I don't know that I ever will. Even if my "prince" does come, it doesn't mean he'll want a woman with the excessive baggage I carry, or that he will be able to carry said baggage. Besides, I don't deserve a prince.

Dammit—I'm tearing up. Fuck!

"Eden?" Lia whines and looks over at me with concern on her lovely face.

"I'm sorry, I don't know what my damn problem is. It's—it's just...fuck!" I pull myself from Everleigh's comforting arms. "I had this picture in my head of how amazing he was and he's..." I trail off. He's no different from any of the others I've tormented in Roxie's Garden of Playthings. He's not special at all. He's a face and body of perfection, but I feel so let down that his personality was so cocky, arrogant, and presumptuous the other day. The polar opposite of what he was that night at the ball a year ago.

"What'd you expect, Eden? He's practically a celebrity. Life's been handed to him on a silver platter!" I can always leave it to my girl, Addison, aka Ember, to give me the harsh reality.

I nod, knowing she's on point. I wipe my face. "Of course, you're right."

"She is, but we know how much you wanted him to be all that you dreamed," Lia gives me a look of pity. I can't have that. It's the same one I got when she saw firsthand how cruel my uncle really was—when he raped me right in front of her after we both pissed him off one night at the club that started this corrupt side of us.

"On to bigger and better things," I retort, pulling my spine up a little straighter.

"That's right. Fuck him. There are other fish in the sea." Everleigh gives me a smile and clinks her lemonade to my wine glass.

"To Mr. Right," Addy states and lifts her own glass.

"You never know," Lia states with a little grin, "he *may* come back."

May hell, he *will* come back. Something in his eyes told me so while I left his naked ass in my chair. But my wall is already up, and he's not going to hurt me next time—heart be damned.

"And when he does, *Roxie* will be ready." I give a devious smile back, getting a laugh from my girls.

Ah, this. This is what I live for.

My girls.

My family.

And to hell with men because they all suck!

I'm walking down the sidewalk on my way to work the next day and drop into the jewelry store on the corner to grab the gift I got for my sisters. It's close to our Friend-versary, and I found lockets I couldn't pass up.

I see none other than Ethan Freeman at the counter

looking at engagement rings. I grin as I see him bite into his lip while the jeweler shows him two different ones. He looks stuck.

I swoop in and shove at his hip with my own, getting his brown eyes piercing into mine.

"Hey there, stud, looking to get engaged?" I tease, and he runs his hand through his brown hair.

"This is almost the hardest decision of my life." He sighs.

"Well, step one: you found 'the one.' This can't be tougher than that, can it?"

"There's just so many to choose from." He has a point as he motions to the sparkling diamonds cut in various styles.

"Yeah, I see what you mean." I tilt my head at a lovely princess cut one. "That's beautiful and simple."

"Well, you know her as well as I do, Eden. Think she'll like that one better than this one?" he asks, pointing down to the art deco one in his hand.

"Addison is timeless, as well."

"Dammit, Eady." He's practically glaring at me, and I can't help the giggle at my throat. "You could be of more assistance, ya know?"

"I know. But this is your game, big boy. Can't take the ball out of your court, now can I?" I wink at him and pat his back with a laugh.

I back away and walk over to the opposite counter where the necklaces are, smiling at the ones I've picked out for my sisters. Lockets with four slots for the four of us.

"Pick up for Riser," I state when the woman behind the counter asks if I need assistance.

She moves off and comes back in a few minutes with my packages. I grin at her and pay.

I pass by Ethan on my way out the door, who looks like a scolded puppy dog.

"C'mon, Ethan. She's gonna love whatever you choose and you know it."

I wave and leave, smirking as I think about how excited Addison is gonna be when her man proposes to her.

Then a cold shudder passes through me that has nothing to do with the March cold. Once again, I'm reminded that I'm the last single one of our Core Four.

2

EDEN

"Happy fucking St. Patty's Day, bitches," I say a little too loud as I clink my green beer with the girls' glasses and get a tight smile from Ev, who motions back to Rory in Luca's arms. "What?"

"Eden..." Lia looks at me like the sweet mother she is, putting a finger up as she looks around.

I laugh, feeling my buzz strengthening.

I know what happens tonight. Ethan has told me his proposal idea, and I plan to be good and sloshed before dinner is through. Even Addy is frowning at me as I down my beer and motion to the waitress to bring me another.

"Sheesh, E, calm your inner drunken ho." She rolls her eyes.

"You'd know all about bein' a *ho*, wouldn't you, Addy?" I snort back, getting a heel to my shin.

"Ladies, ladies, play nice," Landry insists and places a hand on my arm, even as Aliana giggles and reaches for me. Sweet girl, she's so damn cute. Her and the gorgeous red-headed doll of Everleigh and Luca's. I want one. I grab her and pout over at Lia; she seems to sense my sorrow.

I get her arm around my shoulder, and I want to run to the bathroom and cry it out. I'm pathetic tonight and should have told them I wasn't feeling well or something so I didn't ruin it for the rest of them.

It sucks being the seventh wheel all the time, and tonight is one of those nights where my pity party can't be contained.

I look up at Ev, who gives me her best teacher's frown, and I have to look down, pretending to decide between shepherd's pie and fish and chips as Aliana smacks at the menu and blabbers a mile a minute.

If they only knew how heavy my heart has been since seeing Callan again, they would understand my mood. It's as if the void in my heart has enlarged, and now I can't be happy no matter what.

I see Ethan glance at Addy, love shining in his eyes, and it physically hurts.

Luca does the same with Ev, and Landry with Lia. I love that my sisters have found true love; they deserve it, and so much more, and I truly don't envy theirs. I just envy that *I* will never know it. And I know why... because ten years ago, I was forever marked by sin, scarred for life by the Devil.

I hear Addison gasp as Ethan kneels on one knee.

As if my heart wasn't bleeding already, now it's gushing. I don't even hear the words coming from his mouth, I only see the conviction in his eyes. And when she pops up into his arms and squeezes him, I look away to keep from crying. Good for them. One more happy couple. One more lonely night for me. Wishing for something I'll never have.

Ev scoots closer to me. "Want me to have Zeus take you home?"

I realize I'm crying and wipe my eyes. I shake my head and hand Ev the toddler.

"No, I'm good. Really. I would never ruin this for Addison."

I straighten my spine and smile as Addy showcases her new engagement ring; it's as beautiful as she is. I pop up and pull her to me for a hug.

"You did good, Freeman." I elbow Eth and get a blush in return.

I watch as Ev and Lia take their turns oohing and aahing over Addy, Ethan, and the ring before asking for my check from the frazzled waitress.

"You ok?" Addy asks, pulling me to the side.

"Yeah, I think I just need to go blow off some steam, ya know?" I nod my head to the barrage of beers sitting in my spot at the table.

Addy nods. "I'm sorry, Eady."

"Don't you dare, Addison. You two love each other and you're happy together. I would never take something from you you've wanted for almost as long as I've known you. I'm so proud of you, and I'm so glad you finally got your man."

I hug her to me and throw some bills down, not even waiting for the check.

I start to pull away when Addy whispers, "I know, but when the hell do you plan on getting yours?"

I hold her intense gaze before she kisses my cheek and releases me.

Zeus takes my elbow then and guides me out. "Where we going, E?"

"RISE."

RISE, where I can let loose.

RISE, where I can lose myself to the music that is as much a part of my soul as my sins are.

SIX YEARS AGO...

"Can I ask you something?" Addison puts an arm around me as we stumble into my apartment, our night of drinks and merriment taking their toll.

"No fair. You know I'm drunk, and I can't lie when I drink this shit." I hiccup and laugh maniacally.

"I do, that's why I'm taking advantage." She throws me down on the couch, and I look up at her as she puts her hands on her hips. "We've never discussed it and the more time that goes on, the more I want to know... Why did you try to kill yourself that night in college?"

Wow! She went in for the kill with that one. As much as I want to dismiss this, I don't. It's the reason we went out drinking tonight, to celebrate life as survivors of suicide attempts... and me as a survivor of abortion.

I look down. What will she think of me when I tell her what happened? Baby killer, whore, murderer. All these words dance through my head, and I let the silent tears fall before I say, "Vince..." Shit, that name pierces my heart. I never say it aloud, and neither do the girls. It's been five years, and I still can't help but quake at that one vicious word and what it does to my soul. "He forced me to...have an abortion."

Addison's green eyes flash with surprise. "Oh, Eady." She sinks down on the couch and pulls me to her shoulder. "That bastard...I'm so sorry."

"I don't know if it was his or Marco's, not that it mattered. It would've been mine *either way. Not that I would have even known what to do with a baby at eighteen or could've even raised one in— Still, it hurts so much to think..."*

She strokes my hair for a time and soothes my sobs. I don't feel any judgment from her, none whatsoever, not that I expected any, but it feels good to tell someone, to finally get it off my chest. "I know what it feels like to lose your entire family. But you know what? You have me and Ev and Lia. We're your family, always and forever."

CALLAN

"Here, let me help you with that," I say as I lean into the back of the shy yet stunning Eden Riser while she's hanging a banner on the library bulletin board.

I'm sure she's wondering why the hell I'm here. It's been three months since I've seen her, three months since my sister had a talk here, but there's something about the fiery, brunette librarian that makes me enjoy bantering with her. She's so damn closed off, like she's wound tighter than a bag of cats.

Samantha has another signing here today after releasing the second book in her series just yesterday, so here I am, back in the library helping my big sis and watching my little man—my nephew, Caleb.

"I've got it," she grumbles even as my pelvis presses intimately into her plump bottom. My hand falls to her hip and lower—seriously, it was an accident.

Her curvy ass is firm as fuck, and I tell her so, "Damn, Eden, your ass is like a damn Clydesdale's." I brush my right hand down it, subtly admiring how tight it is. She bucks me off and whips around to face me, a scowl on her face, her big brown eyes narrowing.

She doesn't have to say it. The fire in those eyes tells me, "Get your fucking hands off me, asshole."

God, I love getting a rile out of this stuffy librarian; it doesn't take much to rattle her.

But, fuck, I think I might have just sexually assaulted her. Oh, boy...

"Sorry, I—I umm...you must work out a good bit, huh?" I look down over her tall figure, hidden behind an oversized sweater and trousers, her eyes framed in a pair of black frames.

Her brow goes up, and I can't help but smile at the mystery in her eyes. "Six days a week, not unlike you."

My grin deepens. "Wow, you wouldn't be able to tell it in that baggy-ass sweater of yours, though. Why are you hiding a body like that under there?"

"People come here to read books, not see my cleavage," she smarts and crosses her arms.

"Depends on the people, I guess." I shrug and look down at her chest.

She rolls her eyes and turns away from me with a shake of her head, as if I'm the biggest imbecile who ever lived.

C'mon, Cal, recover. Get back on your A-game! "Well, why don't we go work out together some time, then?"

"So you can act like a narcissist in the mirror taking self-ies?" she throws back as she moves to the table, grabbing another banner to staple to the bulletin board.

"I swear, I won't take a single selfie."

I'll be the first to admit my IG feed is full of pics I've taken of myself in the gym. And in my travels. And in bed. The shower... Not to mention my photographer who loves to tag me in the most provocative poses, too. Well, shit...

"Not interested," she mumbles and reaches back up, adjusting the laminated paper and stapling it to the board.

"I have a hard time believing that. You have a thing for me, I know it." I hope, anyway.

"Narcissist," she mutters under her breath.

"Oh, c'mon, Eden. What's a guy gotta do to take a lady like you out to dinner?"

"Man, your ego is as big as your biceps, huh?" She turns

back around to look at me, the flame in her chocolate brown eyes still burning just as bright. Damn, she's a hard-ass.

"So, you *have* noticed my biceps. I freakin' knew it." I grin. Little victories.

"Not. Interested," she states again, dismissively.

"Oh, c'mon, Eden…"

"No, don't you 'C'mon, Eden' *me*—"

"What do you have to lose?"

"Besides my lunch?" A perfectly arched dark eyebrow goes up, and she crosses her arms over her ample chest again.

"Ouch." I grab my left pec, dramatically. "That really hurt my feelings."

"Cal, are you harassing the librarian…again?" comes my sister's voice from behind us. "Leave her alone. Caleb was asking for you, anyway. I think he's gonna try to bribe you into getting him a snack from the vending machine."

I smile. That little boy is totally wrapped around my heart. I love him like he's mine and have since I held him in my arms for the first time. We bonded immediately, unlike he and his father, Drew. Drew stayed busy and practically away from home all the time after Caleb was diagnosed with cerebral palsy at the age of four. For one, because personally I think he was afraid and two, let's face it, Drew was a shitty caregiver…and, well, a shitty person at that. He didn't really know what to do when Caleb lost control of his motor functions, couldn't eat like normal kids, or even use the restroom. His seizures were the final straw—that and Caleb's inability to communicate with his father. As if the toll wasn't taken on poor Caleb and Samantha as equally. But that's Drew for ya, always thinking of only himself. Yeah, Caleb is probably stuck in a motorized wheelchair for life and grunts because he can't speak effectively, but the kid is the cutest damn thing I've ever seen with his thick brown locks and big blue eyes. He looks so much like Sam did as a kid, it's uncanny.

Personally, I can understand him just fine, and he's got a great sense of humor, not unlike his Uncle Cal.

"You know he'll probably succeed, right?"

"I know," my sister smirks and elbows me. "Just nothing with too much sugar, he's already hyper."

"Yes, ma'am." I give her a wink as I move into the main library to a little nook where Caleb and Sally are. I see my little man sitting there, listening as Sally reads *Winnie the Pooh* by A.A. Milne. It's one of his favorites, and I smile as he laughs at something Piglet says.

"Hey bud, you want a snack?" I ask, and he nods vigorously...well, as vigorously as a kid with CP can, anyway. "Well, let's go see what they got you can eat." I silently pray I'll find something. Not that we don't carry snacks around for him—squeeze tubes of various foods like applesauce, baby food, and sometimes yogurts, in addition to foods that are easy for him to chew, swallow, and digest. I'm sure he gets tired of them, though. He's like any other seven-year-old; chocolate chip cookies are right up there with lightsabers. Mrs. Fields cookies are soft enough, and when I stop at the vending machine and see a package of them, I silently rejoice. "Well, well, it's your lucky day, pal. Look here." I point up at the glass and hear my nephew squeal in delight. I may just be his favorite person right about now as I put a dollar into the machine, and he watches in glee as the rotary arm does its thing.

I glance back down at him and smile again. God, he's such a blessing. Innocent, sweet, everything that makes me see that there *are* angels on this earth. I pull out my phone and snap a pic of him literally drooling at the machine, hand to the glass. I write a quick caption, throwing out my recently rising emotions, and post the picture to my IG profile. I don't do this often. Usually, it's me I showcase, being a practical celebrity and all. It's not that I don't enjoy sharing and raising awareness of my nephew and his condition, but I don't want to exploit him, either—or have people think I am in order to get more likes and followers. I'm really *not* that guy. I adore this kid and would kill for him. And if people start hating on this post I just made, well, guess what? They'll get blocked because no one, and I mean *no* one, is gonna make me regret sharing my love for Caleb.

Eden

I can't help the smile that crosses my lips as Callan walks away from me and Samantha and into the library. Despite this big jerk's massive ego, he has a soft spot for the adorable little Caleb, and it warms my icy heart...a little, anyway.

"My brother is majorly crushing on you, it would seem," Sam says.

"Why?" I scoff. Like that matters, I don't plan to give him the time of day. She grins over at me and shrugs. My curiosity is piqued, though. Honestly, what does Callan Manning see in a quiet, subdued librarian?

She, in turn, shrugs. "You aren't like most women he knows. I mean, he's so used to women being smitten with him. He has that sex appeal...or so I've been told." She laughs and her curly brown locks fall around her face. "Women practically throw themselves at him the minute he walks into a room. And you, well...you could care less."

Oh, if she only knew.

I could have literally melted into a puddle on the floor when I saw Callan Manning walk into my library three months ago. His broad, six-foot-five inch frame seemed to take up the entire foyer as my shaking hands nervously opened the doors. I pretended to be unaffected by his words, his deep voice, and his overwhelmingly manly scent and appeal; but on the inside, I was swooning. Then when I saw him in my club two nights later, I felt like I might pass out. Having him all to myself in my private room was more than I'd ever expected. He'd shown up and my all-encompassing desire for him couldn't be contained. Tasting his desire for me and having him panting over my naked form and ministrations was more than I'd ever dreamed it would be, despite that I'm sure, for him, it was nothing more than a routine BJ...and that upset me to no end.

After leaving him tied to the chair, I'd gone to hang with my girls at our penthouse apartment. Then later in the wee hours of the night curled up on my bed, I masturbated with ferocious need, remembering his sexy lips around my nipple, his tongue circling my hungry flesh, wishing I'd let him kiss me as I plunged the dildo deep inside myself. The dreams I had that night were so sinful and decadent, I awoke feeling like he'd actually been there.

Nothing could be farther from the truth.

I haven't had a man in my bed in a long while. I didn't even have sex with Washington, although my sisters are none the wiser. I play with the men at the club and on occasion, I've slipped a condom on one of them to fuck my cares away. It didn't happen but a few times, for my PTSD still controls me far more than I want to admit. What my uncle did to me all those years ago still affects every fiber of my being, dominance and intimacy being the ones it's affected the most.

I haven't been taken from behind or beneath a man since Vince, and I like it that way. I'm in control, *always*. And I have Marco to thank for bringing me out of my nightmare. But despite that I'm no longer tormented physically by him, my Uncle Vince's face and eyes are forever burned into my memory so deeply that I'll never be the same.

Yes, I've had therapy. Yes, I've tried to let it go, but I have panic attacks just thinking about it. When I'm on top, I control my own needs and desires and fears...and if I get scared, I'm able to stop the whole thing.

I swore after Uncle Vince died that no one would ever again have the upper hand. After Marco showed me how to pleasure myself atop him, I knew I'd never allow a man to get the best of me, hurt me, or even touch me, unless I said it was okay. I have the power, I have the say... I have serious damn issues.

"He's really not as bad as he seems," Samantha says after a time of me being absorbed in my own thoughts. I realize I never responded to her and feel like a bitch because I didn't.

"He's famous, they're all that way." I shrug.

"Don't be so sure," she says and motions to Callan and Caleb over at the vending machine in the hallway across from us.

The raw emotion on Cal's face as he smiles down at his nephew and snaps a pic literally makes my heart hurt. His love for this precious little boy is endearing and humbling, and I find myself wondering if he *is* different. Perhaps I'm wrong, and he's not the cocky halfwit I think he is.

Then my memory, always reminding me of the pain of being naive, flashes me back to the moment my innocence was taken from me by a man who was supposed to protect me, a man who was my last living relative—by marriage, anyway—a man who claimed to love me.

FOURTEEN YEARS AGO...

"Don't be afraid, sweet girl. Uncle Vince is here." I hear my uncle say as I cry into my pillow.

The pain of losing my parents is so sharp and poignant. I can't sleep, and when I do sleep, I dream of the car accident. The charred and mangled metal are a grim reminder that there wasn't anything left of them to bury, thus why my uncle had them cremated, their ashes sitting yards from me on the mantle in my ridiculously over-sized room. I miss them so much and hate the big house I've been brought into with a man whose eyes frighten me even more than his dark mansion does.

"*I'm here, Eden,*" *he simpers again, and I want to recoil from his slimy touch. But he doesn't stop as I thought he would and moves into the bed with me. I don't want his comfort, I want him to leave me alone. I want to cry and grieve and go home.* "*Shh,*" *he coos into my ear and I turn my face away from him, his overwhelming cologne so strong that I can't breathe. I've never liked him, not really. I've tolerated him, truthfully. My sweet aunt should never have married a man so vile and repulsive. His voice, even, is maniacal; his words manipulative. Anyone who's been in his presence long enough can tell that.* "*Let your Uncle Vince soothe you now, sweetling.*"

I feel his palm cover my back, and again, I flinch. I can't stop the sobs, though, as my predicament overfloods my senses once more. Why, God, why did this have to happen? *I ask, even though God doesn't respond to me. I've asked Him this question for three days now, the sorrow of losing my loving parents more than I can bear.*

"*Eden, you need to stop this. I can't take your anguish, darling. Please stop crying.*" *When I don't immediately do so, his fingertips on my cheek grow rougher, and he jerks my chin in his direction.* "*Did you hear me? I said to dry it up!*" *His voice is sharp and without sympathy, and I start, my eyes finally rising to his face. It's shadowed by the darkness, but I see the tight line of his lips. He's dead fucking serious.* "*Stop. Crying.*" How can he expect me to do that? Doesn't he understand how distraught I am? I've just lost my parents, my home, my world. What a prick!

"*I—I—*" *I'm stuttering as he moves closer to me, pulling my frame into his. He turns me so our chests align.* What the hell is he doing? "*Uncle Vince?*" *I ask, trying to figure out what he's doing here, in my room, in my bed.* What are his intentions? *Then alarm bells start ringing in my head. My mother had a talk with me not long ago, about sex, men, their ways, their bodies... and even at only fifteen years of age, I realize something is not right about this. About* him*.*

The smile on his face is diabolical, and I gulp. "*That's it. You'll get* used to this position soon enough, my bountiful little garden." His voice makes me shiver. Why is he speaking to me like this?

I feel his hand fall from my cheek, down my neck then to my arm.

"You're still pure, aren't you, my sweet Eden?" he asks and licks his lips sending another shiver down my spine. Why does he need to know that I'm still a virgin? That's none of his business. When I attempt to pull back, he grips my waist and slams me back against his chest. I begin to panic even as he growls into my ear. "This will go much more smoothly for you if you don't fight me."

Oh, God. NO! Please? I'm begging the Almighty to rescue me now. What hell have I been sent to? Why has He forsaken me when I need Him most?

Uncle Vince's hands move down my waist, and I whimper as his palm settles on my hip. Tears spring from my eyes again, but I bite into my lip to keep from sobbing as I'm overcome with maddening fear at this point.

The adrenaline rising in my veins doesn't seem to realize that I'm trapped; it makes one last attempt to fight, and I jerk hard away from him, moving my bottom in an attempt to turn over quickly and make a run for it. To where and what end doesn't matter.

The smirk on my uncle's face as his grip tightens on me is one I'll never forget, not if I live a million years. His voice is low, calm, and I realize then that I'm completely screwed. "You're going to regret doing that, little girl."

The hard slap across my face makes my brain rattle and my cheek burn. I'm grabbed up by my shoulders with a guttural roar —rising a foot off the mattress—and violently thrown back down onto the bed. His weight covers me and all the air rushes from my lungs as his rough hands begin to tear at my clothes and grope at my flesh. I feel my soul flee to the recesses of blackness surrounding me now.

That would be the last time I tried to fight him...

"Coming," I say as I reach for my doorknob, assuming it's one of my girls, but I stand in awe and shock as a gorgeous Callan Manning stands in my doorway early the next morning.

He's clad in dark sunglasses, an old blue ball cap, a muscle-hugging white Under Armour UGA tank top—that few men would be bold enough to wear—and a pair of tight, well-worn jeans that outline his big thighs. He holds a drink carrier containing two Starbucks coffees. "Mornin', beautiful," he says with a grin that tells me he *knows* how damn good he looks and isn't afraid to use it against me.

"C-Callan. Wh-what are you doing here? And how did you find my address?" I'm sure half of my stammering is in part to his bulging, tattooed arms that practically shimmer in the sunlight shining in through the windows of the hallway, like he's slathered them in baby oil. I wouldn't put it past him.

"So, it's this little website called Google," he begins with a smile, showcasing his perfect pearly-whites.

"Duh, smart-ass. I mean—"

"I know what you mean, Eady. I actually used Yellow Pages, yes the phone book, and believe it or not, Eden is a much less common first name than you'd think. And well, you're the only Riser in there, so by deductive reasoning and process of elimi-nation... Here I am." He wiggles his eyebrows playfully, and I can't help but giggle at his enthusiasm. "Besides, I brought you coffee, and who can say no to Starbucks?"

I *am* a sucker for Starbucks—*and* this hunky stud-muffin so nonchalantly standing at my front door like he owns the damn thing.

"I think this is considered stalking on a few levels." I cross my arms over my chest and prop myself in the doorframe. I'm so close to him, I can almost feel the heat coming off his smok-ing-hot frame.

"Nah, I'm a public figure. We can do shit like this and get away with it."

"Oh, ok. I'll be sure to tell the cops that when they get here, big guy." I smirk and raise a brow.

He tilts his head, evaluating me for a second, and I recall what I did to him in Roxie's room not so long ago. My sex clenches at the thought of being so intimate with him again, but I shake it off and motion my head to the coffees. "So, what did you get me? And how did you know I even like coffee?"

"Well," he begins and raises the containers. "I *did* see you with a cup at the library yesterday, so I took a chance and went with a café mocha. I mean what girl says no to chocolate, am I right?"

God, he's downright delectable. I want to devour him. He's absolutely on point. Chocolate is right up there with dancing for me. It's one of my few weaknesses.

"Impressive, Mr. Manning." I have to give him props simply for being so brave, even if I don't really understand what his angle is and why he's here. "But I have to ask again: what are you doing here?"

"Simply breaking down your barriers until I finally crack into that iron-clad fortress you're hiding within." He swipes his sunglasses off and the blue eyes piercing my soul give me pause. I visibly gulp because dammit, if he's not doing a fine job of chipping those walls away each time he's near me lately. "I had planned to bring my nephew with me for back-up. I know you're a sucker for cute kids. Don't play... In fact, I was a bit disappointed that you didn't like my post on Instagram. I rifled through 500 comments, I'll have you know."

"I'm not on Insta—"

"Yes, you are. I checked that, too." He gives me another thoughtful look, and I shake my head at him.

"Alright, *stalker*."

He ignores that comment and continues on about cute kids. "Maybe a neighbor has one around here I can borrow for a minute. Or perhaps a puppy. I think a kitten might even work. You look like you cry at those ASPCA commercials, I bet." He looks around, down the empty hallway like he's actually searching for some helpless animal to torment me with, and I literally crack up. He's hot, funny, *and* swoony—Damn him!

"Well, come in, I guess, since it's probably rude of me *not* to invite you in." I smirk again.

I step back into my threshold and let him into my apartment, knowing I can kick his ass if he even thinks of trying any unwanted moves on me.

He grins again and enters the foyer, looking around at my immaculate, modern, glass-and-industrial-designed loft.

"Whoo-wee," he whistles. "This is fancy, Ms. Riser. Sweet place you have here."

"Thanks."

I gesture to the couch, and he sits down, placing the cup holder on the coffee table in front of him. He pats the leather cushion next to him and reluctantly, I take it, not as close as I imagine he would like for me to be.

"Are you gonna answer my question as to why you're here?" I ask as he hands me my coffee.

"Ah, yes. To break down those iron walls of yours, one needs a chisel—or in my case, a well-thought-out hacking plan."

This is getting interesting, even if I don't have the slightest inclination to take the bait. My brows arch.

"I've come to invite you to have dinner with me tonight."

"No," I answer too quickly, getting a frown from him.

"You don't even know where I made reservations," he scoffs.

"Cancel them. Or take someone else. I'm sure there are many models in great shape like you who would love to go out with you."

"I don't wanna date another model. I wanna take you."

"Why?"

"Why *not?*" He is persistent, I'll give him that. "You know, most women would keel over to have the chance to go out on a date with me."

I sit my coffee on the coffee table and simply stare at him, nonplussed, as my arms cross under my breasts. Cal looks down at my ample bosom for a moment before looking back into my eyes.

"You aren't even giving me a chance, Eden."

"Callan, please don't take this personally, but... Well, you're like all the rest of them," I begin.

All men are the same, and he's a cocky chauvinist who will deeply wound me if I allow him in. I simply can't. I have built these walls for too long to let them be broken into so easily. I have the club, my career, all strong and thriving because I've kept that ironclad mask and foundation in place. He's not coming in and tearing it all down because he's built like a Greek god, has the face of an angel, and is as charming as a prince...even if he is doing a damn good job of trying.

"You don't know me. You think you do, but..." he trails off, and I get a glimpse of a softer side of him that I realize he doesn't show often. Even if I want to believe him, I have to make him work to prove himself, I can't just trip over myself because he's drop-dead gorgeous. That would make me a fool, and I've been fooled before. As if sensing my thoughts, Cal smiles again. "Well, dinner may be jumping the gun, so we'll talk over coffee." He picks up my cup and hands it back to me, touching his to mine before bringing the paper cup to his lips and sipping.

"What did you get?" I ask once he swallows.

"Caramel macchiato. It's my fave."

"Hmm, mine is a dark roast with two sugars and half and half."

"Good to know." He grins, and I gulp. I still can't believe his sexy, delicious-smelling self is sitting in my apartment, on my couch. My mind is taking mental pictures right now to pull out later when I'm alone with Fred, my vibrator. "What about your favorite color?"

"Red. You?"

"Blue." He motions to the hat on his head. "I've been told wearing it makes my eyes pop."

God, his eyes. I don't know what area of his body is sexier —his eyes, his perfect lips, or his chiseled muscles...*or his big, thick cock fucking your throat*, my dirty mind adds. I swallow hard again, flashing back to his moans, the look on his face when he came. God, how hungry I was for him that night.

"I like how your hair frames your face when it's down. It's sexy." He reaches for a strand of my thick, curled hair and pulls it through his fingers.

And just like that, I'm suddenly soaking wet with desire. I know tonight I'll be using "Fred" for sure. And Heaven help me, the visions that will be running through my mind when I do.

"Uh, when's your next photoshoot?" I ask, trying to pull the attention from myself.

"Next week. I'll be in Miami."

"Fun."

"It's just a couple days. I try not to go too far. Sally's been sick and won't be around as much."

"Oh no!"

"Yeah, she's uh, she's got cancer."

"I'm so sorry."

"Well, her prognosis is good, but it's just a lot of treatments and time off, so I wanna stay close, in case Sam needs me. She's got a signing at Barnes and Noble next Friday evening."

"That's great. I love Barnes and Noble."

"Wanna come?" he asks, eagerly.

"How can I pass up a trip to a bookstore and me a librarian?" I wink at him, and he gives me another sexy smile. Fuck me, this man is killing me today. "Thanks for the coffee, Cal."

"Cal, huh?" His eyes are sparkling. "We're skipping right to nicknames now, *Eady*?"

I gulp, loving the sound of this name on his plump lips.

"Guess my chisel is working after all." His grin is triumphant—and how can I shut him down with pearly whites that perfect?

I simply shrug. "Don't know which chisel I like better," I say and look his huge sculpted arms over. Gah, they haunt my dreams; they're literally lickable.

"Eden, you can't do that if you want me to sit here and be a good boy. I don't behave well." Suddenly, his demeanor has changed. And the subservient side of me is terrified, even while the inner vixen is jumping up and down for joy at the prospect of his hands on me again...like they were that night in the club. He must sense my turmoil as he looks away suddenly. "Speaking of..." He clears his throat, "we should hit the gym together tomorrow, what do you say?"

I debate with myself. He's well on his way to breaking in, and I'm well on my way to letting him; there's a part of me that's so tired of coming home to an empty apartment alone. This little bantering and conversing is fun, but it will only be a matter of time before he's expecting me to have sex with him. And I know that I can't...no matter how much I want to. I know the routine; it's the same as it was with Washington. He'll want more. And more is what I can't do. I couldn't do it with Washington. I won't be able to do it with Callan, either...right?

I focus my eyes to the large, patterned rug on the floor, my bruised and battered soul fighting hard against what it needs versus what is safe. I feel Callan's hand cover mine, and I glance up quickly, feeling ribbons of tingling heat curl in my lower belly.

"No pressure, Eden. Honestly. Just two people hanging out. Working out together. Ok? I promise I'll do my best to be a good boy."

"How about you let me think on it?"

"Like, *I don't get an answer today* think on it?"

"You're not very patient, huh?" I stifle a laugh.

"No ma'am. I'm not." His pearly whites bite into his bottom lip in a grimace, but all I see is a flashback of him restrained in my chair back at RISE begging for release. I gulp down a whimper.

Roxie, where are you when I need your backbone?

Step aside, E, I got this!

"Well, guess what, Cal? You're gonna *have* to be." I arch a brow. "I can't just cave the first time you make a gesture that isn't self-serving after all, now can I?"

Ah, she hasn't forsaken me, thank goodness.

He looks away, contemplatively. Then shrugs.

I mentally pat myself on the back and take another sip from my cup, watching as Cal does the same.

"Hey, this is nice. Coffee. Talking. Thank you," I state truthfully.

His demeanor changes once again, and he gives me another of his million-watt smiles. "You're welcome." He toasts his cup into mine. "Cheers. To baby steps."

"Baby steps." I grin back.

I could get used to this. This man. These feelings stirring inside me.

This is gonna be fun. Making him work harder than he ever has for a woman. It's a new kind of torture for him, and Roxie is rejoicing.

Time to have him back in the club to satisfy her sinful cravings. If I can't have him like I want him as Eden, I can certainly have him as Roxie.

3
CALLAN

"*Hercules!* Again?" I tease my nephew even as I sit next to him on the couch and tuck him into my side, pulling the blanket up to our chests.

He giggles, and I feign exasperation even as I click play on the console. I grin down as his eyes focus on the screen, and kiss his forehead, knowing I've just made his night. God, he's precious...and I'm a damn sap and don't even care.

Filling the fatherly role for this kid has been one of the greatest things I've ever done in my life.

The movie plays. I laugh with Caleb and joke when Zeus comes on screen, and soon, he's pointing to me.

"Nah, I'm not as powerful as ol' Zeus, cubby." Cubby is the nickname we gave Caleb when he was just a baby.

Caleb argues, and I laugh again. "I wish," I say, looking back at the TV.

I think back to my last drool-worthy rendezvous with the mysterious and beautiful masked goddess at the club—*RISE*. What a great name for a gentleman's club, ha. My dick seems to follow the command the minute I lay eyes on her tall, curvy frame. I'm drawn into her world and put under her spell. She's a damn seductress, I swear to God, drawing me into the dark, sexual pit of her erotic purgatory. I wish I could understand why she has that pull on me.

Madam Roxie. She's built like something straight out of ancient Greece, a goddess in her own right—Aphrodite, if I can be so bold. Her muscular thighs and voluptuous breasts undo my moral fiber with just one glance, and I can't seem to escape the allure of her. Even while I pine over Eden Riser, the cocky, yet quiet librarian that I can't seem to sweet talk no matter the amount of charm I ooze out. Perhaps that's the problem here. My charms work on all women save for her, so I gotta go and get my rocks off at the alluring club where the elite have clandestine sexual encounters with masked women of the night.

I remember how good her body felt touching mine, scorching my flesh like a branding iron, how amazing she smelled, how aroused she made me with just those flaming reddish-brown eyes of hers. She didn't fuck me—no, she just resorted to tormenting the hell out of my erect cock with her fingers, lips, and tongue until I couldn't take anymore and blew my load all over her face. I think the crazy bitch gets off making me her puppet, but I'm too damn stupid to say, "No," when she comes to dance in front of me and crooks that long, red-nailed finger my way. Helpless. That's what I am. Thirty-three years old and pussy-whipped like a damn sixteen-year-old. I need to get a fucking life!

Caleb points to the girl on the screen—Meg I think her name is, and I grin. He mumbles something that sounds like "girlfriend."

"Yeah, that's Herc's girlfriend."

Caleb points a little finger to my chest, and I grin again. How the hell is he reading my mind?

"No girlfriend. Maybe one day soon. Ya never know." My

mind is thrown from Roxie to Eden, and as I look at Meg, I wonder if all women are manipulative harlots set to ruin men. As Caleb rests his head on my shoulder and I inhale his clean, fresh scent I know they aren't. Drew was the one to walk out on this angelic boy whose heart is bigger than any I've ever known, not the other way around.

No, I'm just the stupid fool all wrapped up in a woman whose face I've never seen. All because I don't stand a chance with the one whose face I can't wait to see again.

***

ROXIE

"HOW LONG YOU PLAN ON STRINGING THIS BOY ALONG, ROX?" Everleigh asks me at the club as I get ready for yet another performance.

"As long as he takes the bait," I smirk, remembering the look on Cal's face as he begged me to have intercourse with him the other night. He was straight putty in my hands, and it was such a turn-on having a man his size dwindled down to a begging little boy.

"Mmm, baby, your mouth and hands are amazing, but I wanna feel your heat."

"Are you begging me, big guy?" I stroke his shaft with such restraint and watch him shiver, fighting so hard with his own.

"Fuck yes. Dammit, yes! I'm fuckin' beggin'. Ride my cock, Roxie baby."

"That's Madam Roxie to you."

He whimpers. "Madam Roxie, jump up here and slide me inside you. Please?"

And yet I didn't. I don't honestly know why...

The inner sadist wants to carry this on...and on. See how far he'll let it go, how often he'll come back to see me, get to know him...like *that's* gonna happen!

"You're sick, you know that?" Ev harrumphs.

Yup, I know! I only shrug in response.

"Well, what does *Eden* think of this?"

I laugh and look around, making sure no one has heard us. We don't use our personal names in the club, but it's just the two of us, and I relax some.

"C'mon, lady, I know you like him. It's obvious. Could you be reminded of a certain someone in Cal's presence?"

I look up into her bright green eyes and balk. Speaking about Marco is something no one ever does with me. They know how upset it makes me, but dammit, she's right. He reminds me of Marco, his size, his sweetness, even in his horndog ways, and especially his eyes. Dammit!

"Hey." She pulls me in for a hug, her business attire rough against my threadbare lingerie-covered skin as her big pregnant belly is thrust against me. I embrace her back; this girl is my sister. She's been there for me when I needed a sister most, her and Magnolia and Addison. My sisters. "It's ok, you know? It doesn't make you a bad person."

When I pull back some, I realize I have tears in my eyes. I wipe my face, hoping I haven't messed my makeup up. It takes far too long for Wendy to apply, and I don't wanna keep my guests waiting. But I smile up into her beautiful face and think of her and Luca, happily married with one child and two more on the way very soon. Everyone in our foursome has someone special now.

Everyone but me.

Everleigh was once an ice queen, like me; we shared our hatred for men together, jaded by our one true love, hardening our hearts over the years and making us crave the blood of their deceptions.

Her craving has been satiated—well, eradicated honestly— while mine still rages like an unspent volcano.

"E, you know that it's ok to let someone in. It's ok to love another man. Marco—"

"Please don't say his name." I shake my head and tremble, her words piercing my heart like a knife wound. She can't say his name in here, and I haven't said it aloud in a very long time; the pain of his loss is still so poignant. The man who was my protector, my solid rock, my only defense against the world, was taken from me to die so that I might live.

"Look at me!" Everleigh clasps my wrist in one hand and cups my cheek in the other. "Sooner or later, you've *got* to move on from him. You can't continue this! You know his intentions weren't always pure and don't you dare stand there and act like he was perfect, because you damn well know that he wasn't! He stood by and—"

"Stop!" I yell and pull away from my friend. "I can't do this right now, Ev. I have a performance."

"Yeah, that's right. A performance. That's all you know how to do anymore, *Roxie*. That's fine. We'll talk later." Her perfectly arched brow goes up, and she crosses her arms across her royal purple dress suit, a beautiful statue of strength.

I sigh and adjust myself, swipe my tears, and check my makeup. My mask is firmly in place, and with that, I walk out of the locker room.

NINE YEARS AGO...

My tears consume me as I sit on the floor of the shower sobbing uncontrollably. I had sex with a man tonight. A very rich, very hand- some, very sexy mountain of a man... The first one since Marco, and

I feel cheap, dirty, and mortified about it. Like I can't scrub myself hard enough. I brought him into my room, went over the rules, tied him down and began stripping, both him and myself.

He spoke such beautiful words to me, and before I knew what I was doing, I was slipping a condom on him and sliding down his big, erect cock. I hadn't realized how much I'd missed the feel of a shaft filling my womanhood, but at the same time I was blind with panic and fear that he would somehow become loose from his restraints and do something I didn't want—like control the situation. So I rode him as hard and fast as I could to reach my endgame, orgasmed, then finished him off with my mouth after shucking the prophylactic. He was as satisfied as a dog served a platter of bacon and threw down an extra three hundred dollars as a "tip." Said I was the most amazing fuck he'd had since his marriage, sixteen years ago.

Roxie was lapping that shit up like it was coated in chocolate, meanwhile Eden is mortified that she just did it with a married man. I'm the epitome of sin...

All the girls are gone for the night, the club is closed; it's four in the morning, and I sit here in hysterics, fingering the brand on my labia, the welt that reminds me of all the shame and resentment Vince brought into my life.

"Eden?" a soft voice calls, but I'm numb to anything but the pain I feel right this moment.

I don't even gasp in surprise or bother to cover myself, overtaken by my grief.

"Jesus, honey, are you ok? Did someone hurt you? You know I'll cut a bitch." Everleigh tilts her head, and I know she's dead serious on the matter.

I shake my head and just look into her piercing eyes, pleading for understanding.

She moves off, and when she returns, she has two towels and is cutting the shower off. She squats down even as I stay still, looking into the shower drain for the answers to my problems. I'm not aware that I'm still scratching at the mark on my sensitive flesh, wishing I could tear it off, until Everleigh gasps.

"Oh my God! Ead... is that a-a brand?*" Ev covers her mouth in horror and I simply look up, my body tensing as I realize in my carelessness, she's seen my biggest secret. She jerks my hand away so she can read my embedded sin puckered there. I don't fight her, just wait with bated breath.*

A storm passes over her face as shame fills mine. "That motherfucking son of a—"

"It's my burden to bear, and after tonight, I deserve it." *I'm a squalling mess again as Everleigh pulls me to my feet and wraps one towel around my body, the other around my sopping wet hair.*

When we get to the locker room bench, she sits us down and pulls me to her in a warm embrace.

"Listen to me: nothing you've ever done deserves that. I know a good plastic surgeon..."

I shake my head. "No. I-I can't."

She frowns at me like I'm nuts and maybe I am.

"I don't know why you're trying to pull a Hester Prynne, but it's your body, your decision."

"Please please *don't tell the girls?" I beg.*

"Eden, you know better." She taps my nose and kisses my cheek. "Us ice queens must stick together, you know?"

4

EDEN

"I can *not* believe I let you talk me into this."

"Oh, c'mon, Eden. It'll be fun working out with the hottest guy in town. Most women would be downright jealous of you right now." He elbows me as we walk into World Fitness —AKA Ramon's gym, as me and the girls call it, together. How is it that Cal and I belonged to the same gym all along and never saw one another?

I roll my eyes at his arrogance. I may end up walking out before all is said and done. I can't stand cockiness. It drives me mad. Unfortunately, men who look like Callan are cocky. They have every right to be, after all. I see as my eyes skirt down his large frame. *Internal sigh.*

We hand our keychains over in unison, and the clerk at the counter welcomes us while scanning our key tags. We take them back, looking for open benches as we move from the lobby into the workout area.

We find some right away, and the big lug takes his gym bag and gallon—yes gallon—of water and places it beside one of them. "This spot work for you, madam."

My eyes go up at the word madam, and I'm taken off guard for a moment, only to realize it's not because he realizes who I am more than just calling me madam—not an unusual greeting for a woman. I recover quickly and nod, setting my own bag and water bottle down beside the bench next to him. "What are we working out today, Arnold?" I quip, sarcastically.

Cal laughs. "Well, I mean, we *could* work out our lower half." The grin and eyebrow he cocks at me takes my breath for a moment. Damn, he's gorgeous...and damn well knows it, too. But that's why he's been on the cover of so many books.

I cross my arms and give him the haughty look I've mastered over the years. "Let's do chest and triceps. Yesterday was leg day for me."

His eyes fall to my full breasts, clad in a tight pink sports bra that doesn't do much to cover my generous cleavage, and I feel my skin flush beneath his scrutiny. "That's as good a place to start as any," he confirms and stares.

"Oh, stop it," I slap his bulky forearm and move towards the weight rack, all too aware of his eyes moving down my back and backside hugged by a form-fitting pair of yoga pants.

"Just when I thought the view couldn't get *any* better," I hear Cal mutter behind me and just as I'm spinning around to scold him, he moves to my side, grabbing a set of 50s from the dumbbell rack. "I'll start here."

Start there. Jeez! I turn and watch him place the weights on his thighs and lay back, his hulking frame blocking out the entire bench. He extends his arms and the enormity of his bulky biceps and wingspan leaves me speechless. God, he's fucking massive. His pecs—barely covered by a seafoam-blue muscle tank—are inked, thick, and well-defined. He lifts the weights into a chest-fly with such ease that I'm in awe of his strength, so in awe that I almost drop the twenty-pound weights in my hands. Damn him! How am I gonna get through this? What have I gotten myself into?

Callan sits up with a soft grunt and another heart-stopping grin. He eyes my expression and the neglected dumbbells in my hands. "You gonna stare all day or work yourself out?" he smirks, and I blush twenty shades of red.

I balk and avert my eyes, turning as I sit on the bench, and drop the weights to my thighs. I stare ahead, all too aware of his smiling eyes. I want to punch his beautiful face and tell him to go straight to Hell, but instead, I lay back and do my own chest-flys. Once I'm upright, Cal following suit after doing another easy set of twenty, he laughs and mutters under his breath. "I could get used to this view every workout." His sparkling eyes make me smile, and I roll my eyes playfully.

"You see yourself every day, Callan," I tease and nod my head to him in the mirror.

"Ha ha, I mean *you*, silly." With that, he turns my way, puckers his lips at me, and lays back down on the bench.

We continue our workout, beginning to sweat as we increase our weights. Obviously, I can't lift as much as he does, so when he moves back to the rack, I go to tricep curls. I smile at him in the mirror again as he sits down, and he returns it, reaching for his phone on the ground.

"Say cheese."

I have no time to protest as he steps up next to me and snaps a pic.

I gasp and reach for his bicep. "Cal, you can't post that!"

"Oh c'mon, you look beautiful. Don't—"

"No! You *can't* post that. Like at all!" I realize I'm being super loud and look around, knowing the panic is echoed on my face.

Cal is frowning but reassures me, "Ok, Eady, calm down. I won't post it. Jeez! Wouldn't want your husband to see you hanging out with my fine self. He might get jealous," he jokes, trying to lighten the mood.

I relax a little and give him a weak laugh. "Yeah, Mr. Invisible-Man Riser isn't one to share." I wink and try to calm my heart rate as I sit back on the bench, reaching for my weights.

"If you were mine, I wouldn't share you either, Eden."

I'm in awe once more as I just stare back at him. Is this his attempt at sincerity or is he just playing me? I can't be hopeful. After all, I don't know him well enough to ascertain if he's being earnest or simply trying to sweet talk me. I mean, who knows how many pairs of panties he's dropped with cheesy lines like that. I put my guard back up—and my tongue back into my mouth—and focus back on my workout.

I've moved on to inclined chest flys, the weights becoming heavier with each rep. I grunt at the last one and set them down on the ground, grabbing for my water. I look back to my workout buddy as I suck the straw into my mouth and watch his entire body freeze, his eyes are entranced with my mouth. I'd be lying if I said the heat that surges through my core has anything to do with the adrenaline coursing through me. This is how he looks at me in the club with my clothes off, as his eyes adore my naked body, his gaze caressing my flesh with hot flames. This is the look he gave me just a few nights ago as he begged me to let him take me. I gulp into the face that's so intent on mine and let my body be consumed by lust. Aside from the club, it's the first time in a very long time, and I savor it for a moment. I haven't felt this so prominently since...

"You two gonna free up one of these benches soon?"

Cal and I both look up to see another gym member standing in front of us. He's small, like *way* too small to be talking to Callan Manning like that. "Maybe you should head to the bathroom and take care of that," The man says with a smirk, pointing to Cal's well-tented shorts.

Cal's face turns down into a scowl and he takes a step forward, undeterred by the semi-erection that I—apparently—brought on by simply sucking on a straw.

"How about you wait your damn turn, scrawny?" Cal growls and towers over the other man, who looks as if he suddenly might puke.

I move forward too, not wanting to cause a scene. It's one of the many reasons I became a librarian, where I can stay in the shadows as both necessity calls for and to satisfy my inner introvert.

This man obviously doesn't know who Cal is, so I plant my hand softly on Callan's chest and coo to him. "Cal, baby, it's alright. We can move on. There are other body parts I wanna work out, anyway." I bump my bottom against Callan's hip seductively.

I watch the guy's brows rise, and Cal smirks at me. Good, he's not gonna get into a fight today.

"Fine, but I don't like being kicked off my bench by this weasel." Cal's eyes flit over the man one last time before he finally turns and grabs his bag and water jug. His eyes narrow as he turns back to the other man. "And since you couldn't wait, you can wipe it down yourself and re-rack the weights...*if* you can even lift them."

The man just gapes as we walk away to the cable machines for tricep pull-downs.

"Fuckin' prick," Cal grumbles as he sits his stuff roughly down to the side. "You know? I could have really made him regret talking to us like that." He rubs a hand over his scruffy beard and the blue eyes that assess me make my insides clench.

"I know, big guy. You could take him with one easy punch, couldn't you?" I ask and move a little closer to him.

"Damn straight," he confirms.

"Well, I think it makes you the bigger person by simply walking away and not letting him affect you."

"Clearly, I'm the bigger man, anyway." That sexy smirk is back. "Usually, I wouldn't let anyone talk to me—or my lady—like that. I hope you know that."

When he moves even closer in front of me, I can feel the head of his unrestrained shaft pressing against my inner thigh. I could moan aloud, remembering how the hard ridge of him felt being pressed so close to my own sex in my club. God, I want to feel it that close again. He feels the shift in my mood and his burning blue orbs fall down my chest, making me feel both unabashedly sexy and completely vulnerable in that moment.

"He's incredibly lucky I wasn't mad."

"Do you turn green when you're mad?"

"Something like that…" Callan trails off as his hand comes to cup my cheek, his thumb stroking my cheekbone. I sigh, loving how protected I feel in his presence. Almost like when I was with—

"I never would have guessed the gorgeous body you got hidin' beneath those stuffy librarian clothes." The smile that greets me as I look into Cal's handsome face is downright ravenous. I want to throw my arms around his big neck and feel his bulking frame pressed against mine. His lips are so enticing. I've never felt them pressed to my own, and God, I really want to. But I hold back—like always.

He must feel my hesitation, for he looks around and takes a step back, clearing his throat and pulling at his shorts. Damn, I made him hard again. Ha!

I blush and grin at my power over him. It makes me feel confident once more, and I move to exercise my triceps.

We don't come close together again as we move around the machines, continuing our workout of chest and triceps, until finally we're finished and hit the cardio machines, both choosing the bikes.

We wordlessly begin a rigorous forty-minute session, our legs pedaling harder and faster as time goes on, in competition with one another. Cal doesn't speak but eyes me every now and again, and the sexual tension between us feels like jarring electricity that jolts us both.

Once our workout is over, we're drenched and breathless as we get off the bikes. I wanna grab him, pull him into the shower with me, and let him give my womanhood the workout the rest of me has endured at his side. But I haven't had sex like a normal person in... well... It's actually never happened.

Marco never took me in the shower. Never took me from behind. Never took me missionary, not after we tried that first time and I freaked out on him. No, I've always been on top, no matter what. Always in control. Always able to stop if I want to. But something about Callan makes me yearn to want to try. I wanna know what it's like to lose myself to him...but what if I can't? What if my Uncle Vince truly ruined me to any other man? What if he succeeded in destroying me, as he tried to do from the very beginning?

My ever-persistent insecurity rampages through my heart and mind, leaving me shattered. Suddenly, I'm gasping for air, the panic rising in my throat until I'm close to blacking out. I see spots, hear my breaths coming out rapidly, and I whimper, both dreading and welcoming the darkness of Death's cold grip.

A warm palm encircles my waist then and pulls me into a solid chest. I feel another big palm at my jaw and look up into an azure blue sky. I smile, for it is Heaven not Hell I'm being thrust into, and I welcome the warmth against my skin.

"Eden," a sexy, gruff voice calls to me. He's my savior, and he's so beautiful.

My eyelids flutter closed as I let the angel lift me into his strong, capable arms, my head falling to his shoulder. I feel myself flying and can almost hear the flutter of his wings.

Take me away, my angel, I think to myself. Away from the Hell I've endured these past fifteen years. Away from the pain, the abuse, the debauchery, the corruption, the devastation... all of it. *Take me to Heaven in your arms.*

I feel something cold on my face then frigid liquid runs across my lips and down my throat. I swallow instinctively, obeying my angel as he tells me to.

"Eady, come back to me, darlin'," I hear Cal's voice say. "Drink, baby, drink. Open your eyes."

And I do, looking into his concerned and sweat-covered face. His dark brows are drawn over his light blue eyes, his lips pulled in. God, he's so handsome.

"There you are. Jesus, don't worry me like that. I thought you were gonna pass out. Drink up. I think you pushed yourself a little too hard today, huh?" His nervous chuckle pulls me out of my stupor.

I look around at the people behind him and literally balk, pulling my knees in and shivering even as I take the water bottle from him and chug it, needing to wake up fully so that I'm in control once more.

"Hey, back the fuck off and give her some room." Callan stands and shoos the others away. They go reluctantly, and I relax as the last one turns from view. He then kneels back down and reaches a hand out to me. "Are you ok?" The concern etched across his face makes me wanna cry. God, he's so fuckin' sweet...when he wants to be.

Immediately, my internal defenses go on high alert. I attempt to stand, and Cal follows, assisting me with ease, even as he looks me over.

"Whoa, easy there, sweetheart. You came close to passin' out. Take it easy."

I gulp as his touch makes me tingle all over. "I'm fine. Thank you. I just—"

"She must have gotten dehydrated." I see Ramon frowning at me in concern.

"Yeah. Yeah, that's probably it," I stammer, knowing that it was that and a panic attack. It's not the first time this has happened, and I'm positive that it won't be the last. "Um, I'm gonna go shower now," I tell Callan.

"Drink this, first. Here," Ramon demands, running up with a bottle of Gatorade and thrusting it at me.

I do as he says, knowing he's right, and slowly feel my senses return to me, my heart rate and breathing coming back to normal.

"Better?" Cal asks, looking into my face and suddenly, I'm completely embarrassed. He sees it and gives me a weak smile. "Hey, it's alright."

No, no, it's not. I can't lose control. I always have it. This was—

"Eden," his sultry voice pulls me from my inner thoughts. His eyes are so sincere, so understanding, so raw as his thumb and index finger come beneath my chin and tilt my head up to look at him. I don't know what is happening here today but I feel an ache inside my chest that I haven't felt since...Marco.

Marco. That name has so many good and bad memories attached to it, and Cal is *so* much like Marco. Big, strong, sweet, gentle. I long to let him in, but I'm so scared to. Marco died because of me, protecting me. The danger has been mostly dormant for a long time, but I know it's not completely gone. Marco warned me there were more like Vince out there, and with that knowledge, I can't pull someone else into this sordid sin pit with me. Not Callan. Not anyone else.

"I'm gonna go shower now," I insist, pulling his hand down from my face.

He senses my demeanor change, but stands his ground.

"Alright, I'll meet you out here, and we're gonna grab a bite to eat." His tone is firm—there's no sense in arguing with him about it.

I simply nod and turn to head to the shower with my bag in tow.

CALLAN

I GLANCE OVER AT RESERVED EDEN RISER, WHO IS NOW CLAD IN yet another baggy cardigan and loose pants, looking out my passenger window into the dismal summer day. She wears a lot of sweaters, even on this sixty-degree day, and it occurs to me that she doesn't do it so much to keep herself warm as she does to hide beneath them.

I got a glimpse of her vulnerable side. And it brought out the protective side of myself, the one I primarily save for Caleb and Sam. It made me feel good though, as if she needed that part of me—although she'd not admit to it if it would save her life.

I scowl, wishing I could understand why she guards herself so. What frightens her? Why does she think she has to be so strong all the time? I know the incident embarrassed her. Hell, I'd be embarrassed too if it had happened to me, but it's over now and she's ok—thank goodness.

"Well, here we are," I say as I pull up to the little French bistro my sister suggested at the corner of West and 20th streets.

Eden's head comes up and she smiles.

"Oh, wow, look at that. Happiness. Damn, that looks good

on you, Eady." Her smile immediately fades, and I could kick my own ass for my smart remark. I digress. "You know this place?"

"Yes, me and my girls eat here a lot," she answers, her sad eyes lightening behind her black frames.

Her *girls*? Does she have daughters? Wow, I would never have guessed that.

"So, does that mean it's good?" I ask as I look up at the neon sign that deems it, Riverside Bistro.

"It is, if you like French onion soup and Monte Cristos." Her brow raises, and I'm overwhelmed with her sexy look. God, she's gorgeous.

"How about most foods in general?" I tease and get a grin out of her.

I pull my keys from the ignition that I've turned off by this point and step out of my truck. Before I can come around to open Eden's door, she's already out and at the sidewalk.

"Now, come on, Eden. I wasn't *that* slow." I cross my arms over my chest, my pride wounded by her independence, even if I admire the hell out of her. "You could allow me to be a gentleman on our first date, at least."

"First date?" Her dark brows rise once more. I smirk and nod. "Oh, I don't think so, big guy."

"No? That isn't what this is?" I give her a lopsided grin, and it stymies her response. Fuck yes! I rattle her. I fuckin' knew it. Ha!

"I thought this was simply working out together and grabbing a bite to eat." Her wary look is back, and it annoys me. What's her deal with dating, anyhow? Maybe it's because of her daughters? "Besides," she mumbles, looking down, "you've been gentleman enough taking care of me at the gym." Her cheeks flame, a stark contrast to her olive skin tone, and it melts my heart.

"Hey," I respond, pulling her chin up with my finger, "don't feel bad about that." I insist with a shake of my head. "It could happen to any one of us when we workout hard enough. You're, in fact, human, Eden Riser. Even if you *are* built like Wonder Woman." My eyes fall to appraise the tight, voluptuous body I know lies beneath her baggy clothes. She's smoking hot, and I wanna explore those curves of hers more than I've ever wanted anything in my life. I lick my lips, remembering her big breasts bouncing with each rotation of her bike next to mine as I tried to suppress the hard-on she continued to bring on no matter how many times I shoved it down. "Oh how I would love to workout with you in my basement, just me and you. God, the things you were doing to me, Eady. The things I wanna do to *you* in return..." I step closer, my palm coming to her waist, and I grip her sweater in my fist.

Her eyes immediately flash something akin to panic, and I freeze. "Umm, I—"

"Sorry, I didn't mean to be so forward. It's been a...a while for me..." I trail off and pull my hand from her side, rubbing it across the back of my neck. Damn, I'm a fool!

"It's ok," she replies a little too quickly. "Let's go eat." She smiles and opens her hand. I take it, ruefully, and follow her into the restaurant.

Once we're seated, I look around at the dark-red bricks, the deep mahogany wood, and modern lighting, enjoying the ambiance and soft accordion music coming through the speakers. "Well, ain't this cute?" I ask, looking out the large window to the river below us.

She nods before glancing back at the menu in front of her, and I'm taken off-guard once more by her sheer beauty. She's not wearing a stitch of makeup, yet her radiance is undeniable. What is it about her that pulls me in so? Like a damn magnet. I want her feistiness, her strength, her passion, and her weakness. I want her begging beneath me. I want her. So. Damn. Much.

"Anything sound good?" she asks, pulling me from my inner male thoughts.

"Hell, *everything* at this point. I'm starved," I respond, and my stomach growls in kind as I look the vast menu over, debating between salad and a sandwich or a full entree.

She laughs, and I swear it takes my breath away. I look up into those deep brown eyes of hers and get lost. I gulp. She gulps. Fuck, I need her. I need to be inside her. I want to stay lost in her look, her eyes, her smell. What the hell is happening here?

Suddenly, I frown, feeling something so familiar pass between us. As if I've stared into these very same eyes...somewhere else...more than once. I can't grasp it, but I *know* I have. I feel the familiarity, the connection.

We're interrupted by the waitress, who takes our drink orders first as our eyes fall back to the menu.

After we order, cool and collected Eden is back. Deep down I wonder, once again, what she's like in bed. I wanna see her lose all that self-imposed restraint, see her fall apart in my arms, see the inner vixen take over her. I wanna shake that reserve, splinter it, and watch it crumble as I rock her fucking world. My dick twitches in anticipation at the thrill of it, and I contemplate if she would be just as enticing without the calm she holds so tightly to. Fuck yes, she would. She's fine as hell, both her strength and vulnerabilities, and I want to see it all, exposed naked before me.

I grin even as she maintains her aloofness. I'm the first to break the silence.

"So, you have daughters?" I ask, trying to seem nonchalant.

"Huh?" she frowns.

"You said you come here with your girls."

"Oh, no," she states, clearing her throat. "My girlfriends. I don't have any children."

Oh good, I want to reply but hold my tongue. As much as it doesn't matter either way, I don't want to think of another man fathering her children. I don't want to think of another man being with her...at all. *Control yourself, Romeo,* I tell myself. *This is your first date, and you think you own her already? What the actual fuck?*

"Caleb is precious, by the way." Her grin takes up her whole face, and I can't help but return it at the image of my sweet nephew.

"Isn't he, though? God, I love that little squirt." The warmth in my heart takes over my body at that moment. "I don't know what I'd do without him, to be honest."

And just like that, the look on Eden's face lets me know I've just made her panties wet. I continue, "He's the best, really. Has a great sense of humor, like his uncle."

"It's obvious how much you adore him. And he seems to think the world of you, too." Her brown eyes hold mine, and I see I'm one step closer to getting this hard-ass lady into my bed. "He's one of the reasons I agreed to come out with you." She smirks.

"Oh?" I ask, my brows raising. "How so?"

"Well, any man who puts that kid on the pedestal you do deserves a chance." She winks. I grin. But frown as I think about his piece of shit father, who won't even give him the time of day. "Cal? Did I say something—?"

"No, no," I say with a heavy sigh. "It's just... Caleb's dad, he's such a dick. Selfish bastard..." I shake my head.

"He left Samantha?" she asks softly after a moment of silence.

"Yeah, about six months ago. For his secretary. Sam called me all upset, and I'll be honest, it was all I could do not to find the fuckhead and beat him bloody. I only refrained for my sister's sake. I moved in with them barely a week after. I've been there ever since." I smile at the memory.

It wasn't easy moving in with my sister and Caleb since I'd been on my own for such a long time. But our parents haven't been supportive of either of our careers. They're conservative Southern Baptists. My father's an old-fashioned preacher, my mom an uptight teacher. Mine and Sam's lives stray a bit too far from their values—being as Sam's highly violent and sexual fantasy books, and my provocative, half-naked physique on many a product; we don't exactly reflect Christian ethics. I tell Eden all this, and about how Drew couldn't handle Caleb's inability to be a "normal" child, so he up and split when the going got tough.

"But you came in and saved the day, Superman." Eden grins in admiration.

"I'm nowhere near as good as Clark Kent, I'll admit. It wasn't easy at first. But we've always gotten along pretty well as brother and sister. We understand each other and value the other's opinions even if we're both hard-headed."

"Arguments make us human, I think. Me and my sisters, my girlfriends: Addison, Everleigh, and Magnolia, have all seen each other's darkest sides and we've fought— even physically— but I think it's made us more humble toward one another."

I nod, agreeing with her, although I can't see reserved Eden Riser losing her cool easily. I'd like to see her mad and wild. The thought again stirs my sex, and I realize I might need to jack-off when I get home so I can chill out a little bit. It's as if my dick is controlling me today, and as much as this virile man is used to being directed by his cock, I don't wanna blow this thing with Eden by having her think that sex is all I think about. Even if I do think about it at least fifty or more times a day.

"So, tell me about yourself, Eady."

And just like that, I see sweat form on her brow. Why is she such an enigma? What could this reserved librarian possibly have to fear?

"I-I, uh—"

"What made you wanna be a librarian?" I ask, attempting to calm her jangled nerves. Hopefully this question isn't too hard.

Eden clears her throat as the waitress sits our soups down in front of us. I see that invisible mask she holds tight to cover her.

"I loved getting lost in books. I didn't have the best childhood." Her eyes flash something dark and painful, and I can't help the frown that seizes my face. "My parents—" She gulps and looks down. This is hard for her—so hard, I see—and I hate that I've unknowingly touched a nerve. "They died when I was fifteen."

"I'm so sorry, Eden. I had no idea."

"Books were my escape from reality. I enjoyed going to the library, the smell of the books, the silence. My living conditions were...less than desirable. It was the one place I could truly be myself, where the quiet could entrap me, where I was...home." A lone tear falls down her cheek, and I long to come to her side and kiss it away. She looks up at me sadly and brushes it away. She appears surprised she's revealed so much to me, but I want more—I *need* to know more.

"Were you put into foster care?" I ask.

She shakes her head. "I went to live with a family member. H-he was the only living relative I had." She glances back down. "After—after *he* passed away, I was free. So I became a librarian." She's silent for the longest time, as if taken by her reverie. I dare not speak, not move. I know she's done talking about it, but I have so many questions I know I can't ask. She fiddles with her hands before picking up her spoon and sipping at her soup.

I hesitantly take my own spoon and begin eating, my appetite almost gone at this point. I feel, with every fiber of my being, that something terrible—something unspeakable—happened to Eden. I can't say what it is or how I know, but the obscure veil covering her eyes while she spoke about her past has left me dumbfounded. Despite what I've been through, I've never experienced the sheer distress I felt coming from Eden's gaze. I can't imagine the horrors behind those eyes, and God help me, that I never find out. For as protective as I feel for Eden right now, I know if I ever find out what happened to her, I might explode in rage.

We eat in silence for a time, lulled by the mundane daily habits of day-to-day life going on around us.

Eden is the first to speak. "It's good, right?" The mask is back, and as much as I want to pull it from her gorgeous face, I know it's too soon. I smile and nod. "It's one of my favorites," she admits with a blush.

"She-crab bisque. I'll remember that," I wink. "I can actually cook, you know?"

I steer our conversation in another direction then, talking about the books she loves, telling her about the classics I've read. And I get to see a passion in her eyes that I can tell she doesn't show often. I swear my heart is overflowing today. What is this little minx doing to me?

"*Frankenstein* was so poignant. Romantic and tragic, symbolic of true human nature. I thought it was hauntingly beautiful."

"Oh, come on, Eady. It was down-right depressing. Admit it," I state as my lamb shank with pomme puree and roasted vegetables is set before me.

I see Eden smile down at her coq au vin.

"Bon apetit," the server states and walks away.

I nod and raise my water at Eden as she does the same. "To *Dracula*, a gothic novel in all its glory."

"Now, *there's* an epistolary classic and one of my all-time favorites," she says. "Although, I have to admit, Callan, I'm rather surprised that you're an avid reader." One of her perfectly shaped brows goes up, and I laugh.

She would absolutely *cream* her panties if she only knew how much of an avid reader I truly was, and her a librarian.

We enjoy our meals and order a pear tarte tatin for dessert with cafe lattes.

I pay the tab and escort my date back out to the truck.

"So, I uh, I guess I need to take you home, huh?" I ask as I crank my truck. "I know Caleb and Sam would love to see ya, though."

"Actually, I need to go to the library. I have a few things to finish up." She looks at the display on the console. It's almost two p.m. "One of my co-workers can drop me home later."

"This late, huh? No rest for the weary," I state, and her head falls, bashfully. "I, uh, I actually need to grab some books for Caleb anyway."

"Oh?" Eden gives me a knowing smile, and I swear I want to kiss her so badly that my eyes cross.

I reverse my truck and head us to her library, wondering how I can sneak a kiss in, even as I scold myself for jumping the gun when this wasn't even an official date.

Once again, I attempt to be a gentleman. I park, pull the key from the ignition, get out, and run to her side of the truck. She allows me the honor this time of assisting her out. Her lips pull up in a smile as I walk her through the doors and into the main library, enjoying the smell of old books as I do so.

I'm reluctant to let her go, feeling bereft as she removes her arm from mine.

"I had a great time today, Callan." Her face is soft as I look her over, loving that she's not as short as most of my past conquests.

"Me too, Wonder Woman. We should do it again...soon."

Her eyes fall, but I simply can't take no for an answer. If I have to, I'll come here every single day and coerce her. I'll send her flowers, chocolates, cards, telegrams...I don't care. I *have* to see her again.

Before she can answer, I hear a motorized wheelchair coming up to me and turn to see my little buddy and sister not far behind, followed by a man I don't recognize in a suit. I immediately look past Caleb to him and scowl. He looks like a weasel.

"Well, fancy seeing you two here," Sam says with a playful grin.

Neither Eden nor I move as we wait for Samantha to introduce the stranger. My brows go up, waiting.

"Oh, uh, sorry, this—this is..."

"Kevin Stanley." The man with slicked back hair extends his hand, and I firmly shake it, wanting to crack every bone within.

"Callan Manning, Samantha's brother." I practically growl.

"Pleasure, Cal." *Who the* hell *told him that he could call me Cal?* "And you are?" His eyes look to Eden, and I turn to see her eyes widen.

Shock—and something else—flickers there, but she quickly covers her falter with a stiff smile, taking Kevin's extended hand. "Eden. Eden Riser. I'm the library manager."

"Good to meet you both. I was just accompanying Samantha and Caleb here."

He glances over at my big sis and gives her a smile I don't like...not one damn bit. I cross my arms over my chest, feeling my brows raise once again as I look at the exchange.

"Well, uh, I should be going. I'll call you later, Sammie." He kisses my sister's cheek and turns, leaving Samantha to blush as she looks at me.

"What the *fuck*, Sam?" I ask with a huff when he's out of earshot.

"Cal! We're in a library," she scolds and glances at Eden apologetically.

"I don't give two shits about that. Who the hell is he, and what is he—?"

"Callan." A soft hand comes to my bicep, and I immediately feel calmer, looking down into Eden's beautiful face.

"Cal, if you can date, then so can I," Sam says defiantly, hands going to her hips.

I hear Caleb grunt and look down at my little man, book in hand, and my heart melts.

"Alright, buddy, let's go pick you out some books then," I quip and turn to my date. "It was a true pleasure, Eady." I take her hand and pull the back of it to my lips, looking into her eyes as I gently kiss it, wishing it was her lips instead. God, how I want to taste her. "I'll see you soon." I wink again and let her pull her hand from mine as I watch her gulp. I turn to Sam then. "We'll talk later." I growl and follow Caleb into the library.

5

ROXIE

My heart races as my eyes take him in. God, I want him so damn much. But there's a part of me that's jealous. Jealous that he desires Roxie like he does. *He wants Eden too,* Roxie retorts. But he wants *you*—he likes Roxie's wild side. He's cheating on me.

He can't cheat on you, Eden, if you aren't even together. It's true. I know it is, but my insecure—and irrational—mind and heart aren't listening. Roxie wants to punish him for his wickedness, and I let her do so as I move my body over his in the dimly-lit private room that he's once again visiting. I hear him moan so erotically that every ounce of femininity within me wants every inch of him in that moment. I moan with him as my body covers his, and I move my scantily-clad body teasingly over his large frame, savoring his broad chest and arm muscles with my hands and mouth. I flick his dark nipple with my tongue and get a sexy grunt out of him.

"Oh, fuck, Roxie. You really know how to make a man feel good, don't you, baby?" His eyes look me over, and he licks his lips.

I haven't let him kiss me, for it's all part of this sick game of mine that I enjoy far too much to be deemed sane. But behind this mask, in my club, I can be anything I wanna be. And right now, I wanna be Callan Manning's ultimate torment.

I watch him struggle with the restraints I've once again put him in. He's bound to the bed, his hands wrenched up on either side of his massive frame. I had to use two sets, since his arms are too big to be contained with just one. The sheer size of him arouses me so much I can feel the evidence soaking the lace of my thong.

"Oh, Cal, you turn me on. God, you don't even know how much you turn me on. Do you wanna see it, big guy?"

"Fuck yes. Show me, naughty girl. Show me everything."

I smile, a woman way too happy about what she does here. Proof that he doesn't deserve sweet Eden. She's too good for this bad boy, and Roxie damn well knows it. *Torture it is, Callan, honey. And I will torture you until I'm fully satisfied.*

I straddle his waist and feel his erection digging into my ass cheek. I hear him growl in response, and it spurs me on. I lean back, open the side of my panties—the opposite side where my brand is—and reveal my naked sex to him.

He grunts, an animal restrained from doing what is only natural, and Roxie laughs heartily. God, she's an evil bitch.

"Can you smell it? How much I want you, Cal?" I trail a finger through my wet folds and show him my dripping arousal.

"Mmm, yes...fuck yes." He inhales deeply. "I smell that sweet peach... Dammit, Rox. Let me out of these so I can touch you." He growls again, and I laugh once more.

"But you're such a bad boy, Callan. I can't. You know the rules, baby boy."

"*Fuck* the rules! They were made to be broken. Let me taste you, Roxie. Please?"

I smirk and look him over. God, I want to feel his tongue on me. I've tortured myself with wanting to taste his lips, feel him inside me, feel his mouth on my sex...but I've refrained, so that Eden can experience these things first. She deserves it, after all. Roxie has had her fun—many times with many men—but it's not often Eden gets the limelight, and Cal has shown great interest. Eden needs this pleasure; Roxie can't have it all.

"Slide up here and let me savor your sweetness."

I relent for a split second then move astride his chest, letting his head fall to the apex of my thighs, close enough to let him do as he craves, but where I can also pull myself away if I want to. I whimper as his tongue licks a deliciously slow trail from my core to my clit, and I fight the urge to move against him, ride his face. It's so hot—*he's* so hot. It feels fucking fantastic, just as I knew it would. I moan aloud as he licks again and his mouth settles over my aching bud and sucks. God, I need this release. I need him.

"Mmm, Callan that mouth of yours. It feels amazing." I whine.

"You like that, baby? I wanna make you come." He sucks again, and my sex clenches. I shiver as I pull his head back and move off him. "Goddammit, Roxie. You're such a tease. Fuck!" he swears, and I laugh manically again.

"But the torment is so sweet, isn't it, my sexy man?" My fingertips trail his chest as he pulls his frame up to a seating position on the bed. Damn, that strength...

"I want you so much, I'm fuckin' shakin'."

I see him quake as he fights the restraints again, and I silently wish he would fucking break them and come at me. Would I stop him if he did? I honestly don't know. I've never been this turned on in my life before.

I pull my negligee down my shoulders, exposing my breasts, and watch his face as his eyes fall over my curvy body.

He looks so aroused and angry, so damn sexy. His jeans are unzipped—how I left him—his girthy member barely restrained. But damn, I'm having so much fun with him. I smile again, and he swears as I take my breast in my hand and squeeze, closing my eyes.

"Let me do that, please?" he begs. I move closer, the torment and anticipation too much for even me. I sit astraddle of his hips again, making sure my sex is now covered, and lean into him, looking into his handsome face. I cup it in my hands and evaluate him. What makes him so different than other men? So much more enticing? Worthy of my affections?

Nothing! Roxie screams. *He can't even stay true to one woman.* I arch my brow, although he can't see it behind my mask, his fate determined.

I move my hand into his jeans, smiling as his big cock juts out and across my palm. It's impressive in both length and girth. I've seen many over the years. They haven't impressed me as much as his does.

"Mmm, yes baby," he says as he thrusts against my covered pelvis, his big shaft peeking through the slit in his boxers, skirting my fingers. I softly run my fingernails across the tip of him as his head falls back. I kiss his jaw, then his throat. "Fuck, Rox, you make me shiver. God, how do you do this to me?" he whimpers, and the sound of it makes my arousal coat both my lacy panties and his boxers.

"You gonna beg me to fuck this big, hard cock of yours again, Callan?" I smart and grip him in my palm again, squeezing as I pump it in my fist.

"Oh fuck."

I feel his steely shaft jerk in my hand and bring the tip to my swollen bud. I rise and lower myself on it, the torment so exquisite I know I can't hold back for long.

"Beg me, big guy. I know you want to," I tease. "Want me to slide your cock into my hot, wet, little pussy?" I ask, knowing the answer even as I bite gently into his massive neck. "Fucking beg me." My voice turns raspy as my womanhood yearns to feel him deep inside me. God, I want it. I want it so bad, but I won't, I can't! If I do, he might not come back for more...and I can't take that.

Instead, I ride his lap, pushing the head of him against my covered clit as I lose myself to the sweet feel of his velvety crown against me. I arch my back and feel his lips cover my exposed nipple. He suckles, and my orgasm assaults me as I cry out in exquisite pleasure. Pleasure I've not allowed myself with a man in quite some time. I rock and grind and whimper my release, feeling tears stream my cheeks as I return to earth. I moan even as Cal's mouth continues to love my nipple and his pelvis arches towards mine in a futile attempt to push himself inside me, for my tight thong is a barricade between us. I angrily look down into his face as he pulls his lips from my breast.

"You didn't beg me," I accuse.

"Because it wouldn't fucking matter," he smarts back, and I growl. "You can't always have what you want, Rox."

"The hell you say! Need I remind you *whose* fucking room of pain this is?" I pull on his cuffs for effect.

"Fuck that! Let me go. I want out of here."

I laugh again. "I'll say when your time is up, not you." I move off him and grab my whip, snapping it as I flick my wrist. "You don't like to play by the rules."

"There *are* no fucking rules, Roxie. Don't you get that?"

"Why didn't you beg me to fuck you, Callan?" I move forward, gripping his face in my hands as I drop the whip, knowing how much he hates the damn thing. His eyes are dark, and I see something different in them... Is that guilt?

Regret? No. It can't be... "You didn't *want* me to fuck you?" I frown, confused. Then why the hell is he here?

He sighs heavily and looks away, fighting against the restraints once more. I pull the key from the carabiner at my hip and unlock his cuffs, dropping them to the bed. He looks up at me, surprised as I gulp and wait for him to approach, knowing I'm not ready for his advances should he decide to do so. I hold my breath and wait as he stands to his full height of six feet, five inches.

I wait. And wait. I can feel the rush of my blood pounding in my ears... I debate running for the panic button we have in each room in case of emergencies.

He doesn't move. Just towers over me by nine full inches. His eyes hold mine as I look up at him. I watch his sex deflating, and internally, I could cry. He doesn't want me. He doesn't want to fuck me. I don't know how to take this; for this hasn't ever happened before in here.

"I guess if you don't wanna have fun, then you're free to go, Mr. Manning." I turn, biting into my quivering lip as I do so. The heartbreak that engulfs me is as painful as any physical blow I've ever taken.

I feel Cal step up behind me and fight the urge to turn into his muscular, naked chest and cry my eyes out. I feel his hand come to my back, and I flinch. No one has ever been freed from their restraints in this room. This is different, and I don't know how I feel about it. I don't allow anyone to touch me; I touch them. That's the way it goes. I bring them in. I tell them the rules. I restrain them, whether it be to the bed or the chair. Then I'm in control. This. This is *way* out of my comfort zone, and panic begins to rise in my belly as Callan turns me around by my wrist.

The knuckle of his right index finger moves from the edge of my mask down my cheekbone, then his finger tilts my chin up as he takes a step closer to me. I can feel the heat coming off him, and I long to lean into him. "But this isn't *fun* for you, is it, Rox?"

How does he know? How can he possibly see beneath this mask?

As soon as I think this, his hand comes up to it and grips it. I grate out angrily, "Don't!"

Cal stops but doesn't move his hand from the black and gold piece of fabric that covers a fair portion of my face. His big palm could easily rip it off me in one clean jerk before I could do anything to stop him.

"Has anyone ever seen you without this?" he asks softly.

And deep down, I know exactly what he's asking me. I don't answer him, though. I hold his gaze, daring him to defy me. Somehow, I know he won't.

Finally, he pulls his hand away and sighs heavily. He turns from me and goes to the chair, lowering his big frame into it. He covers his face in his hands and leans forward, elbows on his knees.

"I don't know why I keep coming here, Rox," he admits and pulls his hands from his face suddenly. His gorgeous blue eyes hold me captive when he looks up at me. "I mean, you—you're gorgeous. Fucking look at you. God, you're like something out of my wildest wet dream. But damn...dammit, I—" He shakes his head.

I walk toward him and drop to my knees, needing to hear this, needing to know why he can't stop coming to me, needing to know what Roxie means to him, what *I* mean to him.

Callan's big palm comes to my jaw and neck and cups it gently. It's the most gentle any man has ever been with me in this room, and I'm completely in awe. He's one of the biggest men I've ever been around, yet his touch is feather light on me; I close my eyes, loving that about him.

"God, help me. I tell myself that I'll stop, that one more fix will do it, that once I have you that this will all stop... but dammit, it doesn't and I'm back here before I know what I've done. Tasting you tonight... God, it was amazing. I want to taste you again. I want to be inside you. You don't even understand. Fuck, Rox...I..."

He's in love with me. That's it, isn't it? Eden thinks.

Don't be stupid, Roxie! You're a floosy, you don't deserve this man's love!

You belong to me, my sweetling, and now you will always *belong to me,* my uncle's voice reverberates in my head, and I squeeze my eyes against the tears that threaten at the memory of the brand searing my groin.

Callan's thumb strokes across my lips, and my eyes shoot open, feeling his face come closer to mine. Panic seizes every fiber of me as I watch his eyes fall to my lips and he licks his own. "I wanna taste every damn inch of you, Madam Roxie. I can't help myself from being taken with you. I want you with a hunger that I've never felt before. But...I can't." His eyes shoot up to mine, and I see that look again.

He's upset, disappointed, regretful. I frown. It's because I'm a stripper, a slut, a whore for hire. It's because I don't deserve him! I never will. Roxie, Eden, we're not good enough for him.

I knew it!

"Roxie, I can't...because I'm starting to have feelings for someone. She—she actually reminds me a little of you, believe it or not." He laughs.

This bastard has the audacity to laugh at my broken heart. I gulp down the pain that has begun to fill every inch of my bruised and battered soul, unsure how I'm still whole after the many times I've been burned. I should be nothing but a pile of ashes.

No, fuck that! You're a damned phoenix and don't you forget that, Marco's voice ricochets inside my head, and I smirk up into Callan's gorgeous face.

"Does this bitch have a name?" I take his jaw in my hands and lean him back. I move my hands down his neck, his collarbone, his pecs. He shivers, spurring me on, and closes his eyes, letting my hands entrance him as they move lower over his torso. When my fingertips flirt with the edge of his boxers, he grunts, but I reassure him with my finger to his lips. "Don't worry, I won't *fuck* you." I say the word fuck in disgust, and his eyes open. He regards me for a moment even as I move my hands to the slit at the front of his boxers and begin stroking the head of his cock. I grin slyly back at him and dare him to stop me, knowing he won't. No man ever does. They're all the same; manipulative, sexually-motivated dogs.

I continue even as he moans and his dick stiffens in my expert hands. I've won. Of course I have, although I don't feel the least bit victorious.

"What's her name, Cal?" I ask again and pump his hefty cock even as my womanhood hums in excitement again.

Fuck you too, bitch, you damn traitor.

"Eden...her name is...mmmm, Eden." He grunts as my mouth covers the head of his penis.

I stop and look up at his face. I gulp. Oh my God, I fucking knew it. He has feelings for me. Holy fucking shit!

He's noticed that I've stopped sucking, and I quickly recover, moving my hand to the base of his shaft. His eyes assess me then and he frowns. "It's not cheating if she's not my girlfriend yet, right?" he asks.

I shrug. "Whatever allows you to sleep at night, big guy," I retort and cup his scrotum. He grips my wrist, again so gently that it takes my breath.

"Why do you keep calling me that?" His eyes assess me, and I could almost swear he's found me out.

I shrug again and giggle. "Well, I mean..." I squeeze his thick member in my hand. "You *are* a big guy, Callan. In more ways than one." *'At a girl, fan his ego!*

He smirks and moves his hand from my wrist. I continue where I left off, basking in the groans that escape his sexy throat as I do so.

I return my mouth to his cock and begin blowing him, taking him deeper into my throat and hearing him hiss as he loves every fucking second of it. His hand cups my jaw and tilts my face up to look at him as I rock his fucking world with my mouth and fist, sucking, squeezing, and working his rock-hard flesh as Eden has yet to do. She's gonna have one hell of a time convincing him we aren't the same person, though. That's gonna be interesting when she finally does give him head.

"Oh, baby, you're so fucking good at this. My God," Cal whimpers even as his fingers move into my wig. I flinch. No man has ever touched me while I do this; it's another first. He must sense this as his hand moves to my neck, then down to my breast and squeezes. I moan. "Yes, baby, you like that?" I moan again and pop off his cock, licking the head of him like he's a lollipop before going back down on him. "Jesus, your mouth feels incredible." He moans, and I answer him. "Fuck yeah, sweetheart. You love sucking my cock as much as I love you doing it, don't ya?" My eyes return to his, and I swear those blue orbs grow darker, hungrier. I want to hop up and ride him like there's no tomorrow. Fuck this facade. He's gonna figure it out, anyway. I can't hide forever, can I? "Mmmm, baby, spread your legs and touch yourself while I fuck your mouth. I wanna watch you." I smile. I've never done this before, and I'm still in control. Done.

I move my free hand, the one that was cupping his scrotum, down my belly, my hip, and in between my legs. "Like this,

Cal?" I coo as sultry as I can manage as my fists tightens around his shaft.

"You know how to please yourself, Rox. You've spent many nights fucking that little cunt of yours with a dildo pretending it's me. Don't fuckin' hold back now, baby girl." *Oh God, if he only knew!*

"Mmmm, yes, baby... Yes I have," I confess, even as I push a finger into my wetness, pull it out, and circle my swollen bud.

"That a girl. Tell me how tight you are."

"Oh, Cal. It feels so hot. So wet...so damn tight."

"I know. God, I can only imagine. It fuckin' haunts my dreams." He groans once more as my mouth covers his hard cock, and I suck him down my throat. One hand moves back to my hair, the other stroking my breast as his pelvis thrusts up and he begins to fuck my mouth, watching as my fingers torture my own flesh. "Come on, Roxie...come for me, baby. Stroke that juicy little peach."

His fingers squeeze my nipple, and I start to unravel. My world splits, and I tumble again. Moans rip through my filled throat as I continue to gulp down Cal's long cock like it's the easiest thing in the world to do. In two more pumps, he's mine and he shoots his load as his hips thrust hard against my face. I swallow him down easily and move my mouth to the head of him, tormenting him with my tongue all the while I continue to stroke my wet folds and look up into his beautiful eyes.

Fuck him! He thinks I don't have him wrapped around my little pussy—even though he hasn't been inside me yet—he's got another thing coming.

Eden or no Eden, he's coming back here to me.

6

EDEN

I gasp as I see the words, "STRIPPER," "CUNT," and "SLUT" written in graffiti on the back door of the club.

"Well," I ask Zeus, "any eyes on who?"

"Nope, guy in a mask. It took all of ten minutes. And he knew when shift change happened because he came just in the right time frame to avoid us."

"Fuck!" I exclaim. "Cover it before someone sees it," I tell Bruno.

"That's not all, E," Zeus says and motions for me to come inside with him as Bruno steps forward to paint over the vulgar words spray-painted in white on the black door.

I follow him into the camera room, and he hands me an envelope. "This came for you."

I nod and thank him. "Hey, don't tell the girls about this. I don't want to give them anymore reason to worry alright."

He nods, and I turn on my heel to head to my office, fear gripping my heart as I pull out a stack of photos.

They're crude, nasty, visions I've fought to erase from my

memory banks. Vince raping me, over and over again, at *The Devil's Playground.*

"Jesus," I exhale and pull my shaking hands from the graphic depictions I've tried so hard to forget over the years. I swallow down the bile threatening the back of my throat.

Who took these? And where did they come from? And why am I receiving these, ten long years after his death?

Someone is fucking with me. Someone is wanting to get under my skin...and they are doing a marvelous job of it. Marco had warned me that there were more like Vince still out there. And this past decade, I've tried hard to heed the warning and stay in the shadows, where I feel safest. But after the graffiti and these photos—photos that should've been destroyed in the fire I set to burn the sin pit to the Hell it came from—I'm certain we're no clearer of the demons plaguing us than we were as little birdies in Vince's hellish cage of torture. God, I feel so helpless...and angry...and annoyed....and fucking *paranoid* right now.

But I've come a long way from being a captive little dove. I am stronger, wiser, and braver than I was as a girl. And I won't go down without one hell of a fight. I won't be bested by this asshole who's out to scare me. Fuck him!

I shove the photos back in the envelope, unlock my bottom drawer, throw the envelope in and lock it back. I then grab up my SIG Sauer P365. I check the magazine, reload it, and cock it. Then reset the safety. I'm ready for those motherfuckers if they come sniffing around. I know I should call Special Agent Kieran Greene, Ev's older brother and a detective for the GBI; he'll know what to do. This is just a scare tactic, after all. No real damage has been done... yet.

Even though my heart is telling me that assessment is wrong. *Dead* wrong.

ELEVEN YEARS AGO...

Lia and I look at one another, alone in the locker room for the first time in a week, for the first time since she saw, up close and personal, Vince taking me and making an example of me. She feels bad, I can see it in her eyes, for my horrors of his "punishment" as well as for telling the girls. It was embarrassing, I won't lie, but necessary. I'm glad they know what I've had to go through inside the walls of this Hell.

"I'm sorry, Eden." She moves forward and takes my hand. "I didn't know that he... he did that to you. I never would have..."

"It's ok, Lia. I'm glad you know. Is that weird?" I give a humorless laugh.

"I don't think so." She looks down. "You're not mad at me, are you?"

"No, of course not."

"I know what it's like to be taken by force."

I think of her marriage to Giacomo and how mean he's been to her about getting pregnant. She's been raped, too; she understands all the emotions that go along with being helpless.

"I'm sorry. But hopefully you'll never know that feeling again. So long as I'm here, Vince won't hurt you ever again, I swear it." I'll take whatever he dishes out if it means these girls won't have to endure it. With that said, I slip her the bag of roofies that I already crushed up and have ready to go, in case they need to be dumped into a drink or two tonight.

I smile at her, trying to improve our moods before we go on stage. Uncle Vince wanted his birdies extra primped tonight, for we have "special guests." We're to be on our best behavior, wear crotchless panties, and flash our dazzling smiles at all costs. I didn't eat dinner because I thought I might puke. These men have graced our establishment before, and I dread having to sit on their laps, feeling their erections digging into my ass and hips, and having their hands wandering my body like I enjoy it when I don't.

"Ready, my sweetlings?" his irritating voice sounds as he enters the locker room, not even bothering to wait to see if anyone is decent.

Thank God, we are ready and stunning as I look at us in the mirror holding hands. Our skin is flawless, hair curled, outfits sparkling, our smiles fake as we greet him.

"Gorgeous, as always." He looks us over and his eyes linger on Magnolia a little too long. "Magnolia, such a beautiful name for such a ripe flower."

She gulps but her smile doesn't falter, and I admire her backbone —I know the deep void that echoes inside those dark eyes of his. "Th-thank you, Mr. Perelli."

"And Cordelia, the secret garden of delights that awaits me so abundantly." His muffled laugh makes my stomach burn. He licks his lips. "Ladies, don't disappoint me tonight. Ms. Greene and Ms. Snyder are already playing such great hostesses to Don and Gio. And I expect the same out of you two." He grips Lia's bicep tightly, "Do whatever they want, got it?" I look up at him in warning to let her go. He sees it, grins, and his eyes narrow before he releases her. "I think I might need to uh...relax before the show. If you would be so accommodating, E?"

I see Magnolia's jaw drop and she begins to speak, but I interrupt her. "Of course. Anything you need, Vince." Anything to keep my sisters safe... anything.

CALLAN

FUCKING SHIT, I'VE DONE IT AGAIN. I DON'T KNOW WHY I CAN'T stop myself from going to see her. But I can't. There's something about her that just keeps pulling me in. I don't know if it's the mask, the secrecy, the allure, the unknowing. It's the fact that I haven't slept with her. That's gotta be it. Once I finally fuck her, all this will end.

But it won't. Somehow I know it won't. I keep telling myself the same lies. Like somehow it will make them true. But they're not, and I know they're not. There's just something about Roxie that keeps pulling me back—no matter how fucked up the situation is. I mean, men pay her to sexually torture them, and I wanna be completely consumed by her, fuck the living hell out of her. What kind of person does that make me? Sick!

I sigh even as I work out that morning, taking my frustrations out on the weight machines and elliptical before showering and heading to the library to see the other woman I can't seem to get enough of. I had a photo shoot yesterday, and all I could think about was Eden Riser sucking me off because I had this insane dream about taking her on Roxie's bed in her kinky garden of pain. She had that damn wig of Roxie's on, sans the mask, and I swear I've never woken up so hard in my life. I had to take a cold shower and unburden myself, all the while seeing Eden's deep brown eyes as I plunged inside her over and over again, unable to quench my thirst for her.

I don't know what the hell is wrong with me. Even Sam and Caleb have given me shit about how obsessed I am with this damn library. I don't give a fuck though. I'm asking Eden out on another date, so I can be one step closer to these dreams and fantasies I can't shake.

So here I sit, in the library of Eden's, trying to be inconspicuous in my hat and a pair of glasses as I sit reading a romance novel with a ripped half-naked biker on the front of it, like some pansy. It's a good book, though, and I'm thoroughly impressed by the sex scenes thus far. I remember asking Sam how difficult it was to write the male POV in these scenes, of which she laughed and said all men were the same so it was quite easy. I recall shooting her a bird and leaving the room to enjoy my book in silence following that.

A throat clears, and I look up to see the sexy librarian of my yummiest dreams smirking at me with three equally as beautiful dark-haired women standing behind her. I lower my book. "Mr. Manning...I'm surprised to see you here." A slight blush paints her olive cheeks, and I long to kiss the warmth right off them.

"You shouldn't be, Ms. Riser. As I recall, I told you I was a big reader." I clear my throat and sit up a little straighter. I give her a wink and a grin and watch as her eyes fall bashfully.

"Eady," a voice behind her says and a fair-skinned brunette with piercing green eyes—Snow White, eat your heart out—elbows her. "Aren't you gonna introduce us?"

"Oh, uh, yes. I apologize," Eden stymies. "Cal, this is Everleigh."

I stand and take Everleigh's hand, shaking it softly, noting her opposite hand falls to a big, pregnant belly.

"You already know Addison here," Eden opens her palm to a more familiar fair brunette with green eyes, "and *this* is Magnolia." And yet another brunette! This one is olive-complected, like Eden, but with blue eyes that sparkle as she smiles at me. "These are my girls," Eden finishes proudly.

"Ah, yes, the sisters you mentioned." And sisters these four stunning foxes could be. "Well, ladies, it's very nice to meet you. I'm Callan Manning."

"Indeed, you are." Addison gives me a grin. "I remember you, Mr. Big Shot Book Model."

"Ah, yes, Ethan's fiancé, right?" I wrinkle my brow, knowing I've met her before. "The ball." I point in recognition.

"Yup, we all went to the masquerade ball together last year." She nods.

I smile remembering that night and the sexy masked date I had. "Speaking of, how's your friend Roxanne?"

Addison breaks into a coughing fit, and Eden elbows her, looking testy.

"Nice to finally meet you, Callan. Landry's told me about you," Magnolia states, stepping forward and taking my extended hand with a little giggle.

Eden eyes Magnolia as if she knows something I don't, and Magnolia drops my hand abruptly and steps back.

"Gals, let's give our girl here a minute to talk. Eady, we'll be up front." Everleigh grips Eden's arm softly before turning, and the other two follow, Addison giving me a wink. Why do I feel like I'm the butt of a big fat secret all of a sudden?

"Motorcycle romance, huh?" Eden crosses her arms over her ample chest and smirks.

"It's really good," I insist, my eyes moving from the top of her head down to her flats. She's stunning today, not like any other day, her hair up in a perfect bun, black frames propped on her nose, and dressed in a dark gray pencil skirt and red blazer that flatters her curvy, tall figure. I wanna loosen that bun and pull those long, thick locks through my fingers as I take her from behind. Dammit, wasn't that just the scene I read? God, what is wrong with me? I clear my throat and adjust myself, looking around to make sure no one else can see me.

"Charming," Eden scowls. "Now, I see why you read romance."

"Oh, c'mon, Eady. You read them too... Right?"

"I prefer fantasy, but romance is ok every now and then. It's a bit too unrealistic, though."

"Yeah, 'cause fantasy ain't?" I roll my eyes. I have a point, and she knows it. She stifles a laugh.

"What are you doing here?"

"I came to check out...books." I recover even as my eyes rove her frame again.

"Right. Of course you did."

"And to ask you out on another date."

She's already shaking her head and I frown, not wanting to take no for an answer. "Why are you so difficult?"

"Why are you?"

"It's complicated." She looks down, biting into her lip.

"You aren't married, are you?" I frown. Oh God, what am I gonna do if she says yes?

"No, I'm not married."

"Engaged? Betrothed? Divorced?"

"No, nothing like that. I just—I don't... I don't date, Callan."

I give her a confused look again. "I'm not your type, huh?"

She shakes her head. "No. You're...too cocky."

"As you've said. And you're not a lesbian. So... What's the problem? You like small men you can boss around?" She laughs, it's soft and sexy and I step forward. Her eyes warn me back; I don't heed it. "Listen, Eden," I whisper when her finger covers her lips for me to do just that. "Just, please give me a chance. I want—" I look around, making sure no one hears us. "I want to take you out. I want to court you. I wanna have you come have dinner with my family."

She literally balks and steps back, surprised is an understatement. "Why?"

"Because I like you...like I really, really like you. I want to know you. Sam and Caleb, they like you too. You're a breath of fresh air."

She just stares back at me as if I grew horns, and just as I'm about to reach up and make sure I haven't, she speaks. "I shouldn't, Cal. I shouldn't get involved with you."

"Why? Eden, you don't—" I step forward again, and this time, she doesn't shy away. I grip her wrist softly and pull her hand up to my chest, resting it there, just gauging her reaction. "You don't have children, you're single, you're a *fucking* librarian for God's sake. Give me a chance, will ya?"

"You don't know me, Callan." She whispers back, and I can see fear on her face and sadness in her eyes.

"I *want* to know you, Eden Riser. I want to know everything there is to know about you. Please?" I'm begging now. Dammit, this woman has a strange power over me, and I can't understand for the life of me why.

"Just don't say you weren't warned, Callan."

I simply smile. Victory is mine!

"WHEN'S YOUR HOT DATE, CAL?" ROXIE ASKS ME THE FOLLOWING night as her fingertips run through my hair. My entire body is humming, and I long to kiss her breathless.

"Tomorrow."

"Good, I would feel strange seducing you on the night of your date with another woman." She smirks and deep down, I highly doubt that's true. "With *Eden*?"

I look her over, she seems sincere enough, but I detect a note of jealousy and call her out on it. "Why do you care? You haven't even kissed me or let me inside…"

"And I fucking *won't* either," she growls back, and I huff.

"Then why the fuck do you care?" I ask again, needing to know.

"I don't." She sasses back and moves from my side on the bed we're laying atop. Her long, golden hair cascades down her back as she faces away from me.

"The hell you say! What's your fuckin' problem, Rox? You aren't mine. You know you're not. I don't think you even *want* to be, so why do you care who I take out on a date?"

"You don't know anything," she replies softly, and I can tell I've hurt her feelings. But dammit, she gives me nothing so what can I do? "Would it matter, Cal?" her tone changes, and she looks back over her shoulder at me. Her eyes burn into mine, and I swear I've seen the same eyes before...not here but... "I'm a whore, Callan."

"No, you're not."

"Yes, I am! I fuck people for money, that's what a *whore* does. News flash!"

"Roxie..." I have no words. I can't argue with her. It's no use. "I don't care!" I finally say and sigh as I run a hand down my face.

"Everyone cares...at some point or another," Roxie mumbles under her breath.

"How can you say that? You know I can't stop coming back here."

"You're seeing another woman tomorrow. So, obviously what you feel with me is only physical. Don't deny it, Callan. I may be a lot of things, but I'm no fool."

"I care about you, Rox. You feel it. I know you do...but yes, I care for Eden."

"Tell me about her."

I grin, thinking about the sexy librarian even as Roxie moves back to my side and begins to stroke the light scattering of hair across my chest then traces the tattoos running there and along my arms. I don't touch her back, for I've learned my lesson the few times I've tried. She's free to touch any part of me, but I can't return the favor. She's off limits, and it tears my heart in two, knowing I can't take her how I want to.

Roxie's eyes come up to mine; she's waiting for me to divulge.

"She smart, and beautiful, shy but feisty too. She's brunette with these eyes that are so deep and brown and big. She's tan, and tall, and curvy, not unlike you, Rox," I say because I can feel envy spike through her.

"Have you kissed her?" she asks.

"No, not yet, but I really want to." Those lips of hers are so kissable...

"Just take things slow, Cal."

"Why?"

"Because it's your first date...and from what you've said, she seems reserved."

"She is... I don't really know why." I ponder, recalling all the hesitation I've encountered from Eden thus far. I remember what she said about her childhood.

"Perhaps she has a past."

"We all have a past," I offer.

"Not like her," she whispers as she looks away.

"Do you *know* her?" I ask and look deeply into the colored contacts of my paramour. I know her eyes aren't red-brown, any more than her hair is gold. She's hiding behind a disguise, and I crave badly to know why.

"I'm just saying, from all you've told me... I think you need to take it real slow with her."

"From all I've said, or all you *assume*?" I scoff. "Why won't you let me touch you, Roxie?" I ask, wondering for the millionth time but finally asking.

She shakes her head. "I—I can't talk about it." Her eyes lower, and I see a flicker of panic cross her face.

"Rox, did someone hurt you?" I ask as I gently cup her cheek—touching be damned, she needs to see that I care—and she winces. I know she's second guessing why she didn't restrain my hands tonight. I would never betray her trust, but her fear upsets me...more than I want to admit aloud. "Are you...afraid of me?"

The eyes that come up to mine still my thoughts; I know I've seen this same look before. The same. Exact. Look...

A knock sounds on the door, and our moment is broken.

Roxie gasps and hurries to the closed door, opening it slightly. I hear hushed voices, and Roxie huffs. She closes the door and comes back to my side.

"Callan, I'm sorry, I won't be able to finish you off tonight. I-I have some business to attend to. I apologize, but—"

"*Finish* me off?" I smirk. "Roxie, contrary to what you may believe, I'm not only here for the pleasure of your mouth and hands...but because I actually enjoy your company."

I jump off the bed and pull her to me by her wrist. I feel her tense even as I press her frame into mine. I hold her there for a moment and whisper in her ear. "Take care of your business. I'll see you soon."

With that, I kiss her cheek softly before she gapes up at me, pulls away, and leaves.

EDEN

"Washington!" I feel my cheeks flush as I look up to the big mountain of a man who used to work here at the club as one of our security guys. "What's going on?"

"E-Rox," he recovers and looks around. "We need to talk."

"Look, I—"

"No, I know, I know. But we *need* to talk," he persists.

I nod sternly and look toward the back hallway, where my office is.

The last time I saw him, I said some hurtful things that I knew were harsh but needed to be said. He wanted more. I couldn't give him that. I lied and said it was because I didn't have feelings for him. I mean, I did, just not feelings quite as strong as his were for me. Besides, I don't usually mix business with pleasure. He was getting jealous of some of my highest-paying clients. I couldn't have his possessive demands ruining years of building up my reputation.

As we're heading down the red plush-covered hallway, my mind flashes back.

"Rox, let me out of these cuffs. I wanna slide myself into that wet, little—"

"Shut up and lower your head like I told you." I growl and crack my whip against my side, looking the man over that I have strung up like a sacrificial lamb. He's on the leopard skin rug I ordered from Africa, on his knees, facing me. His arms are spread wide, tied and cuffed. He can't touch me. Just how I like it.

"Mmm, baby, you know I love when you hold the reins, but c'mon let's switch it up tonight. Let's trade spots. Let me pleasure you, please?"

"If I have to tell you again..."

"Eden."

"Don't say my fucking name in here, Mount." I hiss and reach for a gag. "You've been warned. I don't play games. I think it's time I showed you that I mean what I say, in case you weren't sure."

I move forward, taking his head in one of my hands. His brown eyes flash something unreadable as he opens his mouth obediently, and I insert the gag and tie it behind his head.

Now, I don't have to hear his incessant demands. I can do what I want with no lip.

And I do, gripping his erect shaft in my fist as I slowly kiss every inch of his chiseled torso, letting my tongue curve over each sinewy muscle until he's practically whimpering and arching his hips. I grin back into his face, pleased with myself.

Then I fall to all fours and begin rocking his world with my mouth, hand, and fingertips, gulping his decent-sized cock down with a skill I've honed over the years. Soon, he's thrusting against me and grunting as I bring him to climax. I pull his member from my mouth, and he ejaculates all over my tits with a muffled roar that leaves me sinfully happy.

When he comes back down from his high, his broad chest expanding and contracting as he pulls deep breaths in through his nose, I finally pull the gag from his mouth.

"Fuckin' hell, Ead—I mean, Roxie. That was..." he trails off, looking my scantily clad body over. "Ok, my turn now."

"Dammit, Washington, I've told you over and over again..."

"I know. I know, but dammit, why can't I touch you? Why can't I be the one to bring you to orgasm? I don't understand. Let me make love to you, I promise I won't—"

"No, means fucking no, asshole!" I yell, feeling a pit open up in my stomach. "If all you men knew what the fuck that meant, we wouldn't be here. Roxie wouldn't even exist!"

Washington gulps, his Adam's apple bobbing in his thick throat. He frowns.

"Alas, she does though. And the fun in this room belongs to me. The sooner you realize it, the better." I soften my tone, attempting to dampen down my anger at him—at men in general.

"I know you've fucked men in here before, Rox. I've seen it."

"When?" I raise my brows in question. Zeus is our eyes in the camera room and "sees" what goes on behind our closed doors. But only for our safety, not because he's some perv who gets his rocks off during a free preview. Or is he abusing his privileges to spy on a girl he has feelings for that has, obviously, let those feelings go too far.

"Let's just say, I've kept my eye on you."

"Possessive much?" I sass and turn.

"Tell me you don't feel something for me, and I'll gladly leave."

"You mean aside from lust?" I ask and sit on top of my bed, adjusting my heel clasp so I can avoid his eyes.

"You do. How many times have we been in here? You want me for more, I know you do."

I laugh maniacally at him. Bless him. He just doesn't understand.

"Oh, Mt. You know Roxie plays games. You're merely a toy. Sorry to disappoint you, baby boy."

"Don't fuck with me. Tell me the truth."

"The truth would have even you running scared, Mount Washington." I scoff at the nickname we've given the bulky man who guards the front door of our club. "This is the way things are, if you don't like it then you know where the door is." I point and shrug.

"Ead—"

"Don't!" I warn again and wave my finger at him.

"Please? I don't—"

"You clearly want more than I'm willing to give you. I can't give you something I don't have, Washington."

He looks down then back up. "Then I guess it's time for me to move on."

His reverse psychology doesn't work on me.

"I hate that you've come to that decision and you will be sorely missed here at RISE." I rise from the bed in the corner and my heels click as I begin to walk away.

"That's it, then? That's all you're gonna say? After all we've been through?"

"All *we've been through?*" I try not to smirk.

"Nine years, Rox. I've been here for nine fucking years."

"And your leaving is regrettable."

"Regrettable? I'm flesh and blood, and I'm kneeling here right now, telling you that I want you. Isn't that enough?"

"Bless your heart, Mount. Are you in love, honey?" I walk back over and kneel before him. I take his face in my hands and tisk, feeling his jaw clench in my palms.

"Roxie, please? Give me a chance?"

I lean in and kiss his cheek. I wish I had love in me, but I'm too far removed from it. I've built my life on controlling my surroundings, my circumstances. And I'm in hiding. So how can I have a normal life, a normal relationship with a man? It isn't possible. Even if I wanted it to be.

My eyes flash many things, trying to get him to understand without words.

When I rise again, I hit the panic button on the wall I had installed in the event of an emergency. The door immediately unlocks, and Bruno rushes in, looking ready to tear Washington's head clean off his massive shoulders.

"C'mon, Rox..." Washington whines.

"You ok, Roxie?" Bruno asks, confused as he looks from me to Washington and back, clearly observing that the man is restrained and not a threat.

"Thank you, Bruno. If you'll see Washington out, please?"

I nod at Bruno and begin my exit but turn when Washington calls for me once more.

"You may have everyone else fooled Rox, but not me. I know deep

*down you're just a scared little girl who wants to be loved. I could be
that person, if you'd let me. I know you feel something..."*

I turn and bring my finger up to my lips, shaking my head.

*"Remember your NDA that you signed and don't make me get my
lawyers involved because if I have to, I will, and it will get ugly."*

"I would never hurt you, Eden. You fail to realize this."

*"Good, because you don't know the wrath you'd incur on yourself
if you did." My brows raise in a final warning as I exit my room.*

THAT WAS SIX MONTHS AGO, NOW THE TAN, BROWN-HAIRED,
brown-eyed mass of muscle stands before me as I move to my
desk and prop my bottom there, extending my fishnet-covered
legs in front of me.

"You look...stunning as always. How...how are you?" he
asks, pink tinting his cheeks and I can't help but grin at him.
He was always sweet, charming, and handsome.

"I'm well. I hope you are." I lift my chin as he attempts to
move forward stopping him in his tracks. The look in my eyes
says "Stay back," and he heeds it, thank goodness.

"Listen, uh, there's been a man asking questions about you?"

"What man?" Immediately my hackles raise and fear fills
my belly.

"I don't know his name. All I know is that he was asking all
kinds of questions about you?"

"Me?"

"And the club. But mostly you."

"Washington, so help me God, if you—"

"Eden, like I told you, I would never hurt you. I just wanted
you to be aware that someone is curious about you and what's
going on here?"

"Can you describe him?"

"Sure, he looked like every other mafia guy from every gangster movie you've ever seen before. Starched crisp black suit, slick-back hair, dark sunglasses."

"Young, old, fat, skinny? I need details, Mount."

"God, I've missed seeing you."

"Please don't do that. Focus, Washington. Tell me who this was and why they were wanting information on me."

"It was at another club, the club I work for now, *The Pussycat Lounge*. He strode up while I was working last night and asked if I knew about *RISE*. It seemed awfully suspicious. Hey, maybe we should go to the cops."

I sigh. I'll talk to Luca and Kieran later. In addition to the pics and graffiti, now someone is attempting to get info out of my old employees. *Great!*

"Hey, why don't we go get a bite or...?"

"Washington, I appreciate you coming here and giving me this information, but I...well, I..." I can't stop the smile at my lips. "The truth is: I'm seeing someone."

His brows raise in surprise. "Wow. I'm surprised. But good, good for you, Madam Roxie. I'm glad to see you aren't hiding behind that mask anymore." He smirks as he moves forward and points to my mask.

Little does he know just how much I've kept hidden from Callan.

7

EDEN

I clear my throat as I open the door for Callan the following evening. This is our first official date and I can't hide my nervousness.

Just last night, I was hanging out with the girls, discussing how nervous I was to have a date. Lia had Aliana asleep on her breasts as the rest of us sipped our wine and conversed.

"J*UST BE YOURSELF AND TAKE THINGS SLOW, E," M*Y FORMER FELLOW ice-queen, Everleigh, states with weary green eyes.

"I think he's adorable," Lia adds with a grin.

"I wouldn't kick him out of bed for eating crackers," Addy smirks. "He may be Ethan's buddy, but Eth fucks up, and I might just have Cal come console me." She winks playfully. Addison is far wilder than her easy demeanor would ever reveal. She cackles and clinks her glass against Lia's.

I smile back at my sisters, grateful for their advice and approval.

"I'm not rushing into anything. God knows." I look down, and *they can all sense my hesitancy. After all, it's been ten years since Marco died, and I'm still not over it; I might never be.*

I get hugs from them all, knowing that they've gotten their HEAs with men who utterly adore them; perhaps now it's my turn to pursue mine.

I ATTEMPT TO WIPE MY THOUGHTS CLEAR AS I LOOK OVER Callan Manning's big frame. I can't help but be swayed by the sheer power he exudes as I practically stumble back on my wedges in his overwhelming presence.

His big palm reaches out and grabs mine, steadying me, and I blush ten shades of red. Jesus, how am I ever going to get through this night? I gulp and give him a smile, pulling every shred of confidence I have within me. I can do this...right?

"You look amazing, Eden." Cal's approval of my red dress, ribbon-curled locks, and ample makeup makes me happy that I spent so much time primping.

"I hope I'm not overdressed."

"Not at all. You're perfect."

I give him another smile and reach for the purse and leather jacket I've set aside. Cal steps out, and I follow, closing and locking the door behind me.

He takes my arm and steers us towards his truck, helping me onto the nerf bar and into the passenger side.

His truck smells like cologne, potent and masculine, and I inhale, letting it engulf my senses.

Madam Roxie could handle this night, no problem. She deals with men all the time at the club. Even Eden has put the girl's men and husbands in check, making sure they're protected. But this is a side I've not encountered but a time or two before. I don't usually have to deal with men in this setting. The fact that there are usually more women at the library than men is one of the reasons I became a librarian in the first place.

When Cal jumps in, cranks the truck, and heads down the road, I try to relax, but my nerves feel jangled by his massive size. I look over, taking in his light blue collared button-down shirt and black slacks. Two buttons are undone, showcasing the tattoo that spreads from one side of him to the other, right below his collarbone and the upper three inches of his chest, an ink collar with many colors and designs. I bite into my lip, clenching my legs together as my eyes appraise his muscled frame, the shirt hugging his bulky biceps, the trousers tight across his big thighs. He's every fantasy I've had of him in the flesh, his bearded jaw trim, his hair spiked, and his tan perfect like always.

He smiles, seeing me evaluate him, as if reading my thoughts. "Like what you see, baby?"

Fuck him! He's so cocky. Of course I like what I see! What fool wouldn't? I think back to the times he's been in Roxie's room, how his skin tastes, how his hands feel on my body. I gulp. I can't think about that right now.

"You look very handsome."

"Handsome, huh? Your eyes are undressing me. Kinda like you know what I look like naked."

I snort, dismissing his comment, even though I suddenly recall what his massive muscles feel like beneath my palms, how his thick sex feels down my throat, how it tastes... *Stop right there, Eden.* "It's, uh, it's been a long time since I had a date," I confess, knowing I'll be tripping all over myself if I don't let him know this now.

"That makes two of us, just so ya know." He winks and reaches for my hand.

Do I take it? Is it too soon to hold his hand? I don't know how to act; this is ridiculous!

I take it. It's big and warm as his fingers interlock with mine, and the peace and excitement of it makes my stomach tingle. I smile back and just enjoy the warmth spreading through me as I hear Aerosmith on the radio.

I don't ask where we're going, although I assume it's for dinner when we turn into the parking lot of a restaurant on the Chattahoochee River. I grin as he pulls up to valet and my door is opened. I take the hand extended to me and thank the attractive young valet as my date joins me at my side.

"Take care of Beast for me," Cal states to the young man with a wink.

He escorts us in, and we're led to the back of the restaurant almost immediately upon coming to the hostess stand.

"Perks of being a celebrity," I murmur as we are seated at a booth with a great view of the river. Cal smirks as we sit down, and our menus are handed to us. I thank the hostess and look up at Cal. "This is beautiful."

"Best riverfront steaks in town, or so I'm told." He winks again, and I wanna melt right here in my seat. God, he's scrumptious. "Wanna order an appetizer?"

I nod and when the waitress comes over, he orders a shrimp cocktail, a mojito for me, and a beer for himself. We continue to peruse the menu and place our order once our drinks are set before us.

"So, as a romance reader, I got to ask…" I begin, "What did you think of *Fifty Shades of Grey?*"

Cal gives me a brow. His blue eyes move over my body, leaving a heat trail in their wake. "I'm sure the literary side of you would love to tear the book to shreds, Eady." I give him a knowing grin and cover my smirk. "I, however, personally thought it was hot as fuck," he answers.

I roll my eyes. He *is* a man after all; what did I expect?

"What about you, Ms. Riser?"

"I'll just put it this way, I liked the movies much better."

"Oh, I'll just bet you did," he whispers, leaning forward. "Bet you almost ran the batteries in your vibrator out after you saw them, huh?"

I simply blush, a vision of him in Roxie's room flashing in my mind's eye.

"I bet there's a whole side of you that no one knows about, isn't there? The quiet librarian is a cover, I bet."

I can't help but think of my past and the secrets I hide. Secrets even my girls don't know about. Secrets I don't want to bring to the surface for fear that it will arouse the darkness I've been hiding from for far too long.

"How about I pull a Christian Grey and tell you to take your panties off, right now?" Cal's grin is devilish, and I can't help but laugh at his enthusiasm, my dark thoughts stuffed down for the time being.

I take a sip of my cocktail and arch a brow, pulling out something Madam Roxie might reply—channeling my inner bravery. "And what if I were to say, Mr. Manning, that I'm not wearing any?" My eyes hold his, and he almost chokes on his beer. I can't help the giggle at my throat as he wipes his mouth.

"Jesus, Eden, you can't say things like that. Fuck." He looks around before grabbing under the table, assumedly to adjust himself. "First date rules be damned, lady. You're killin' me tonight."

"Killing you, how?"

"First, you look incredible dressed in a tight dress that accentuates your body *so* freaking well. I mean, my imagination is running *rampant* right this moment."

I look down at my ample cleavage, barely contained behind the plunging V of the neckline of this crimson silk dress. He's right, it is pretty form-fitted. Perhaps, I should have worn something different. I frown, my insecurities sprouting.

"Don't get me wrong, baby. Daddy is liking, but shit, do you see the eyes on you right now?"

I gulp and look around to the men, even the ones who are accompanied by women, and catch a few eyes, feeling them darting down my curvy frame. *Oh shit!* I've drawn attention to myself. That wasn't my intention.

"I bet they wish their dates only looked *half* as amazing as you do." I get a wink from my hunky date and smile again, my hesitation tucked back in place as my confidence soars. "That shrimp cocktail isn't half as cold as that woman over there." Cal points to a tight-lipped woman in a conservative dress suit, and I stifle a laugh, my mind taking off as the liquor begins to buzz through my system. "I bet they haven't slept in the same bed together in ten years."

"Ok, Mr. Mind Reader. Who are you, the Long Island Medium?" I snicker as he leans closer to me, whispering.

"I've become somewhat of a people watcher, what with traveling alone so much over the years. I'm fairly good at it. See. She has yet to look him in the eyes. I bet there are cobwebs growing between her legs. He's probably been watching PornHub since Jr. moved out."

I shake my head and roll my eyes, but know he's probably not far off the mark. In fact, I'm certain I've seen the older, balding man in my club not that long ago.

"He's sitting there, bored to tears with her, thinking of all the incredible, hot sex we're gonna be having tonight." Cal winks. "Let's give him something to ease his lonely night, E."

With that, Cal throws his arm around me, pulling my side against his. I gasp, my tummy fluttering from his closeness and the excitement of exhibitionism. I balk and playfully scold him, "Callan."

"C'mon, it'll be fun." He leans in and moves the hair off my neck. I feel his breath tickling my flesh and break out in goosebumps. "Besides, when was the last time you played, you quiet little thing, you?"

Oh, if he *only* knew. I love to play, and with him especially, but I realize this *is* fun as his lips press against my pulse point and I moan when his tongue licks there. It's been so long since I allowed a man to love my body. I never let them have control, but Cal is so commanding, and outside my room of torture, I'm an entirely different person. Besides, I like this new Eden without inhibitions, I realize, as I let Callan make out with my neck with the gentleness and patience of Job.

My flesh is quivering as I close my eyes and lose myself to his smell and his hot mouth on my sensitive flesh. I feel his tongue at my collarbone and reach my hand down to grip his knee, my fingernails digging into his thigh. I get a chuckle, then a growl as I move my hand up a little higher.

"Easy, Eden," he whispers into my ear. "Or, I'll be forced to pull you onto my lap and *really* give Mr. Rodgers over there a show he won't forget."

The thought makes my center clench, but a thousand painful images run through my head, and I find myself pulling away from Callan. We are in a restaurant, after all. We need to cool our jets. I clear my throat and move my hand.

I feel shame coming off of Callan and smile over at him, trying to regain my composure as I replace my hair and let collected Eden come back.

"Perhaps, it was a mistake to sit next to you, Mr. Manning."

"Mistake isn't the word I would use at all, Ms. Riser. You're as enticing as the forbidden fruit, and all I wanna do is devour you whole." The heat in his eyes ignites a hunger I haven't felt in far too long, and I simply gape back at him.

It takes a manager coming to thank Callan for his patronage before I can get my heartrate under control. I can't let this get so out of hand. This is date number one—well two, unofficially—and he has no idea what he's gotten himself into with me. I'd be wise to remember that. I scold myself and try to keep my wits about me, remembering that I told the girls I was gonna take this slow.

When our appetizer comes, I can see my coolness has rubbed off on my date. Even as his arm goes around me to rest on my bare back and I shiver in response, his demeanor seems more relaxed than before.

Our entrees come, and we take our time enjoying our food, talking about his nephew, Samantha, my girlfriends, my work and his. Then his face becomes devoid of all emotion when he asks me, "So, what's the scoop on Stanley? You know him, don't you?"

I can't hide the panic on my face. What do I say? Kevin Stanley is a slime ball. He pays to sleep with women at my club, and from what I've been told, he thinks he is King Dick. He's shady and demanding and has come close to getting the boot a few times. I've had to have the bouncers throw him out on more than one occasion, had to call Uber on his drunk ass, and well, he's just a creep. I truly don't know why we put up with him.

"I, uh—" I try to think of something quick, something logical.

"Shoot straight, E, I know he's not a good guy. I feel it in my gut."

"I've just heard he's bad news, that's all. He's not a nice person."

"Yeah, anyone can see that. Sam has always been attracted to the losers." Cal scoffs and rolls his eyes, taking another sip of beer as we wait on the waiter to bring Cal's credit card back.

"She'll figure it out." I shrug, hopeful.

Cal shakes his head. "He could be Jack the damn Ripper himself, and Sam wouldn't see it. I don't know why her creeper radar is broken. I must have gotten both doses." He sits quietly, thoughtful for a moment before asking, "Hey, you wouldn't try and talk to her about him, would you?"

"M-me?" I stammer. What could I possibly say to Samantha to convince her?

"Yeah, if I say anything, I'm the bad guy. But you're a girl. Girls have like a sixth sense about those kinda guys, right? Just say something like you saw him checkin' you out or he gives you the heebie-jeebies or some shit, I dunno."

"Cal, I really don't wanna get involved."

"Please, Eady? I don't wanna see her get hurt again. You don't know how hard this past year has been for her." His gorgeous blue eyes pull me in, and I can't stop my nod of agreement after a moment or two. "Thank you." He pulls my knuckles to his lips and kisses them, so gentle for the giant he is. I can't help but smile into his handsome face, feeling his allure reeling me in like a fish in a net.

Before I know what's happening, my chest is hitting his, my eyes are closing, and his soft, plump lips are touching mine. I moan aloud, the feel of his lips on my own so foreign and good and sexy. I part my lips slightly, returning his kiss, and let his tongue slide into my mouth. I cup his jaw and angle my head, my desire yearning to be quenched, a raging inferno blazing deep inside.

I haven't been kissed with this kind of passion since Marco, and damn, have I forgotten how amazing a kiss can be. Callan's strong tongue tangles with my own, and my head reels—from him or the alcohol, or both, I'm not sure. I lose myself to this beautiful man who's invaded so many of my fantasies.

Soon, I'm gripping his shirt and fighting his tongue for control as I feel a big palm cup my head, another at my waist. How could I not have known how good he would taste, how mesmerizing his feel and smell would be? My senses are completely overloaded. I'm in trouble, serious trouble, as I feel myself falling into a pit of hunger that I don't ever want to come out of.

Finally, Cal pulls back as we hear a throat clear, and we look at one another, dazed at our reactions to the other. I watch Callan's Adam's apple bob as he swallows and turns his head to the waiter, thanking him and taking the check and his card. He pulls a deep breath in and looks down to sign.

I immediately glance around to see the attention we've unknowingly drawn to ourselves once more. I see the old man who'd been eyeing us earlier is staring at me as if I'm naked and his next meal.

I'm used to these looks in my club—hidden by my mask, not in real life—not as Eden Riser. For a moment, I'm disgusted with myself for allowing my desires to rule my head. I look away and stand as Cal looks up at me. He gives me a tight smile and stands himself, taking my arm and leading us to the exit.

Neither of us says a word as we wait for the valet, and Cal's hand falls to my lower back. I visibly shiver and not from the cold either, but Callan doesn't move his hand.

Once we're in the truck and headed down the road, Cal is the first to break the silence. "I'm glad you came out with me tonight."

I look over at him and take his extended hand, squeezing it. "Me too. It was lovely. Thank you."

"I, uh, I'm not really ready for it to end, though."

"Cal." I look down, not sure how to let him down easily. I can't sleep with him, not tonight, not for a long time—if ever. The fear of intimacy, of being overtaken by this huge man, immediately takes over me and I gulp.

"Hey, no pressure. I know, we, uh...we kinda moved a bit faster tonight than I expected to, honestly." I nod in response, glad he wants to take this slow too. "But, you know, I recently signed up for Disney+, so I wouldn't mind hanging out with you a little longer and watching *The Swiss Family Robinson*. I mean it was a great book, after all, and I've never seen it."

I laugh, a real genuine laugh, for the first time in a long time. "Cal, I would *love* to go back to my place and watch *The Swiss Family Robinson* with you."

CALLAN

I AWAKE TO THE SOUND OF THE DRONING TELEVISION IN THE background and feel a warm body against mine. Eden's head is resting on my shoulder, her curvy frame pressed into me. I smile, loving how this feels right now. She's so peaceful when she's sleeping, that tough outer exterior gone, a vulnerable angel taking its place. Her dark hair swirls around her face in ribbons and her thick, dark lashes rest on her high cheeks. Her lips are utterly kissable, and if I didn't hate to wake her, I would lean in and sip at their warm beckoning.

We both fell asleep watching the movie and the laptop must have shut off, leaving the television to return to cable mode, showing "No Signal" on the receiver. Its droning is soft and constant, not enough to wake Eden, so I just continue to stare at her beautiful face, her cheek resting on my pec is sweet bliss. As good as this feels, I really need to move; my arm around her is starting to cramp, probably being in this position for hours now.

I glance at my Apple watch and see that it's past one in the morning. I should go home. A gentleman would lay this lady down on her couch, place a blanket on her, and leave. But I'm no gentleman, never have been. I know Eden set the alarm, and

I don't know what the code is. I also don't want to leave the door unlocked when I do leave, so I may as well stay. At least this is what I tell myself as my knuckle brushes across her soft cheek and down her hairline.

She stirs a little, mewing like a kitten, and I feel my heart swell. God, I want her so much. I've enjoyed our night together. She's broken out of her shell more easily than I imagined she would. We have a good bit in common, and there's a side of her that's less conservative than the stuffy librarian I originally assumed her to be. There's also a secret side, I realize again, as my hand moves up her lean back and I hear her say, "Mmm, Marco."

Marco? Who the *fuck* is Marco? Anger flares in my gut, and I could almost growl aloud before I remind myself that this is our first date. I need to chill the hell out. He could be anyone, but I get a feeling he's an old lover, boyfriend, someone Eden was intimate with. I feel rage build within me. *Whoa, relax Cal, I tell myself. You don't own her, first off and second, she has a past, just like the rest of us!*

I pull a deep breath into my lungs and begin peeling myself away from her. I grip the back of Eden's head and move it from my pec, easing my chest from hers as I scoot my bottom over. She gives a cute little grunt as I stand and begin gently guiding her to a lying position. "No, don't go," she whines, mostly asleep, and I grin again.

I place a pillow beneath her neck before removing my palm from the back of her head. "Shh, I'm not going anywhere, gorgeous." I kiss her cheek and get another coo from her, my heart and cock reacting, in kind. I grab a blanket from the back of the leather couch and pull it over her thin, sleeveless red dress, doing my best to avoid gazing at her enticing bare thighs. God, how my lips and hands would love to explore that olive-toned flesh that goes on for miles. I avert my eyes and adjust my crotch as I move to the recliner adjacent to the couch Eden is now sleeping restfully on.

I watch her as I grab another blanket, cover myself, and get comfy as I lounge. I may sleep tonight, but damn if I won't be dreaming of that sexy sasspot just six feet away and all the yummy things I wanna do to her.

I AWAKE WITH A START AS MY PHONE BUZZES IN MY POCKET. HOW the hell did I sleep with that bulky thing in my pants all night long? Oh, wait, that's not my phone. I tuck my morning wood aside and pull my phone from my pocket. It's only a dozen Instagram notifications for the photo my PA posted earlier this morning, a half-naked photo of me modeling for a photo shoot in nothing but a towel. It's now approaching twenty thousand likes and the comments go from racy to rude, nothing I'm not used to by now. I roll my eyes and stretch.

I catch Eden's eyes roving me as she, herself, awakens and begins to stir.

"You stayed the night, huh?"

"Well, I would've left, but the alarm was set, and you were sleeping so good."

"Sure, sure," she smirks with a beautiful smile, and it's all I can do not to run and pounce on her. Her hair is a mess of curls and her dress is bedrumpled, looking like she's been thoroughly fucked. All I can think about is how much I want to see this again...with her naked and me beside her.

I gulp, attempting to rein in my wicked thoughts. She's just an innocent librarian. I need to behave. "So, uh, you hungry? Wanna go grab some breakfast?"

She smiles again and evaluates me with an arched eyebrow. "Yeah, I'd like that."

"Mind punching in the alarm code? I wanna grab my bag and shower real quick, if that's ok."

Eden nods again and peels the blanket from her legs. She moves to the keypad and my cock suddenly stands at full attention. *Fuck me!* Her dress has ridden up her thighs and I get a glimpse of a plump, round ass cheek that her black thong doesn't cover. Librarians wear thongs like that? Dear God, that's sexy as hell!

I have a fleeting vision of her tall, voluptuous frame clad in only that tiny black thong, her black glasses, and a pair of strappy heels, and groan aloud.

Good thing she's disarming the house alarm and doesn't hear it, but as I adjust my tight trousers once more, I know my arousal isn't going anywhere anytime soon. He's got a mind of his own, after all. "Fuck it", I think, and stand, pulling the blanket from myself.

Her eyes hold mine briefly before falling to my unhidable morning wood and stop there. I shrug at the surprised look on her face.

"When your ass cheek is hanging out of your sexy as hell thong like that, I have a difficult time controlling the inner beast," I lean in with a playful growl and she steps back, almost as if she's afraid of me.

"I...I'll, uh, I'll make us some coffee," she states as her hands move down her back, to smooth her dress down, and she moves off, even as I frown and head out the door, going to my truck to retrieve the overnight bag I always keep there.

I can't help but feel bad. Maybe I frightened her, but damn, I was only kidding about the beast thing. She has to know that, right? Fuck, I'm an asshole. I smack my head and turn to head back inside.

Eden

I smile at Callan as he enters the kitchen and hand him a cup of coffee. He's fresh from the shower, his big body clad in an old Star Wars t-shirt and well-worn jeans, looking scrumptious as all get out. I clench my legs together to quiet the hum that seems to come whenever he's near. His face is solemn, and I don't understand why he's frowning. He rubs the back of his damp head and reaches for the mug in my hand.

"Thanks," he mutters and avoids my eyes. "I'm sorry. I didn't mean to offend you earlier."

I know my face appears confused as I draw my brows.

"About the inner beast...controlling him?"

"Oh!" That's what he was worried about? Seriously? "Callan, you didn't offend me."

"You looked like I'd slapped you, Eady."

I frown. You'd think I would be used to men—the way they talk, the way they act, the way they talk and react to *me*. But I'm not, and especially never in my house. I keep my personal life separate from the club, I always have—for more reasons than one. I never bring clients here, so having this stud muffin in my personal space is unnerving me. I feel out of sorts, out of control, insecure. I need Roxie's bravery right now.

"I... You just took me off guard, is all. I guess I was embarrassed."

"With an ass that looks like that, you got *nothing* to be embarrassed about, baby doll." He grins, and I swear I'm melting. God, he's so beautiful and his freaking big-ass inked biceps stretching out the sleeves of that shirt. O.M.G. I'm drooling, literally drooling.

I don't stop his approach as he cages me against the counter, even as my alarm bells are ringing off the walls inside my head. My heart is deaf to their pleading. His finger pulls my chin up, and he looks me in the eyes.

"I would love to see more of it, in fact."

I gulp but hold my ground. How can he make me such putty like this? Damn it!

"I-I..." Fuck, I'm a rambling idiot right now. I need food. I need to think. I need for him to not be so close to me. I think I'm running a fever. "We should—"

"Who's Marco, Eden?"

My face falls, and immediately, I'm on the defense. "What? How—?"

"You called me Marco last night when you were half asleep."

I look down, unable to hide the blush on my cheeks. Well, this is truly embarrassing. First, Cal has seen my ass cheek hanging out and now, he's gotten a brief glimpse into my soul, the dark place where my secrets are hidden—well hidden. I don't like this, and he seems to sense it as he takes a step back. Thank God, too; I think I'm actually hyperventilating right this moment.

I take a deep breath in, relaxing some as Cal turns to grab the creamer in front of the coffee pot. I wonder how long this is truly gonna take, for me to give in, for me to trust him, for me to open my heart once more. All I know is that when I do, it's gonna threaten to bleed out.

8

ROXIE

I smirk as I look over at Callan Manning sitting in his usual spot, eyeing me as I dance and crawl on stage. Will tonight be the night I give into him? Will he beg me, and I'll relent? I don't know.

It's been three days since he last saw Roxie. And he's called and texted Eden each day since their first date and come to see her at the library twice, giving some lame excuse as to why he's there. As if I can't see right through his antics. It's endearing, but he's still a man, and I can't fully trust his intentions yet. Although the way he is with his nephew, Caleb, makes me wanna spit out baby after baby just to see that goofy grin on his face. It could work between Eden and Callan, but where will that leave Roxie? And what will he do when he realizes we are one and the same?

But you aren't *the same, are you?* I ask myself. Roxie and Eden are two separate entities, as different as night and day. Roxie is the girl behind the mask, but she also *is* the mask. The one who has protected Eden following the darkness she was thrust into. Roxie is the phoenix, the rebirth from the fire that destroyed Eden's demons. Eden is quiet and collected, introverted, while Roxie basks in the spotlight. There's nothing reticent about Roxie; she takes charge, she doesn't submit, and she doesn't fall in love. Eden hides, Roxie flaunts.

And tonight, Roxie feels like a predator, fixing her cat-eyes on the delicious Callan.

I lick my lips as I stop in front of him and squat down as the song changes, noticing his eyes don't stay on mine but fall between my legs. He wants it, he knows he does, and I smile in victory.

"Feeling frisky tonight, tiger?" I ask as I pull my bottom lip in and bite it gently. I watch his eyes follow my tongue as it traces my top lip.

"What'd you have in mind, Madam?" His eyes betray him as they flash heat.

Indeed. He's mine. Hook, line, and sinker, just as always.

"Why don't you come to my room, and we'll play?"

He gives me a hesitant smile, but he'll cave. They all cave to Madam Roxie at some point or another. She has an uncanny power over them.

I move to sit on my bottom and come off the short distance from the stage to his seat, not far for my tall height. I take his hand and lead him to my room, nodding at Bruno as we enter.

I can almost feel the sudden change in demeanor, oozing from Callan's pores. I turn, looking him over even as I fiddle with his unbuttoned shirt collar.

"What's the matter, baby?" I ask boldly. Like he's my baby. I've had my mouth on him and dry-humped his lap, but he's not by any means mine.

His Adam's apple bobs, but he doesn't answer.

"Cal, why are you here? We both know that you don't wanna be." I fish.

"And we both know that's the biggest fuckin' lie of all, don't we, Rox?"

I cross my arms over my chest and exhale, waiting. "Well, are we fucking or what? Time is money." I smirk.

"You know we aren't goin' to. It's like our unspoken rule," he mumbles and sits down in the chair adjacent to the made-up bed. "Dammit, Rox." He plants his face in his hands as he leans his elbows onto his knees.

"I sense a therapy session coming on," I sigh. "Maybe I should charge you more."

"I keep coming here and I'm gonna be broke." His voice is muffled in his big palms.

I have the audacity to laugh, even though there's nothing funny about any of this.

"I can't do this anymore, Rox." He pulls his hands from his face and looks up at me, a serious expression on his gorgeous face.

He's breaking up with me. *Wait!* We don't have a relationship, so how can he be breaking up with me? God, I'm such a fool.

"It's Eden. She—"

"She doesn't know about me." Of course not, and I know this. Why am I asking him stupid questions I already know the answers to?

He gives me a withering look, saying the exact thing I just thought. "How can I start a relationship with her if I have someone on the side? It's not fair to her...and it's not fair to me."

And what about me? Roxie wants to scream. But I don't. I just look him over. Eden will get hers, and Roxie needs to back off.

"You really care about her, huh?" I ask and squat before

him, resting my palms on his knees as he moves back to a sitting position. This could work to my advantage...

He nods. "She's..."

"Not like me. Quiet. Soft. Not in your face."

"She's hiding her own demons."

And I balk. How can he possibly know this?

"What kind of demons?"

"I don't know. I just sense a hesitancy from her. I think she's afraid to get too close to me, which is why I need to focus on *her* and stop living this fantasy of ours, Roxie." His hand falls onto mine, and I can't help the grin on my face. He's being so sweet and thoughtful. It makes tears spring to my eyes. I knew he had deep feelings for me, but this is a surprise. He's gonna give up Roxie...to be with Eden.

"You might be the most genuine man who's ever walked in here, Callan."

He shrugs. "I'm just growing a conscience, I guess."

"It's sexy as sin and makes me want to fuck your brains out," I growl in hunger.

He laughs humorlessly. "We both know you won't."

"It doesn't mean I can't think about it."

"You are so twisted, Roxie." He cups my cheek as he says this, and his eyes burn into mine. "What man hurt you so much that you love to punish the rest of us?"

"Wouldn't you like to know?" I sass hotly, my hate for my Uncle Vince overpowering the softer side Callan has been petting.

"I did ask, didn't I? Tell me why you hate me and all men in general."

Hate. Such a strong word... I hate that I feel the need to restrain them in order to keep myself from their reach because they might undo years of me repressing what was done to me in order to hold my shit together, and I love that I have the ultimate control and power to elicit the responses I want from them: pain, pleasure, surrender. The girl who was once weak has been transformed into a goddess they now worship. A goddess who loves her power.

Because I wanted revenge. Revenge for the girl that lust, force, and greed destroyed. Revenge for the innocence I was robbed of. Revenge for the first love that was taken from me far too soon and the baby my uncle had ripped from my womb because it wasn't convenient for his club, livelihood, or reputation. But revenge has become my life's blood, and my bloodlust should be all but quenched by now. In ten years, I've kept them all at arm's length, fearing they'd topple my empire in their need to conquer, overtake, and pillage as men are known to do, and yet...

Here he sits, taking my hands in his and piercing my soul with his achingly bewitching blue eyes, the one and *only* man who's ever been freed of his bonds in the presence of Roxie.

Callan must sense all the emotions boiling in my veins because he leans down. I gasp as I realize he's about to kiss me. God, I want his kiss, his lips, his bandage over my badly-damaged psyche, but he'll know I'm Eden. He'll recognize us.

But I can't back away as his mouth falls on mine and I arch my back into it, pressing my lips harder to his. He moans, as do I, and I wrap my arms around his neck. His hands grip my back as I move to straddle his lap. I lean my chest into his and let my desire for this strong, sexy man fuel me on. I've never wanted anything more than I want him inside me at this moment, and I'm desperate to have him. Desperate to find retribution for the crimes I've been punished for. Desperate to feel what Marco made me feel so long ago, as I haven't ever felt this way with a man here before or since.

"Oh, God, Cal, I want you. Please, baby, take me." I'm

begging. Dammit, Roxie is the one begging now. *Look what this man has done to you!*

Fuck, but I can't stop myself as I rub against his restrained crotch, grip his shirt, and fuck his mouth with my tongue. He moans, and his hand moves into my hair as he kisses me back, and I relish in it. I need release, sweet release in his arms. There I'll find it, I know I will. I reach for his jeans, my hands shaking as I pull at the button, but his hands are stopping me, and I gasp as I look into his eyes.

He's shaking his head. "No, stop, Rox. I can't, I'm sorry."

What the *actual* fuck? Is he serious right now? I wanna pull the mask and wig off right this second and show him who the hell I am. I want this facade to end. I want to find solace in the arms of this angel of a man who has touched my soul with his sincerity. But it's too soon. I'm jumping the gun, and I know it. This is only temporary. He'll hurt Eden. She's gotta stay guarded. And Roxie has to ensure that. I slap back on that ironclad mask of ours.

"Fine." I shove myself off him, planting my hands on my hips as I stand. "Go to your perfect little *Eden*. But if you show your face back here in my club again, I'll have you thrown the fuck out. Remember that." I point my finger in his face and turn on my heel.

Alright, Eady—you're up, babe!

9

EDEN

After last night's rejection, I woke up feeling resolved to get my shit together. Roxie is taking a back seat where Cal is concerned—as long as he doesn't come back to the club any time soon—so hopefully Eden can reap the benefits of having a boyfriend for the first time in a decade.

Washington was the last "conquest" I've had—if one could even call him that. He was a fuck buddy that I played with for years, one that I didn't even actually fuck. I gave him head and dry-humped him, orgasming on his covered lap, but never had intercourse with him. Goes to show how messed up I really am, but I'm trying to sort out my issues and move on with my life.

I've not had sex much since Marco. Maybe less than five men at the club, if I'm being completely honest with myself, have sampled Roxie's "goods." The few times I finally indulged and slipped a condom on the random guy I was entertaining in my room, I was weak, needing to see if I could actually go through with it, making it more a test for myself than to pleasure him.

Each time was more difficult than the previous—nerve-wracking, even—the fear that they would break out of their restraints and overpower me enough to ruin my moment. I orgasmed a couple times because it'd been so long since I'd felt a hard shaft deep within and I succumbed. But for the most part, it was uncomfortable, anxiety-inducing, and awkward, despite my nighttime profession as a stripper.

Which is why it surprised the hell out of me that last night, Roxie was throwing herself at Cal, begging him to fuck her. Why would she do that? Sex hasn't ever come easy for us. It's always been so tense and stressful. How can it be any different with Callan?

It has to be. It can be like when you were with Marco, I tell myself.

But he isn't Marco, and I'm not the seventeen-year-old girl that he made love to all those years ago. Since his death, I've not been able to let go, not been able to trust any man. The sex I want, I can't have. The sex I have had, I don't want. I want more. I want to give myself fully over to a man, I want to be open, but the fear overwhelms and overpowers me. I know it's the fear that I won't be able to have what I had with Marco, that I'll be disappointed. That I'll have a panic attack and freak the guy out. But Callan doesn't appear to scare easily. He could be the one to help me, help me move on, and he seems to genuinely care for me and wants to see where things go. *So maybe you should let him!* I tell myself.

And I've decided today that I will, truly. I plan to open my heart and my mind and let him woo me, let him attempt to heal the broken soul buried within bruised and battered Eden Riser, the burning little birdie who rose from the ashes to become a phoenix—a fucking flaming-hot phoenix named Roxie.

I pull my big ass truck up to Addy's and honk my horn.

It's Saturday, and we're getting pampered today. It's girl's day so we are getting our mani/pedis, having lunch, and going to watch a chick flick.

"Get in, bitch. Starbucks is calling my name," I yell at Addy as I roll the window down and get a pouty duck face in return which makes me laugh. I didn't have time to make coffee because I woke up late, and my head is already hurting from lack of caffeine.

"Well, you must not have gotten a healthy dose of cock last night like someone did," she boasts.

"Yeah, yeah, quit your bragging, nympho," I grumble, not desiring to hear her and Ethan's latest sex-capade story.

"Sheesh, E, what's your deal? Sounds like you need to hop a ride on the dick coaster in the worst way, grumpy cunt." She climbs in and throws her purse on the floor board.

I cackle at the name and pull her in for a hug. "Sorry. I'll be good once I eat."

She proceeds to tell me about how excited her and Ethan are for their wedding. They are planning a fall wedding this year, quaint and cozy.

Again, I'm reminded that all my sisters are getting their forever loves, all but me. *But you're working on it*, I reiterate to myself.

I smile and let her ramble on about flowers and decorations, the dress, the bridesmaid's gowns...until I pull into Lia's, and she and Everleigh are heading out the door in a hurry.

"Don't even park, just reverse, I'll meet you in the street," Lia says, hustling down the driveway like she's evading a police raid and pointing to her street.

"What the hell, Lia?" Addy asks, perplexed.

Ev and Lia run to get into the truck and settle in.

"Aliana just fell asleep. If she hears Aunt Eady's truck, she's bound to come with us, and I need a girls' day without her, Lord knows."

"All the pregnant woman wants to know is where the hell are we eating? Luca's takin' Rory to Six Flags, and these twins are about to rumble right out of the birth canal if I don't feed 'em soon."

God, I love my sisters! What would I have ever done without them? Even though I pulled them straight into the worst Hell imaginable, they were able to forgive me and understand that it wasn't entirely in my hands. I did the best I could under the circumstances. It's not like I even had a choice in the matter. Vince was gonna bring them into his ring; I just did it with the least amount of bloodshed possible.

I pull up to our nail salon, and we're ushered to our usual chairs where we begin chatting.

"So, Eady, you gonna tell us about that hot date of yours or what?" Everleigh is the first to ask.

I blush. "It went well. Really well, in fact."

"And?" Lia coaxes.

"And we're hanging out again tonight," I admit and pull my lips in.

"Really? Well good. I'm so glad to hear it. He may be full of himself, but he seems totally into you, lady." Lia grins.

"All I wanna know is: did you fuck him?" Addison asks, getting a giggle from Magnolia as the nail technician begins on her toes.

"Rude! Just because you're a sex addict doesn't mean everyone else is, Addy," Ev scolds.

"Ok, there is nothing rude about getting your healthy dose of vitamin D, Ev. You should know." She points to Ev's pregnant belly and shrugs, getting us all to laughing.

"Seriously though, I-I think I could try and move on...with

Callan," I admit, perking my girls up as they focus on how solemn I've become.

"Well, it's about dang time, Eady. You've needed to move on for a while now." Ev pats my leg and smiles at me.

"You know we'll support you, so long as he's good to you." Magnolia nods.

"But if that fucker hurts you, you know we'll tear his balls off and feed them to him through a funnel," Addy adds, narrowing her eyes in promise.

"Osiris has been itching for a thrill, just sayin'," Ev adds and Lia grimaces, knowing that once-icy, ice queen don't play; she can actually filet a bitch.

"You girls are the best," I say. "I'm so glad you're supporting me about dating him."

"We've always supported you, woman. You're our sister," Lia reassures.

"Core four," Addy reiterates.

"We aren't friends, we're family, Eden." Ev takes my hand in hers. "Now, that isn't all you wanna tell us, is it?"

I look down and shake my head. They don't know all my darkest, deepest secrets. Most of them but not all... That I haven't been dominated by a man since Vince, that I can't have sex like a normal woman, that I'm a big fat liar when it comes to being the sexual fiend I portray in my dominatrix outfit at *RISE*. That I can't sleep at night, that a searing memory burns in my brain alongside the scar at my groin. Well... Ev knows that harsh truth, but not Lia and Addy. Addy knows about the abortion Vince forced me into, and Lia saw firsthand the cruelties Vince inflicted on me, that rape was used as the penalty for *their* punishments.

"It's hard, we know, but you're not alone," Magnolia says.

"You aren't the only one with demons, Eden. We know this

is difficult, but you can talk to us, you know that," Addy murmurs and puckers her lips at me.

I nod and wipe at the tears falling down my cheeks. It's so very hard for me to show anyone my vulnerable side. I've been the tough one for so long. Solid as a rock, as the earth element my name and stage character represents, but I'm not made of stone. I am a living, breathing human who feels, and I've felt so alone for so long, despite that I've had my sisters by my side all this time. They've shared in some of my lowest of lows, but the shame still overwhelms me at how wrong I was done at the hands of my guardian. Vincent Perelli did a number on me.

"What is it, hon?" Everleigh asks. "You know you can tell us anything. This is a no-judgment zone."

I inhale and say, "I haven't had sex in almost a year."

Three sets of brows draw.

"But you just…" Addy begins only to get interrupted by me.

"Cal and I haven't had intercourse." I'm met with silence that draws on for ages before I add, "I never even did it with Washington." I focus on Lia who looks stunned.

"Why?" she asks.

"I-I can't. Have sex like…like ya'll…like normal w-women." I know my face is smoldering red, I can feel it.

"Oh, Eady." Ev sighs.

"I'm a liar. I lied to my best friends because I didn't want y'all to think I'm abnormal. I mean, you know I've been through a lot, but I didn't want you to think I was totally batshit crazy."

"We don't think that," Addy confirms, and Ev and Lia nod their agreement.

"You don't think it's fucked up that I can't let a man *fuck* me?" I ask, my voice raising.

"Eden…" Lia begins, looking down as she chooses her words. "After what Vin…" she trails off. "After what *he* did to you, I can't imagine that would be an easy task. I know it sure as hell wasn't easy for me and I…I understand more than you think I do." She reaches her hand out to take mine.

"You are the strongest person we know," Ev says. "And you've had to deal with things no one else we know has ever had to. Things that no one should ever have to deal with. What was done to you was unforgivable. You've dealt with it in the best way you could. Don't think you're abnormal for not being able to give yourself to someone, not being able to make yourself that vulnerable again."

"I'm sorry," I whimper.

"Don't you dare be sorry," Addy coos.

"We're sorry you've had to endure what you have," Lia states.

"We're sorry you've felt the way you do." Ev pats my hand again. "But it sounds like you're willing to give it a try?"

I grin and nod. "Callan seems different… At least, I hope so."

"Then you give him a chance and yourself a chance. If anyone can do this, E, it's you!"

With that, my girls embrace me in a group hug.

I INHALE SHARPLY AS THE RING SOUNDS AT MY DOORBELL, AND my breath whooshes out as I lay my eyes on my sexy date. Damn… A dark blue polo shirt never looked better on a chest and biceps, and I immediately wanna tear it off his big frame and palm the muscles and tats I know lie beneath.

I gulp as a bouquet of stunning red roses is handed to me.

"Hi there, beautiful," his deep voice states.

"H—" I can't even finish the word as he steps in and pulls me against him, his nose hovering at mine.

Fuck me, I want him. He takes my breath away. I'm not sure if it's his overpowering presence, or his smell, or my fear, or a combo of all three, but I like this heady feeling of being out of control. For once in my life, I don't feel intimidated in a man's presence, despite that this man outweighs me by a lot and I don't think I'd win, even though I could probably be considered a worthy opponent.

"You look downright delectable." His hungry eyes rove my silk shirt and skirt clad body, and I feel scorch marks on my skin where they settle. "Where's the bedroom?"

My eyes go wide and I can see realization darken Callan's face. He covers his blunder with a big grin.

"Baby girl, I'm just playing. It's too early for that." But I know as he takes a small step back to look me over once more that he would take me in a heartbeat if I said the words.

"Uh, what's in the bags?" I ask, realizing he holds grocery bags in his left hand, his duffle bag is over his shoulder.

"Dinner, of course."I raise a brow and he laughs. "I'm cooking for you, darlin'."

God help me, he's delectably gorgeous, reads, smells like pure masculine heaven, is built like a Sherman tank...*and* he cooks? "The bedroom's right there," I croak and stifle a moan as I point to where my bedroom is.

He belts out in laughter at that and pulls me back to his frame.

I grunt, loving how hard and solid he feels pressed to me. My hands settle on his thick pectoral muscles and my head lifts to look up at him. Gah, those eyes and lips.

His nose swipes mine again before he whispers, "I should feed you first. Wine, dine... then we'll see what comes after?"

Oh my, he wants to sixty-nine? No, I can't. He'll see my...

"Relax, Eady, you're as flustered as a horde of cats in a doghouse."

I snort with laughter, and he follows then he lowers the bags to the floor and cups my cheek with his massive palm. "I missed you."

I gulp. Damn. Really? He just saw me... what yesterday? And when he hasn't seen me, we've FaceTimed, texted, talked on the phone.

I sigh and my breathing accelerates as he leans his head down to kiss me.

Wow. I missed his kiss, him, his hands holding me up so that I don't fall into oblivion.

The lips on mine are soft, sensual, and long to be explored as my tongue darts out to taste.

A deep rumble vibrates through his chest and suddenly my thong is soaking wet with desire.

I answer his masculine call as my mouth opens to his. My tongue slides in and sweeps across his, and I feel his palm move across my back and into my hair.

This is the most exposed I've ever been to a man, since Marco, but instead of feeling cornered, caged like the bird I was, I feel free, weightless, powerful. I slide my hands from his chest to his sides, then his back as I grip him, still somehow holding the bouquet of roses.

His other palm settles on my waist, gripping my shirt in his fist as a growl escapes and he angles his head, his tongue plunging into my mouth to feed my raging desire.

Our teeth clash, passions war, and I moan again as I feel his hard manhood digging into my inner thigh. God, I remember what it feels like, tastes like, the thick weight of it in my hand as I loved it with my fist and mouth. My center begins to throb desperate for it, longing to feel his shaft nestled deep within.

But you can't! You're ruined. You're marked. You're unworthy!

I pull back suddenly and Cal releases me, as if I've just screamed bloody murder.

I lick my lips and my hand moves to my breast, attempting to keep my heart from beating out of my chest.

"I'm sorry, Eden. I—"

I'm shaking my head and give him a weak smile. "No, it-it's alright…"

"Too fast," he answers my unspoken statement.

I say nothing, just reach my hand out to his and calm my jangled nerves and sex.

"So, what'd you bring to cook, Chef Manning?"

He gives a laugh, runs his hand through his hair and takes my outstretched hand before reaching for the bags.

"Pizza."

I look suspiciously at the bags. "You mean there's no box?" I snort.

"Nope." He follows as I lead him into the kitchen and motion to the island. "It's gonna be homemade. Only the finest culinary treats for *my* date."

"Oh, impressive. I've never had a date cook for me."

"Really?" he frowns.

"Really," I insist. Speaking of dates, I haven't had many of those either.

"Well, you're in for a real treat, Ms. Riser. I brought stuff to make a delicious peach and arugula salad and margherita pizza." He pulls items from the bags, showing me.

"Yum. My fave."

"Score for me!" His arms raise in a touchdown gesture and I giggle.

"I was hoping you liked sausage too," he teases and bobs his brows.

"Oh, I'll just bet you did, stud." I shove at his shoulder as he pulls out a package of Italian sausage.

"Best homemade sausage this side of NYC."

"You really know the way to a girl's heart, don't ya, Cal?"

"All those romance novels I read, darlin'." He winks and I feel my knees weaken.

From the bottom kitchen cabinets, I pull out a pan for sausage, a pizza stone, and a cutting board at Callan's request.

He starts the sausage on low, washes his hands, and grabs his phone as I grab a vase for my roses. Cal turns on some music, attaching it to my Bluetooth speaker on the countertop.

Frank Sinatra's smooth voice fills my kitchen, and Callan pulls me into his chest. One big palm cups my own and the other settles on my waist. I grin up into his handsome face as our feet move to the rhythm of the music.

He feels good against me, solid, steady, unshakable, and I feel safe here in his arms. For the first time in a very long time, I'm comfortable in a man's company.

Sensing my ease, Cal says, "Thanks for giving me a chance, Eady."

His gorgeous blue eyes rove my face and I'm spellbound at the tenderness of this gentle giant as his hand moves from mine to cup my face.

He turns abruptly in the direction of the sizzling meat, as if he's just remembered, and I giggle as he swears and begins stirring it.

I could get used to this feeling...and dancing in the kitchen with him while he cooks for me.

"Crap, I almost forgot my apron."

"Apron?" I snort.

"Can't be staining my favorite Ralph Lauren polo, now can I?"

He pulls an apron from his duffle bag, and I stifle another laugh as I read what it says, "Kiss the Chef... and he'll melt your butter."

"Nice. I rather enjoy having my own personal chef." I prop

my hips on the island counter and fold my arms beneath my breasts.

"You like wine?" he asks when he turns from the meat on the stovetop.

"What do *you* think?" I ask as I point to my wine rack and bar in the corner.

"I brought a Cab/Shiraz mix that's gonna make you cream your panties." His enthusiasm is contagious.

He pulls a bottle from another bag, and I grin as he moves to my charging wine bottle opener. I open the cabinet to my right and pull down two red wine glasses as he reaches for my aerator.

That he's gone to such lengths to impress and please me makes my heart soften...a lot.

Cal pours our wine and we toast. I moan when I sip mine, and he nods as if to say, "Told ya," before looking down at the apex of my thighs, getting a laugh and swat from me.

He pulls the dough from its bag and sets it on the cutting board to rest, then retrieves some gorgeous heirloom tomatoes along with some fresh mozzarella and basil.

"Man, what else you got in that bag of yours?" I nod to the duffle bag he just pulled the ingredients from and he smirks.

"In due time, my dear." He gives me a wink before he starts slicing and dicing.

Meanwhile, I feel useless and ask, "Can I help with anything?"

He looks around. "Wanna make the vinaigrette?"

I shrug and grab another cutting board and knife. I begin cutting herbs and we work in companionable silence as Callan hums along with the music. When he begins to sing and serenade me, I laugh again.

I don't usually laugh this much in the company of anyone other than my sisters and the realization makes me happy.

Once the meat is browned and the toppings ready, Cal rolls out the pizza dough and places it on the pizza stone. I put the ingredients for the balsamic dressing into my shaker bottle and give it a good shake before setting it aside. I slice the juicy peaches Callan brought as he tops our pizza and ooh and ahh over how pretty it is when he's done.

Cal places it in the oven and together we finish getting the ingredients into the salad bowl. By the time it's ready, my belly is rumbling and the pizza is smelling like an Italian dream.

Cal grins and pulls me back into his arms as a Dean Martin song comes on. I lay my head on his pec and his bulky arms cover my back. I hear his heart beating, steady and lulling, and I'm taken back to Marco. His was the last relationship I've had, the *only* relationship I ever had apart from the one I have with my sisters, since the one with Uncle Vince was so dysfunctional I'd hardly call it a "relationship."

I don't realize there are tears falling down my cheeks until I hear Cal grunt and swipe at one with his thumb.

"Eden, baby, what's wrong?"

Gah, how he says the word baby makes my lower belly flutter. I simply look up into his entrancing eyes and shake my head, unsure how to voice my emotions.

He watches me for a time before he asks, "Marco was your boyfriend?"

I nod.

"What happened?"

Jeez, do we really have to do this now? Everything was so great. Then I go and ruin it with my tears. But I haven't spoken about what happened. I don't even talk about it with Lia, Ev, or Addy anymore. And I say the only thing on my heart at the moment, "He died."

Cal gulps. He wasn't expecting that. His eyes widen before

he pulls me back into his arms and settles me against his chest. "I'm so sorry, sweetheart."

I let the tears fall. Maybe it's good to let the emotions out that I always hold in so tightly.

But this is only like our second date. I can't be that girl. I need to get ahold of myself.

"I'm sorry. I don't mean to ruin our night, I just—"

"Hey, c'mon, Eady. You aren't ruining anything." He lifts my chin with his thumb and index finger then plants a soft kiss on my lips. My tears stop immediately and I calm. Wow, that was easy.

His grin says he's thinking the same thing. "I have a surprise for you."

He kisses me again then disentangles himself from me as he walks back over to his duffle bag.

"I was gonna save this for later, but I think now is the perfect time."

I wait as he pulls a big thick paperback book from his bag and grin as he turns it around so I see it's him on the cover. Cal is a stern and sexy warrior, his bulky half-naked torso is on display with his tattoos shimmering amid a distant sunset, leather pants cover his big thighs, and his arms are raised with an axe in one hand and a crown in the other.

It's Samantha's debut novel, and I laugh because it's my favorite—and last time I saw Sam, I told her so. She must have signed one for me and sent it with her brother tonight. She's such a sweetie.

I jump up and down as Cal opens it and sure enough it's customized with my name and autographed by not only his author sister, but by him too. I'm over the moon!

"I mean, as the girlfriend of a famous book model, I thought it imperative that my woman have a signed rendition of my work."

Did he just call me his girlfriend?

I laugh and hug the book to my chest as he hands it over. "Oh, Callan. I love it. Thank you."

He chuckles in turn. "Now you can set it next to your bed at night and look at me as you masturbate."

I roll my eyes and he laughs.

"This is wonderful. Thank you." I flip through the pages and stop when I come to the section where the figure of a woman is sketched onto one full page. "I always loved these drawings. Who does them for her?" I touch the signature, but it's more of a scribble that I can't make out. I note, too, that Sam's never made mention of the artist in her backmatter or copyright page.

Cal's cheeks redden, and I frown. Probably some ex-girl-friend of his or something, I'm sure. He stays silent so long that I elbow him, coaxing it out of him. He thrust his hand through his thick dark hair before he finally relents and says, "I do."

My jaw drops. "No way, really?" I ask and watch his blush deepen. "Cal, wow! That's amazing."

"It's just a little hobby. I don't make a big deal out of it, but Sam does."

"And for good reason." I press. "You're incredible."

"Well, you already knew that," he teases, and I see in his eyes that he's pleased with my reaction to the sketch.

The timer on the oven goes off, saving him any further embarrassment, and I smile to myself realizing that maybe Callan isn't quite the total self-absorbed, alpha-hole I originally thought he was after all.

Our dinner is delicious, and Cal is good company. He's funny, quick-witted, and I find myself seeing him for the first time as more than just a sex symbol, despite that he is delectable and damn well knows it.

We clean up, loading our plates into the dishwasher before

heading into the living room to watch TV, opting for a rom com, and I badger him about being in touch with his feminine side. I snuggle into his side as his arm rests above my head on the couch.

"So, why is that?" I tease.

"I dunno. Having a big sis who had lots of slumber parties and having her boss me around about what Disney movies we had to watch." He shrugs. "Most chicks don't like scary movies so that was always out...and action movies, too." He frowns.

"Not this chick." I wiggle my brows.

"That's right, this chick is adventurous."

I giggle as he swoops in for a searing kiss. I kiss him back and revel in this new feeling he's invoking in me. He doesn't deepen it, but I can feel he's anxious to do more than kiss and relent as his tongue skirts the opening of my lips. I moan and let him in. He doesn't take advantage though, just shifts his chest ever so slightly as he explores my mouth with his tongue. It moves softly over my teeth and caresses my own tongue, and I moan again. I feel Cal's hand move to my face, where he cups my jaw and angles it up.

When my tongue delves into his mouth, I get a growl from him and immediately my center hums.

He's so unhurried, like he has all the time in the world, and there's a part of me that's eating this shit up and part of me that wants to unleash the inner Roxie and attack him, but I hold back.

First, this isn't Roxie's show, it's Eden's, and second, it's only our second date...but damn, I really want to inhale his tongue and feel his hands on every part of me, even if I'm terrified of him doing so.

He pulls back for a brief second to breathe, his nose nudging mine gently.

"Just how adventurous is Miss Eden Riser?" he whispers in a raspy breath.

And damn if I'm not suddenly showing him.

I grin. This is my big moment. My in. And I'm not going to let it slip away. I arch a brow and stand, pulling him with me as I lead him to my bedroom.

Holy fuck, Eden, what are you doing? My brain screams. My alarm bells are ringing, blaring a warning that my womanhood seems to be oblivious to.

I know that once we cross that threshold and he's on my bed, he can overpower me, thrust me ten years into the past, and leave me that frightened little girl from *The Devil's Play-ground*, but there's this part of me that wants to push the envelope. See just how far I'll let it go. See how far he'll go...

Callan looks surprised as I guide him to my bed, and I realize he's glimpsed my damn stripper pole in the center of my room. *Well, fuck!*

"Is that what I think it is?" he asks, in both surprise and fascination.

"Uh, no. It's uh... it's for support for the..." I point to the ceiling, but Cal's eyes are back on me and I gulp.

Shit, now that I'm here, I don't have the first clue about what to do.

How do normal adults mess around? He must sense my hesitancy because he reaches for my hand as he sits on the edge of my bed. I look at it but don't take it. Instead I turn and do the first thing I think of.

I turn the lights off, and close the door.

IT'S COMPLETELY SILENT, AND FOR A SECOND I THINK I'LL chicken out and run in the opposite direction. I hear Callan swallow and know he's waiting for me to move first. I pull in a shaky breath and peel my shirt over my head. I throw it aside and let my eyes adjust to the darkness.

I can see his silhouette, so broad, so immense on the edge of my bed. My heart is pounding right this minute and my lungs burn with the need to breathe as I uncomfortably hold in my breath.

"Eden," my name is said so softly that I sigh in response. His voice is sexy, deep, easy.

I'm thrown back to *The Devil's Playground* for a moment, remembering Uncle Vince's voice with it's malicious tone... such a stark contrast to Callan's.

"You're the first man in my bedroom," I confess, needing to expel the memories bubbling to the surface.

"Since Marco?"

Shit! Why does his name keep getting brought up tonight? I don't want to talk about Marco.

"He was never in this room," I answer, dismissively.

When Cal stands and removes his shirt, I gulp, panic echoing in my soul, threatening to draw me down.

I'm frozen as he approaches and bite into my lip to keep from whimpering. He's unleashed, not tied down, not restrained. This is a first. I'm miles out of my comfort zone.

"Cal..." I warn. "W-we need to..."

"I know, baby."

How does he know? *What* does he know? Before I can think any further on the matter, his hands are at my shoulders, his chest is pressing into mine, and his lips are on my cheek, moving down to the corner of my mouth, seeking my own.

I moan as his palms move to my waist, and my arms wrap around his neck. This feels good. So good, feeling my bare skin against his. He answers my moan with a beastly one of his own as our lips connect.

He doesn't press, doesn't goad, just awaits as I control the pace, my tongue diving in to explore his delicious mouth. I can feel his cock hardening against my clothed thigh, and I moan again as I press my breasts into his broad chest.

I grip his scalp with my hands, digging my fingernails in as I love his mouth, the taste of him fueling my desire until it's threatening to consume me whole.

My passion skyrockets as I absorb this moment in all its glory. I feel empowered, freed, and I don't have to be in Roxie's room of pain to obtain my power.

This feeling and knowledge are new, exhilarating, and I soar as I feel the invisible cage I've had wrapped around me for so long begin to break apart, bar by bar.

My hands move to Callan's broad shoulders, and my fingertips trace the lines of muscle, the firmness of his pecs, the carving of sinew that ripples with each shaky breath he takes. He's quivering as I pull back and see his frame bathed in the moonlight seeping in through the windows of my bedroom. I'm doing this. Me. Eden. Not Roxie. I'm just as powerful as she is, I realize, and smile up at Cal.

I can see his restraint and willpower are being tested, but he doesn't protest. He has no idea. He simply knows that we must go slow, not rush into things. And I love that he's respecting my boundaries...now to test his.

My fingertips move down over his tattooed flesh, his chiseled abs, to his beltline. He swallows hard, his head falling back as I finger his exposed skin horizontally, caressing his bare belly.

His fists clench at his sides, and I look up again, seeing fire practically dance in his dark eyes.

"Eden, please?" If he's asking for reprieve or more, I'm not certain, but I give him more. I lean into him and take his lips again. My kiss is passionate as I angle my head and stroke his tongue with mine.

His hands move to cover the expanse of my back as I revel in his fervor, one that matches my own.

When we pull back for breath, I'm urging Callan backward toward the bed.

He falls, and I land atop him with a grunt. He chuckles as he holds me to him, then adjusts us so I'm beside him.

All I feel is giddiness, eagerness, and freedom as my fears are damped down and his kiss takes me higher.

We make out for a time, his big palms stroking my back, mine caressing his sexy, muscled chest, before his hands begin to move out of my comfort zone.

At first, I inhale sharply, unsure whether to swoon or panic as his fingertips tease my bottom and the zipper there. His eyes hold mine in the darkness, awaiting further instruction before his mouth moves to my shoulder.

I close my eyes and relax my nerves as his tongue licks a trail across my collarbone, and his lips settle at my throat.

"Oh, Cal," I whimper as his kiss melts my hesitancies in one fell swoop. His mouth is a sexual blowtorch, scorching my flesh and opening my mind to all sorts of erotic fantasies. His tongue dancing across my pulse point wreaks havoc on my womanhood and leaves me breathless.

I haven't noticed he's pulled my skirt up until I feel his bare hand on my upper thigh. I'm hyperventilating even as my sex-starved body is relishing his mouth sucking at the plump mound of my half-bared breast, his tongue licking the edge of the lace.

Desire uncurls inside me, even as my heart trips when I open my eyes.

Callan's chest is now covering mine; he has the upper hand.

He can overpower me. He can take this further than I want. He can…

Immediately my hands tense on his chest, and Cal pulls back. His hands still, and his eyes are riveted on my face.

I gulp, paralyzed.

"You ok, E? Do you want me to stop?"

No. Then Uncle Vince has won. I bite into my lip, unsure, as Cal cups my jaw and swipes his thumb across my lips.

He has such patience compared to the man who I tortured in Roxie's room. He must really want me, want this.

He only wants that sweet little garden I marked as mine, Vince's voice fills my head.

Cal's lips are soft as they kiss me again, the passion slow and sensual as I'm taken back to the present, sucked from the dead, dark memories that haunt me.

His hands return to my back and bottom. He grips it and aligns me to him; we're side by side again, and I can see he's feeding off me, trying to instill trust and calm even as his mouth and hands pull me further and further into lust.

It's as if he knows exactly what I need and how I need it, despite that I haven't told him or guided him, aside from answering his kisses and caresses with curious ones of my own.

He doesn't cross the line again, and as much as I want more, I won't, not tonight.

For at least one burning question has been answered; I *can* move on from my past.

I may be marked by sin, but I have not been destroyed by it.

10

EDEN

"So, tell us about the date with that stud of yours, E," Ev says into the phone as us girls have our weekly FaceTime call.

"Yeah, I need juicy details," Addy insists.

"Are those lips as kissable as they look?" Lia asks.

I blush and clearly, they can see it through the screen.

"Awww, look at that face! I love it. So... I take it that's a good sign?" Everleigh insists while feeding Rory some oatmeal.

"Yes, yes, and yes," I say, feeling my heart melt as I remember Callan's lips on mine, my neck, my collarbone, those big hands stroking me with such gentleness that I swoon right here on the couch.

"Aww, I'm so glad," Lia confesses and grabs up Aliana, who grins and waves at us from the other side of the screen.

"Hey, sweet girl..." I wave back. "He's... y'all, he's just... gah, he's sooo hot."

"Someone got her rocks off, I take it." Addy smirks. "Good for you, lady. Glad to see you are stepping out of your box of tricks."

But I'm not, not yet. We didn't go very far last night. But

baby steps though, right? It's ok that I didn't get him off...right? I mean, I will in time. It's just... Well, I enjoyed the making out part. I don't know that I've ever *just* made out prior to now. I mean, not like a real girl who doesn't have the pressure to do more. It was...freeing. I felt free to explore his mouth, his chest, his arms without feeling the need to rush to the ending. It was slow and sensual and chiseled down some insecurities of mine. Well, a few anyway.

"Sooo, when are you seeing him again?" Lia asks with mischief in her smile.

I shrug. He's already texted me this morning with:

Sexy Studmuffin: *Good morning, gorgeous. I can't WAIT to see your beautiful self again. Tonight? My place?*

And how can I say no? When I want nothing more than to have those big, ripped arms around me and those delicious lips devouring mine?

"Probably tonight. I mean, I shouldn't but..."

"Oh, you've got it bad," Addy states with a giggle. "Good for you."

I mean, men love the chase, right? Maybe I'm too hasty. I should make him crave me a little harder...

No, fuck it. I'm seeing him again...*tonight.*

CALLAN

THESE LAST TWO WEEKS WITH EDEN HAVE BEEN AMAZING. SHE'S beautiful, smart, funny, and makes me desire her more than any woman ever has before her. We've worked out together, hung out together, had breakfasts, lunches, and dinners together. She's come to the house to eat with Sam, Caleb, and I, and we've made out like a pair of teenagers. I can't get enough of her, and I even made up my mind that I'm gonna wait to sleep with her... Well, for a little while yet, as I sense something is off.

She doesn't seem as eager to go at it as I am. Yeah, we've kissed, we've made out— and I finally rounded second base the other night when I fingered her, but the problem is... it's all been in the *dark*. She runs to turn the lights off like we are hiding from parents who might walk in on us. The first time it was kinda fun, but now, I'm getting annoyed. I wanna see her body, I wanna watch her face as she splits apart, see her nipples harden as I suck on them. I wanna explore every inch of her, and I want to take her, but she gets this panicked look on her face each time I begin to move like we are gonna take it further than kissing and heavy petting. This has started to grate on my last nerve. I know she stated that she had a hard childhood, but my suspicions are starting to darken when I see the fear take her captive as we become more and more intimate.

Tonight, we lay facing one another on my bed, tongues tangling together, lips hungry. My mouth moves to her collarbone, my hand cups her breast, and I begin to pull at the hem of her shirt. She grunts, but I don't stop as I peel it up her chest and go for her lacy pink bra. I'm quick as I pull it down roughly and lean in to take her nipple into my mouth. Eden moans, and I swear my entire body is humming like an engine brought to life. The only thing I can think of in those moments is how much I want to claim her. I'm a dying man, starving for oxygen, and she's the air that I need to breathe. I flick the succulent little pebble with my tongue and have her bucking against me as I pull her leg across my hip, gripping her bottom and giving it a firm squeeze; it's so plump and delicious, after all.

After ravishing one breast, I move to the other, the sight of her gorgeous curves making my member go rock solid.

"Oh, Eden, you're so fucking gorgeous, baby doll," I state before assaulting the breast in my grasp. She feels so good; I can't wait to be inside her. I rock my erection against her pelvis, craving that warmth between more than my next breath. I feel her melt into me as her hand grips my shoulder and moves up my neck and into my hair. With that reassurance, I begin to make my descent down her body, wanting to taste her sweetness. I can smell it as my hand falls between her legs. My desire for her gets kicked up another notch when I move a finger through her wet folds. "Fuck, Eady, you're so wet for me." I get a gasp as I move my finger into her silky heat, and her head falls back.

"Mmm, Cal," she whimpers, and I move faster, lowering my head from her breast to her taut belly, kissing her perfect skin. I move lower, lower as my other hand moves up her skirt to grip her ass. My head is at the waistband of her skirt and I'm licking from there to her navel when I feel her thighs clench and her hands tense in my hair. "Cal," she warns. I grip the fabric, ready to pull it down, when her hand grips mine and I look up. I see fear darken her chocolate brown eyes, and she whispers, "Stop. Please?"

I don't know how to react to this—I feel like a teenager again all of a sudden. Then a thought occurs to me: Is Eden a virgin? I can't imagine this is true, but it's not impossible. She's only in her late twenties. Perhaps she never went this far. That thought has me reeling. I don't wanna stop, but I guess I have to. I don't understand this, she seems to be enjoying it...or was until my head came to her waist band. What's she hiding? She's beautiful, the bare skin I've seen of her. Doesn't she understand the torment she's putting me through every time we stop before we get to the good part?

She really knows how to build up the sexual tension between us, huh?

She didn't let me make her come last night when I fingered her either. *Odd*, I think. I had thrust in a couple times and she stopped me, as if it were...

"Eady, baby, am I *hurting* you?" I frown, hating myself so much in that moment. If she's a virgin, maybe I'm being too rough.

She looks down, avoiding my eyes. But just as I'm about to demand a confession, she answers, "No."

"Are you a virgin?" I ask, my voice cracking.

She almost smirks but holds her composure. "No, Cal, I'm not a virgin. I just—"

"I'm going too fast," I answer and feel like a total jerk when she nods with a blush. "Jesus, E," I sigh heavily and run my hand through my hair, pulling back and removing my finger from inside her. "I was about to freak the hell out, baby. You gotta tell me these kinds of things."

Her eyes are rimmed in red as I move back to where our bodies are aligned, facing her as I cup her cheek. She begins to pull her top up, covering herself, and I frown.

"Eden, I—"

"I'm just tired, Callan. I'm sorry."

Tired? What the actual fuck? Now, I've got a mild version of blue balls, and I'll have to take care of it in the shower later. I'm disappointed—so damn disappointed—but I know I'm being a dick and tell her so.

"Damn, Eady, I'm really sorry. I didn't mean to—"

"It's ok." Her hand cups my cheek. "I know you want to." She's blushing. Damn, she's so fine, so innocent, and I wanna make her dirty.

"But you're not ready. I'm moving too fast, I know. I can't help myself. You're just so damn beautiful, sweetheart." I kiss her nose and softly run my finger down her cheekbone, giving her a big grin. "All I can think about is all the naughty things I wanna do to my sweet, innocent little librarian."

She was smiling, but now it's turned into a full out frown—and it's all because of what I said. Dammit!

Eden looks down, her brown eyes brimming with tears I don't understand. I feel like a straight-up asshole. What did I say? I again feel something dark that she's hiding from me, and my gut twists. I want answers, but I know I can't demand them. I can't. She'll have to tell me in her own good time. And I'll just have to be patient.

I'm not a man known for his patience, though, and I wonder how long I can wait to hear her confessions.

I'M IN A PISSY MOOD THE FOLLOWING MORNING. I HAD TO JACK off in the shower last night after Eden left abruptly, maintaining her claim of being "tired." Armed with a vision of my sexy librarian in nothing but her red-framed glasses, curly hair spilling down her smooth olive-toned back as I took her beneath the spray of the shower head. I could still feel her hands on my shoulders, her lips on mine. I imagined how sweet they would feel around my cock, and immediately, I was coming, hard and fast—then I was swearing. That could have been us, coming together, but she won't let me pleasure her. God, she felt so good too. Her heat, silky and sweet, her moans reverberating in my ear. God, I wanna fuck her so badly. But I'm being a pig. I can't push her, can't rush her. But fuck, I've never wanted a woman so badly in all my life. Even as much as I wanted to have Roxie, Eden has me straight up tripping and as soon as I get some coffee in me, to where I can think and not text gibberish, I'm gonna text her sweet ass something romantic. She deserves it. Dammit, now she's turning me soft. What is this woman doing to me?

Sam is up and smiling at me as I walk in, her brown hair mussed. I immediately hope she didn't bring that dick Kevin home with her last night. I frown.

"Good morning, grouchy," she says with a giggle.

I grunt and move to the coffee pot she's thankfully already brewed. "Mornin'." I begin to doctor my java, as usual—more creamer than coffee.

"What's the deal, little bro? Didn't you and Eden have fun last night?" she giggles again. I think back to how loud we were, but again, we didn't go far before Eden was stopping me. I don't know what and how much Sam heard, despite that her room is on the opposite side of the house. "You two are so cute together, I swear. What?" Sam sees my head drop, and I quickly sip my coffee, hoping she hasn't seen my eyes but my sister can read me like a book. She's talented that way. "Cal?" her hand comes to mine, and I look up into eyes as cerulean blue as my own. I gulp, and Sam frowns. She turns, grabs a chair and sits, giving me her full attention. "Tell me."

I love that about my older, by two years, sister—always in tune with those around her. A heart even bigger than that big, smart brain of hers. A man would be blessed to know and have her, and I think once more about the undeserving douchebag she's dating. But it's me she's looking to talk about, not Kevin Stanley, so I blurt it out, "Something's off, Samantha. I can't put my finger on it." I huff out. "Eden is gorgeous and sweet and...amazing. But..." Ok, obviously, I don't usually talk about sexual stuff with my sister, but I need a woman's input on this. "She's stopped me twice now from being intimate with her. We've made out, like horny teenagers, but almost always with the lights off and I..." I'm blushing as I look away. "I fingered her the other night, but...she hasn't let me finish her off, and last night, I was kissing down her belly when she stopped me from going down on her. I don't get it." I run a hand through my hair and finally get the guts to look back to Sam. "What am I doing wrong? She's not a virgin, I asked. Am I just going too fast or what?"

Sam smiles in understanding; she was once a teacher. "Have you ever considered the fact that she was raped or abused?"

Raped? Abused? Like hit on, *beaten*? I know the look on my face is of sheer horror because my sister pats my hand. I finally answer, "Jesus Christ! You don't think…"

My darkest, deepest suspicions have been voiced aloud. Was Eden raped? I hadn't thought it was quite that bad, but now with Sam saying what the back of my head was screaming at me to deliberate on, I have to say it's not out of the realm of possibilities.

Samantha is nodding her head. "The signs are there, Callan. She avoids being intimate with you, doesn't have conflict in her life, she rejected you over and over again before finally agreeing to date you… She's a tough egg to crack. I bet it's been a while since she had a date before you too."

Damn, if she's not spot on with all her assessments. I'm a blind fool.

Sam continues, "Perhaps you're putting her in predicaments she was in beforehand. Have you noticed any scars on her?" Scars? No. Her skin is flawless… I think. "Fear of intimacy is a dead giveaway. Nightmares. Fear of confrontation. Doesn't see how beautiful she is."

I gulp. Sam is on point. Now what can I do? There's a nagging inside me to push the envelope. See how far Eden can be pushed and what will happen if I expose the secrets she's been hiding. As I said, I'm not a patient man, and the thought of someone hurting her is more than I can bear. I need to know what happened to her, who did these horrible things I'm suspecting, and I need to know *now*.

EDEN

I TRY NOT TO THINK ABOUT HOW DISAPPOINTED CALLAN WAS last night after I left so unexpectedly. God knows I want him, with a hunger that won't wait, but my demons are so dark sometimes I fear that I'll be swallowed whole before I can expose my secrets. I have so many, after all, and I'm scared to death of what Callan will think of me when he knows the entire truth. I'm ashamed—no, mortified. What if it's too much for him to take on? And he will *have* to be patient with me on the intimacy part. I want to let him claim every inch of me, but the visions in my head haven't gone away, as much as I've prayed and begged and shouted them away. Vince is always there, in the back of my mind—reminding me of the darkest times in my life, his voice an endless echo, his black eyes burning into mine as he takes my body, ripping a piece of my spirit away with each violent thrust. I lost count of the dozens of times he made me bleed, the times he bruised me, the scars he put on my soul that are invisible to the naked eye. It was only three years of my life, I remind myself. But those three years haunt every facet of my being. I can't look in the mirror without seeing the damage he did even if no one else can. That malignant man ruined me to sex, to men, to trust, relation-ships, love...

I go into work today and try to clear my mind. I'll apolo-gize to Cal later and pleasure him, at least, next time I see him. Only one of us needs to be tortured after all, right? Jesus, I'm so fucked up in the head. Obviously! What kind of woman is beaten within inches of her life, burns the shady club down where she was victimized, only to rebuild another, then becomes a masked stripper once more, chaining herself to the sin pit that she was born into?

One with two faces, I remind myself. The sick, sadistic one gets off on hurting men for the damage done to her as a teenager, the other one is hiding in the shadows of the other's wings. I'm riddled with duality at every turn. Roxie needs Eden, and Eden needs Roxie. They balance each other out, but part of me knows that the longer I keep Roxie around, the longer I extend the sickness I'm plagued with. I can't heal if I can't let Eden be herself; after all, I'm both Eden *and* Roxie. I just have to learn how to merge them back together.

But even if I do that, will Callan accept me? Will he be able to look past the outer shell of who I am? Will he be able to love the corrupt side of Roxie, the sinful side of me, the one who is as much a part of me as the introverted librarian? Can he accept that Eden *is* Roxie and Roxie Eden? That, in essence, is what I fear the most...his rejection of my duality.

I don't deserve him. He's beautiful, good, and worthy of a wonderful woman. A woman with a clear past and conscience, not one with a dozen skeletons in her closet and two faces. And furthermore, can he *handle* the ugly truth once I tell him?

11

CALLAN

I walk into the library, my heart heavy and my mind wandering. I wonder if my sister is right and recall every little detail of my intimate times with Eden. My stomach begins to knot thinking that something awful has happened to the woman I'm starting to fall for. The anger rising in me is building, like the storm in the distance as I approach the desk and try hard not to let Eden see how riled up I am as I greet her.

"Cal, what are you doing here?" Her smile is sly, and I can't help but smile back at her. She looks gorgeous today wearing a black pencil skirt and matching blazer, and my hungry sex jolts to life as she leans into the counter, the gold tank top beneath her blazer giving me a great shot of her ample cleavage.

"Well, I just couldn't wait until our date tonight, so I had to stop by and see my gorgeous girl," I admit, my statement genuine despite that my true intentions are a bit less obvious.

"Are those for me?" She motions to the bouquet of colorful flowers I picked up for her on my way here.

"They certainly are, pretty lady. Come kiss me, and I'll give them to you," I schmooze, for I crave the touch of her lips on mine like the tides crave the moon.

She blushes, and it tears another notch into my heart. I'm not sure if she's blushing because she likes my flirting or if she's bashful about our closeness these last few weeks. She looks around and moves from behind the counter.

When she reaches me, I grab her and pull her stark against me. God, she feels good, her curvy and muscular frame contouring to mine so perfectly. I cup her cheek with my free hand and lean my face into hers. Her lips are soft against my own, and I moan at the contact, savoring the smell of her spicy-sweet fragrance as I deepen the kiss.

All too soon, Eden is pulling back and gripping my shirt, giving me another blush.

"Easy there, tiger. I *am* at work, remember?"

I raise my left brow and remark with, "I mean, it's a bit quiet. We could sneak off to your office and mess around a little."

She gives me a giggle and adjusts her black-framed glasses, her dark hair bobbing in its usual French twist as she shakes her head at me. "Callan…"

"I'm dead fuckin' serious," I smirk.

Her smile slowly fades, and I evaluate her eyes, her face, her demeanor, trying to figure her out.

I plunge ahead, my goal of wanting to get to the bottom of the mystery that is Eden Riser feeding my morbid curiosity. "I wanna kiss more than your lips, baby. Daddy's feelin' a little naughty today." I tighten my grip on her waist, lowering my hand to her ass and giving it a squeeze. "Haven't you ever fantasized about messing around in a library?"

Her eyes turn playful. She looks around and pulls on my shirt again, leading me toward the hallway to the left.

Step one, I've gotten her alone. Now, onto the next phase of my devious plan.

Her lips crash against mine as she shuts the door behind us, then cuts the lights. I drop the roses to a desk and pick her up with ease, sitting her down beside them as she gasps and her fervor increases. My cock responds in kind as my tongue plunges into her hot, eager mouth.

"Fuck, Eady, I want you," I admit, the statement not a lie. She tastes and feels so good. I want to have her in every way possible. And I don't know if I can wait any longer.

She moans as my hands move over her back, and I take this moment to push the envelope. My hands fall to her breasts, and squeeze gently, savoring their plump softness in my palms before moving into the blazer and slipping the jacket down her shoulders. I look into her eyes as I do so, trying to see if this is okay. Her eyes on me don't waver so I continue and unburden her of it. I kiss her again and angle my head, letting my finger-tips flirt with the line of her tank top, just above her breasts.

"I've been dying to see your sexy body, Eden. Touch you. Kiss every single inch of you," I whisper as I dip my index finger into the slit of her exposed cleavage. She moans again and my dick jumps in my pants. I frown. Step two. "But I can't see you in the dark, now can I?"

I don't give her time to protest as I quickly—in two strides —flick the light on and move back to the desk, stepping in between her knees. My palms settle on her panty-hose clad thighs and I move them up ever so slowly. I see the flicker of doubt on her face as my hands come to her waist and I begin to pull on the hose.

"Cal, I really should—"

"Take these off. I wanna taste you," I insist and kiss her lips again, even as I lift her from the desk. I slide my palms into the tight hose and begin moving them down her hips.

"Cal—" Eden protests again, and I start to hate myself for what I'm about to do.

"C'mon, baby. Your clit will thank me in a minute," I tease and shove the hose off. I pick her back up, sitting her down onto the desk once more.

I remove her shoes and throw the discarded hose aside. I touch her bare legs, admiring the smooth, olive tone of her skin. I smile at her, but don't miss her hard swallow as her dark brown eyes hover on mine. She's anxious...and I've made her that way.

I try to keep to the task at hand and lean her backward onto the wooden desk, my chest hovering above hers. Her eyes change, a look of panic taking hold of her. Why is she so frightened? What does she fear I'll do?

My lips return to hers as I cup her breasts again, my fingertips pinching at her clothed nipples. My hand slides down her waist as I deepen the kiss, and I feel my member jerk again as her tongue tangles with mine. "Mmm, let's see how wet you are, baby girl."

She whimpers, and I can't tell if it's from pleasure or fear. I don't meet her eyes, for I'm starting to feel like a terrible person now.

I slip my palm into her lacy panties and groan as my fingertips slide in between her folds. God, it feels amazing...the slickness of her desire for me. I slide a finger inside her, wishing it was my cock instead and pump it a few times, using my thumb to stroke her little bud, getting a hiss out of her. The heat of my own desire assaults me, and I move my lips to her collarbone then her breasts.

Step three is here, and I remove my chest from hers, sliding slowly down her torso. I pull my finger from within her and move to kneel on the floor, my hands cupping Eden's firm bottom.

"Callan, I have to get back to work," Eden's breathy voice calls to me.

"Not before I give you a mind-blowing orgasm, Eden."

"No, I can't. You have to stop. I—" She moans as my mouth nibbles at her silk and lace covered center, my tongue darting at her through her undergarment. I can taste her through the fabric, and the sensation makes my arousal even more pronounced. I groan and move the crotch of her panties aside. "No!" Eden protests and moves to sit up, but not before I see the raised welt at her groin, the one that's hidden behind the edge of her panties.

"Eden." My stomach clenches as the realization of what it is. "Jesus Christ...is that a—?"

The look of horror on her face stills my blood, making my anger all the more poignant. "I want you to leave, Callan."

"Goddammit, Eden. Who *did* that to you?" I growl and cross my arms over my chest as I stand up. Eden huffs out as she pulls her skirt down and jumps off the desk.

"I. Want. You. To. Leave. Right the fuck now." She points her finger in the direction of the door.

But the damage is already done. I've already seen it. Proof of what, I have no clue. But proof that there's a whole other side of Eden Riser that I never could've imagined. A past filled with horror. A past of unspeakable acts. Like opening Pandora's box, I've unveiled something that I wasn't meant to see. At least not yet. And I don't know how to take it or how to react. I'm horrified, angry, disgusted...and have a sudden need to pull her against me and tell her how much I care for her, that I'll never let her go. But I'm kidding myself if I think that Eden hasn't discovered my ploy. She's onto my trick and she's as angry as I am.

"Fine. I'm leaving. But this is far from over, sweetheart."

"*Over* is exactly what this is." The daggers shooting from

her eyes could pierce my soul, but I feel that I'm the first person Eden has gotten this close to in a very long time. I'll be damned if I run away like a coward. It's gonna take more than her attitude to scare me off.

"I don't think so, darlin'. Whenever you're ready to talk about that," I point to her groin, "I'm ready to listen," I say in finality as I turn on my heel and bolt out the door, needing to hit the gym so I can destroy a punching bag with the anger inside me at this moment.

Eden

I HOLD MY BREATH AS CALLAN WALKS OUT OF THE DOOR. THEN I fall to my knees into the floor as my heart breaks into thousands of pieces. Not since my Uncle Vince was alive have I been as mortified as I am in this moment. Now Cal knows about my darkest secret. The one I've kept even from the girls I consider my sisters because it represents the lowest time of my life, when my soul was finally taken from me, my body marked for all eternity by the very devil himself. The initials of my evil captor branded into my skin, welts and shame I've hidden and never let anyone see—well, Ev did, but only because she stumbled upon me in the shower that night.

When Uncle Vince said he'd mark me for life, he'd been as serious as a heart attack. He'd done it the very day he'd been made aware of mine and Marco's deception. It was our punishment for loving one another, for deceiving Vince. First, he'd forced the man I loved to bear witness to him violently raping me. Then he took his brand, held it over a flame, and put it to my tender flesh—if Marco had ever doubted who I belonged to —marking me with his initials, V.P.

Now, it's my scar to bear, my shame, my humiliation. It's

my own personal scarlet letter. And Callan has seen it despite my many attempts to hide it for as long as I could. I sought darkness the few times we've been intimate, and as always, remained in control. No man has taken me on my back since Marco. Marco, the man whose death reminds me of my own torment here on earth, the man whose life was essentially snuffed out by the hands of those he deceived.

My past—and present—are too sordid, even for me, and I find myself bawling on my hands and knees as my emotions overtake me. Thinking of Marco, of how truly alone I am in this world, of all the offenses that have been committed at my hands, to me, and to those I love the most. It's too much to bear. The sins. The secrets. The lies. The deception. The betrayal. And now I've brought another innocent soul into the fold.

Now, I have to tell him, expel my burden onto him when all it will do is hurt him and make me feel as empty as I still do to this day, years after the fact.

Callan deserves better even though he deceived me to get this information. But I owe him an explanation for my secrecy, for hiding in the shadows. I could have come clean, but I was too ashamed. If I had only told him sooner, he wouldn't have had to find out this way. If only I had been honest. But honesty is something I haven't known how to express since before my parents died. It's a difficult expression now that I live a life of polarity.

I rise, pulling my panty hose and blazer back on and pressing my feet into my shoes. I have to get out of here.

I move toward the door, wiping my eyes. Seeking escape, seeking reprieve, seeking forgiveness—an outlet for my anger and self-reproach.

I search my half-empty library for the other librarian, Angela. When I find her cataloging, her jaw drops at seeing me so distraught. *No* one sees me as anything but composed and collected.

"I have to go," I mumble. "I'm so sorry."

She just nods, and I turn, absorbed in my own anguish.

Soon, I'm in my truck, driving to an unknown destination as my reeling mind forces me through a series of unwanted memories. They're flashbacks of Marco, the man Callan reminds me so much of, the first man whom I, willingly, gave myself to. The man who taught me how to love my body. The man who taught me how to fight, how to love, how to be loved. The man whose love also tore me apart.

I shake my head at the recollection of Marco's face flooding back to me and realize I've driven to the cemetery where he's buried. I can't recall how long it's been since I've visited this place, this plot, where I buried my first love. All I know is that I need to speak to him, no matter that he's gone and has been for ten long years.

I park my big truck and turn it off, yanking the key from the ignition. I lock it as I walk amid the lonely gravestones on this cloudy day, a fitting day for my mood.

I fall to my knees as I see his headstone, and my heart jerks in my chest as I read his name—Marco Harliss Bentley. "Oh, Marco. I'm so alone. I've messed up so badly."

I cry on my former lover's grave, wishing for many things, having many regrets, and feeling my heart bursting as I pour my soul onto the grass in torrents of emotions. I close my eyes and let the memories take me back to the day I knew what love truly was.

"PLEASE, DON'T GO. NOT YET," I PLEAD, HATING BEING ALONE IN THE *dark on a night like tonight.*

"You know I can't stay, little dove."

"Why do you call me that?"

"What?"

"Little dove?"

Marco gives me a soft laugh, his big frame shaking, and my eyes fall to his broad chest. I bite into my lip just as a rumble of thunder shakes the house. I shudder, and my eyes jerk back to his.

"I guess it's my pet name for you, Eady."

Pet name, huh? I must be his pet then.

"Do you like me, Marco?" I don't know why this storm has made me so darn brave all of a sudden. Perhaps my fear of him leaving me rivals my fear of Uncle Vince catching him here in my room.

Over the last several months, my hands and words have gotten ever bolder where Marco is concerned. I am totally crushing on him, I can't help myself. He's kind and handsome, and the only man in my life right now who makes me feel like I'm actually a person instead of a possession.

"Of course I like you, Eden, you're my boss's..." His face grows serious, and he takes a step back.

"No, you know *what I mean."*

"Ead—"

"Tell me the truth. No one else has to know."

Lightning cracks outside, and I gasp and visibly shake beneath the covers.

Marco takes a step towards the bed. *"Why are you frightened of thunderstorms?"* he asks as I frown.

I look down for a time before replying, *"It reminds me of the night Uncle Vince...p-punished me for s-starting my period on the stage. It was storm—"*

"I remember," he growls and looks away, taking in a deep breath. He glances back down at me and his eyes soften in the dim light. *"Want me to lay with you?"* he asks and knows what I'll say before I say it as his knee hits my bed.

Internally I squeal, delighted that I won't be alone to bear the memory of that awful night Vince took me out into the thunderstorm to teach me a lesson, telling me that no one got to bleed on his stage unless he was the one bringing the blood.

"You have a way of weaseling yourself into my skin, you know that?" Marco teases, but there's no conviction in his tone. I have this monster of a man exactly where I want him, and he knows it.

My bravery seems to know no bounds as my hand cups his jaw and my eyes linger on his big lips. Is there anything small on this man's body? Suddenly, I don't know why, but I'm dying to know.

"You didn't answer my question, Marco."

"Would it matter if I did like you?"

I shrug. "It matters to me."

"I can't do anything about it, now can I?"

Was that supposed to be an admission? "Soooo...." I persist.

He looks me over, his sparkling eyes almost sad as they move over my body. I'm all too aware of the tingling that has begun in my core. "I wish things could be different, Eden. But they aren't."

"But if they were?"

"If they were, there would be nothing stopping me from loving you right now."

My heart soars at his words, and curiosity gets the best of me. "When you say loving me..."

"I mean making love to you, my little dove. I would be buried deep inside you this very instant."

I gulp. That's what I thought he meant. I bite into my lip again, wondering if sex with Marco would feel different than what my uncle does to me. The girls at the club, Kara, Caleigh, and Nichole, all talk about how awesome sex is and about having multiple orgasms. The experiences I've had disgust me in every sense of the word, especially the forced orgasms which shame me more than anything else. Taking any pleasure in such vicious and perverse acts makes me consider that maybe I deserve to be in this Hell after all.

Marco's kiss felt amazing, alive—not that I've kissed him beyond *the peck kiss I did two months ago. But it stirred me in ways Vince's touch never has...so surely having him inside me would feel just as good, right?*

Marco appears to know my thoughts as he says, *"I would make you feel good, Eden. It can feel good. Different than with Vince."*

Is this truly possible? How? *"Show me...please?"* My desperate plea is just above a whisper.

His brows draw as he looks into my eyes, a mixture of fear, desire, and angst fill his orbs. My heart hammers suddenly in my chest, threatening to escape through my throat.

We both know that no one else is coming here, we are alone for the night. Uncle Vince won't be home until morning... He trusts Marco to protect me. This is the one room where the cameras aren't allowed, for fear that someone might spy on Uncle Vince's little treasure.

"Eden, you don't know what you're asking..."

"I do." I know very well.

"If I take you, little dove, I'll be here all night."

"I want you to be."

"I don't know that you know what you want."

"I want you, Marco," I admit and realize that it's true. He gives me an escape from the void that is my life. He's the one constant in my sea of turbulence. My stable, solid Marco.

"Oh, my sweet little dove. Once I start, I'm going to be unable to stop." I comprehend his double entendre even as his head falls and his lips capture mine. I moan as I unleash the full force of my passions upon him. My arms wrap around his neck instinctively as his body moves into mine. His big hands move over my bare arms and I shiver at the contact, at how gentle my giant really is. My mouth opens, and his tongue gently moves across mine. The invasion is unhurried, unforced for a change, and I revel in the ribbons of desire uncurling inside my lower belly.

"Oh, Marco," I whimper and push my body even further into his,

my breasts crashing against his massive chest as his hands fall down my waist to my short-clad bottom. He gives a good squeeze and moans again, and I feel his growing length pressing into my thigh. He thrusts it against my bare flesh, and for a moment I balk at the realization of what I've done, the onslaught I've brought upon myself. I pull back suddenly and gulp as I look into his lust-filled eyes. But I don't find the usual darkness I see in my uncle Vince's and give Marco a weak smile.

"I'll stop if you want me to, Eden. You just say the word."

I shake my head, and my hand grips the back of his neck as I pull his face back to mine. I kiss him, making sure this isn't a dream, that it's real, that he's real. Here. In my bed. Kissing me. His groan of satisfaction spurs me on, and for a time, we make out. His hands move over my quivering skin in awe. His mouth moves to my neck, and I break out in gooseflesh as he nibbles at my sensitive pulse point. I feel my desire quickly dampening my panties and long for him to be there, unsure how I feel about all this. It's happening so fast...

One of his big palms moves to cup my breast, and he watches himself knead the full mound. My insecurity grows as his hand moves to the hem of my shirt and beneath, to the bare flesh of the breast he was just fondling. I blush as his fingertip strikes my bare nipple then moan aloud when his head lowers, his lips finding my erect flesh, pulling the rigid peak into his hot mouth. I've never felt pleasure like this before. My uncle has conditioned my body to orgasm from response alone, but this... This is something different, something incredible. A new side of me has been unleashed, and I can't stop the moans of satisfaction hurling from my throat. My reactions only encourage Marco on as his other hand moves up my shorts, his fingertips sneaking into my panties and in between my legs to the throbbing bud at the delta of my thighs. I'm surprised to watch myself arch against his palm as his finger enters me, and I cry out his name.

"Yes, my little dove. Feels good, huh?"

I whimper in response and press my breast further into his

mouth, my head falling back in wanton indulgence. My body and mind are so stimulated that it's overwhelming. I reach for Marco's beltline, wanting to touch him, pleasure him like he's doing to me. He chuckles and moves atop me, aligning his body with mine even as his mouth and finger stay where they are.

"I'm gonna make you come now, baby. Then again while I'm inside your sweet little body."

I nod even as his lips pull my orgasm from me, his finger pumping into me with slow sensual strokes. My climax comes violently, and I'm wracked in spasms. I whimper out as his lips move over mine, kissing my pleasure cry while his finger thrusts harder and faster inside me.

When I come back to earth, I'm shucking my shorts as he's unbuttoning his slacks and unzipping his fly. I grab for him, wanting to have him filling me, wanting to orgasm while he's inside me more than I've ever wanted anything...save for my freedom from the bondage of my uncle.

Marco kisses me again as he shoves his pants down and grips my hips, pulling me toward him. He's thrusting inside me and hovering his big frame over mine when panic seizes every inch of my body, and I freeze. I'm not sure what has me so afraid, but Marco immediately sees it and pulls my face to look at him.

"Eden, baby, look at me."

I do and feel my eyes flood with tears.

He's not Vince. He's your Marco. Your sweet, loving Marco. Let him in.

I try to will my body to relax, will myself to breathe, but I'm frozen completely.

"Little dove, come back to me," he whispers and cups my cheek. He kisses my lips softly, but it's no use. My uncle has destroyed me, I'll never be able to do this with anyone else. "Eady," Marco calls to me again and begins to withdraw.

"No," I protest and grip the shirt still clinging to his shoulders.

"Eden, I won't force—"

"Just do it. I'll be fine. I just—" My legs—wrapped tightly around his hips—quake despite my pleading. Marco shakes his head and begins pulling me from him, untangling me as if I'm a vine. "No," I beg. "Marco..."

"Shh, it's ok, love. I have an idea." He grins slyly at me, and I relent as he shucks his shirt and moves off the bed. He lays his dress shirt over my desk chair and removes his slacks, doing the same with them. He stands before me, gracefully naked, his erect sex impressive to a girl who's only seen one other up close and personal. I look at him approach, feeling equal parts apprehension, solemnity, and disappointment. He takes my hand and pulls me upright and toward him. I follow his lead and let him peel the shirt off my torso. I feel my cheeks flame as I wonder what he thinks of my now naked body. I don't have to wonder long as he says, "God, you're stunning."

He's seen me naked before, at the club, with my uncle Vince atop me. Seeing me unclothed is nothing new, but he's never seen me naked when we're alone together, and I realize he's telling the truth as his shaft pulses in response. I give him a bashful grin despite the fact that I've grown to hate my disproportionate body even more over the years as my uncle uses it to his advantage, here and at the club.

"Eden, you have to see how gorgeous you are." His eyes come back to mine, but he knows how insecure I am of my Amazonian-type build. I have body dysmorphic disorder, after all. "See my eyes?" he asks, and I nod. "See my cock?" he asks, and I can't stifle the laugh at my throat. "Your body is breathtaking. Embrace it." As if his words need verification, his hand falls back to my breast and reshapes it in his big palm. It then falls to my hip, my ass...

Soon, we're kissing again and my hand falls to gingerly test his manhood. He moans and pulls back just enough to let me play, pleased that I'm eager to satisfy him. And I am. I want him to fall apart to my touch. Love me the way I have only dreamed.

As if sensing my thoughts, his knee moves back to the mattress *and his chest hits mine as he pulls me into his arms. I relish the feel of our bare skin touching, his lips kissing me, his hard sex pressing into my thigh, his hands on me.*

"Eady, I want you. All of you, but I know this isn't easy..." When I don't respond, Marco continues, "There's a way you can be in control, of the penetration, of your orgasms."

I don't even have to ask him to show me as he moves us together. He lays down on his back, taking my hands and pulling me astraddle of him. This is different. I've never done this before; Uncle Vince always takes me on my back.

Marco smiles, pleased at my surprise and excitement. He guides me, moving my hand to his shaft, shows me how to prepare myself, then how to mount him. I slowly impale myself on him and moan as my body takes each inch of him inside me until I'm to the hilt. I stop and grin down at him, watching his eyes dance. "You're on top now, little dove. You have the power. All of it. I'm yours to command, Madam."

"OH, MARCO. I OWE YOU SO MUCH," I STATE AS I REALIZE THE impact his selfless gesture had on my life. "I don't know what to do. How can I explain any of this to him?" I ask, knowing how difficult revealing my secret double life to Callan is going to be, but I have to do it if we're to have anything real together. It's been hidden so deep for so long. My fear encompasses me.

Something Marco always said comes back to me as I pull myself upright and touch the headstone, tracing his name with my fingertips.

Life goes on, Eden. Even when we think it's over.

How right he was, for my life has gone on despite thinking it was over many times and the many times I *wished* it was over. It's as if I hear him speaking to me, as if he's not really gone, and I can hear his voice in my ears, encouraging me to unburden myself. And I know that I have no choice but to do so. I can't have a relationship with Callan if I can't be honest. But trust is hard to come by in my life and unloading my insecurities may be the hardest thing I've ever had to do.

I KNOCK ON THE DOOR, BILE RISING IN MY THROAT. MY EYES burn and my heart feels like it might just explode in my chest. I want to vomit and run in the opposite direction as I hear the door open. But it's not Callan who greets me, it's Samantha, and I relax—though not much.

The look on her face is disappointed, anxious, and sympathetic.

"Eden, I'm glad you're finally here. Cal has been downstairs for hours now. He's madder than I've ever seen him."

"I'm sorry, Sam. I—"

"Come in, please?" Samantha grips my hand and pulls me inside. "He's been giving that punching bag hell so just be prepared. I can hear him all the way from the kitchen." Her brown hair bounces as she turns and walks through the living room, motioning to the basement door. "Good luck," she grumbles and opens it.

I gulp as I hear Callan's heavy grunts and the sound of his fists assaulting the punching bag.

"Thank you, Samantha," I say and begin walking downstairs, hearing the door close behind me.

I'm on the last step before Callan sniffs and turns, hearing my heel hit the mat covering the carpet. I freeze as I see him. His burgundy muscle top is drenched in sweat, and his face is red. His brows draw, and I don't know whether to swoon or shy away in fear. His wrapped fists drop to his sides, and he exhales hard as he looks me over. He takes in my own red face and swollen eyes, and his lips draw in, a pained expression that isn't lost to me.

I speak first, unsure how to begin. "S-Samantha let me in, I—"

He nods and motions for me to have a seat on the couch across from the TV, while he takes the leather ottoman across from it. I sit and look his big, sexy build over. His tan skin is blotchy from his workout and his inked biceps are swollen. His black shorts bunch as he leans forward on his knees, sweat dripping from his temples, his dark hair as wet as the rest of him.

Immediately, my female parts hum and I want to throw myself at him and beg for forgiveness, but I realize that sex isn't going to fix this. He deserves answers.

"Cal, I'm sorry. I should've—"

"Who did that to you, Eden? Who's V.P.?"

My eyes lower, and I feel my cheeks flame. "My uncle."

"Did he...?" Callan looks down, his hands move to cover his face. "Jesus, Eden, did he...?" He can't form the words, and I gulp as I realize what he's asking me can't even compare to all the hell my uncle put me through for over three years. Rape. Torture. Beatings. Torment of the mind, body, and soul. Yes. Yes, Uncle Vince did all that to me and so much more. He marked me in more ways than I ever could've imagined, and to this day, I'm still affected by it. No amount of therapy or prayers or moving on has completely healed me...and probably never will.

"Yes." I manage to say. "He did."

Callan's hands move, and the pain on his face matches the tearing in my heart. God, this is so much harder than I thought it would be. And his expressions aren't going to make it any easier. His mouth opens to speak, but I cut him off. "I guess I should start from the beginning." A tear falls down my cheek, and I shift in my seat, discomfort seizing every part of me. "My parents died in a car accident when I was just fifteen years old. The only living relative I had was my maternal aunt's husband, Vincent Perelli."

"*The* Vincent Perelli? The 'godfather' of Atlanta?"

I nod. One and the same. "Crime boss. Sex trafficker. Kingpin. Rapist. Murderer. Sociopath. Paranoid control freak. I would go on, but I think you get the idea."

"My God, Eady." Callan's big blue eyes burn into mine and shame eats into me.

"He began raping and beating me the very night I came to live with him and grew more possessive as time went on. The atrocities he committed were endless. I won't *beguile* you with all the gritty details, but needless to say, it fucked me up royally."

Callan blows out, and I can tell this is difficult for him to hear. I flinch as his hand comes to my knee and cups it ever so lightly. "I had no idea, baby. I'm so sorry."

"I haven't been able to have sex with the lights on or..." My lips tremble, again, the shame eating me alive on the inside.

"I had no right to trick you like I did."

"It's ok. I-I'm kinda glad you did. Now you know the extent of my dysfunction. Cal, I—I'm not normal. Nothing about my life is normal. I—"

"I don't want normal. I want *you*."

"I have another man's initials *branded* to my pussy lip, Callan...and I wish his corruption stops there, but it doesn't! It's affected every facet of my life, to the point where I can't even have sex in the missionary position. I haven't since—"

"Eden, I care about you." Those beautiful baby blue eyes

scorch my soul. "I-I'm not usually a patient man when it comes to what I want." His hand moves from my knee up to my face. "He may have marked your skin, sweetheart, but he can't mark your soul, Eden. You're beautiful. As beautiful inside as out. I'm not intimidated by the scars left from a dead man. If you want me, Eady, I'm willing to work at this. I'm willing to be patient because you're worth it to me." The smile he gives me is the most genuine thing I've ever seen, and I can't help the tears that spill forth. To hear someone say that I'm worthy is mind-blowing and humbling, and my heart soars.

I throw myself into his arms and sob. I sob as all the wrongs feel righted in Callan Manning's solid embrace. He tucks my head into his shoulder and kisses my temple. "My sweet, sweet angel. I'm so very sorry." His words undo something inside me, unravel the insecurities, the doubts, the fear, the anguish. I feel whole again for the first time in so long, and I can't contain the satisfaction of finally telling someone, unburdening myself of this secret past of mine that keeps me caged like the little bird I've always been.

I pull my head from Callan's shoulder and look into his face. He cups my cheek and leans in to kiss me. It's a soft, sweet kiss of understanding, of compassion, and hope, and I melt into it as my mouth opens to his. He deepens our kiss, but it's not rushed. He kisses me slowly, as if he has all the time and patience in the world, and I find myself falling...falling hopelessly...into him and in love with him. He's my beacon in the dark storm that's been my life; he's my warmth in a room full of cold. Callan is the man I've been waiting for, and I long to give him everything I've held back for far too long.

When he pulls back, he holds my face in his hands and smiles at me, pulling one from my lips.

"I've got you, Eden Riser. No one can ever hurt you again.

You hear me? I'm here for you. Always. I'm not going anywhere."

I continue kissing him, throwing my passion, desire, fear, and doubts into the wind as I let him take me away—somewhere only the two of us exist. Soon, I find myself rocking into him as my body starves to be comforted by his.

He lets out a soft chuckle and pulls back again, seeing my body thrown astraddle of his. "Easy there, little bookworm. Don't be so eager." He gives me a wink, and I swear, my heart stills.

"Sorry, I—"

"It's alright. I just... It's no surprise how much I want you, Eden." He gulps even as I feel his length growing against my thigh. His eyes rove my face, and the blush on his face is precious. If only I weren't so hesitant, I would fully give myself to him, fully and completely. But I can't. Not yet. I still have more to tell him, in due time.

I gulp and he smiles again, a man of patience indeed. He cups my cheek and kisses my forehead, looking into my eyes with so much sweetness that it makes me wanna cry again.

He falls back and pulls me with him, resting my head on his chest. I listen to the steady beating of his heart against my ear, letting it lull me as he rocks me and wraps his big arms around me, making me feel safer than I ever have before.

I'm in love with him. I don't know how I can be this way so quickly—and before I've ever even made love with him, even though we've been intimate many times...well, he and Roxie have. Although, now, I guess I need to tell him that too. Soon. There's been enough surprises for one day, I think.

Yes. I'll tell him...and soon.

Just not today.

Callan

My chest literally aches right now as I hold my girl in my arms. My girl. Eden is mine. And for the first time in my life, I feel a sense of completeness as I hold her that I've not felt before, ever. She's come clean to me about her past, why she was so hesitant to be intimate with me, and as much as it breaks my heart, it feels good to know she trusts me with her deepest secrets.

God, what a monster her uncle Vincent Perelli was! What kind of man would do such a thing to his wife's niece? A child he was entrusted to take care of, protect, and keep safe? A psycho who died in a fire intentionally set at his club, that's who. He literally branded her, raped her, and did God only knows what else while she was in his care.

I breathe in deeply and fight the nausea that threatens the back of my throat. I can't even comprehend the sheer hell this beautiful woman has been through living with a notorious mobster, but as she pulls back to look into my eyes, I know one thing—she's safe in my arms now. I won't let anyone hurt her ever again. I felt utterly helpless when she told me, sorry for the girl that was robbed of her innocence, terrible for the wrongs put upon her, and swore to myself she'd never have to feel that way again. I'll take this relationship as slow as I need to, so long as she's comfortable with me, nothing else matters.

"Eady, baby." I kiss her forehead. "Are you hungry?" Shower be damned, even if I stink, I'm taking care of this woman right now. Nothing else matters.

She nods and gives me a sweet smile. My lips find hers again, softly giving her a reassuring kiss.

"Come on. Let's go get you something to eat, sweetheart."

She moves off me, and I stand, taking her hand. I walk us

up the stairs, hands interlaced, and when I open the door, my sweet nephew and sister are seated at the table in front of us.

"Oh, hey, I—I thought you guys would be a little while," Sam says with a blush. "Help yourself."

"You like spaghetti?" I ask, and guide Eden. She nods as I motion to the empty seat next to Caleb.

"Hey, buddy," she says and pats his hand. He gives her a grunt, and she giggles. "Yum, this looks delicious. Did your mom make it?"

Caleb grunts in glee, and I grin as I begin to plate spaghetti and meatballs, salad, and garlic bread for Eden and myself.

I hand Eden her plate. She thanks me as I take the seat opposite her at the table.

We all eat in silence for a time before Caleb starts to communicate with Eden. I smile as she speaks back to him, not understanding him but glad she's attempting; it warms my heart.

"That's right, buddy. Eden is my girlfriend." He murmurs that she's pretty, and I laugh. "Yes, she's *very* pretty, isn't she?" I wink over at my "girlfriend" and get a blush from her. Caleb garbles again, I'm sure it sounds like nonsense to her, but I laugh once more. "Yes, that means you *can* check out all the books you want from the library now."

"Uh, Callan," Eden protests.

"Cal," Sam scolds me. "No, that's not what it means, son. Don't you listen to Uncle Cal!" Samantha tells Caleb.

Eden laughs, and the sound is music to my ears. Caleb then says that he's gonna date a librarian too, and I laugh in return.

"What's he sayin'?" Eden asks after she swallows a bite of spaghetti.

"He wants to date a librarian too," Sam admits with a big smile.

"Aww, Caleb, you're so sweet. I love that." Eden coos.

"Sweet just like his Uncle Callan." I wink at Eden, whose smile melts me once again.

"Kevin was going to come tonight, but his meeting ran longer than he expected."

I watch Eden flinch in response and frown over at her, but she shakes it off. She knows something about the guy my sister is seeing, something that bothers her, and I don't like it. I don't like him, and I realize my gut has never been wrong before.

Once we're all finished with our dinner, little Caleb is asking for dessert. Sam, of course, made a big bowl of home-made banana pudding, Caleb's favorite.

"Yum," he says as Sam puts his helping down in front of him.

"You plan to share that, cubby?" I ask.

"Nope," Caleb says, and Sam gives him a bite.

"Good stuff, isn't it?" Eden asks, taking a bite of her own serving. "Thank you for dinner, Samantha. It was delicious."

"My pleasure. I'm glad you stuck around for it," Samantha says, and I know it's in earnest. She sees how I feel about Eden, how much I've wanted to get closer to her.

Afterward, Eden and I are washing the dishes up as Sam gets Caleb ready for bed. When I, once more, ask Eden about Kevin, the plate she's washing suddenly slips from her grasp to the floor and shatters in a dozen pieces.

"Oh my gosh, Cal. I'm so sorry."

"It's alright. Don't move. I'll grab the broom," I insist as I step across the mess and over to the broom and dustpan in the corner. "Hold still, sweetness."

She does as I say while I discard the larger pieces into the trash and sweep the remainder into the dustpan then empty it in the receptacle.

"Callan, I'm so sorry. I—"

"It's ok, baby. No harm, no foul," I say as I take her face in my hands. I kiss her lips, savoring their softness against my own, and move in closer to her. I deepen the kiss and feel her lean into me. I run my hand up to her head and unfasten the clip in her hair, letting it fall down her shoulders as I run my palm into it. I moan as I grip her scalp and bring her head closer to mine. She reciprocates, and I feel her palms flatten against my chest. My sex aches to be nestled against her, and I feel it fill with blood as my body tingles from Eden's closeness.

"Oh, Cal," she murmurs as my other arm encircles her waist and my grip tightens on her shirt.

"Eden, baby, do you know how good you feel against me?" My brain is humming along with the rest of me as I bury my face into the crook of Eden's neck, inhaling her sweet scent and licking her throat.

"Tell me how good, Callan," she whispers and I swear, I could rip her clothes off right here and take her on the table we all just ate off of. I can't, though, not yet. We have to ease into this, as I've well seen today.

"So good I wanna lose myself to you, Eden Riser, over and over again." I grip her waist in my palm then splay my hand across her back as I pull back and look into her face.

She's so beautiful. Her dark hair now framing her face, her olive skin, her plump lips, and deep brown eyes. I grin even as I pluck the glasses from her nose and set them aside. I tilt my head and study her.

"You're stunning, sweet angel. And I can't wait to eventually get entrapped in you, my sweet little garden," I confess with a smile.

Suddenly, Eden stills. The look on her face has me reeling. Her lips quiver, and I frown, unsure what I said or did to invoke this reaction in her.

"E?" I ask and cup her cheek.

She closes her eyes and shakes her head, momentarily

somewhere else. When she opens her eyes again, she gives me a weak smile. "I'm sorry, I—"

"Tell me, what happened?"

"No, it's nothing, I—"

"Eden," I scold. "You *have* to talk to me. Don't shut me out. If I did or said something—"

"You didn't know. It's...the name, garden, I—"

"Someone else called you that?" I scowl once more, my stomach tightening as I think of the pain she's been through. She closes her eyes again for just a moment and nods, her head falling. "Sweetie, I'm sorry."

"Cal, please don't apologize, ok? It's still new and—"

"One day at a time, right?"

"Right." Her eyes lift, and I smile again, capturing her lips with my own. I slant my mouth and simply love hers, trying to pull away the anguish and pain from her, attempting to instill love and trust. I know that this is going to take time and won't be easy on us, but I meant what I said. I'm willing to try to make this work. I won't push her, and I'm going to be here for her.

Time heals all, or so they say anyway.

EDEN

"HEY, ZEUS, WHAT'S UP?" I ASK INTO MY PHONE AS I WALK INTO my office at the library the next morning.

"So, I wanted to discuss something with you."

Damn, he's got that serious tone to his voice. This can't be good. What now?

"Ok," I answer.

"Last night there was a man here that I didn't recognize. I

don't have him listed as a guest or a member, so I don't understand how he got admitted in the first place."

"*Excuse* me?" I ask, anger painting my cheeks. All our doormen, security guards, and employees know the rules of the club. No one gets in that doesn't have prior approval. "Who the fuck let him in?"

"I don't know, Eden. I'm checking into it but... he was asking questions that were suspicious."

"Zeus, I want you to stay diligent. I don't want anyone in the club that doesn't have proof of membership. Not even guests. Refuse them at the door. We have to figure out what's going on. I'm calling Kieran when I get off the phone with you. Someone is seriously fucking with us."

"I know. I—"

"When you find out who the hell let him in, I want him fired on the spot. No excuses."

"Done."

"And Zeus?"

"Yeah."

"Don't—"

"I know... don't tell the girls. I got it."

"Thanks for calling me, Z."

"Eden... stay safe, alright?"

I hang up and flip through my contacts until I find Kieran Greene, Everleigh's older brother. It's time to tell him what's been happening at RISE.

He answers on the second ring. "Eden? You ok?"

"Hey K, listen, we need to talk."

12

CALLAN

"Oh baby," I grunt as Eden's hand comes to my crotch and I pant, like an animal over a meal, but fuck, she's turned me into one. "Jesus, Eden, you're killing me, sweet angel. I can't. Fuck. I can't." I practically whimper as she squeezes. "Please?" I'm begging, but I don't care. It's been two weeks and I need to be inside her, fill her, have her mouth on me, *anything* to satisfy this pounding ache in my loins.

I've been gone the last week to Paris, and I've never missed anything in my life more than I missed this sexy little goddess of mine. Now, I have her pressed against my body and I want more, God I want so much more.

I grip her shirt and pull it apart, ripping the buttons even as Eden balks, shocked by my actions.

"Whoops," I murmur and move my mouth to her collarbone as my hands grab for her breasts, covered by a lacy black bra that I'm simply dying to see beneath.

"Callan! That was a new shirt."

I chuckle. "I'll make it up to you, darlin'. Just let me have my fun."

She moans in response as my fingertips find her hard nipples, and I tease them. "Mmm, I missed you."

"I missed you too, love. So much."

The voice calls and FaceTime helped, despite that she practically tortured me as we had phone sex while I was away, and I got to hear her sexy voice orgasm for the first time ever. I came so hard I thought I would have a brain aneurysm, but fuck, it felt so good. I told her afterward that I wanted to hear her come in person, and she told me it was definitely happening when we saw each other the next time.

Now, here we are. Our first time finishing what we started...hopefully.

"No pressure, Eady. I'll stop if you need me to." I assure her even as I pull her hair back and claim her mouth with a deep kiss.

I gauge her reactions to me, feeling her body melt into mine. She's unbuttoning my jeans and freeing my erection as we fall to the bed. I instinctively move between her legs as my hands move to her back, freeing her from her bra. As my eyes fall over her big mounds, tipped with brown nipples, I smile and my head falls to suckle her. She bucks hungrily against me, and I pull her hips against mine, gripping her ass as I torture her nipple with my tongue, loving the sounds flying from her arched throat. I move my hand up to her neck, then my mouth follows, and I pull back as I look into her eyes. Just as I'm about to ask if everything is ok, she stills and I see the hesitation hit her eyes. She's afraid, and once again, I've done something wrong. I feel like a total fucking asshole as I roll off her and swear.

"Dammit, Eden, I'm sorry. I didn't think. I—"

"I-I don't wanna stop," she whispers, and I look back at her. She stands, I follow and move to stand next to her. I know she can't be on her back. It brings back the memories. I have to try something else. I see the mirror on her wall and smile, getting an idea.

"Come over here, baby." I have her stand in front of the mirror as I step up behind her and move my hands over her big breasts, giving them a squeeze. She moans and her head falls back onto my shoulder. "Look how gorgeous you are, baby doll. Watch my hands love this beautiful body. Fuck, you're so damn sexy, Eden." I breathe out as my mouth moves to her long, slender neck. I nip at her, feeling her skin break out in goosebumps as I pinch her nipples with my fingertips. "Mmm, does that feel good, baby?"

"Oh, Cal, yes."

"Be a good girl now and unbutton those jeans for me. Let me love the rest of you."

Eden hesitates for a moment and I see her eyes flicker to mine in the mirror. But she finally does as I request and moves her hands to unbutton her jeans. She slides the zipper down slowly, and I growl in her ear. I lick a trail down her neck to her shoulder.

"Pull them off your hips, darlin'. I wanna see your sexy little panties."

"And what if I'm not wearing any, big guy?" The sassy little minx that answers me makes me grin. I love that Eden is gaining this confidence. It's becoming and turns me on like nobody's business.

"Mmm, even better, angel. Let's see, shall we?" My hands move down her sides, and I slide them into her jeans, shoving them down to the floor. I feel my dick twitch against her bare ass and moan again. "Fuck, yeah, that's what I'm talking about. Look at you, you're a fuckin' sex goddess. I can't wait to explore every inch of this beautiful skin." I move my hands over Eden's hips and let one palm cup her peach-fuzz covered sex, my middle finger sliding in between her soaking wet folds as she parts her legs, while the other returns to torture a breast.

"Mmm," she murmurs and her head falls to my shoulder again. "Callan."

The sound of her pleasure makes me so damn hard I could explode, but I only arch my hips against her, craving the feel of that plump ass against my erection. "Spread your legs wider, baby. Let me in." I murmur as my mouth moves over her shoulder blade, and I nip it with my teeth. She does as I ask, such a good girl, as I explore her slick folds, her arousal propelling me onward. "Fuck, Eden, you're so wet baby. I love it." I arch my hard cock into her bottom once more, loving the feel of her naked flesh against mine, my sex aching to be buried deep within her.

Eden whimpers again as my middle finger slides inside her. God, she's so wet and tight. I swear I'm coming on her firm ass any second now. "Fuck me, your tight as fuck and beautiful, so beautiful," I say as her face crumbles in pleasure, accelerating my desire as I bend her slightly forward, her hands bracing on either side of the mirror, and pump my finger into her harder and faster. My other hand falls to the delta of her thighs, and I circle her clit with my fingertips, watching her tits bounce as I pump my cock against her tight ass. "Yeah, sweet angel, come for me now. I wanna see your face as I rock your fucking world." I chuckle in equal parts pleasure and agony.

Suddenly, she's crying out in orgasm, and her body is quaking against mine as I propel her into sweet oblivion, biting into her shoulder as I love her body's reaction to my stroking. "Mmm, yeah gorgeous. Get yours, baby." I continue to move my finger inside her, kissing her from one shoulder to her other and gripping her breast. I tweak her nipple and bite back into her throat, practically making out with it as the heel of my hand grinds against her clit. She's whimpering and reaching and just as my teeth bite again, she comes again. I hold back every restraint inside me not to thrust my cock into her and take her right here and now. But fuck, I can't. She isn't ready.

I whimper, myself, and watch as her eyes change in the mirror before she removes my finger, turning swiftly. Eden kisses me hard, and I press her to the mirror, ravishing her mouth and body in a way that leaves her panting. But before I can move, she does. She's kneeling before me and gripping my cock in her hand and bringing it to her lips. "Oh, Eady, yeah baby. Ah, yeah, right...fuck...yeah, just l-like that. God, that mmm...mouth. That mouth is so d-damn hot...ooohh." I'm a stammering fool as her deliciously warm mouth loves my shaft in such a way that I can't even fucking speak. God, she's got me all wrapped up in her. She looks up at me and grins, mouth full of cock, and I can't help the chuckle at my throat even as I whimper again.

"Watch your face, Cal. See how you crumble as I devour your huge cock. Mmmm, I wanna swallow your cum, baby."

Whoa! Who the fuck is this, and where's my girlfriend? But if this isn't the hottest damn thing I've ever experienced. Her words thrill me as much as her hungry mouth and gripping fist, and I tighten my grasp on her thick, dark hair as I watch her practically inhale my dick like she's done it a million times before. I'm literally putty as I look up in the mirror and see her going wild on me. God, it's one of the sexiest sights I've ever bore witness to. I rock my hips into her and feel my thighs tingle before I cry out and thrust hard into the mouth that's adoring my cock. I feel my seed burst into her throat and watch her eyes darken as my head falls in exquisite bliss. She continues to suck and squeeze, milking every last ounce from me as I groan and my pumping into her mouth finally ceases.

"Holy fuck, Eady. That was damn incredible," I say as I pull her to her feet and hug her to my weak frame.

She giggles, and I kiss her shoulder again. I pull back after I gain my breath and look into her eyes. "Was that ok?" I ask.

"More than ok," she answers with a blush, and I kiss her nose. "Maybe...maybe next time, we can..."

"I'm sorry I got a little carried away in the beginning, I—"

She stops my words with her finger and a shake of her head. "No sorries. I... I think I might be ready, Cal."

My brows raise and the surprise on my face can't be hidden. I mean, I want to. *Believe* me, but I just want her to be comfortable above all else. Her happiness is my one priority.

I'M ON THE SET OF A LOCAL SHOOT THE NEXT DAY WHEN I GET A call from my buddy Ethan Freeman.

"Whazzup, my entrepreneurial friend?" I ask and laugh when he snorts.

"You sound like you're in a good mood."

"Hell yeah I am, I got a fine ass woman who can't get enough of me... You know how it is." I smirk.

I think back to Eden last night and how she made me cum so hard I thought I was gonna explode from the intensity. She's everything. Her body, her intelligence, her overwhelming appeal... Man, I can't wait until I'm buried inside her. It's gonna be mind-blowing.

"Well, if you can get your head out of the clouds for five minutes..."

I'm the one snorting this time; not like he can talk. He's obsessed with his fiancée, Addison. And I understand, she's beautiful too.

"The girls are having their girls' night tonight, and I was wondering if you wanted to hang out."

Well damn, so I guess that means Eady's out for dinner tonight. Does it make me a pussy that I'm uber disappointed?

Fine, I guess I can make room for my old friend.

"Sure. What'd ya have in mind?"

"A big fat juicy burger from The Vortex. And I got tickets to the UFC fight at Philips Arena, front row."

"Hell yeah, count me in," I say as my photographer motions for me to unzip my jeans and get off the phone.

"Cool."

"Alright, I gotta go. Got sexy pics to take and all. Pick you up at six?"

"Sounds good. See ya then, *stud muffin*." Eth cackles as he hangs up.

Fucking dick, I think as I set my phone aside and turn to the camera, flexing my bicep.

Asshole's just jealous that I got a billion and a half women who've masturbated thinking of me.

Then I think about the one and *only* woman I want to masturbate while thinking of me and grin.

EDEN

I GIGGLE AS I OPEN THE DOOR, KNOWING IT'S CALLAN BEFORE I answer it. I'm not prepared for the intense hotness assaulting me as my man stands there in a ball cap, tight jeans, and red polo shirt holding an adorable, fluffy, little tan, black, and white Bernese Mountain Dog puppy.

"Happy birth—Oh. My. God. Cal." I pout as I look at the sweet baby in his big, inked arms. I don't know which one is melting my heart more right now. I pet the sweet little puppy who whines at me and look up to see my handsome bearded model grinning like a possum down at me. "You got me a puppy? What in the world am I supposed to do with a *puppy?*"

"Love him and pet him...and let him stick around. You know? Kinda like a boyfriend." He winks and leans in to kiss me. I pucker my lips and smooch him back, feeling a muscled bicep come around my waist to draw me closer.

When I pull back slightly to stroke the whimpering pup, I shake my head. "I dunno. I'm not home often enough and…"

"Oh, c'mon, Eady. He's just too damn cute, and he was out on the street. Well, he was gonna be. My friend's allergic and can't keep him. He needs a home and look, he likes you."

The puppy licks at the exposed cleavage my V-neck is showcasing, getting a mischievous chuckle from my boyfriend. "Easy, boy, now *those* are mine. Daddy don't like to share." Callan looks up at me, and I've forgotten every thought in my head.

"I guess we'll need to go get him some stuff before we head to Lia's, huh?" I ask with a frown, knowing that we don't have time.

He smirks. "Well, he comes with a crate and a litter box and all that stuff."

"Litter box?" I laugh. "Dogs don't use litter boxes."

"Well, everything but the litter box then." He winks again. He's not as oblivious as he wants everyone to think he is. He's intuitive and listens well for a man, plus he reads a great deal, which makes him smart as hell in my eyes. He may use his physical appeal to earn his money, but he has an intelligent mind and knows how to use it.

I step aside and let Callan through to sit the puppy down on my Persian rug, letting him adjust to his surroundings. He wags his tail and walks around, sniffing and exploring and I grin.

"He's *our* puppy, we'll own him together." Cal wraps a big arm around my waist and pulls me into his side. "One big happy family."

I laugh again and elbow him. "When he poops on my floor, you're cleaning it up, *Daddy*." I arch my brow.

"I like when you call me that. Say it again. I mean it *is* my birthday and all." He practically growls in my ear as he pulls me into his broad chest, and I swoon as his mouth falls to my neck. I moan and feel his cock growing at the apex of my thighs. I say, "Daddy," once again—only much more seductive this time—and a deep rumble fills his chest. I smile even as his lips take mine, and I feel his hands lower to my hips. "Dammit, Eden, you're good at torturing me, you know that?" he says breathily as he pulls back to look in my face.

For a moment, I forget everything and drink him in. I don't deserve him. He's too good for a stripper like me. I gulp. He senses my hesitations and strokes my damaged soul with a kiss to my forehead. He's been so good with my secrets, but I have more to tell him, so much more, and I'm afraid he may run for the hills once he knows the entire story—Hell, I would if I were him. He's been patient, sensitive to my insecurities, slow with his advances. He's been perfect, and I tear up, realizing how wonderful he is.

"I'm eager to hang with your peeps today," he says with a grin. He should be, I've talked about them relentlessly, eager for him to spend time with them. I smile. "Think they'll mind if we bring Cujo along?"

I laugh. "Cujo? We are *not* naming this sweet baby Cujo!" I look down at the precious pup who has now stopped in front of us, wagging his little tail and barking.

"Beethoven?"

"He isn't even a St. Bernard, Cal." I playfully swat my boyfriend's bulging bicep.

"Fine, let's name him after one of my favorite fictional characters."

I wait, laughing when he has this silly smirk on his face, loving the anticipation. God, I love this man. I just need to tell him so. I will...eventually. "And that would be?" I say, the wait becoming too exciting and I laugh.

"Maximus!" At that, the puppy barks and Callan and I both laugh. "And there ya have it."

Cal pulls me in for another smoldering kiss, and I wish we had more time to spare before we're off to the party at Lia and Landry's in celebration of Cal's birthday weekend.

We celebrated him—just us—last night with dinner and wine on the balcony and he opened the gifts I'd gotten him before he got whisked away this morning to an early sunrise photo shoot downtown.

I pull back regretfully, remembering our night of fun, and step over the puppy as I move into my kitchen to grab the potato salad I made for the barbecue.

I open the fridge and retrieve the bowl, making sure to jut my ass out at him.

"Well, look at you, all domesticated and shit. That's hot, E." He gives me a sexy grin as he props himself in the door frame with Maximus in tow, and I swear it's all I can do not to drop the bowl and rush him, potato salad and party be damned.

Cal's one of the "sexiest men alive" according to *Red Carpet Raves* magazine. He's muscular, bearded, tattooed, on more book covers than I can count...and he's mine. I can't believe it. Damn, I'm a lucky woman. I smile back and ignore the yearning in my center as I move up to kiss him once again.

"Let's go, or we'll be late." I look at my Apple watch and frown.

"Yes, ma'am. Don't want our little Ms. Punctual to be tardy, do we?"

I roll my eyes at him and grab my purse from the couch as he grabs up Maximus. He knows I thrive on routine and organization. It's my two hang-ups—alright, two of my *dozens* of hang-ups.

Once I'm seated in Cal's truck, I take Maximus in my arms as Cal places the bowl of potato salad on the back floorboard, ensuring it won't slide around. I stroke the sweet pup's head as he settles into my lap and closes his eyes. Maybe having a dog will be good for me.

Cal cranks the truck and glances over at me as he heads down the road, looking like the happiest man in the world. His hand comes over and settles on mine, and he chuckles softly. "We did good, baby. He's beautiful."

I laugh back and look down at Maximus. He *is* beautiful, and I'm eager to have a companion for when Cal is traveling. He'll be on the road soon, and I dread being home alone. My demons flood me when I'm alone, which is why I read a lot.

Cal must sense my seriousness, for he looks over and a solemnity darkens his handsome face. "Eden, when are you gonna tell me about Marco?"

Are you fucking kidding me? I wanna ask. *Horrible timing, Cal!* In the car ride on the way to Lia and Landry's is not where I wanna do this, but I know I've kept him in the dark for far too long. I owe it to him to give him answers.

I sigh heavily as I begin, letting the stroking of Maximus's fluffy little head comfort me as Cal's fingertips stroke my arm. I close my eyes and go back in time.

"Marco was one of my uncle's henchmen, my bodyguard. He was thirteen years older than me, and the only person who treated me kindly amid all the darkness. By seventeen, I was head over heels for him, and it didn't take long for me to realize that the feeling was mutual. Our relationship was completely platonic for two years, but as the debauchery surrounding us got worse, we needed each other for comfort...among other things. He'd seen me at my worst, been there for me when no one else was. We finally..."

I pause here, breathing deeply as I remember the good and bad of my first love. "We *consummated* our feelings for one another on a stormy night, despite the danger, despite the consequences." I'm crying. Dammit, I knew this was gonna happen, but I can't stop the flow of tears as I relive the night Vince finally found out about us. The gun to Marco's head then my own. The fear in my heart that my uncle was gonna destroy the only hope I had in a world of pure hell. I tell Callan all this. "Deep down, I always knew Vince would catch us eventually, and a part of me didn't care because I was so in love with Marco that it didn't matter what Vince did to me. Hell, he'd already raped, assaulted, and tortured me for years, what was one more beating? Or death even... I knew death would've been better than the life I had, but his cruelty was far worse than I'd ever imagined it could be that night."

"That was the night h-he branded you?" Cal asks, barely above a whisper.

I nod in reply. Among many other vile things...right in front of Marco, badgering and spitting on him as Vince violently defiled my body in every way imaginable—all the while my head splitting from the blow he'd given me with the butt of the gun, my ribs, torso, and sex aching in pain from the damage done at his hands.

Over the years, I've tried so hard to forget all the horrible things he did and said to both Marco and I as he made Marco watch every second of the awful torment, threatening to staple his eyelids to his forehead if he dared close them.

But I'll never forget the tears streaming Marco's face, how

many times he apologized to me, begged Vince to stop hurting me, pleaded with him to kill us both and finally put an end to the agony, once and for all. At that point, I was begging too, praying for death's sweet relief, my entire body and soul pained and shamed beyond words: bruised, broken, cut, and bleeding from every orifice it seemed. I can't repeat the things my uncle did that night, for no person should have to hear those vile words and phrases Vince said. Just like his other playthings, I was just another puppet in his crazed game. I was his toy, his caged little bird, the replacement for the woman he'd always wanted but could never have—my mother, Lydia. I became his obsession, the ultimate possession he could manipulate, bend, and break to his will—and he did so with great success.

"The next morning, I was so bruised I had to cover every inch of skin in order to go to class, even my face. I caked makeup on myself and donned a hoodie to cover the damage he'd done, but that was finally the straw that broke the camel's back for Marco. He couldn't do it anymore and decided, finally, that Vince had to die."

"He would've been a dead man the minute he touched you, if I'd been him." I see Cal's fists grip the steering wheel in anger as he growls.

"There were things I didn't know, people who were worse than Vince. Marco wanted to—"

"But he didn't! He let that shit continue on for years. Fuckin' coward…" He growls again. "This is making me physically sick, Eden." I understand what he's saying, but he doesn't know the half of it. Marco's physical strength was no match for what we were up against.

"I'm sorry," I whisper. I know. It makes me sick, too. *But you need to hear it.*

"What did he do?" Cal asks after a long moment of silence.

"Marco shot Vince in the head at point blank range right in front of me. One minute I was sitting on Vince's lap in his office, the next I was pulled off him and his head was exploding." I gulp at the memory. Despite how satisfied I'd been to see the evil destroyed, it was revolting, and I remember puking all over the desk.

"Jesus, Marco. That was—"

"Not what I'd planned, I know, but time isn't on our side, my little dove." He pulls me to his chest and cradles my head. "I love you, Eden. Do you have any idea how much?"

I begin to cry because I know this is the end for us. He cups my cheek and brings my head up to look into his sky-blue eyes. I see pain, defeat, but also victory there. He kisses me. It's a soft, sweet, sensual kiss. A goodbye kiss. I know I'll never get another one. This is it! This is the last time. I don't want it to end as he pulls back and tears flood my eyes as I see Marco crying.

"I've loved you since the moment I saw you, Eden Riser." I love that he calls me by my real name, not Cordelia Perelli like Vince has for years now; God it feels so good to hear it after all this time. "One day, I pray you'll forgive me, forget him, and finally be able to move on. You must be strong now, my little phoenix. You be strong and you fly away from these ashes. You hear me? You live your life like it was meant to be lived and love again. Promise me?" His voice cracking makes me sob. God, I don't want him to leave me, even though I know he must. The bad men he spoke of will come for him after what he just did. As he said, time isn't on our side.

Just as I think this, the door bursts open, and Rocco comes in guns blazing, looking from us to the mess now sitting in Vince's chair. He gags. "What the fuck—?" he doesn't get to finish as Marco shoots him in the head, too, and my stomach lurches even as I gasp.

"Eden, here. You light the first match. You've earned it, baby."

I swallow hard as Marco places a box of matches in my hand and moves swiftly around the room dosing the contents of a container on everything. When he's done, he comes back to my side.

"The rest of the club is soaked too and ready for you to set fire to the other three corner closets. Go in order, from this room in a circle, from the north closet to the south then go out the exit door to the parking lot. You'll have time to get out and call for help before the alarm sounds. Then you'll finally be free." He grins even through his tears.

"But what about Cordelia?" I ask.

"Taken care of. After tonight, you're Eden Riser again, and Cordelia Perelli is as dead as her captor."

I smile. "Thank you, Marco. For setting me free, for loving me, for getting me out of this Hell."

"Anything for you, my love. My sweet Eden."

"Come with me, Marco?" I beg one last time, even though I know he can't. He's a dead man, no matter where he goes or where he tries to run because they will find him... If he lives, then I'll be in danger. He knows this and shakes his head.

"You know I would if I could. With everything in me." He pulls me to him again and kisses me one last time. "Now, send the Devil's Playground to Hell where it belongs and get the fuck out of here."

With that, I pull a match from the box, mesmerized by the red and orange flame I've just brought to life with one strike. I stare into Marco's eyes as I toss it at the kerosene-soaked curtain.

"I love you, my dark knight." I smile, and without a second thought, I move swiftly out the door.

Even when I hear the last gunshot sound, I don't look back. I move to the north closet, and do as Marco told me to, praying for God to let my lover into the pearly gates as I destroy the cage that held me. I'm free, and tonight, I fly.

. . .

Cal gulps as I finally look back up at him. He's shaken by what I've just told him, and how could he not be? After several moments of silence, he speaks. "Jesus, Eden. That's so fucked up. I'm sorry."

"I'm sorry, too."

"For what, baby?"

"My past is...well it's freaking catastrophic." I blurt out on a sob and lean down, resting my head onto the snoozing pup in my lap. As much as I've tried to move on, it's been so hard. When I'm not reliving this nightmare, I'm reliving the time before it, my life before Uncle Vincent's corruption a distant memory. One I wish I could remember more vividly than the horror. I sob for a time before I can speak again and when I do, it's yet another confession that only one of my sisters knows. "Marco was also the father of the baby Uncle Vince forced me to abort. Well, if I had money to bet on, I would say it was his. I don't actually know for a fact which one of them..."

The anger on Callan's face has turned to pure revolt as he pales and places a clenched fist at his mouth. His eyes close, and he looks like he might be sick. Hell, I think I might be sick by his reaction to what I've just told him. He turns his head and takes a deep breath in, then bows his head and cups his hands over his face. He leans over the steering wheel as I realize we're stopped and parked at Lia and Landry's house now.

"I don't know that I can take any more, Eady." His voice is muffled through his palms. He moves them down as he turns to me and extends his hand, interlacing it with mine. "Baby, to know you've lived through all that madness and come out in one piece... Dear God, you're so strong. So very strong."

But I'm *not* in one piece, I split apart into two separate entities to deal with the tragedy of my past. I continued my life as a masked stripper. How can I tell him the rest? He might leave me now that I've told him about Marco and Vince. Does he want to run in the opposite direction as far as he can?

I crumble again as I attempt to look for an answer in his eyes. My tears and quaking are violent as my emotions erupt within me. I see Cal frown; he looks angry, which makes it worse. He's gonna walk away. I know it. Why would he wanna stay in the afterbirth of the bomb I just threw at him?

I gasp as a pounding comes to the truck window, and we both jump as if we've been shot.

"What the fuck, Eden? Did this asshole make you cry? Get out of the vehicle, motherfucker. I'll beat your ass!"

If I wasn't so distraught, I might actually burst into laughter at Addison's reaction to my tears, but I'm taken off guard for a moment; so is Callan as he looks from Addy's angry face back to me.

"I said to get the hell out of the truck. Are you deaf?" Addy continues.

I laugh this time and hold my hand out to her and shake my head. "Bad timing, Addy," I state and give her the cut it out gesture. I see her eyes narrow, and she purses her lips at Cal before turning on her heel and walking off.

"Well, that was a great second impression!" he says with a frown, and I laugh again.

"I'll tell her later, don't worry."

"Don't *worry*? I'm the bad guy."

"No one could *ever* beat Vincent Perelli when it comes to being the 'bad guy,' so again, don't worry."

"Good, that makes me feel better," he grumbles before giving me a serious expression and taking my hand once more. "You're amazing, in case I haven't told you recently, Ms. Riser."

"So, does this mean you're not leaving me?"

"Why would I leave you? Simply because you told me about your past?" Cal looks shocked that I would ask him this question. I shrug and he says, "Like I told you, E, I'm not going anywhere, and I meant that. In fact, I admire the hell out of your bravery, sweetheart." He kisses my knuckles and gets a smile from me.

I begin to wipe my tears. I pull the sun visor down and check my makeup, grateful for waterproof eyeliner and mascara. I reapply my lipstick and cradle Maximus as I step out of the truck.

Cal has the bowl and locks the truck door, taking my elbow and giving me a kiss on the head before we walk to the door and knock. I grin and lean up to kiss his lips just as the door opens and Landry's laugh greets our ears. "*There* you are! I was afraid Addison was gonna bring us all out to tear your door off the hinges."

Cal blushes twelve shades of red before he finally smiles back, and I roll my eyes. "She never was one for patience, or good timing." I pull Landry in for a hug, and he looks down at the puppy in my arms and pats Maximus's head.

"Well, you know why she's called Ember," Ethan states with a wink, knowing he was the one to coin her club name, as he's next in line for a hug.

I give him a wary look and his eyes widen for a split second in realization before he glances back to Cal, trying to blow it off. "Happy birthday, buddy, how are ya?" I pray Cal doesn't connect the dots because I don't know if he *can* handle any more of my secrets today.

"Eth, long time no see, man." Cal laughs and pats his old high school buddy on the back.

I squeal when I see Aliana and Rory running toward me and sit Maximus down as I scoop them up. "Come to Aunt Eady, baby girls." I give the little dolls smooches before placing one on each hip and leaning forward to kiss Lia's.

"Sweet Lia, I've missed you."

"Missed you too, sis," Lia says and hugs me back, grabbing Aliana who squeals in glee at Maximus. Lia looks down at the puppy now sniffing her rug. "Did you bring a dog?"

"Yes, he's our new pet. Cal brought him to me today. Isn't he cute?"

"Puppy," Rory points and shimmies down my hip, reaching for the pup.

"Cal's adorable. The dog, yeah, not so much, he's chewing my rug." Lia grins from my boyfriend to the pup and extends her hand to Callan as Landry steps up behind her, taking the bowl and gift from Callan.

"Lia, you remember Callan Manning? Callan, Lia and Landry Laurent." I smile as they all greet one another before Cal grabs Maximus's chewing mouth off the rug.

"Hope y'all don't mind. Wow, that is one gorgeous head of hair you got there, kiddo," Callan states, motioning to Aurora's red locks. I grab her back up as she glances bashfully back at Cal and tucks her head into my breast. I kiss her cheek.

"Nah, we got a fenced-in backyard. It's cool." Landry motions to the backyard, and Cal follows, pup in tow. "Want a beer?"

I watch them walk off and round on Addy, who comes around the corner then, arms crossed. "What the hell, *Ember*?"

"Jeez, I'm sorry. I didn't know I was interrupting story time." She rolls her eyes.

I shrug. "It's fine." I give her a laugh. "It's good to know my sisters are as protective of me as I am of them." I smile into Rory's sweet face and kiss her plump little cheek again, getting giggles from her. Aliana runs up, wanting her turn before I set them both down. I open my arms to Addy, who hugs me reluctantly before I get a laugh out of her.

"Of course we're protective," I hear Everleigh's thick accent coming in from the kitchen as she waddles towards me. "No one messes with our girl and gets away with it."

I smile and move to embrace my very pregnant friend. It's good to have all my family in the same room again. It's almost like Vince never was. Almost.

CALLAN

DID I HEAR ETHAN SAY "EMBER" AND WHY DOES THAT WORD— no, *name*—sound familiar to me? It's like I can't place it, can't connect a piece somewhere, and it's not because of the beers I've had; I've had four to be exact. No, there's something here I can't quite put my finger on and my senses tingle as I feel a strange sort of deja vu.

These four women are sisters in every sense that counts. It was clear within the first few minutes of seeing them hugging, laughing, and interacting that they all share a common bond together. Eden mentioned she got close to Lia and Ev while attending dance classes and Addy was her dorm-mate in college, and I'm glad my sweet Eden has them to love and protect her.

God, when she told me about Marco and Vince and the baby that was taken from her, I was sure I was gonna lose my breakfast. The vast amount of tribulations this lady has been through blows me away. You'd never know from the outside that she's housing so much pain, regret, torment; she has such a sordid past. The reserved librarian is a complete mask. And I can understand now why she would seek a career like that. There's so many layers to her, and I want to peel back each one until she's completely exposed before me, naked and raw. I want to peel those layers back and soothe them, one by one.

Even still, as much as I desire her body, I want her trust, her love, her complete submission even more. She's slowly but surely giving it to me with each confession, each moment we spend together, and I'm reciprocating, but I still feel she's holding something back. I don't know exactly what it is, but after the bomb she dropped on me in the truck, surely this last thing can't be worse. Can it?

I pull Eden to me as I approach and nod over at Eth as he does the same to his girl, Addy. They seem super happy together, all these couples do. Lia and Landry are nice and Everleigh and Luca too; they banter like they're best friends as much as husband and wife, and I can't help but hope that Eden and I will be like that too one day. Wow! The future. This woman has me thinking about the future, and as I look down into her big brown eyes, I can almost see it. Her, a couple kids, Maximus, a big house, a picket fence. Settled down. It's perfect. BBQs and birthday parties, daddy-daughter dances, and trips to Disney World. It's heavenly, and I want it all. I want it all with her, my sweet Eady.

I grin and lean down to kiss her plump lips, wrapping my arms around her and squeezing her into my frame. She feels so good here, so right.

"Hey, the bedroom's back there if you need to use it, man," Luca jokes as I come up for a breath, and I can't help but chuckle. I guess it is a bit off-putting having the new guy making out with his girl in front of everyone. I blush and shrug.

"Ah, don't let him fool you," Everleigh states with a playful shove at her hubby. "That's exactly how this—twin boys, mind you—happened." She points to her pregnant belly and everyone laughs including the toddler, Aliana. She's adorable with her light brown hair and fat cheeks, and when four-year-old Rory takes those cheeks and kisses her square on the lips, I swear I want to go procreate with my girlfriend right this second. I'm gonna blame all my warm and fuzzy inner dialogue on those little stinkers if I start to voice aloud how I feel tonight.

We end up having burgers and dogs. Landry mans the grill and fishes out an occasional beer for the other guys as I watch Maximus run in the backyard and Ethan tells me about his newest business venture. Luca plays hide and seek with Rory, and all is right as rain.

That is, until I head back in to grab a platter for Landry to put the meat on and overhear the girls talking in the dining room nook. I'm out of sight behind the wall and freeze as I hear what they are discussing.

"Are you dancing with me tomorrow night, Lia?" Eden asks.

"Yes, it's finally date night, and Landry can't *wait*. Aliana has been cock-blocking him all week. We can't wait to head to Siren's Grotto and finish what we started on Monday." Lia giggles.

What the fuck did she just say?

"I hear Roxie's garden has been vacant as of late," Everleigh says with a smirk.

"Oh, shut up, Ev. She's simply letting Eden have some fun...for a change," Eden giggles.

"It's about damn time, control freak," Addy says. "I was afraid you were gonna grow cobwebs down there."

I inhale sharply as the door opens behind me, and I turn to see Landry's smiling face.

"You get lost, Cal?" he laughs.

"Uh, no, sorry, I—"

I'm a damn stammering fool right now. I don't know whether to be pissed the fuck off, turned the fuck on, or blown the hell away because right now I'm all three and a hell of a whole lot more.

"Platter's right here, dude," Landry scoffs and grabs the large tray sitting directly in front of me. He pats me on the back. "No more booze for you, lightweight. You've been cut off." He laughs again, shakes his head, and is out the back door before I can even respond. But dammit, right now I'm tripping all over myself.

I just came in on a super awkward conversation and now, I remember where I heard the name Ember. It's the same place where I heard the name Roxie. The same place where I spent months of my life pining over a woman I wasn't allowed to touch or fuck. The same place where I almost lost my mind thinking I was going crazy over that sadistic little vixen. The same place where I'm gonna head tomorrow night to confront the next confession in Eden's little Pandora's box full of the motherfuckers—Motherfucking *RISE*.

13

CALLAN

The next night I'm completely fuming as I walk into the dark nightclub, the one I haven't been to in over a month because I was trying to give up Roxie and embrace Eden. God, I'm such a damn fool. I've gone over it, over and over again. How did I miss the connection? How did I not see it? How did I not notice the similarities before now? How did I not see the proof that was right there in front of me, time and again?

I was able to get through the barbecue without showing how angry I was last night. And I'm not angry at Eden, I'm not. Well, ok, I *am*. But how could I not be a little angry? She completely duped me. I'm mostly mad at myself, though, for being so blind. I made a dumb excuse about being sick to my stomach after we got back to her place, put the new pup in his crate, and headed home to do some research on Eden Riser.

Turns out she's one of the club owners. Ding ding—first bell rang. I had to do a *lot* of digging but was able to find the record after paying a hefty amount to a PI.

There's no history on her prior to ten years ago; it's like she didn't exist. But there *was* mention of a Cordelia Perelli, and Eden *had* said she was Vince Perelli's one and only relative. So, I've put two and two together.

After getting barely three hours of sleep, I camped outside Eden's apartment around four PM, watched her go on a jog with our puppy, and then later followed her to the club. She parked in a reserved space and went in the back. Ding ding— second light bulb went off.

Then I swore up a storm and once more, I waited. I waited for her to get settled into her costume and comfortable before I waltzed in to confront "Roxie." I got a sweet little text from her about thirty minutes ago:

Eden: *Feel any better, baby? Want me to stop by later when I leave Ev's? I think I might have some medicine that will get you all better ;-)*

Callan: *No, I think it may be a bug :-S Stay far away! BTW, how's my boy?*

Eden: *:*-(I'm sorry... He's good. Finally stopped crying around 3 AM. I'm exhausted. :-/*

Callan: *You go home and rest, love :-* We'll talk later.*

I just got a dozen kissy face emojis and a GIF saying, "Feel better."

Oh, I'll feel better alright, once I've had it out with her for her deceit. There's a part of me that understands, but there's also a part of me that feels betrayed.

I inhale the familiar scent of booze, perfume, fog machine juice, and the lemon scent of cleaning spray. I immediately see her on stage, and my heart literally turns over in my chest. I wanna rip her off that pole and cover her half naked frame from all the eyes on her, but I can't. One, I'm mesmerized. Two, the show must go on.

I'm not here to piss her off or expose her. I simply want answers. And I want her to know that I now know about her dark secret—her dual personalities.

I move ever closer to the spotlighted stage where she's front and center. The way she moves over that pole it's as if she is one with it. Now, I know why she's in such great shape. She's practically an athlete.

When her dance ends, she dons a crown of diamonds. If she's not the hottest thing I've ever seen in my life... Her gold wig and matching black and gold mask, her ridiculous excuse for a teddy, and those sexy as sin platform heels. I wanna scoop her up and devour her.

She doesn't see me as she goes the opposite way off the stage and down the stairs, parading herself for her clients. I watch as a patron grabs her wrist just as I'm moving toward her. I see who it is and rage suddenly encompasses me, every other emotion gone in that instant.

Kevin Stanley is stroking his hand up Roxie's arm, and I'm within inches of grabbing it and breaking it. The thought of him being in her room and her doing the things with him that she's done with me make me murderous.

"Roxie, you up for a little extra fun tonight, sexy lady?" Kevin asks, his eyes on her voluptuous breasts, the ones that are barely covered by a piece of black lace.

"Ha," Roxie says with a smirk. "You can't afford me, Kevin."

He gives a hearty laugh and leans in. He's loud as fuck, no doubt from all the booze sitting on his table and his attempt to speak over the music blasting out of the speakers. "I'd take out a second mortgage just to have one night in your room of pain."

"I'll just bet you would," she smarts back and pulls at the hand around her forearm.

I see Bruno approaching from out of her line of sight and hold my hand up, motioning to him that I have the situation taken care of. He recognizes me, for how could he not the many times I've been here, and gives me a nod.

I move slowly to the opposite side of Roxie, ever closer, within inches of them.

"Keep your shit up, Stanley, and I will *ban* you from this club once and for all, do you hear me? I know exactly how you work, and *RISE* isn't the place for your antics."

Just as he's about to respond, he looks up to see my growling face. He balks and stands from his seated position. "Uh, Cal! Hey man, uh…"

"Get your hands off, Madam Roxie, right the fuck now." I huff out and take the final step, separating the distance between myself and them as I grab the wrist he's gripping Roxie's arm with. He loosens his grasp, and I literally growl. "You piece of shit! I knew there was something about you that rubbed me the wrong way. If you ever try to contact my sister or lay a hand on her or my nephew again, I'll end you, comprende?" My eyes burn into his as he steps back and gives me a simple nod. I turn my attention to Roxie, whose mouth is slightly ajar in surprise, and sigh. "Rox, I believe we have a prior engagement."

She closes her mouth, gulps softly and nods, turning on her heel in the direction of her room. I follow.

We're in the hallway and out of earshot when she says, "I thought you were *sick*."

Aha! Caught her! "Roxie" wouldn't know that tidbit of info.

"I am sick, Rox. I'm sick of these games we've been playing. Or do you prefer *Roxanne*?"

She turns again, and I stop walking. Her red-brown eyes are burning into mine despite the dimly light hallway. "I told you not to come back here or I'd have you thrown out, do you not remember that?" Her eyes narrow, and I can't help but give a humorless laugh.

"What's the matter, baby, you jealous...of *yourself?*"

We have a stare-off for a moment before I hear a throat clear behind me. It's Bruno, but he's not looking at me, he's looking at Roxie. For a moment, I think I'm gonna have to fight him in order to get her alone. Finally, she looks over at him and gives a slight nod. He turns and heads back to the end of the hallway.

"Why are you here, Callan?"

"Oh, we both know why I'm fucking here, Roxie. So let's just cut the bullshit and have a conversation about it."

Her eyes narrow again. *Ready or not, baby girl, your secret is out.* As if she's heard me, she grabs my shirt and turns on her heel once more, pulling that vanishing key from its mysterious location—I swear it's a magic key—to unlock her private room. Once we're through the door, she shoves me inside, slams it behind her, and plants her hands on her hips.

I watch her, evaluating her, and for a moment, I'm afraid I've made a huge mistake. What if I'm wrong? Jesus Christ, I *better* not be wrong!

"How many men have you brought to this room since me?" My first question comes out accusatory, and I hate how she flinches as I ask this. I know I really don't want the answer. The thoughts of another man touching what's mine makes me see red.

She raises her head defiantly. "That's none of your fucking business!"

"The hell you say." I growl as I take a step forward and watch as she recoils. Fuck! I'm a fucking asshole. I want to apologize for my brazenness, but I *have* to face Roxie if I'm to get to Eden. I have to show her my dominance, once and for all. "Tell me!" I shout, and she flinches and pulls her arms across her chest, protectively.

She gulps, and I'm afraid she's withdrawing and won't answer me. Finally, she says, "There's been no one since you, Callan. I swear it."

Oh, thank God! I can breathe easier now. I inhale and exhale, attempting to rein in my anger. She doesn't need that. She needs understanding. She needs empathy, which prompts my next question. "Why?" I practically whimper out. "Why, Rox, when you had a way out of all this, didn't you take it? Why go back into a world of sin and secrets?" I shake my head.

"How could you possibly understand the why of all this?" she grates and looks down. "It was what I knew, what I excelled at. My power. My way to stay hidden from a world that didn't understand me. Once the darkness has touched you, Cal, you're never really *free* of it. Plus, it was a way we could help girls like us. Keep them safe."

"*Safe*? By parading them around like peacocks, hooking them up with dirty, wealthy pigs, and having them shuck their clothes for money?"

"You don't understand... Besides, it pays the bills," she growls.

"Yeah, well an elite club owner doesn't *need* to strip for money, now does she? Not one with the fortune Perelli left you! You do it because you want to—you enjoy it."

"Yes! I do." Her chin raises again defiantly, and I can't help but grin at her fortitude. God, I love this woman. Her strength. Her vulnerability. Her sass. Her sweetness. Her softness. Her determination.

"Oh, Rox. You are a damn enigma, you know that?" I laugh.

I'm not mad. It bothers me to know she's showcasing her beautiful body as guys whack off under the tables to her naked form exposed before them. To say it doesn't would be an outright lie, but at the same time, I know it's a release for her—a way to have power in a world where she's been otherwise powerless.

"I don't need your fucking approval, Callan." And there, she's hurling that power at me now.

Time to show her.

"No. No you don't, do you, Rox? What *do* you need from me, baby girl?"

She's taken off guard as I move closer. I see panic in her eyes as she takes a step back.

"I think I know. I know exactly what you need, darlin'."

I see her gulp as the back of her thighs hit the bed. She's trapped and realizes it, but the fear isn't of me. Roxie doesn't fear me. She fears no one.

I move up and close the distance between us, cupping her cheek. I'm not tied down, I'm unleashed. I'm the only man she trusts to have free rein in here, and I'm going to savor every minute of this.

"How long did you honestly think you could keep this a secret from me, huh?" I see her gasp. My smile deepens. "It's time to take the mask off now. It's time for you to embrace my love for you. And I do, with everything in me, love you."

She gulps again, and I see her shiver. My hand moves to her hip and I trace the line of her high-cut lace lingerie.

"Let me make love to you, baby. The way a man was meant to love a woman. The way I'm meant to claim you. Submit to me, Madam Roxie."

I see a tear run down her cheek, and I swipe it away, bringing it to my lips. I lower my face to hers, kissing her. She moans aloud, and I feel her palms against my chest. At first, I'm afraid she's gonna push me away—like she always has—but she doesn't; she grips my shirt tightly.

I unleash the full force of my passion as I pull her against me and touch her—her hair, her face, her breasts, her waists, her legs. Soon, we are a tangle of limbs as I love her mouth with my own, and we're falling to the bed. I lay her down softly, letting her head fall to the pillows and position her beneath me, aligning our bodies as I cup her cheek.

"Cal," she whimpers, and I look into her eyes. I don't see hesitation there as I usually do. I see relief, I see freedom, I see trust...and I can't be happier at this moment. I grin. "I-I'm ready but—"

"But what, baby?" I finger her jawline, her cheekbones, her lips...and let her adjust to my weight on her. I kiss her softly, coaxing the last ounce of hesitation from her.

"I don't deserve you," she admonishes, and I smile.

"Oh, but you do. You're everything I've ever wanted." I take her lips again and thrust my tongue in, loving the responses coming from her throat as my hands move over her body. I moan as her fingers come to the button of my slacks, and I realize how hard I am, how much I want to be inside her, how much I've *always* wanted to be inside her. When her palm grips my rock-solid shaft, I groan. "Oh, my sexy angel."

She pumps my bare cock gently as I squeeze a breast in my palm and with the fingertips of my other hand, move the lace of her garment aside, splaying her thighs. I lower my head to her round breast and feast on her nipple, making her back arch off the bed as I slide a finger into her wet folds.

"Let's get you ready for me."

"Oh Cal," she cries.

I love her with my mouth and fingers, all the while arching my hips into her stroking fist, close to losing my mind—and my load—before I finally move lower down her body. I lick a trail across her belly and down to her thighs before tracing the scar marking her groin with my tongue. I breathe a sigh of relief as I kiss it and lick it and love it, love her darkness as much as I love the goodness that is my sweet Eden.

I begin to tongue her clit and thrust my finger into her silky heat and soon, she falls apart to me. I love the sounds of her pleasure as my own sex screams in unrequited release.

I'm peeling the fabric from her skin and shucking my clothes before she pulls me to her, running her hands over my shoulders and back. She kisses my lips with reckless abandon as I position her beneath me, opening her thighs to accommodate my big frame.

"I love you," I say, and she smiles.

"I love you, Callan."

She moans as I gently guide myself to her wet opening and rest the head of my cock there. My head falls to hers at the sensation of our sexes kissing for the first time before I begin to slowly press inside. It's so much sweeter and hotter and silkier than I ever could have imagined—the true garden of Eden—and I hold myself back from the orgasm that wants to burst forth. My legs shake as I look into her eyes and try so hard not to give into my bodily demands.

"Oh baby, you feel so damn amazing."

"Mmm, you do too." Her hips arch up into mine, and if I'm not coming right that second, I'm dying. Dammit, I may be a lot of things, but a selfish lover isn't one of them. I hold back and hold back as I sink further into the most exquisite place I've ever been.

That's when I do it. I move my hand up and pull the wig off, gently because I know she pins that shit on tight for her dances. Once that's done, I pull the mask up and over her head and look upon her gorgeous face. The eyes are still red-brown, but I know beneath those contacts, her eyes are a beautiful, chocolate brown.

"There you are." I grin, and she laughs even as a sob hits her throat.

"Oh, Callan."

"My beautiful Eden." I moan as I withdraw and plunge deeply once again. "My sweet, amazing Eden." I hear her gasp and see that she's taking my sex easily, not repulsed or afraid of my bulky body atop of her. Her hands grip my shoulders as I make love to her, arching my hips nice and slow so she can acclimate to the stretch of my member inside her. "God, I love you."

And just like that, she's orgasming around me.

I groan, a man in bittersweet agony and continue to thrust into her, pleasuring her.

For I've found my Heaven, within the garden of Eden. Eden, *my* Eden.

EDEN

TO SAY THAT I'M SHOCKED THAT I—THAT ROXIE—SUBMITTED and succumbed to the man I love is an understatement. How is it that I couldn't do this with Marco, yet Callan came in, guns blazing, demanding I yield to him...and I *did*? As if I never had an issue before. As if the pain of my horrific past is gone, and my soul is now unbroken. How did he do that?

I smile up at him as he strokes my face with such tenderness. He took me bare, he came inside me...and I didn't stop him. I didn't *want* to stop him. It never even entered my mind. I simply wanted his love in any form he chose to give it to me, and I accepted it—willingly. It's as if a huge weight has been lifted from me, despite that he's on top of me now, his big body covering mine, basking in the bliss of our sexual union, and yet I don't falter, or flinch, or recoil in fear. I'm in awe, shock. He's conquered my fears, he's conquered the sadistic dominatrix Madam Roxie; instead of griping about relinquishing my control, I'm honestly super relieved. Relieved that I don't have to battle my dark demons alone, that another shares my burden. A man I love and trust with all my heart now sees inside the dismal pit that has been my life for the last thirteen years and he's still here, smiling down on me like I've given him the key to Heaven.

"Are you ok?" he asks and tilts his head to evaluate me.

I nod and stifle a sob. "More than okay."

"Good. Me too." He pulls my hand from his chest and kisses the back of my knuckles. "Roxie didn't put up much of a fight." He smirks and dammit if I'm not swooning. He's so damn handsome...and cocky.

"Don't make me put that mask back on and grab my whip, Mr. Manning," I scold playfully.

He laughs heartily and whimpers in pleasure as I do the same. "Mmm, damn that felt good, baby." I can see in his eyes that he wants to make love again...and to be honest, so do I.

"It's hard to fight off a man as big as you, Cal." I arch a brow.

"Eden, you and Roxie have had me on my knees since the night I met you both, and you damn well know it."

It's true, Cal is a big teddy bear. All I'd have to say is the word, and he'd release me. But I'm comfortable in his arms. I love him. I feel protected by him and deserving of his love. The girl that was marked by sin has found a salve for her wounds; his name is Callan, and she can't get enough of him.

I lean up and kiss him, loving how he sighs in peace and arousal at my mouth on his. As much as I've surrendered to him tonight, he's surrendered to me too, I know with certainty.

Our bodies move again, desire stirring within us once more, and he relinquishes control as he moves me over the top of him. I love his hard, chiseled flesh with my hands then ride his rock-hard shaft growing harder and harder still inside me, relishing in every inch of him. This has never felt as good as it does now, so freeing, as if I'm flying and he's the wings keeping me in the air.

I love him with abandon, rocking my hips and focusing all my efforts on simply embracing this moment with him, hearing him groan and say my name like a mantra. His big palms cup my breasts, and he pulls my mouth to his even as I lose myself to him once more. Having him here, in my bed, inside me, is far better than any fantasy of him I've ever had. He's big, he's bold, he's *mine,* and I fuck him like I'll never have him again.

Soon, we're coming apart together and looking into one another's eyes. It's poetic, it's incredible. It's love. Wow. I never knew it truly existed or that I'd find it again, but here I am experiencing it in all its mind-blowing glory.

As our hips stop moving and I still atop this Adonis of a man, I smile happily down at him. He returns it, and I can feel my heart melting even as its rhythm accelerates.

"You're incredible," he says in awe.

"No, you are," I say. Then curiosity gets the best of me. "How'd you know?"

Cal never told me. I never asked.

He points to the tattoo on my neck, the one all of us girls have. I realize he probably felt it more than saw it, as it's a unique UV tattoo. "This was my first suspicion. Ethan said Ember yesterday, and I couldn't place it until I overheard you ladies talking at the table. But I think I knew before then."

"Oh?" I smirk as my hands move over his chest, tracing the tattoo across his pecs.

"Your mouth gave you away, your moans. The undeniable chemistry I had with Roxanne, Roxie, and Eden; I thought I was going nuts."

"And what would you have done if Roxie wasn't Eden?"

"Ménage à trois?" He shrugs, and I can't help but laugh. "I mean, you *are* a sadist, maybe you were willing to open your mind."

"Roxie doesn't share," I sass, and he gives an overexaggerated pout.

"I have a feeling Roxie is *all* out of her comfort zone right now."

"Surprisingly, not as much as you'd think." I begin to stroke his lower abdomen with my fingernails and get a hiss out of him as his head falls back on his shoulders.

"Mmm, well, I'm glad the mask is finally off." His grin is so genuine that I lean down and take his lips again.

"Me too, love, me too."

"Not to say Roxie might need to put it back on every now and again," he smirks.

I laugh. "Oh, I would expect it no other way."

Cal wraps me in his arms as he flips us over. "So tell me, *Roxanne*," he begins, "was your night at the masquerade last year as amazing as mine was?"

Ah, my Prince Charming. Looks like he found my glass slipper.

"How could you?" I ask Marco as I pace the floor, bile rises in my throat. After all the horrible things he and my uncle have done, one would think I would be immune to evil, numbed by the extent of

corruption. But this, this is unacceptable. *My heart hammers in my chest and my head throbs. My lungs burn and my eyes are pouring tears like a fountain.* "I... I can't even. Get out. I don't want to see you right now. I'm disgusted with you. You both make me fucking sick."

"Shh, my little dove, please try to—"

"Understand? *How the fuck can I understand what you've done, Marco? She was a goddamned librarian. What would she have done? You're a piece of shit!*" I scream and shove at his chest as my anger takes over me. *How could the man I adore do this to me? How could he!*

"You don't understand."

"No, you know what? I don't, and I never fucking will understand the shit you do for that bastard. He tells you to fucking jump and you say how high."

"Don't, Eden. Don't go there." *Oh, he's angry now, fucking good. Let's hash this shit out right now.* "You can't fight him any more than I can!" *His voice raises, and I thrive on the adrenaline I'm feeling right now. I can't fight Vince, but dammit, I can fight Marco, and right now I wanna taste his blood like nothing else I've ever wanted.*

"You can! Dammit! You weigh a hundred pounds more than he does!" I shout at the top of my lungs, years of pent-up emotions have led me to this moment.

"I can't! You don't know what you're saying!"

"You didn't have to murder her. She was a good person." I break into tears, the loss of my sweet Mrs. Stewart bitter in my mouth.

"It was quick and painless, baby, I swear." *He pulls me into his arms even as I fight him, clawing and screaming, but I'm no match I quickly realize as he pins me to my bedroom wall, the fight in me unable to expel itself from within.*

Finally, I cave and let him tuck me into that spot that was made just for me, beneath his collarbone, against his bulking pec, tightly in the arms that appear taut enough to explode. I sob and sob and sob. The innocent lives that have been lost to Vincent Perelli seem never ending. I think of my sweet girls and how I second-handedly betrayed them. God knows I didn't want to, but I didn't have a choice in that either, any more than I'd had in the baby Uncle Vince had torn from my womb before it even had a chance at life. Although, in hindsight, I'm glad a child didn't have to come into this world only to suffer the sins of his family, of his father or his mother, of his sick as fuck great-uncle.

I pull back, thinking of Marco's baby he unintentionally planted inside me. We'd been careful, but in the end, it had been completely unexpected. Vince looked at me strangely when I'd told him. His black eyes had somehow gotten darker. Deep down, I knew that he knew I was deceiving him somehow, even as I prayed to the God who never seemed to hear me that He continue to keep my love for Marco a secret; Vince would kill us both if he found out. Vince hadn't reacted quite as I'd expected—his response had been far too calm— although in the end, I hadn't been surprised he wanted "it" gone.

"That's alright, my sweetling. I'll take care of it. No need to disrupt our lives with an unwanted burden." *The disgust in his tone felt like acid on my skin. I realized then that he was suspicious about whether the baby was his or not. After all, he'd been taking me bare almost daily for years and not gotten me knocked up. It had only taken Marco mere months.*

I couldn't prove it was Marco's child. But in my heart, I believed it was.

I didn't fight Vince on the decision. If I'd protested, it might have made me look guilty. I hadn't even needed to tell Marco, for he was the one who'd driven me to the clinic two days later even as tears fell silently down my face, and my soul hurt with what was coming.

"I-I'll go with you, my little dove. If you want me to." He'd cleared his throat, a shadow of the strong, formidable giant he was. He'd taken my hand, but I'd jerked mine away and thrown open the door. I'd hated him that day. Truly hated him...almost as much as I hated Vince.

I didn't speak to him for over a month after. I went through severe depression and contemplated killing myself; just as I attempted to do so, Addy stopped me. A part of me wishes she'd never heard me come in, never heard the bottle opening; if she hadn't, I'd be free of this horrible darkness I'm fully encapsulated in.

When I finally spoke to Marco again, we fucked first, hard and violently. Clashing like waves hitting a cliff, angry and with a force we never had before. But we didn't speak of the baby again or the abortion.

Now, I'm seething as I look up into his face with angry eyes, pulling back in his arms so I can see his face. "Get out, Marco," I say calmly.

"I'm not fucking leaving, Eden. And guess what, you can't fucking make me either."

The fierceness in his blue eyes makes me shout. He's too big to fight, but even without physical power I can use my words to chop him off at the knees. Fuck him!

"Why don't you go suck his dick even harder than you already do? You both might enjoy it." I spit in his face, my fury the only thing keeping me grounded to this earth.

He grunts, surprised at the venom, but grins. The motherfucker is impressed by my boldness. "Go ahead, get it out of your system. Tear me to shreds, little Roxie. Tear that mask off and let the red out, baby. Hit me where it hurts." He laughs maniacally, and if his arms weren't holding me up, I would fall. I scowl back into the face I love more than anything else in the world, but I'm a sobbing mess again.

"You let him kill our baby, Marco. You've let him destroy us both. You've blackened your soul for a man who may just be Satan himself. And for what? Because you fear him? Why? What hold does he have over you so that you can't break it? You're gonna let him kill me, aren't you? Too fucking late. I'm already dead. You just threw the last spike into my heart. You. Not him." Marco shakes his head, but I continue. "Yes. You're no better than he is. You're just as monstrous."

He gives me a wary look. If it's a warning, I don't heed it. I just plunge the knife further into his chest as my eyes narrow.

"Eden, baby, you're angry. You don't mean that."

"I do. I feel nothing *for you anymore. You're not a real man. A real man wouldn't have allowed it to go this far. Now let me go, and get out of my room so I can grieve for the caring lady you took from me in peace."*

Marco regards me for a long time, quietly. I don't know if he doesn't speak because he doesn't have anything to say or if he just doesn't have the energy to fight with me anymore. His next words will haunt me for years to come.

"Eden, as much as you see the monster, you have no idea what I've spared you from. As bad as things have been for you, they could be worse."

I scoff, what the fuck is he even saying?

"Go ahead, I don't expect you to know or understand. You've only dealt with him for four years now. I've been here for over a decade. I've never loved anyone, Eden. Any. One. And the love I have for you will be the death of me. So you go right ahead and you grieve, my sweet little dove. Grieve for that lost soul. But grieve for this one, too." *He points to his chest and tears spring into his eyes. "If it's the last thing I do, Eden Riser, so help me God, I will free you from this hell. It may mean that I have to burn for my sins for all eternity, but baby, you won't ever have to."*

And with that, he releases me and leaves.

I wake with a start as thunder rolls in the distance. A shiver runs down my spine that has nothing to do with the coldness of my bare flesh.

"Eden, baby?" Callan's deep voice calls to me in the darkness. I feel his arms reach for me. I whimper and throw myself into his chest. "Sweetheart? What's wrong? Did you have a bad dream?" He coos even as his lips seek my temple. "It's ok. I'm here, angel. I'm here."

I wish I could say it was simply a bad dream; no, it was a memory. One of the worst fights Marco and I ever had. It marked me just as deeply as the brand at my groin did. I haven't thought of that night for a very long time. As Everleigh said recently, Marco wasn't perfect; he allowed things to happen that he shouldn't have. But there are so many things that we don't know: about the things Marco kept from me, about what else Vince was involved in, about the men Marco warned me about, the ones who were like Vince.

I have a nagging suspicion that it's not a coincidence that on the night I give myself to a man for the first time since Marco that it's also the same night the memory of what he said comes to me in the form of a dream. I shiver again despite that Cal's naked flesh is warm against my own.

"Sweetheart, you're trembling. What is it?" He comforts me, and I take it from him, but I can't stop the quivering of my lips or the hammering of my heart. "Eden, baby, talk to me. Are you afraid of storms?"

I realize this is the first storm we've encountered together and nod against his chest. I kiss his pec, thankful for his presence, closing my eyes even in the darkness.

"Oh, sweetie, I didn't know. I'm sorry. Want me to turn the TV on?"

I nod again, remembering that we left the club hours ago and came back to his house.

"Ok." He releases me and turns, his broad back displayed by another flash of lightning. I gulp. He grabs the remote and turns the TV on giving us a little noise and some light. He then pulls me back into his arms and tucks my head against his chest. He chuckles light-heartedly. "Don't worry baby, Cal will protect you from the mighty Thor. I may not have a hammer, but I can sure throw him my *Zoolander* look. That'll stop him."

I laugh despite my fear, an image of Callan Manning in my head, puckering his lips into a duck face while walking down a runway. God, I love this man. *Thor, eat your heart out, baby.* Cal almost has you beat...almost.

"There's my sweet girl. Talk to me." And the hand that cups my cheek and tucks my hair behind my ear breaks every barrier I've ever put up, those blue eyes gazing into my soul.

"It was a memory of Marco. H-he killed someone I cared for."

"Oh Eady," Cal murmurs. Even in his darkest imagination, he can't picture the hell I went through all those years ago.

"It was Vince, I know. I mean Marco was just another puppet in the game. We all were. I...I know Ev says he was a bad man deep down, but there's a part of me that believes Marco didn't have a choice in most of what he had to do. Vince had leverage over him of some kind...just like the rest of us. Our families. Our loved ones. He was manipulative and evil and..." I trail off. "Something Marco said has stuck with me over the years. More than one thing he said." I'm rifling through the memories like a library catalog. I shiver again, his warnings still fresh in my mind. Vince wasn't alone. Marco had to die along with Vince and so did Cordelia Perelli. But why? And who were these other men? What did he mean?

As protective as the girls and I have been over the years, keeping the secrets we have, keeping our identities hidden, even building firewalls for all the possible loopholes, attending to any source of exposure to the point of paranoia, there's a part of me that worries I'm missing something, some detail, some smear in the ink... What if every stone hasn't been turned over? What if every "i" hasn't been dotted nor every "t" crossed. What if we're still somehow in danger? Someone has photos of me they shouldn't have and someone graffitied my club door.

"Eden?" Cal's eyes burn into mine. He asked me something, and I spaced out.

"Cal, I'm scared." My lip trembles again. I fear for myself, for my girls, for Callan.

"Shh, I'm here baby. No one is gonna hurt you ever again. Hear me?"

I do hear him, but I can't quiet the all-encompassing tingle of doubt clinging to me like static. What if he's wrong? What if he can't protect me any more than Marco could?

What if I'm destined to be a pawn in Vincent Perelli's never-ending game?

14

CALLAN

"Yup, that's an elephant," I say to my little man, Caleb, as he points to the elephant down in the pit in front of us. Eden and I have come to the Atlanta Zoo today to enjoy this beautiful day with my nephew while Sam has a book signing not far away in a local bookstore. She practically forced us out after we helped her setup since the place was so small. Sam doesn't really need us there to crowd her. She does well on her own, without her family as an audience. So, we decided to come here instead; she's got the better part of the day to read a portion of her book, sign, and network.

I'd rather be outside than cooped up in such a small space, especially on a day as beautiful as today is. It's sunny, it's warm, and love has made me a softy as I hold Eden's hand and smile down at my angel of a nephew. He loves animals and being outdoors, and I'm glad I have the opportunity to do both with him today.

I pull Eden against my side and inhale her scent, grateful that we no longer have any more secrets between us. Our relationship has gotten even stronger, and I long to take it further than I ever have before. I love that she's getting closer to my sister and nephew and that they seem to adore her as much as I do. I kiss her jawline and tickle the bottom of her ear with my nose, feeling her shiver as I do so. I could growl with the lust that fills me. God, I want her so much. I'm insatiable when it comes to her; she's got me all wrapped up.

"Cal," she scolds playfully as my arm wraps around her waist and my hand settles on her hip.

"What?" I feign ignorance.

"Behave." Her brow arches.

"Not if I can help it." I lean in to kiss her and do so, soft and sweet, a promise of what's to come later, despite that we've been intimate every day for the last three days. I can't get enough, don't know that I ever will, and I love that about us.

When she pulls back, we linger just inches apart looking into the other's eyes.

"Wanna invite the girls over for dinner?" I ask, eager for her family to meet mine.

"I would love that." She smiles big, and I kiss her again. I only pull back long enough to respond to Caleb, who eagerly claps as the elephant he was pointing to raises his trunk and bellows.

Eden tenses in my arms then gasps, gripping my shirt. I'm immediately alerted and look to where her eyes are transfixed. I see a man with jet black hair smiling deviously at her with a finger to his lips as if saying, "Shh." I feed off her fear only a moment before I'm pissed and prepare myself to confront the motherfucker.

I growl and take a step forward, watching the stranger's eyes narrow. Eden pulls at my arm, and he moves away before I have the opportunity to ruin his day—and his face.

I turn to her, frowning. "Who the fuck was that?"

She's shaking her head in horror and confusion, and I'm at

a loss when she says, "I...I don't know. H-he looks like... No...it *can't* be." She covers her mouth with her hand, her terrified eyes seeking mine.

"Eady, who the hell is he?"

"He looked like...like Vince, but V-Vince is dead. I saw... I saw him die." She closes her eyes briefly before opening them again.

I can say with certainty that I'm unnerved by what just happened. Clearly, the strange man was looking at Eden and shushing her. And my gut is telling me that neither of us wants to know why.

Eden

LATER THAT NIGHT, WE HEAD TO EVERLEIGH AND LUCA'S. Instead of them coming to my apartment, Ev volunteered her house because the entire crew decided to crash in—Caleb and Sam, in tow, to meet my family. My family, consisting of my sisters and their families since my parents have long been gone. I have butterflies in my stomach, hoping my girls love these two as much as I do, but I know deep down they will. If I adore them, then Everleigh, Lia, and Addison will follow suit.

Cal kisses the back of my hand as he parks and turns the ignition off. He then hops out and assists Caleb. Sam and I grab the containers of food we brought to the get together. Grape salad for Sam and baked mac and cheese for me.

When Luca opens the door, he gives us a handsome grin.

"Come on in, y'all," I hear Ev say and smile at her familiar voice.

"Luca." I nod to Ev's hubby and introduce Samantha.

"This is Samantha, Cal's sister. Sam, this is Luca Giordano, Everleigh's Italian male counterpart."

Sam gives him a smile, and he reaches for the bowl in her hands. "Nice to meet you, Samantha. Let me get that for you."

"Training him right, Ev." I smirk and get a furrowed brow from Luca before he looks to Caleb.

"And this is my little buddy, Caleb." Cal smiles down at his pride and joy. I can't help how my ovaries sing with that face. God, I want to pop out some babies that look just like this man. He's fucking yummy and even yummier when he's doting over his adorable little nephew.

In fact, I think I'm gonna have to run to the bathroom with him before the night is over if he doesn't stop looking at me like he has been all day.

"I told you not to bring anything," Everleigh drawls, taking the mac and cheese from me, Rory's hand never leaving hers.

I tickle her belly and get a laugh out of the cutest redhead I know.

"Pregnant women gotta eat. Besides, your ungrateful ass will be glad for it when you taste it. I put gruyere cheese in it and added a secret seasoning. It's gonna make you wanna slap your mama." She takes the casserole dish as I rub her protruding belly lovingly. "How are my boys tonight?"

"Kickboxing, it feels like..." she trails off and breathes out heavily.

"Baked cheesy goodness, that's what I'm talking about. Eth's had us on a grilled veggie kick, and I need carbs," Addy adds, moving to embrace me.

"Did you say gruyere cheese?" Lia walks forward with a toddling Aliana in tow, and the sweet girl squeals when she sees me.

"I did," I add, hugging Lia before scooping up Aliana. I kiss her plump cheek and blow raspberries on her neck, getting sweet baby cackles out of her.

Caleb grunts behind me, and I turn to introduce Aliana, Rory, and my Core Four.

"Caleb, this is Aliana, Lia, Rory, Everleigh, and Addison." I point to each of my sisters.

He grunts, and Aliana giggles at him, reaching for him.

"Aww," moves around the girls as sweet Aliana hugs him then sits back into my arms.

"Dang it, Li Li, as if my ovaries weren't bursting already," I coo in her ear, getting another giggle out of her, then feel said ovaries explode when Rory leans up to kiss Caleb's cheek. Fuck, my heart.

Luca scoops Rory up and moves over to Sam who oohs and aahs over her.

I move to the couch, Caleb following behind me in his motorized chair.

I set Aliana on my lap and glance at the baseball game on TV as Addy says, "How old is Caleb?"

"Seven," I respond and pat his hand. "We went to the zoo today and saw elephants, didn't we, buddy?"

Which reminds me, as much as I don't want to be a Debbie Downer, I need to tell the girls about the stranger that I saw.

"Ev, get over here." I motion for her as she comes back in from setting the dishes on the dining room table. I see Cal making the rounds with Sam, introducing her to Landry, Ethan, Kieran and the Greenes. I whisper as I gather Lia, Ev, and Addison in a circle, "I need to tell y'all something." I lean in so Caleb can't hear me.

"I saw someone at the zoo… someone who looks like…like Vince." I steel myself for their reactions.

"Now wait just a cotton-pickin' minute," Everleigh croaks. "Say that again?"

I look back, making sure Cal can't hear me. "He looked like Vince, I swear to God. A younger version of him."

"What could that mean?" Lia sighs.

"Oh, c'mon. We *know* Vince is dead." Addy reassures. "Right?"

All eyes look back at me. Eyes filled with apprehension, concern, and uncertainty. I know he's dead, for sure. I saw his head explode. I saw the fire... Hell, I *started* the fire. I nod. He's dead. That I know for sure.

"Well then maybe you've had too much to drink," Addy teases, trying to lighten the mood, as she nods to the glass in my hand.

"It could just be a coincidence." Lia shrugs.

"Eden, I know your demons are never happy when things are going right for you. Is it nerves? I mean, you and Cal seem so happy..." Everleigh takes my hand, and I feel scalded.

They don't believe me. *Or they don't want to believe you*, my mind says. I look at Li Li in my lap, giggling at Caleb who attempts to make funny faces at her, and I frown. They all have their happy ever afters, the fear is over for them, the worry. They are forgetting why we were hiding in the first place, why we had to keep our identities secret.

Vince is dead and has been for a decade. Antonio and Giacomo are dead, relieving Ev and Lia of their misery with the Cervelli family. For my sisters, it's over; but for me, I'm still living on eggshells, waiting for the next skeleton to pop out of some random closet. I know that the tentacles of Vince Perelli have stretched on endlessly, inescapably, even after his death. The scared little dove within wants to beg for their under-standing, to make them see that this is still very real, but the strong phoenix is hearing what they are saying...and what if they're right? What if I'm just finding things to worry about because it's all I've ever done. Fear is all I've known since burning that damn club to the ground, and these girls—and the need to protect them from villains like Vince—has always kept me going. And now I'm the only one in the club still dancing, still working, still a slave to my past.

I gulp and nod at Ev, trying to smile. "You're right," I lie and pop up to stand by Cal.

My brain is telling me to think things over, but my heart is warning me that something isn't right.

I smile at my handsome man and look over at Sam, who gives me a big grin.

I hear the door open and see Kenton Breckinridge walking in. He's Ev and Kieran's cousin on their mom's side and a fellow law enforcement officer, following in the family footsteps. He's tall, broad, and auburn-headed with blue eyes—he reminds me of Sam Heughan—and I almost cackle as I turn to see Samantha's jaw drop.

Kent walks up, shakes my hand, and I smile at him. "Kent, how are you?"

"Eden, good to see ya. I'm well and you?"

"I'm good. This is my boyfriend, Callan," I say as Kent pumps Cal's hand, "and his sister, Samantha, the soon-to-be famous fantasy author."

Kenton's eyes fall on Sam's, and I swear I can almost hear the sizzle in the air as he reaches out to take her hand. "My my, what a lovely author she is." He pulls Sam's hand to his lips, kissing her knuckles delicately as her cheeks turn into bright red apples.

I giggle but feel Cal's fist clench around my waist, and his pec flexes beneath my palm. I look up to see his jaw tick, and I'm suddenly engulfed in licking hot desire at his dominant stance. It's so freaking sexy...

I tilt my head at him as if to say, "Lighten up," and move my hand to his fist, softening it until he flattens it out. Sam laughs at something Kenton says, and I arch my brow at Callan. *See, it's all good.*

But I know how protective he is of his big sister after what her ex put her through. With Kevin being out of the picture now, Sam has been having a hard time as of late, which is why we brought her out tonight. It's good to see her smiling so much, and Cal tends to see my way of thinking as Sam moves Kent in to meet Caleb, who is laughing at Lia and Aliana playing with him. I even get a slight smile from him as I poke his thick pec.

I lean in to whisper in his ear, "Bathroom, big guy. Now." I lick his earlobe with a hungry tongue.

His brows raise in surprise, and I stifle a laugh as I pull him to the back hallway.

As soon as we enter the bathroom, I slam the door and reach for his jeans.

"Mmm, Eady, what about Sam and...?"

I interrupt him with my tongue shoving down his throat. "Mmm, they're fine, having a blast," I say between breaths. "I simply have to have you... right the hell...mmm, now." I groan as one big palm cups my breast, the other gripping my ass in a death grip as he grabs me up and plants my bottom on the countertop.

"Fuck yeah, now works for me," he mutters as his hand moves to my jaw and tilts my head, his lips taking mine in a searing kiss. "But everyone's gonna hear us." He pulls back with a mischievous smile.

"Ask me if I care?" I smirk and grip his belt, even as I loosen it and grope for the zipper.

Our kiss is needy, desperate, as we grab for the other's clothes in an effort to get our sexes naked and connecting, in a call that supersedes all else. He pulls the crotch of my panties aside beneath my dress and impales me with a long, thick finger. My head is thrown back and I purr as his hot mouth settles on the pulse at my throat and the heel of his hand hits my aching bud, leaving me a whimpering bundle of nerves.

Once his hard cock is in my hand, I'm pumping it, eager to have it buried deep inside me. All those years without a normal sex life have made my bloodlust for his shaft unignorable.

"God, Eden, you've got me so hard, angel," he grunts as I swipe the precum from the tip of him. I want to taste it and do so as I pull my thumb to my lips, moaning as I suck it into my mouth. "Fuck me, you're gonna make me cum before I'm ever inside you."

"Then you'd better get inside me, stud." I tease as I sweep the head of him across my dripping wet slit. He groans and shivers, and I love what a bumbling fool I make him.

He thrusts his hips as I guide him inside me and wrap my legs around him. He lifts me and we both stifle our cry as his hard cock settles within me. Then we move and our mouths clash. I answer each thrust as his sex loves my own with an urgency I've never felt until him.

Cal lifts me off the countertop and presses me to the wall, my back slamming hard against it, and I grunt. He stills and looks into my eyes, afraid he's frightened or hurt me, but I'm moving on him, seeking my climax, all else forgotten but this sexy beast devouring me as only he can.

I know the others outside can hear us, know they know what's going on, but I couldn't care less as Cal thrusts higher and deeper, pushing me to oblivion in his big, muscled arms. I hold tight, gripping his back in a death grip as his lips kiss my jaw, my throat, his tongue lapping the sweat at the base of my collarbone.

"Oh God, Cal," I whimper as I start to splinter apart. His mouth covers my pleasure cry, and his pace increases, pistoning into me with bone-jarring thrusts that have me climaxing again.

With a mighty roar that I attempt to stifle with a kiss, he empties himself inside me, his pumping hips hammering mine relentlessly until he finally stills. His breathing is ragged, his hairline sweaty as he lays his forehead on mine, spent.

I giggle and kiss his nose. "You're all mine, Callan Manning." As if there were any doubt.

"Damn, I love you, Eden. Look what you do to me."

I glance in the mirror at my arms and legs clinging to his rock-solid frame like a monkey wrapped around a tree and grin. His sexy, muscled ass is clenched, his cock still hard inside me, and I'm horny all over again. *Shit!*

I kiss him with passion, our tongues tangling, deliciously seeking the other.

I rock my hips on him until he stills my movements.

"Eden…" he scolds without conviction. "You're killing me, darlin'."

I can feel his length growing again within me and wish we were home because I'd fuck him all night long, and by the look in my eyes, he knows it too. I grin again.

"Later, lover, I promise. But we still have to walk out of this bathroom." He looks down at the dishevelment of our clothes, and we both laugh.

Before I'm ready, he's sliding out of me and easing me to the ground, straightening my dress. I go to right his pants, and he stills my hands.

"I got it. Thanks though, baby." He winks and God, if I'm not riding his hot ass again, I'm dying.

But I do realize we've probably been overheard as we check our appearance in the mirror, and I wipe lipstick from Cal's face trying not to cackle. My cheeks pinken as he takes my hand and opens the door.

"Jesus, Addy, what the…?" I ask as Addy waits there, Ethan in tow, tapping her foot impatiently.

"It's about *freaking* time..." she mutters. "Our turn."

I see Cal balk and Ethan shrugs as she pulls him into the bathroom while we exit.

"Smells like sex in here. Just like I like it," Addy states and slams the door in our faces.

When Callan looks at me thoroughly confused, I laugh then shrug. "Welcome to the family, big guy." I pull him back to me and kiss him breathlessly.

15

EDEN

That Sunday, I'm in the club dancing, practicing my routine. I've decided not to strip anymore. I'll parade around in lingerie and continue to do what I've been doing, only without removing any garments. I am the last single madam, and this is my club so it's my say—after all, we have plenty of women who strip. And I may still be single, but I'm now in a committed relationship and no longer want to show skin to men who aren't Callan. I made the decision after Cal and I broke the final barrier in the room just a hundred yards from the spot here on the stage, but last night, I told him about it. He, of course, couldn't be more pleased. I know he won't be satisfied until I give the dancing part of it up for good, too. For now, though, he'll have to be happy with this.

I let the music take me as I move from one position to the next, my body flowing as smoothly as water over river rocks. I've danced for as long as I can remember, starting as a ballerina when I was just four. It's an escape for me: balance, poise, discipline, as the pole and I become one. I invert myself, going from a Leg Lock to an Extended Frodo to a Chinese Flag position before I smell a cigar burning and realize, startlingly, that I'm not alone in here.

I gasp as I slide down the pole and gulp at the man standing before me.

He has on a crisp, pressed suit, and his dark hair is slicked back. He has a cigar between his capped teeth, and the way he looks at me makes me feel like I have thousands of centipedes rapidly moving over my skin.

"Eden Riser. It's a pleasure to finally meet you, my dear."

Fuck, he knows my name.

"I-I'm sorry but the club is closed." I hate that I stammer and rub my suddenly chilled bare arms. I look beyond him for Bruno, who was standing watch at the only door this man could have been permitted to enter through.

"Oh, I've incapacitated your bodyguard. I wanted to make sure we're the only two to bear witness to this conversation."

And just like that, I'm the caged little bird again, flashing back to when Vince Perelli was still alive. I shiver and bite into my lip to keep from whimpering.

The man grins. "Oh, don't worry. I didn't kill him. He's simply knocked out." He seems pleased by my distress. "My my, you've been a busy girl. And so successful, too. Vince would be proud."

Oh God, please don't say that name here. This is a dream, it's all just a bad dream. I'll wake up soon in Callan's big arms and tell him all about it. Only, even as I pinch myself, I realize that this isn't a nightmare. It's fucking real!

"I'm sure your uncle spoke of me... Alfieri Costanza, at your service. You look so surprised, lovey." He gives a low, sick laugh that makes my stomach clench. This. This is the man my sweet Marco warned me about. And God, how I wish I had listened.

I'm so sorry, Marco. I'm so sorry I didn't guard myself better. It's all been in vain. His sacrifice. It was a facade—our freedom a lie.

Every instinct I have is telling me to run, but knowing what I know now, there's nowhere to run to. No one to run to. My luck has finally hit a dead end. I will die in the place where Roxie was born—fitting, it would seem.

"I've been watching you and your partners make a thriving business here at RISE, and I must say, I'm incredibly impressed." He sits down in front of me. "Oh please, by all means, don't let me interrupt your dance."

Fuck you, I want to say, but hold my tongue. I won't give him the satisfaction of besting me. I cross my arms over my chest and wait for him to continue.

"Ah well, too bad. I was enjoying the show." He adjusts his crotch—a way to rattle me, I'm sure—but my eyes stay trained on his. I'm used to men attempting to make me feel uncomfortable. I can handle that. "It seems you owe me, Ms. Riser."

"*Owe* you?" I scoff.

"Yes. You burned down Vince's club, and I haven't received payment in ten very long years. Millions are due to me."

"I'm not paying you a fucking dime, you thieving bastard."

"Oh, but you *will*, and do you wanna know why?" His grin chills my blood as he leans forward. "Because if you don't, I'll kill every fucking person you know, and take it from you, anyway." I want to shake my head but don't. I attempt to keep my calm while inside I'm trembling. "Because I'm even worse than your fucking crazy-ass uncle ever dreamed to be."

"I didn't know that was possible," I can't help but sass. If I'm dying, and everyone I know is too, what the hell difference does it make?

"It is, sweetheart. And good thing for you, I'm an extremely patient man, so I'll be as patient as I *have* been. However," he steeples his hands as he says this, "I won't continue to wait too long."

He motions someone in a suit forward. A muscular, bald man with a scar running the length of his face, carrying a tablet.

Al turns the tablet in my direction and shows me a camera system setup on all my girls and Cal. I gulp, attempting not to panic. "There are many lives at stake here should you decide to *fuck* with me. You do what you need to do to get me my money, and I'll pretend that this awkward conversation never took place. But if you don't..." he trails off, and the guy beside him turns a gun into the direction of the cameras and makes a shooting sound with his mouth. "I'll enjoy blowing *all* their brains out, and right in front of you, too. Even little, what was his name, Otis?" Al turns to the man he calls Otis, who responds deeply with, "Caleb," and gives me a gold-toothed grin.

I feel bile rise in my throat, and my legs wobble. I stumble in my strappy heels before righting myself.

"Ah, look at that, the feisty dominatrix has a heart after all! Look at that." Al laughs, briefly looking into the shadows. "That'll be eight million dollars wired to my account by Thursday."

"*Thursday?*" I whimper. That's not enough time to get that kind of money.

"Or cash." He smirks. How the fuck would he know I have that amount of cash? "Oh, the things I know, *sexy bookworm*. The things I know," he whispers as if reading my very thoughts.

I can't help but gulp again, remembering how Cal took me from behind last night overlooking my balcony while calling me his sexy bookworm. Jesus... This sick perv was watching.

My head reels and I feel like I'm gonna hurl at any second, I even pull my hand to my mouth.

"As I said, I've been watching you for years, baby doll." Al winks and licks his thin lips, and I feel like I'm being raped all over again. Oh dear God. I *am* gonna hurl.

"Alright." Al takes the glass ashtray Otis hands him and flicks the ashes from his burning cigar into it with a small tap. "Now that *that* business is done, let's discuss the other pressing matter."

Oh God, of course there's more. There's always more with men like this one.

"You can come on out now, Enzo."

Just as I'm about to ask who the hell Enzo is, the man I saw days ago at the zoo is there. The man who looks just like…

"Ah, I see Enzo needs no introduction." Al gives a hearty laugh when he sees my expression.

"Hello, cousin," a man who could be identical to Vincent Perelli says. He's a younger, less dark version of the man who took my innocence, my spirit, and my joy from me, but there's no denying he's Vince's child. Black hair, narrow nose, dark eyes devoid of emotion.

I prayed that my mind was playing tricks on me. I thought I was seeing things. I see now I was wrong…dead wrong. I can't form words as he walks forward, out of the shadows, and into the light, his angry face looking me over as if I'm trash. For a minute, I'm back at *The Devil's Playground*, the innocent little dove of Marco's, the soiled birdie of Vincent's. Yup. I'm abso-fucking-lutely gonna hurl.

Al laughs again. "Go ahead, son. Tell her."

"I'm Vince's biological son, Enzo Ramirez Perelli. Marco was tasked to kill me when I was born but didn't."

Wait? *What*? Marco was supposed to kill an *infant*? Even as I silently praise my lover for his mercy, looking at this man who's far too similar to his father, I wish now Marco would've added one more innocent life to the tally on his belt. I gulp.

"Yup, that's right, isn't that some *shit!*" Al is laughing again, and I've never hated a sound so much in my life. Except, well, maybe Vince's grunting into my ear while he fucked me. The back of my throat is burning with unspent vomit. "Marco brought him to *me*. Get this—Vince found out he'd accidentally knocked up his housekeeper after Enzo here was born and wanted him dead. See, he didn't want anyone to know. Child born out of wedlock, non-Italian family and all. But someone had to help carry on our dynasty. We needed a back-up plan, so I took the kid in, taught him everything I know, and he's been building quite a vendetta against you and your friends. He wants what's owed to him. All that money you inherited from his father, the money you've made off this *fabulous* nightclub."

"It's mine by birthright," the less intimidating version of Vince says.

"Ya see, that amount we need...yeah, it just doubled." Al's smile is gone, a scowl replacing it. "And I'll expect twenty percent of your earnings every month from now on, which Otis here is gonna collect. And again, you know the drill should you decide to defy me. I'm not your Uncle Vince. You can't fuck your way up the ladder of *this* empire. Sex doesn't talk quite as much as money does for me...unfortunately for you." Al gives me the once over then shrugs. "Tick tock, tick tock, Ms. Riser."

As soon as the three men leave, I find the nearest trash can and evacuate my roiling gut.

This isn't happening.

This isn't happening.

This. Is. Not. Happening.

Not again.

I can't contain the tears that come or the gag that escapes my throat once more. I heave and vomit again...and again...until there's nothing left to hurl.

How am I going to come up with the money Al wants: sixteen million dollars? We might have enough cash between all four of us and the safe to cover most of that, but there's no way I can get that kind of money in four days. I'm completely fucking fucked. I don't know what to do. Who to talk to? Last time, I had Marco. Who do I have now?

"Oh my God, Bruno?" I gasp and move from the floor to the door. I run down the hallway where Bruno lays unconscious. "Bruno!" I yell and begin to feel for a pulse in his neck. I feel one within half a minute. Oh thank God. He's not dead, but he has one hell of a knot coming up on his eye. I should call an ambulance. Yes.

I run and grab my phone. As I'm kneeling back to Bruno's side, I see the back doors bursting open. My heart freezes in my chest as two men in black ski masks approach. I feel panic seize every inch of me. This is it. I'm finally dead. I can finally be free, once and for all, but the torture I'm going to endure at their hands is going to be pure Hell.

Ah, you can take it, Eden, you've been through worse, my inner phoenix squawks. But have I? I hate the darkness. Dammit! But that's all I see as I'm jerked from the floor, a bag thrown over my head. Darkness and suffocation. *Great!* Death can't come soon enough now. I don't fight. Only whimper and yell for Bruno because his face is the last one I'll ever see of my family.

I feel what I assume to be a needle pierce the muscle of my upper arm and yelp from the surprise of it. My body feels weak as I'm being dragged outside. I hear birds, traffic, a vehicle running. I'm pulled up and into that vehicle, I assume, as I hear a sliding door slam shut. I begin to hear murmuring voices as the blackness grows even darker and darker until I feel heavy, my limbs numb. It's getting harder to keep my eyelids open, my ears are ringing.

I'm going…going… As I slide into the seat, laying down, I surrender to my state.

My heartbeat is steady. My body has accepted its fate. After long years of torment, it's finally done.

Death is coming for me.

I close my eyes and embrace it.

CALLAN

"LIA, CALM DOWN. WHAT DO YOU MEAN, YOU HAVEN'T HEARD from her?" I grip the phone tighter as a frantic Magnolia sobs into the receiver.

"I mean, *none* of us have heard from her! We call and her phone goes straight to voicemail. She was supposed to be here an hour ago. You *know* Eden; this isn't like her. Something is wrong!"

Panic rips through me. No, Eden is punctual to a fault, and she was excited about going shopping with the girls today.

"When did you last talk to her?" I ask.

"Yesterday."

"Did she say she was going somewhere first?" She had told me she was going straight to Lia's.

"No. And I'm here at her apartment…and her truck isn't here."

Maybe she's at the club. "I'll go to RISE, I'm right around the corner." I say, fear clenching my heart even as I pray for my girlfriend's safety. If something has happened to her, I don't know what I'll do.

"Cal, there's...there's been a couple strange things that's happened lately. I don't know if she told you but..."

"Like what?" My gut is telling me I'm not going to like what she's about to say.

"Graffiti at the club, sightings of a man who looks...like...well, he looks like Vince."

"Lia, I want you to hang up with me and first call Kieran, then Rian, ok? Tell them what's going on."

"I already have! K's the first one I called." I hear her grunt as my tire wheels squeal when I make an abrupt turn. "What are you gonna do?"

"I'm gonna find my girlfriend. Have Kieran and Rian meet me here at the club."

Lia agrees, and I throw my phone down in the seat, relief quickly flooding my veins as I see Eden's truck in the parking lot. That same relief is just as easily extinguished as the exit doors turn out to be wide-ass open, and Bruno's stumbling out of them with a hand to his bleeding head. "Fuck!"

I park my truck and immediately jump out, approaching Eden's bodyguard. "Where's Eden?"

"Two men took her. They were in a blue van. I was hit on the head with the butt of a gun and awoke as they peeled out. Jesus. We were completely blindsided."

"Which direction did they go?" I ask even as I start to move back to my truck.

"It's too late, Callan, you'll never catch them."

Motherfucking shit! My worst fears have come to life.

When Eden told me her uncle was once the head honcho for one of Atlanta's biggest sex-trafficking, drug-running, money-embezzling crime families, I knew it was bad news. I also knew you don't just get to run away from the mob.

Well, it looks like those assholes found her. So much for staying safe. So much for hiding their identities. If Eden is in danger, they all are. One by one, they're gonna be picked off. I can only pray now that Eden is returned, and alive. Perhaps, these people have only taken her to frighten her into something. Probably something involving money. I can't think about what's being done to her right this minute as I wait for Kieran and his dad, or I'll go insane.

"Stay strong for me, E, strong for your sisters."

Please bring her back to me, I pray to God above.

16

EDEN

I'm surprised that when I wake up, I'm alive. Either that or Hell is very close to an interrogation room with its loud, spinning fan, uncomfortable metal chair, and cleaner mixed with a faint scent of mold and mildew. The bag is still covering me, and I can make out a lightbulb hanging over my head.

This is shady as hell, and I await to hear the clank of torture devices in the background.

Finally, a heavy door opens and closes, and the sound of heels clicking on the concrete floor hits my ears.

"Are you fucking serious, Delgado? Take the bag off her head. What is *wrong* with you guys?" I'm shocked to hear the soft tone of a woman's voice.

"Sorry, we wanted to make it look as legit as possible, Sky."

I gasp as the bag is taken off my head and my eyes fall on a lovely redhead with diamond earrings, impeccably dressed in a taupe dress suit. She gives me a smile and shakes her head.

"I'm so sorry, Ms. Riser. Forgive the *special* agents for their man-handling, we needed to make this look like a kidnapping."

"Excuse me?" I'm so confused right now.

"Let me start over. I'm DA Skyla Redmond."

I knew I recognized her. She's the DA of Atlanta. But why is she here in my own private Hell, and why was I "kidnapped?" She seems to recognize my perplexity.

"Unfortunately, I know Al Costanza all too well. You see, my husband and I were chased down by his associate Giovanni Geraci several years ago. As you know, these men run the Atlanta Cosa Nostra. Their offenses are many, and we're one step away from having enough evidence to indict the last of them. Geraci was put away. Now, his buddy Costanza and his minions are next. That's where I need you to come in."

"Me? I-I just met the guy today, I don't know—"

"You didn't *know* him? Costanza was Vince Perelli's partner." Her brows draw.

"P-Partner?" I stutter. Vince didn't have any partners. He worked alone, didn't he? He…

"Ms. Riser, Vince, Al, Giovanni. They were all a part of the same empire. Along with Antonio and Giacomo Cervelli."

Giovanni… *Gio*, that name sounds familiar…

Wait, Antonio Cervelli was involved with Vince, too? God, things are starting to make so much sense now. Why Lia's father pushed her to marry Giacomo and produce a pure Sicilian heir, why Antonio took the company away from Giacomo when he couldn't. Why Giacomo was murdered in his prison cell when he turned on his father and became an informant.

Italian mobsters thrive on their bloodlines...and secrecy. But I'd never seen Al before. *Wait*...Yes, I have. Don... In *The Devil's Playground*. I didn't know their real names, but their faces. Al's and Gio's faces I can remember seeing around. I *knew* I recognized him. When Vince's club burned, they had to find a new hideout, a new racket. It's all starting to click now. "I'm sorry. It's just...I—"

"It's alright. The boys gave you a mild sedative. It'll wear off soon. I apologize, but the DA couldn't just come waltzing into a well-known strip club and have a talk with you about organized crime. They've been watching you, following you, tapping your phone. We couldn't take any chances. Now can you tell me what happened? Why he finally confronted you?"

"He wants sixteen million dollars from me by Thursday."

I ramble off to Skyla about all that Al told me, about meeting Vince's son, Enzo, about the threat against my family. I begin to cry; this day has taken a huge toll on me. I can't even breathe right now.

"Don't you worry. We have eyes and ears everywhere and guys undercover, but you're the final piece of the puzzle to help us pull it all together."

"*Me*? Why?"

"You're gonna get the confession we need from Al. I need you to meet with him again while you're wired." When my eyes go wide, she pats my hand. "Don't worry. I'm not sending you in alone. We have a mole in their system. You remember Otis?" she smiles and motions over to the guy she called Delgado. He's wearing a ball cap and takes it off to reveal a bald head.

I gasp. "Oh my God." Panic takes hold of me before "Delgado" smiles and waves.

"Not Otis and no gold-teeth." He opens his mouth and sticks his tongue out. "Just undercover."

"Delgado, get out." Skyla rolls her eyes. "Our original informant was actually Antonio's son, Giacomo. He'd come forward about three years ago with a great deal of information on his father's involvement and all the drug and sex trafficking he'd been doing over the years. It would seem he was disowned after he couldn't produce an heir, so needless to say, he was a bit bitter. But then next thing we know, Antonio shuts him up for good and our lead went cold, so Special Agent Delgado went undercover. Gia, Antonio's daughter, was the next to come forth. She was able to fill in the missing pieces we needed about Al and his connection to the ring. So, guess who's getting the last laugh?"

I can't help the relief of laughter at my throat. "So, what is it you need me to do?"

"Well, you'll meet back up with Costanza with your wire while we stay a safe distance back. It will be a simple business deal. Be sure to ask questions, though, as many as you can, about what originally happened with Vince. How it got started, who, where, etcetera. The more he confesses to, the better. Otis here will help the process. I need you to schmooze. Can you do that?"

I smile, hopeful for the first time in a long time that my "freedom" may indeed be obtainable after all. I can schmooze with the best of them. After all, I learned from the best schmoozer of all, my uncle Vincent. I nod. "Let's shut these fuckers down."

WHEN CAL AND I WALK THROUGH MY DOOR LATER THAT DAY, I hear, "Dear God in Heaven, you're ok!" Addy's quicker than anyone else and pulls me against her, squeezing me.

Murmurs echo around me, and I'm passed around like a ragdoll to Everleigh, Magnolia, Kyleigh, and finally Samantha before Cal grips me back against him and encases me in that fortress of a body of his.

Addison hands me a whimpering Maximus. I cradle him to me and kiss his sweet, fluffy head. He licks my tears away, as if he understands what I've been through.

I never thought I'd see them again, and I can't stop the tears that fall, grateful to have so many people who were concerned for my life.

I look up into Callan's face. I've never seen him so worried. His lips hit mine hard before he tucks me back into his chest.

"I'm never letting you out of my sight again, Eden," he insists.

Little does he know, I'll be in the thick of things again—and soon.

I glance over at a frowning Kieran and Rian Greene, whose brows raise expectantly.

I know, we need to talk.

"Who kidnapped you? And where are they now?" Rian asks.

"The Spinellis," I answer robotically.

Kieran crosses his arms over his chest, giving me a frown. He knows I'm keeping something. *Fuck!*

The DA and DEA agents had left me in a parking lot several miles away with a few bruises to make it look legit, and I had to call Cal from a payphone. He was panicked and livid when he answered, keeping me on the line the whole time before he got there. He held me so tight I was sure I was going to pass out from not being able to breathe.

I hadn't really understood the whole point of making the kidnapping look real. If it was to look as though I was taken by a rival mafia family, wouldn't that make Costanza even more suspicious of me?

Oh well, I have to trust in the DA and Special Agent Delgado if I'm going to pull this off.

I sit down and tell the Greenes, the girls, their guys, and my boyfriend my rehearsed version of the false kidnapping, leaving Al and Enzo out all together, per the DA.

Your girls don't need to know the entire story. It's only gonna make them worry about you. This has to stay just between us for now. All *of it,* Sky's words echo through my head.

So I lie. I lie like I never have before. Kieran, Luca, and Rian are the hardest to convince, though, wanting every minute detail of the incident for evidence and such. Cal looks ready to kill someone as he holds my hand and strokes my back, a perpetual scowl on his handsome face.

I tell them all, per Skyla, that I was blindfolded, taken to an interrogation room, and asked questions about Vince—nothing more, nothing less.

Even though I see the questions lingering, it's all I can give them for now.

I hope and pray my backbone holds out as I pull one lie out of another. Then I give some lame excuse about being tired and just wanting to rest, holding in my tears.

Keeping things from them all these months—the graffiti, pictures, someone asking questions at the club—has been the hardest thing I've done in ten years, and it has truly taken so much out of me. I love every one of them, and I tell myself that these lies are to protect them.

I hug my sisters tightly, and Kieran tells me that he'll be in touch as they all leave.

Cal moves me into the bathroom where he's drawn me a bath.

His face is solemn as he strips me naked and assists me into the tub, pulling my long dark hair over the lip as he moves a wet cloth over my arms and shoulders.

"Jesus, Eden, I've never been more relieved in my life than when I heard your voice," he whispers into my ear, and I feel a tear fall from the corner of my eye.

I, too, thought I was a goner the moment I saw Alfieri in my studio.

Cal continues to murmur sweet nothings in my ear, telling me of his undying love for me and promising to keep me safe.

My sobs catch in my throat as his gentle touch stops at my bruised wrists, and he growls.

"I swear to God if I ever see the bastard who took you..." he doesn't finish as I turn my head and catch his blue eyes sparking in anger.

Delgado actually did that. I told him to. He was hesitant but even Skyla insisted that it needed to look like I was bound with rope, and bruises would help the legitimacy. He gripped both wrists tightly, but it was me who told him to squeeze even harder. His beautiful blue eyes reflected the same look I'm seeing in Cal's now.

"Oh Cal, I'm so sorry." It's not a lie. I'm sorry for the lies, the deceit, the past that has followed me and the girls for the last ten years—a veil of darkness always clouding our sunny days. A looming shadow that won't escape us no matter what we do.

Now, it's up to me. I have to end this, once and for all. I thought I had, but it was just a front. Now, I can finally put a real stop to it all.

When my tears are spent, Cal pulls me from the tub and wraps a towel around me.

I'm numb as he dries me off and throws one of his big shirts over my frame.

He leads me to the bed where we get in, and he pulls the covers up around us as he tucks me into his solid arms where I feel safer than I ever have in my life.

For now, I take solace in his presence. For now, I am at peace.

But soon, I'll be putting my life in danger once again and I pray once this is over, me and my sisters can finally be free of the cage the Devil put us in.

My heart begins to hammer in my chest as I see a black Lincoln pull in, and I get out of my car. I unlock the trunk and move to the back, stating into my wire, "It's showtime."

It took two phone calls to convince Al to meet me again, face to face. "Otis" helped out a lot with that. Everything was set up in record time. I have two duffle bags full of "money" and a wire—which is much smaller than I anticipated— strapped to me. I've never been so nervous in my life as I was when I pulled up to this rendezvous point and cut my engine.

I can only pray I'm not walking into the mouth of the lion now as Al steps out and looks me over with renewed interest. He licks his lips, seeing me dressed provocatively in a black mini skirt and white V-neck button down. I approach as "Otis" moves to my trunk to get the bags of money. He gives me a wink.

"Well, well, forget what I said about sex not talking, lovey. Perhaps I need to come have a private show in Roxie's Garden. I've heard the delights in there are *well* worth the price tag."

I could gag aloud, wondering which man I've taken in there over the years has been a spy for this sleaze-ball. There's prob- ably more than one. Dear God.

"Please tell me that's why you're here, kitten? You, wanting another *private* meeting?" His teeth practically have feathers coming out of them. Yup, the lion's den for sure, and I'm the stupid little bird who's fallen right into his trap. I literally want to die as he steps forward and moves a calloused hand to my hip and down my bare thigh. "You are enticing, I'll give you that. I can see why Vince was so obsessed with these curves. I'd love to feel every one of them." His whisper in my ear makes me shiver...and not in a good way.

Seal the deal, get the fuck out, Eden. Don't let him intimidate you.

"Al," I pout and plant my palms on his chest. "I must say, my desire for older men is rather...sinful." I purr and force myself to look up into his disgusting, wrinkled face. I get a satisfied chuckle from him and continue. "I had hoped there was more bargaining we could do." I attempt to look seductive instead of scared out of my mind, which is all I feel in this moment.

His eyes trail my face and his grip tightens on my hip. "I'll bet you'd like that wouldn't you? You little *slut!*" His eyes turn malicious, and he grits his teeth.

Shit, I've awakened something I never intended to. Al grips my hair and turns me to face "Otis."

"Ya see, kitten, I'm no fool. Not like your uncle Vince was. You don't have me by the dick like you did him. I'm on to your wicked ways."

With that, I watch as a gun rises beside us and he shoots Otis in the chest. Otis grunts as he's blown back, bags in hand, and falls to the ground.

I scream and watch as he lands awkwardly. Oh God, what have I done?

I'm turned rapidly around to face a spitting mad Al Costanza. "You were fucking kidnapped by the fucking Spinellis! And I'll bet they forced all kinds of information out of you, didn't they?" he spits out. I gasp, too afraid to move. "Did you think I was fucking kidding about your loved ones? I'll kill all of them. Did you think I was as stupid as Vince was? That I didn't see right through your games, Eden?"

"I...I don't know what you're talking about," I whimper.

"Vince was the power, the money behind the operation. Cervelli had all the resources. Geraci, the muscle. And me, guess what *I* had?"

I couldn't guess if my life depended on it; I'm frozen with fear.

"I'm the brains of the entire operation! And I didn't get where I am today by letting conniving bitches like you trick me. Now, you're gonna tell me everything you told the Spinellis or that club of yours is gonna turn into a house of a thousand corpses, capeesh?"

I nod. I can do this. I'm strong. I'm a phoenix.

"They wanted to know about Marco and...and Enzo."

"Of fucking course they did. Ah, Marco. Such a loyal henchman, wasn't he?"

I frown, unsure if I understand his meaning. He grins. "Well, I'm gonna kill you anyway so it doesn't matter if I tell you or not. And hell, I guess you deserve to know the truth about your lover." My eyes give me away, and he smiles diabolically again. "Yes, love, we knew. We *all* knew. We had such power over him. He couldn't have kept it from us if he'd tried. The other three of us wanted to kill you both, but Vince, God he was such a fool when it came to you. He honestly didn't believe his perfect Eden would ever deceive him. Thinking with his dick instead of his head. Which was why he had to die."

Wait? What? It wasn't Marco's idea to kill Vince? It was *Al's?*

"Oh, Eden, don't look so shocked. You knew how unhinged your uncle was becoming. He was starting to get too messy, too bold. A family needs stability, discipline. A true leader, not a wannabe like Perelli. Had I but known Marco would end his *own* life and burn the club down, I would never have planted the idea in his stupid fucking head. So much money gone," Al growls. "Then *you* come along and take everything from us. You greedy slut. Well, now you'll pay, won't you?"

I gulp as the gun raises to my forehead, centimeters separating the metal from my flesh. My life flashes before my eyes. My wonderful life before my world went dark, my parents' death, Vincent taking me in, the horror of living as his captive, his whore, his dancer, meeting all my precious sisters, Callan,

Caleb… My entire life has been completely marked by sin and now that's how I'm going to die…in sin.

I begin to pray that God takes me in exchange for my family, bargaining that damning my soul is equivalent to saving all of theirs.

I close my eyes against Al's smirk, even as he moves closer and grips the back of my hair with a clenched fist.

"I'm not done yet. Killing you wouldn't be any fun if I didn't play with you first, now would it, little dove?"

Oh God, *why*? Why can't I just die with some small amount of dignity left?

He pulls me to the trunk of his vehicle and slams my upper body down, my chin hitting so hard against the surface that I bite my tongue, teeth crunching together. I can feel the blood running from my mouth, taste the metallic liquid pooling over my tongue and down my lip. I lick it away and attempt to stay calm despite that inside, my heart is ripping apart at the seams.

I feel his rough hands thrusting my skirt up. Earth, swallow me, please? I can't stomach being violated once again by another man with a soul just as black as Vince's was. It sickens me, not just the act of sexual assault itself, but the shame, the hate, the submission of my soul and body to someone whom I don't love. I think of Callan, my gentle giant. I'm glad he's not here to witness my defiling like Marco was. God, that memory haunts me even now.

I hear Al's pants unbuckle, his zipper gives as the cool breeze blows against my bare bottom. Tears flow from my eyes, tears of anger and rage and disgust. I want to fight this bastard, not unlike how I fought Vince the very first time this ever happened to me. But I remember how that turned out. And I didn't have a gun pressed to the back of my head as I do now. One wrong movement, and I'll be dead. But being dead is better than being raped again, I suddenly decide.

"Now, let's savor the fruits of Eden and see what had Vince so enthralled with this sweet little cunt of yours." I feel soft flesh touching my inner thigh and cringe. It's all I can do not to whimper, but I won't give the asshole the satisfaction.

I have all of a couple seconds to decide my fate now. Rape or death. Rape or death. Rape...

NO! Not today, motherfucker.

I raise my arm, elbow out. If I turn very quickly I can shove that jointed bone right into his nose and pray I won't miss. I'm preparing myself to do just that as I hear a voice. A voice that's all too familiar to me.

"Get the fuck away from her, you sorry piece of *shit*."

"Callan!" I scream, tears streaming my face, and turn to see Cal along with Kieran and Rian, their department-issued firearms raised toward Al.

Everything happens so fast, I don't have a chance to think. The restraining pressure that was against my back and thighs is now gone, and I hear the buzzing of the blood in my ears... God it's *so* loud—*how is it that loud?*

It's not blood pumping into my ears, it's helicopter blades.

A huge spotlight lands on Alfieri and blinds him, momentarily thwarting his attempt to shoot towards the man I love. In a split second, my knee comes up and shoves into Al's crotch.

His cry is muffled by the droning of the helicopter, the sounds of metal, and a thousand screaming voices.

I take off, seeing my freedom, seeing my savior, Callan. I smile as I run to his open arms, but I don't miss the look of sheer terror that suddenly crosses his handsome face.

Too late, I feel a burning in my back as a blast so sharp and intense assaults me from behind. I jerk at its force and look down, my white shirt is being stained ruby red.

Oh my God! I've been shot. Holy shit! Al fucking shot me. Wow. So, this is really it? I'm dying.

But at least I didn't have to experience another man taking something from me that wasn't theirs to take… Well, my life was forfeit either way…so long as we shut these bastards down once and for all, so long as my family could be saved.

"Eden, baby, oh God." I see tears in my lover's big blue eyes. "Kieran, fuck, what do we do?" Cal's hand is pressing firmly into my left side, but I feel numbness and cold, so cold.

"Cal, you came." I reach up and cup the handsome face I adore so very much, my head resting against his shoulder as he cradles me in his big arms.

"We followed you," he says, looking at Kieran, whose concern seems to grow as he runs off, presumably to get help. "Eden, baby, talk to me. Don't leave me, please?"

I didn't realize I had closed my eyes until I look up at the contorted face beckoning to me. At least if I have to die, I can see this beautiful face one last time.

"Cal, take care of my sisters."

"Don't! Don't you dare. You're *not* dying. Eden, I'm not gonna let you. Help! Somebody help!" he screams, looking ahead of us.

An aura surrounds him as I shiver. I can't feel my legs anymore, but I won't tell him this. I can die happy, knowing that Al is not going to hurt anyone else.

"Keep them safe, my love."

"Eden, baby, please? I can't lose you." His sob startles me awake again.

"Don't cry, Cal. It's ok." I smile as he brings my hand to his lips.

It *is* ok as I see light, feel warmth, hear voices and something is pulling me. Pulling me away from this darkness I've been drowning in for so long. I feel at peace as I close my eyes.

Death, sweet and serene, takes me away on the wings of a beautiful angel in the form of my precious Callan Manning.

I AWAKEN TO THE SOUND OF BEEPING. MY HEAD POUNDS AND I feel like I'm in a dream world, memories are dull as I try to recall the last thing I remember.

Callan, a helicopter… Dying.

My eyes burn when I open them. Everything is blurry, but I focus on my left side where I see a brunette head laying next to my thigh. It's Addy, her arm is thrown across my blanketed shins. Movement draws my attention beyond her where I see Everleigh pacing and frowning at the phone in her hands, tears glisten in her green eyes. I gape in wonder as Magnolia enters the door to my right, giant bags of Chick-Fil-A in her hands.

"Ev, can you grab the door for me?" she asks as she sits the bags down on the tray in front of me.

Everleigh moves to the door to shut it behind Lia, and I hear a gasp as Lia sees that I'm awake.

"Cal!" she shouts as her blue eyes search mine. "Callan!"

I hear a manly grunt and a groan. "Yeah? Wh-What's wrong?" I hear the creaking on thick leather and a whoosh to my right as I see Callan spring up off the settee, big body ready for the next battle he's about to face. His eyes are stuck on Lia's, fear and fatigue shadowing his features. She nods to me, and he turns his head in my direction. He inhales sharply and his hand covers his mouth in a mixture of relief, surprise, and emotion. His blue eyes are sparkling with tears even as he laughs and moves to my side. "Oh, baby. You're awake. Oh, thank God."

His big frame moves to the bed as softly as he can where he

sits and takes my right hand in his. Plastic tubes extend from the back of my palm as he pulls it to his lips.

"Eden, can you hear me?"

Of course I can. I'm not deaf.

"Baby, can you nod?"

Of course I can nod. Why is he acting so strangely? I feel movement to my left and see Addison smiling at me, tears streaming her beautiful face. "Oh, Eden. You're alive."

Alive? Alive. Yes. I was dead, wasn't I? So if I'm not dead then I *must* be alive.

I gulp and look up at Everleigh and Lia who are now embracing, happy tears painting their cheeks.

My sisters are okay. I'm okay. Callan is okay. Or he would be if he wasn't sobbing like a baby. What aren't they telling me? And where am I?

"Cal?" I look back at him. That goofy smile on his face too. "Where am I? What happened?"

"You're in the hospital, my love. You were shot in the back, but you're going to be fine now. Just fine."

I frown. "Al?"

"In custody. Thanks to you. And he's going away for a very long time if Skyla Redmond has anything to say on the matter —and she has lots, believe me."

I wiggle my shins, something is squeezing them, and they itch like a thousand bugs are crawling on them.

"What's on my legs?" I ask, starting to feel panic rise in my gut.

"Oh, I'm sorry, I didn't mean—" Addy trails off as she sees me scowling, and I begin to shove at the blanket around my hips.

I see the wraps with air tubes leading to a box hanging on the bottom of the bed.

"What are those? Get them off me."

"Calm down, baby. Let me grab a nurse."

"Get those damn things off me now!" I cry, and shove at Callan to do as I ask.

"Ok, Eady, ok. Just chill your jets," Lia answers and begins to unstrap the leg wraps. Relief comes as my legs "breathe" from the constricting, sweaty material. "They had them on to help with the circulation in your legs since you've been bed-bound for days now." Lia has the kindness to rub my legs for me, making the itching practically disappear, that inner nurse taking over her.

"Oh, thank you, Lia. I love you. I could kiss you." I sigh in gratitude.

"Well, thanks but I'd rather you kissed him instead." She winks and points to Callan, who grins at me.

Cal leans in then and seeks out my lips, kissing them with a softness that I've come to love. I moan in content as he pulls back and gives me another beautiful smile.

"You worried us, my angel." When I frown, he elaborates. "When you were shot, the bullet hit your spleen. You were knocking on death's door when the helicopter took you away."

"You died twice before you ever got here, Eden," Addy informs me and takes my hand, crying again.

Oh wow.

"The surgery began quickly. They were able to stop the bleeding, but we were told that you might not…" Cal trails off with a gulp.

"You lost a lot of blood, and they weren't sure if you had any brain damage. We weren't given the best prognosis for survival," Lia answers.

All is quiet as I look at the faces of my loved ones surrounding me. Their concern for me, their love for me.

"Guys. Do you honestly think I would leave you all without a fight?"

Everleigh is the first to speak up, "Of course not, Eady. You're our backbone. Core Four, remember?"

I smile, getting one out of all of them. "Core Four. Where would I be without my sisters? And my handsome knight in shining armor?" I squeeze Cal's hand in my own.

My knight looks down. "Sorry excuse for a rescue attempt."

"You did stop him, though. You stopped him from raping me, Cal." I cup his cheek, wincing as the needle in my hand bends with my movement.

"But he shot you, and I was helpless to do anything but watch you die in my arms."

"I came back, didn't I?" He nods in response, and I finger the tear running down his cheek. "Besides, I'm a phoenix, remember? I always rise from the ashes. Even death can't hold me."

The girls all laugh, save for Addy who rolls her eyes. "Drama queen," she teases and leans in to kiss my cheek. "You scared the hell out of us, Eden."

"I'd take another bullet any day to protect those I love."

"Hey, don't be so hasty," Everleigh scolds and flicks a finger at my foot.

"Well, first things first...do I get to eat? Because I'm fucking starving."

17

EDEN

ONE MONTH LATER...

I laugh, "No, Cal, fish sticks are fine." I tickle Caleb's little nose and then kiss it, getting a giggle from him. "Who doesn't like fish sticks?" I shrug at Caleb and get another sweet cackle from him. I hug him to me and kiss his fragrant shower-fresh hair. God, I love this kid.

Cal wrinkles his nose at us, and I stick my tongue out at him. Cal raises his hand. "This guy right here doesn't. So, I guess it's chicken nuggets for me," he mumbles as he turns the airfryer on. "Babe, sit, I got it." He points to the barstool, and I huff.

"Callan, I'm fine. I feel great." I touch my nose to Maximus's and set him in Caleb's lap, where he loves to lay.

"That's because you're still on narcotics," he adds when I move to embrace him and inhale his heavenly fragrance as I plant my nose into the middle of his t-shirt clad chest. He kisses my forehead and enfolds me in his arms.

"Am not. I'm healing nicely," I add as I look up and kiss his chin.

"You are, and when you've healed up completely," he whispers as his hands fall to my short-covered ass cheeks and grab, "I'm gonna enjoy coating your insides with essence d'Cal."

I laugh heartily before his lips fall on mine for a soft, sensual kiss.

We are pulled from our moment when the doorbell rings. Max barks, and Cal says, "I got it."

I move back over to Caleb, helping him with his cup. I kiss his cheek again, and when I pull away, I see Cal entering the kitchen again. Only his face is solemn, followed by my sisters, their guys, Kieran, Rian, and DA Skyla Redmond.

"Oh wow, we're having a party." I clear my throat and try to calm my suddenly racing heart. "Wish I would've known." I look down to the big shirt of Callan's I'm covered in, braless, and my Daisy Duke shorts that barely cover my ass cheeks. I pull the shirt down, self-consciously.

Skyla smiles at me and motions to the living room. "You might want to sit down, Eden."

Oh God! What can that possibly mean? Nothing good, right? I look to Cal, who moves Caleb over to a little table in the corner to color, while I walk into the living room and take a seat next to Lia and Addy. They smile and take my hands. I look to Cal who sits across from me on the ottoman of my L-shaped sectional and pats my knee. He hands Max over to me. The pup seems to feel my tension and curls into the crook of my arm.

"Wanna start, Sergeant Greene?" Sky asks.

Rian smiles over at me and nods. "Eden, Al is going to be put away for a long time. Enzo, too, if we have any say in the matter. So I don't want you worrying anymore about hiding in the shadows. Every last connection to the Atlanta mafia is going down."

I feel tears hit my cheeks, and my sisters squeeze my hands as I look at their grinning faces.

"But we found some connections...and you and the girls deserved to hear the truth and have closure," Kieran adds and nods to a file in his hand.

"Lia, Addy, Ev, Eden, you all knew that Vince had a hand in bringing you into the club for a reason, even if you weren't sure the reason at the time. Eden, you weren't as in control of that as you originally thought."

When I frown at Kieran, he continues, "See, thing is, Vince was so obsessed with having 'little birdies' in his menagerie that he didn't care the lengths he had to go to get them there. Eden and Addy, what he did to get y'all...was downright diabolical."

My blood stills as I ask, "He killed my parents, didn't he?"

Kieran looks down but nods as his eyes come back up to mine. I knew it. Deep down, I knew he was behind their car accident.

"The breaks were cut, Al confirmed it. Vince told him what he'd done in order to get you in," Rian answers.

"And *my* parents, he—?" Addy asks, gulping her sorrow down as I squeeze her hand.

"Yes, Vince had the fire started. He knew your father, Addy, and decided you were the next, following Eden."

Jesus.

"Ev, he threatened to kill us to get you involved. He relished having the daughter of the police chief in his club. Lia, you were simply a win/win for him, seeing as you were the daughter of Giordano, who owed Vince and Antonio a lot of money. He loved having something else to dangle over your father's head."

Ev and Lia inhale sharply, looking at one another in equal parts anger and pain.

"When his obsession with Eden continued to become more and more unhealthy, Al started questioning his sanity—and loyalty—and knew Vince would be the downfall of the entire organization if he continued down the path he was on. He had to go."

"So, he convinced Marco to murder him," I finish.

Rian and Kieran both nod, and I feel Cal's big palm squeeze my thigh. I look at him and see sadness and understanding in his beautiful eyes.

"Al didn't account for Vince leaving everything in his will to one Eden Riser, his only living relative, following the demise of his adopted daughter, Cordelia Perelli. So he hid in the shadows, waiting for Enzo to come of age, and when he did, he brought him into the fold. By then, Geraci was rotting in prison, fearing retaliation from Costanza. Then the Cervellis were murdered by the rival gang, the Spinellis. That left you, Eden, and all the money you girls had accumulated over the last decade."

"But he didn't know we'd been investigating him for the last four years," Skyla adds in. "That accident you and Landry were in, Lia, was no accident. They've been at you ladies for years. His business is a sham, and he's been laundering money, hauling drugs and illegal weapons, and committing murders and fraud for decades now. His reign is over."

I look around at my sisters, all of us are tight-lipped, solemn, but also relieved.

I'm the first to speak. "I'm so sorry," I say first looking to Addy, Ev, then Lia.

I'm embraced in our group hug, and we begin to sob, for all the loss, all the pain, all the suffering we endured at the hands of Vincent Perelli and his fellow mobsters.

We are all spent when everyone decides to go, needing some time to process what we've just heard.

Kieran motions for me to follow him as everyone goes before him. He pulls me to the hallway and sighs.

"Al said a few things that I thought you might want to know...regarding Marco."

I nod for him to continue, not sure what else I can handle right now, but know I want to hear everything; once and for all the truth will be out there.

"You always wondered what hold Vince had over Marco," he eludes. We've talked prior to now about things, Kieran and I. Vince. Marco. The Devil's Playground. "It was Marco's sister he held over his head. His little sister, Emma, the last person alive from Marco's family. After rescuing a young Marco from the wrath of the Spinellis when their father got killed for unpaid back payments, he used her as leverage should Marco ever get out of line."

I cover my mouth and my lips quiver, thinking of how awful that would be.

"She was just ten years old and Marco sixteen when Vince took them in. If it weren't for him, hers and Marco's fate would have been death, for sure. He felt beholden to Vince, as you can probably understand."

I nod. "Thank you for telling me, Kieran."

He gives me a nod and turns to leave before I grab his hand and stop him.

"Hey, what happened to her?"

Kieran smiles. "She's under witness protection now. She's safe. For whatever reason, Vince never hurt her. He gave her to a good family who cared well for her and raised her as their own." He shrugs, and I thank God for the mercy shown to the little girl, grateful that one of Vince's "little doves" never felt his wrath.

I don't eat while Cal feeds Caleb, saying nothing the entire time, even when Cal puts Caleb to bed later. I feel far away, distant, my mind a million miles away, years ago to the perfect family and past I had...before Vincent Perelli ripped so many lives apart in his pursuit of becoming the Devil we knew him as.

"Hey," a deep voice interrupts my internal reverie, and a warm palm covers my back.

I look up into the handsome face that never fails to steal my breath and the deepest glacier eyes I've ever seen.

"You ok?" Callan asks, even knowing that I'm not.

I reach out and cup his perfectly-sculpted square jaw, running my fingertips over his beard. I don't answer, he doesn't expect me to. I trace the lines of his neck, his collarbone, his chest. I cup his pec in one palm and let my other hand settle on his hip.

Suddenly, his arms wrap around me and hold me so tightly to his frame, I'm convinced I'll melt into him and we'll become one being.

When he finally pulls back enough to look at me, I gaze up into his eyes again, mine shimmering with unshed tears.

"Make love to me, Cal," I whisper.

He says nothing, just simply leans in to kiss me. It's slow, sensual, soft. Softer than any kiss I've ever had, softer than Marco's lips ever were, and a hell of a lot softer than Vince's.

I absorb his love, his passion—my gentle giant of a man— even as his hands begin to rove my body. I'm amazed at how much I've opened up to him over these last several months, how I don't flinch at his touch, how receptive I've been to having his body on top of me, loving me, holding me, penetrating me. It's as if my past isn't so. As if I was never raped or beaten or tormented beyond all sanity.

I whimper as his tongue caresses mine, so unhurried, so

sweet, so giving. I thrust my own into his mouth, loving how it unfurls ribbons of desire deep within me.

Cal carries me to my bed and aligns his frame with mine, careful to keep himself above me, his massive body centimeters from mine as he shucks his clothes and continues to kiss me.

I love how his hands own my curves while he undresses me, the way my skin shivers at his touch, the way my belly flutters in anticipation of our sexual union.

When he enters me, I cry out in wanton desire, my womanhood reveling in being taken and conquered by him. I grip his shoulders as I wrap my legs around his hips, anchoring him to me like he's my lifeline. Pulling him ever closer, the need to feel his dominance a stark contrast to the fear I always had when being overcome by Vince.

Cal loves me, loves my body, thrusts within me, driving me toward my salvation from the demons that threaten me still. And I answer his moans with my own, looking into his eyes as he makes love to me as I asked him to.

When we succumb to one another, tears fall from my eyes and he kisses them away. He spills himself inside me and I absorb him, loving that he's the stoic man I've always needed. The warrior angel that will fight my battles with me, the one who'll chase the darkness away.

"I love you," he says, "I will always love you. He may have taken everything from you, my sweet Eden, but you're mine now, and I won't stop until I've given it all back."

EPILOGUE
CALLAN

SIX MONTHS LATER...

I grin at Eden as I take her hand and we move into the tattoo shop.

"Eden, are you sure about this?"

"I've never been more sure in my life, my love." She leans in and gives me a long, slow, sexy kiss that leaves me wanting more than I can give her in a shop filled with people.

I laugh. "Alright. It's your choice then."

She's called back by the guy named Lou, and I take her hand as she takes her seat. She pulls her shorts up as Lou tucks the towel, covering her crotch.

I feel my jaw tick and my brows furrow as I look him over. He's in my territory, and I almost growl as I watch his hands on her.

"Down, tiger," Eden warns and giggles as Lou readies the station with ink and the stencil that's been prepared.

"It's still not too late to change your mind, my sweet."

"I'm not going to." She looks at me confidently as I watch

the little stencil attach to her skin with my initials C.M. in bold, thick font. "I think you're more anxious than I am."

"Not anxious, just want to make sure you're ok with having my initials on your body for the rest of your life."

"Only until I tire of them and have them covered by my next book hero," she winks.

"Ha," I belt out a laugh and take her hand as Lou begins. "These will be the *last* initials to cross your skin. I assure you of that fact."

"If you say so," she teases again.

"Hey, you better be sure because I only intend to have my heart branded once and only once."

She gives me a funny look, her beautiful brown eyes dancing in humor. She has no idea. I leap for joy on the inside.

Lou isn't between her legs long, good thing for him, because my anticipation grows as the minutes extend into a half hour. I pace, I can't help myself. I can hardly be contained.

When Eden pulls on my hand to chill my jets, I huff. She's completely clueless and thinks my frustrations are because another man is seeing a part of her only I see now.

As Lou finishes, he looks up at me with a nod, and I come to Eden's front, squatting to see the work.

C.M. now covers the scar where V.P. once stood in red welts on the sensitive skin of Eden's groin. We found an amazing plastic surgeon who repaired the mark on her skin and gave it enough time to heal so that we could "rebrand" her. I smile, pride and love swelling in my heart.

"Does it look good?" Eden asks in anticipation.

"Indeed! But not as good as this is gonna look."

I bow to one knee and pull out the ring that's been heavy in my pocket for weeks now, showcasing a big solitaire to the woman I'm head over heels in love with.

"Cordelia Adaleden Riser, I, Callan Oliver Manning, can't live another day without asking you to be my wife. The sun was never brighter, the sky never bluer, and my heart never fuller than when you came into my life. I know nothing is ever certain, and there are battles still to be fought, but if you promise to be mine, I'll always love you with every beat of my heart." I replace the poem I wrote into my pocket and thrust the ring up at her.

I smile up into the most gorgeous face I've ever seen, her beauty never ceasing to stop me in my tracks. Tears are glistening in those chocolate-brown eyes and a hand covers her mouth, but she's bringing it down as she begins to laugh.

I start to frown as her laughter echoes around me, my confidence is shaken, rattled as the sound peals and dampens my mood. "Dammit, Eden, this isn't really the response I was going for." I look around at the faces staring back at us and sigh. I stand and cross my arms over my chest. "What the *hell* is so funny?"

"Oh, Cal, I'm sorry. I'm not—" Another round of laughs grates on me, and my patience is a thread away from snapping.

Eden sits up slightly, pulling the towel from her short-covered crotch and motions to Lou, who is still on a stool in front of her. "Cal, I'm sorry, but I never expected to be proposed to while I'm spread-eagle before a tattoo artist. That's all." She's trying to hold back another laugh, and I look down to see Lou turning ten shades of red.

"Jesus, Lou, could you give us a sec?" I sigh and throw my hands up.

"Damn, man, I do apologize, but it's not like you gave me a chance to get out of the way." He has a point. I kinda went in for the kill. "Eden, do you like your tattoo?" Lou's attention is now on Eden. He's placed a mirror on her leg and she looks down at it. He snaps a picture and removes himself as I growl out my irritation to his retreating form.

My mood is furious now as I blame myself for ruining this perfect moment and look down, knowing I'm unable to salvage it. I feel Eden's hands on my beard-covered cheeks. I'm simply ready to pay my regular tattoo guy for the job and get the hell out of dodge when I feel lips on my chin.

"Hey, don't be mad. I wasn't laughing at you. I was laughing at the situation."

"Well, I feel like a fucking idiot," I whisper even as she moves into my opening arms.

"Please don't. You have no reason to. You have my full attention. Do you want to finish your proposal?" Her eyes are playful, and I feel a faint smile tugging at the corners of my mouth.

"How do you know I wasn't finished?"

"Because you have a flare for the dramatic, and I know you have something else up your sleeve."

"Oh you do, huh? You're the one who's dramatic, and you damn well know it."

"Touché, my love."

"Fine. But can we go to the bathroom or something at least. I feel like I'm in the center ring of a three-ring circus."

She giggles again but shakes her head. "You're gonna propose to me in a bathroom?"

Dammit, this was all so much better laid out in my head. I close my eyes and count to five.

"Eden," I grip her face in my palms and look deeply into her eyes. "I fell in love with you in a strip club." Jesus, *really*? I hear snorts behind me. "Actually, I fell in love with you when I saw you in your masquerade mask." Not any better. "Fuck. I love you, okay. I love everything about you. Your sweet side, your naughty side, your strong side *and* your weak side. I love that you get me and put me in my place. I love that you've touched my heart." I move the hand of hers that I've pulled over my heart to raise my shirt. I've been hiding this tattoo for two days and now I can finally show it to her. The word RISE is there in the same bold font as my initials are on her flesh, and it's right over my heart. "Rise is a word that makes me think of you and how strong you are, of how we met and its symbolism to you...and to me. You see." I point to the R. "R. Roxie. I. S. is. E. Eden. Roxie is Eden. Rise."

Her brows go up, and she smiles brightly, understanding my meaning and why I did this.

"It also means to rise, like my sexy little phoenix has in the face of adversity. Time and time again. And now you don't have to be alone to do so. You'll never be alone again. Do me the honor of being mine, being Mrs. Callan Manning. Marry me, Eady?"

She nods, looking like I just handed her the moon. I lean in to kiss her sweet lips, the lips that tear a hole inside me and put me back together all at the same time, lips that soothe and torture, lips that comfort and seduce. Lips that I love, that belong to the woman I can't be without. Eden is the love I've always wanted but never knew it until I met her and she opened my heart to a new world. A world of sin, secrets, satisfaction, suffering, and salvation. A world of love, hope, justice, and happiness. A world with dual meanings, double the pleasure, double the rewards.

With the past behind us, we can now move forward into the future. And I want so much for our future, starting with a playmate for Maximus and Caleb.

I think I'll work on that first.

Eden

I smile as I stop in front of the headstone I've seen dozens of times before. God, it stills my breath even now, but I've come to terms with our sordid past, our sordid love, our sordid life together.

Even now, almost eleven years have passed, and my soul can finally let go of what was done to me, to us.

Cal stands at my side as I look down on Marco's gravestone. His big arm is around me as I place the flowers on my former lover's grave and step back. Cal knows this is hard for me still. The pain of losing my first love in the way I did, the anger at him for keeping things from me, all the unsaid words between us.

But I'm healing and growing, and Cal has been by my side, overseeing my progression.

I look up into his handsome face as he wipes my tears from my cheeks.

I can finally forgive the man who freed me from my bonds as Vince's captive, even if his motives weren't always selfless, in the arms of the man who loves me beyond measure. I have learned what true love is, what letting go means, and what unconditional love represents. Loving one despite their flaws, despite their scars, despite being marked by the sins of their pasts.

Callan has helped heal my still-raw wounds, and I will love him forever for it.

I feel a presence behind us and turn to see a woman.

It doesn't take me but two seconds to realize who she is, and I gasp.

The dark-haired beauty smiles at me. She doesn't know who I am, or so I think until she steps forward and takes my hand.

"You must be Eden." I flinch and look around cautiously. "It's alright. I wouldn't be here if it weren't safe. Special Agent Greene sent me."

I know I'm gaping as I look her face over. She looks so much like Marco that it overwhelms my senses.

"I just wanted to meet the woman my brother cared so much for."

I'm spellbound as I glance from the woman to my fiancé and back. She laughs. "Marco sent me letters, telling me about you. You freed us both, you know. And I want to thank you for your bravery." When I shake my head in confusion, she continues. "If it weren't for you, I'd still be in hiding from them. Al never knew my whereabouts. Why Vince didn't tell him, I'll never know, but Special Agent Greene and I thought it best to keep me in witness protection until we knew for sure. Now, he's going to prison for a long time, and I'm free to live my life, safe from their retribution... thanks to you."

I'm pulled into a tight hug and my arms wrap around her, feeling an instant connection to someone I've never met.

"Here," she says and pulls an envelope from her purse, "you should read this."

I look at the handwriting; it's definitely Marco's.

"Let's get together soon. I'd love to talk to you some more."

I'm still gaping as she walks away and Cal elbows me, grinning.

"Looks like you're still turning little birdies into phoenixes, Ms. Riser," he says, admiration sparkling in his eyes.

"And here I thought I'd leave my past where it died." I look regretfully down at the letter from my former lover. I open it hesitantly, as if it's a bomb that needs disarming, while Cal patiently waits.

My eyes scroll through it, and I know I won't be able to read it.

"Here, do you mind?" My hands shake as I pass it to my handsome fiance.

"Of course not." His grin gives nothing away.

"Dear Emma, my precious baby sister,

It is with great sadness that I say: This letter will be my last. I must ask your forgiveness for what I am about to do. But as a former captive, yourself, you must understand the extent of my love and that I can no longer simply stand aside and continue to watch the man who holds all our lives in his hands go unpunished for his evil deeds. One day, I hope you can look back and realize that it *had* to be done. For you, for me, for Eden, for all the innocents held in Vincent's grasp. Love makes you do things. I pray you'll see what I mean, eventually. Do not grieve for me. Live your life as it should be lived, freely. And one day when you can, find Eden, meet her, and tell her just how deeply my love went for you both. I wish I could have been there to see you two fly free. I bet it was such a glorious sight.

With all my love, Marco."

When he finishes, I'm sobbing and apologize for my mess. "I'm sorry, Cal."

"Hey," he takes my face in his palms and kisses my nose, "I know you want to let your past go. But there are things that you deserve to know, Eden. You deserve closure, and perhaps this is how you can get it. What kind of man would I be to deny you that?"

"I don't deserve you, Callan Manning."

He shakes his head. "You deserve everything I have to offer and so much more. You still don't see yourself as I do, as Marco did, as all the women whose lives you've helped fortify do. You are so much more than just a brave and beautiful woman, E."

"That's right. I'm a fucking phoenix." I smirk, getting a laugh out of the man I adore with my entire soul.

"Exactly, Rox!. You're a fucking phoenix... and don't you ever forget that, my love."

A soul-scorching kiss is planted on my lips, and I soar on the wings of the phoenix I've gone through Hell to become. I will power on. Because I'm strong. Because I can. Because sin didn't break me, nor the Devil...

Even death couldn't hold me.

I am a phoenix, and I will continue to fly.

THE END

EXTENDED EPILOGUE
EDEN

"...So, it is with great honor on this ten year anniversary of its founding that we welcome to the stage for one final performance, the founding madams of RISE: Madam Roxie, Madam Isis, Madam Siren, and Madam Ember," Zeus announces over the overhead speaker.

The song "Back in Black" by AC/DC comes on; it's a remix, and the beat is hot and pumping just like we like it. Lia, Everleigh, Addison, and I take the stage like old times and move to our respective poles while swaying our hips. We're decked out in our masks, wigs, tiaras, and sparkling costumes we had made just for our big night. This will be our final performance as madams, and we aren't stripping tonight, much to both ours —and our men's—delights. We caged birdies are finally free, free to indulge in the art of dance, like we've always loved; the love of expression that brought us all together all those years ago.

I see my sexy man, my real-life book hero, Callan Manning, grinning lovingly at me. The desire is tamed—for a moment, anyway—and pride fills his eyes. He knows this is bittersweet for me. It's my final hoorah in the club that me and my sisters founded ten years ago today. Sure, I'll still be helping on the business end. Hell, it's my club, I will always have a hand in it. But now it's time for me to focus my life where it really matters, outside the walls of my self-imposed cage, with my family and my man.

Me and the girls decided to make this a charity-type event to raise money for Hope House, along with a few other local charities. We brought in some big names in the entertainment world of Atlanta, including several of the Gladiators pro football players: Brett McFadden, Travis Redmond, Paxton Guthrie, and Quillan Layton to name a few. Gods they call themselves and gods they are in looks and legend both; with their presence, our club is at max capacity and the amount of money we've raised is unprecedented. It was actually Lia's idea, and she threw out the DA's name first before saying, "Hey, isn't she married to that football player? Maybe we could get him involved somehow."

From there, the party just increased in size and extravagance. Raffle tickets were sold for a trip to a beach house in Cancun, along with a new car and an all expense paid Gladiators game. I tell ya what: these football players know how shit's done. In less than a month we've sold close to a hundred thousand tickets. Hope House will be funded for decades at this rate, and the night isn't over yet. We've drawn quite a large amount of interest, and I have a feeling we won't be having many "slow" nights for years to come.

Lia, Addy, Ev, and I dance our hearts out, swaying to the rhythm and wrapping our poles in perfect synchronization before we do our own free-style moves as the music morphs into one of our favorite Billie Eilish tunes.

We weave our spells, the madams of stripping, the moves

and allure we're known for, all the while my eyes don't leave my soon-to-be husband's.

Applause rains around us as we bow then look at each other before Madam Siren grabs the mic and begins serenading our audience with her notorious and beautiful, siren-like voice. She belts out a slow and sexy version of "Crazy in Love" by Beyonce. I watch as Landry's eyes mist over, a sailor caught in her fishnet for sure.

Afterward, we come off the stage and intermingle into the crowd. We shake hands, sign autographs, and are finally ushered to the front tables where our men are, along with Skyla and Travis Redmond, Brett and Madi McFadden, Pax and Rebecca Guthrie, and Quil and Veda Layton. They all sit drinks in hand.

Zeus is joking with the other Zeus, fighting for dibs.

"But I see and know *all* that goes on in the club, you—what —throw *thunderbolts*, c'mon? Clearly, I'm the true Zeus." *Our* Zeus flexes a bicep and gets a snort from all the Gladiators.

"You *obviously* don't know our QB or you'd be careful, imposter Zeus," Travis "Ares" Redmond jokes.

"Yeah, thunderbolts aren't all he's known for throwing," Pax insists. "You should go back to your cameras."

"Fine, fine, but only because I know my madams are well cared for." Zeus winks over at Luca, Landry, Callan, and Ethan.

Tall, dark, and handsome Quillan Layton eyes Zeus before raising his chin. "Leave us, mortal." It's no wonder he's called Hades as his narrowed gaze watches my employee walk off. Zeus turns at the last minute and shoots Quil the bird, causing Sky and Becca to burst in laughter and the rest of us follow suit.

"Pass the guacamole over, Poseidon," Travis says and elbows Paxton.

Sheesh, these athletes take their god names seriously, I see.

"I'd say it was a good turn out," Ev states and interlocks her hand through Luca's.

"Great idea, sis," Addy looks to Lia, who grins over at Landry. Ethan rubs Addy's shoulder and kisses it softly.

"It really was. Who knew a ten-year anniversary celebration would turn out like this," I state and smile at Callan.

"And we got to meet *these* guys," Landry says, motioning to the Gladiators who, in turn, give him a nod. Although I know deep down he enjoys college ball better than pro, it is quite a treat to make their acquaintance. Their wives remind me of my sisters; they all seem to have a close friendship.

"Sooo…" Cal whispers in my ear, "Madam Roxie, wanna go see what's happening in the garden of pain?" That sexy smirk tells me all I need to know, and I give him a brow raise.

"I'm always in the mood to whip my man into shape," I sass.

"I thought Roxie had reined it in a bit," Veda teases, and I elbow her.

"Oh, she has. No worries, *Obsidian*, I'll go easy on him." I give her a wink and take Cal's outstretched hand. "Y'all don't wait up. And enjoy the rest of the party."

I wave to more people who are dancing and watching the next performers come out on stage as Cal leads me to the back hallway to my former room here at RISE.

I motion that I don't have my key on me with a frown, and suddenly, the door jolts open. I look up at the camera over the frame and give the thumbs up to Zeus, the all-knowing.

The room looks foreign to me now, as if I'm in an alternate universe all of a sudden. My eyes fall on the walls of crops, floggers, and devices I've used over the years on countless men, at the bed that was as much my prison as my freedom. I take a deep breath in and feel my fiancé's large hand come to my back.

"You ok, my love?" he asks.

I turn to him and nod. "Fine, just… It's weird being in here now."

After all, it's been so long.

"Wanna go home instead?" he asks, and I shake my head.

"No, I'm good. I'm in here with *you*." I trace the lines of his gorgeous face, over the mouth and beard I love, getting a grin from him.

"No pressure, Madam Rox. You know you own every inch of me. You say, 'Jump' and I say, 'How high, your highness?'"

I snort because as much as I've taken this alpha down a peg or two, he owns me as much as I do him. But that snort dies on my lips as Cal leans in to kiss me.

I get wrapped up in his smell, his size, his power over me as I throw my arms around his neck and melt into his big frame. It's almost magical how much I've grown to love it. The girl who feared being dominated is now gone in the wake of my giant model.

"I can relinquish control…"

Cal cocks his head thoughtfully.

"Tie me up. You play the Dom in Roxie's room of pain tonight."

Cal scoffs. "Seriously? You trust me enough to let me do that?"

"I'm about to become your wife. Of course I do."

He looks me over, assessing me for a moment before moving to the rack to grab a set of cuffs.

I don't protest as I'm led to the bed and laid down. Cal pulls my hands to the bed frame and restrains them in the cuffs. I give my soon-to-be husband a grin, and he returns it before his lips cover my exposed flesh in languid kisses that have my skin quivering. I moan as his hands follow suit, and he moves lower down my body. His kisses leave a searing trail in their wake, hovering at my lower belly.

"Do you know how much I love you, Eden?" He looks up, his eyes so tender.

"Enough to absolve me of all my darkest sins?" I ask in turn.

"Absolutely." He spreads my thighs, and his lips settle over the former mark that is now covered by his initials. I sigh in both relief and desire equally. "You were the first to unmask me. See beneath the facade."

"So, you're saying I conquered you, Rox?" That delicious crooked smile is back, and it makes me eager to have him inside me.

"You did, big guy. You destroyed the mask. Freed the phoenix."

"So long as that phoenix doesn't fly without me."

I laugh even as his tongue traces my groin, lapping at the sensitive flesh that aches for him.

"Are you kidding? You're my wings, Cal. A bird can't fly without her wings."

ONE MONTH LATER...

"Mmm, Cal, the girls will be here any minute," I protest even as Callan takes my lips again.

"Then we have plenty of time," he teases. His hand grips the ties of my bikini bottoms and pulls them off me, plopping the wet garment onto the side of the pool. "Whoops," he chuckles as his mouth falls to my neck, and I whimper.

I feel his fingers tickle my thigh before he's probing the entrance of my now-bare lower body.

My head falls back as I reach for the crotch of his swim trunks.

"Oh shit," I moan as his thick finger thrusts inside me and grip his hard cock.

"Yeah, baby. I wanna be inside you," he growls as he tugs at his trunks then plops them down next to mine.

We're frenzied as he lines himself up and thrusts deep, in one smooth motion, and I grip his broad, naked shoulders as my head falls back once more.

I cry out with each lunge of his hips while his lips on my neck destroy my resolve and shiver as his shaft fills me in glorying pleasure. I whimper as his mouth encloses my nipple and pulls.

"Shit, Cal, ahh, they're so sensitive, damn," I whine even as my womanhood clenches him, and he growls again, thrusting deeper and faster.

"I know, Eady, it's sexy AF. Come for me, angel. I can't hold back much longer."

And I do. Splitting apart as Cal's cock hits my walls in just the right spot—as it always tends to do. It's like it has a built-in sonar where my G-spot is concerned.

My husband's mouth covers mine in an attempt to stifle my pleasure cry from echoing off the rooftop bar area. He climaxes with me and clutches me tight as he shivers and spasms.

When we finally come down from our sexual high, Callan rests his forehead on mine and grins at me.

"Fuck, I swear our sex life is even better now that you're pregnant, wifey."

"Or you're just hornier, Daddy." I chide and finger his pec.

He shrugs, and I laugh. "That or you're just even more irresistible with my baby in your belly." His big palm cups my lower abdomen, and the love I see in his blue eyes makes tears come to mine. I can't wait to be the mother of his child, hold the sweet babe in my arms, and see this look in his eyes forever.

"Fuck, is that sex I smell in the air?" A familiar voice calls, and I grunt.

"Shit," Cal grumbles and grabs his trunks from the poolside. I follow suit, and we quickly cloth ourselves beneath the water.

"Dammit, Addy, you freak. Give us a second," I adjust my bathing suit top and look up to see Addison and Ethan moving toward the big table we have set up for today.

I look back to my sexy man, kiss and hug him before swimming to the ladder. We get out and grab our towels to dry off.

"Jesus, you two. Now the kids can't swim in there because of y'all. Gross!" Ev says with a sneer.

Cal shrugs and gets a laugh out of Landry who sets the pool floats to the side, Aliana on his hip.

"Actually, semen can't survive more than a few seconds in a pool..." Sam says carrying a bag and a bowl of macaroni salad, "I researched it once. But that doesn't mean I want to swim in my brother's." Sam smacks Cal's bicep with a scowl, and I laugh as I greet Caleb with a kiss to his cheek.

"Careful what you say around little ears," Lia says pointing to the kids. "And she's right. There's no worries about microscopic baby makers. Within seconds, they were dead."

"I mean, mine might be Herculean though, so let's eat first, just to be sure," Cal brags and flexes a bicep, getting my female parts to humming again.

Luca rolls his eyes, Rory, Corvin, and Gavin in tow, and Addy raises a brow at him.

"Good thing, you don't have to worry about getting knocked up twice, baby," Ethan says and wraps an arm around Addy, who balks at his Freudian slip.

"Wait, what? Why?" Ev asks, hands on her hips.

"Add... are you?" I ask.

The big smile on her face is answer enough and Lia, Ev, and I all squeal as we pull her into our Core Four hug.

"OMG, how long have you known?" Lia asks.

"We literally just found out last week. Eth is over the moon."

We squeeze her again, and Ev and Lia's eyes are watering.

"Well," I begin. "Looks like you and I are gonna be pregnant together then?" I say to Addy, and her jaw drops.

"What? Seriously? Oh my God, Eden!" Addy squeals, followed by Lia and Everleigh.

We're hugging again, and there's not a dry eye in our foursome when we pull out of one another's embrace.

"Girls, this is incredible. Can you believe it?" Ev asks.

We're holding shoulders, our heads leaned in to one another's.

"I'm so damn excited for y'all," Lia says and covers her mouth, her emotions high.

"To think, our lives were so horrible ten years ago. And look how far we've come," I say, reverently.

"We all got our knights in shining armor," Addy says.

"I love you girls," Ev says and puckers her lips.

"Core four, sisters. Always and forever," I answer.

THE END... no seriously this time ;-)

ACKNOWLEDGMENTS

I want to thank God for the gift of writing: without Him, I would be nothing.

To my husband for all you do so that I can stay on my computer for hours—and sometimes, days—on end.

And last but *certainly* not least, I want to give a shout out to my girls: Nicole, Kali, and Cara for all the awesome collaborating that went into this series. The long and (most times, winded) VM's, the video chats, the laughs, the fun *and* sadness of writing these girls—It has been an ABSOLUTE blast and I can't wait to do more with y'all in the future.

Writing Eden's story was heartbreaking at times because as a fellow sexual assault victim, I felt her pain in more ways than one. The Me Too movement and RAINN are near and dear to my heart.

Therefore, a portion of my profits from this book (20%) will go to both the organizations, so that awareness is garnered, our voices can be heard, and victims of assault can be supported.

Like the girls in these books, never back down, always RISE up. You are a fucking *phoenix* and don't you *ever* forget it.

SNEAK PEEK- QUINLIN AND KIERAN'S STORY

Here's a sneak peek at a Sin and Secrets spin-off by authors Nicole Rodrigues and Kali Brixton... COMING SOON

QUINLIN

I laugh with Emlyn in my arms, perched on my hip, and Magnolia's birthday gift hanging off my other as Em's little hand reaches forward to ring the doorbell to the Laurent house. Within seconds, Magnolia's husband, Landry, opens the door with a panicked look on his face and my smile fades.

"What happened?"

"She's not leaving!" Landry whisper yells. "Everyone is going to be here in an hour, but she's been in the bathroom all morning."

"The bathroom? What happened?" I ask as I put Emy down on the floor. She waddles inside, searching out her best friend, their daughter of practically the same age, Aliana.

"I don't know, she's claiming it was one too many glasses of wine at *RISE* last night. We haven't been in a while and thought we needed a change of scenery because...she's getting frustrated," Landry sighs, running his hand down the front of his face.

"Not getting pregnant?" I whisper, shaking my head, feeling so sorry for the woman who has become one of my closest friends. I know Lia has Addison, Everleigh and Eden, but I've never had girlfriends in my entire life. Getting sucked into the toxic world of my ex-husband's at such a young age, he made sure to cut me off of anyone that might fill my head with thoughts of leaving him, becoming brave enough to do exactly that four years ago. *Leave him.*

"Yeah. I told her it'll happen when it happens. We have Aliana, and she was a miracle to begin with after Lia thought she couldn't have children. You know her though, the—"

"Perfectionist," I finish with a nod. "Addy and Eden are already at the Bistro. Let me see if I can coax her out."

Landry nods as he moves to the side, and I take the stairs up to the master bedroom, opening the door and hearing the sound of vomiting coming from the bathroom.

"Lia?"

"Go away. Let me learn my lesson in peace," she moans. I stand in the doorway of the bathroom and see her on her knees, hovering over the toilet as she vomits again. I rush forward, holding her hair back from her face and smile at her.

"You know when people turn thirty, their hangovers last a few days now, not just a few hours like when you were younger. No one told you that?"

"I'm turning twenty-nine not thirty yet so screw you, Quin," she groans, throwing up again as I turn my nose up to the smell. Yeah, that's definitely a hangover.

"Did Landry take care of you or do I have to kick his butt?"

"Everything I'm eating is coming back up. He tried but...dammit, why did I drink all that wine?"

I take the hair tie off my wrist, collecting her thick brown hair in my fist and tying it back before I walk to the sink and wet a rag. I gently pull her to her feet, pushing the toilet lid down and make her sit as I press the rag to her cheeks and the back of her neck.

"Does this have anything to do with the fact that the gang is getting knocked up like a herd of fertile myrtles and..." I press my lips together, not wanting to divulge the fact that Landry may have let it slip a minute ago. She doesn't look up at me, but her lips press together and I see a tear drop to her bare thigh.

"I'm happy for Everleigh, I am Quinlin, but Landry and I have been trying for so damn long and...how? How did it happen so easily with Aliana?"

"You weren't thinking about it. As much as you wanna say it isn't in that medical brain of yours, getting pregnant is just as much psychological as it is physical. Don't think about it. You and I both know that it happens when you least expect it to," I say with a smirk. That gets a laugh out of her and she nods. "You're young, Magnolia. Enjoy Aliana, be happy you don't have to split your attention and can give it all to her right now. It'll happen when it's meant to happen."

I brush a piece of hair away from her face, and she squeezes my hands, broadening her smile at me.

"And here I am, the supposedly older and wiser one, yet the twenty-four-year-old protege is giving me a life lesson."

"Hey," I scoff, "I haven't been a protege in a long time. In case you forgot, I'm the manager now."

Magnolia laughs and pulls me in for a hug.

"No one else I would trust to continue to run that club like we intended. Although, I am quite disappointed in Danny. He should have cut my butt off long before I entered the Grotto."

"Well, you didn't see the look Landry gave him when he

tried to hold you up off the barstool. He doesn't like Danny very much," I laugh.

"He's protective. As much as he's understanding about it all, the most understanding out of all our men, he's still a man. Possessive and jealous when his wife is half naked dancing on stage, even if her eyes are only on him."

Her blue eyes lift to mine, and my mouth drops open a little, my brows furrowing.

"What...what are you saying?"

"I'm saying I think I may...I may just teach the pole routines and self-defense classes from now on if that's okay with the manager?"

I study her, owing so much to the woman that gave me hope, gave me strength, a way to make a living, skills to defend myself, the career I'm now striving for at the GBI and smile at her.

"I think if we had a full-time teacher like you, that club can become something none of y'all imagined it could be. They'll learn from the best." I pull her to me in another hug and then my nose scrunches, pulling away. "Now you smell like crap, so let's get you cleaned up and to lunch with the girls. We have more than just a birthday to celebrate today."

KIERAN

Before I can knock on Landry and Magnolia's front door, it opens and my sister stands there with a big scowl on her face.

"About time, idiot. You almost ruined the surprise. She's two blocks away!" she sasses, pulling me by my t-shirt through the door and slamming it behind me.

I laugh, shaking my head as I say hello to everyone. Saving my parents and Miss Greta for last, my favorite little redhead jumps into my arms from my dad's embrace before the sound of a door opening startles us all to silence. As Magnolia opens it with a shocked look on her face when we all yell "Surprise!", Rory throws out a belated "Prize!" which garners a laugh from everyone. Even though she's only been in my life technically for a few months, it's amazing how quickly something so small can take up such a large space in your heart.

Lia starts to cry as Landry pulls her into a hug, and they whisper back and forth to each other as more tears stream down her face. The moment is touching, maybe to someone who believes in the type of love those two have. It's the same type of love my sister and my best friend have together and now their friends Addison and Ethan—the kind that so many people in my life seem to have found lately, but not me.

I learned a long time ago I'm not meant for that type of life.

Rory catches sight of Aliana, and quickly wiggles out of my hold to go play with her cousin and the little girl that's toddling beside her. Dad gives me a shrug like, "What're you gonna do?" and laughs as I furrow my brows. How the hell did I just get one-upped by a couple of toddlers? With my semi-bruised ego in tow, I turn to head toward the kitchen to grab a drink when the woman behind Magnolia comes into view.

I know Addison and Eden, but who the fuck is...

"Pick your jaw off the floor, brother, unless you plan on mopping up all that drool," Ev teases in a whispered tone, roughly lifting my chin up to close my mouth.

I scoff as I brush her off me and ignore her warning. *Drool, my ass.* Taking in her gorgeous form, I'm sort of mesmerized in a way I haven't been in a long time. Dark hair, curvy back-side... Fuck if this girl wouldn't be worth every drop. From this view, I can only see her side profile, yet it's enough to let me know the entire package is amazing.

Hmmmm. How to play this?

Not like old Kieran used to, dickhead.

It's no secret I was quite the player in college and half of high school—charm a girl, have some fun, then move onto the next one. My sister constantly gave me hell over it for years, but I was serious when I told her last year after our big blowup that I wasn't the same guy who lost his mind at the sight of a beautiful woman all those years ago. Although, seeing this beautiful creature here? Damn it all if my dick isn't singing a slightly different tune right now, though.

You're now the nice, non-dickish version of Kieran. Remember?

Easing my way toward her, I slap on an easy grin and muster up a little charisma. "You must be new to the group. I'm--" Her beautiful side profile turns to face me and I'm met by a set of clear blue eyes I'd recognize anywhere. "Quinlin?" Problem is they're too good for me. *She's* too good for me.

Her eyebrows raise, then lower just as quickly. "Quinlin, huh? What a coincidence, mine is too. I could have...could have sworn your name was Kieran, though," she teases, stuttering a little as she puts her hand out for me to shake, a beautiful rosy blush tinting her cheeks.

I crack a smile at her jab. "Sorry, I didn't..." I pause, taking an appreciative view of her fully, noticing how her figure seems to have filled out over the years. *Wow. What a fox.* "You just look...different." I clear my throat to dislodge the knot that somehow got tangled up in it. *Weird.* "You change your hair or something?"

"It's longer, yeah. I've been growing it out," she says, nodding down to her dark hair hanging a little past her shoulders now. It was a lot shorter when I first met her, a couple of years ago. "And I think it's been awhile. I...I didn't know you'd be here. I thought you'd be...working?"

"Nope, not today. How've you been? You have a baby...right?"

Her cheeks grow noticeably redder as she glances away

quickly then back at me. "I do, yeah, although she's not a baby anymore. She's running around here somewhere. She's...she's a year and a half now." She swallows and looks away from me again, smiling at someone and waving. "I should go find her. See you later, Kieran."

With that, she leaves and I'm stuck in place, dumbfounded. Shit, did I strike a nerve or something? My phone buzzing breaks me out of my thoughts, and I reach for it out of my back pocket and swipe to answer it, stepping out towards the backyard.

"Special Agent Greene," I answer.

"Greene. We want you to come in tomorrow and help with the training. We have some good prospects this round. Three made it through, but there's one in particular that we may ask to shadow you," my commanding officer, Monroe, barks.

Ah, fuck. "Babysitting duty?" I snap. "After the shit I just put behind bars for you, you're assigning me to *babysitting duty*?"

"It's more of a trial run. Whichever of the three we feel is the most qualified will become your partner on the next assignment."

"Fine," I growl, "Who are the stupid assholes?"

"Jeremy Holland, Royce Owens, and Quinlin Kincaid. Kincaid is the one we're hoping pans out."

I glance up, my eyes landing on the gorgeous brunette that's giggling with the little girl I saw tagging around with Aliana earlier, spinning her around. A woman I want with every fiber of my being but know I can never have, can never ruin...despite me ignoring my sister's warning and waltzing right up to her.

"Quinlin Kincaid? Brunette? Blue eyes? Mom?"

"You know her?" Monroe asks.

"Yeah," I sigh. "Yeah, I know her."

"Is that gonna be a problem for you, Greene?"

I shake my head, swallowing down all the doubts I have. I can't ruin this for her. If she's one of the three that means she's more than qualified and this would be a great opportunity for her, a good way to help with her kid. I know from talking to Everleigh that the dad was never in the picture, so she may need this job to help raise a kid on her own.

"No, sir. No problem. If you say she's as qualified as she is, then I trust your judgement. I'll see you tomorrow."

I hang up the call, feeling a smile pull at my lips. I may not be able to make a move on her without my sister cutting my balls off, but spending more time with her because of work is out of my hands. I glance over to my side and see Everleigh make an "I'm watching you" gesture and pat her right hip. Nice to see motherhood hasn't kept her from packing her balisong Osiris along for the barbeque. I pity the poor kid who tries to fuck with Rory.

Watch all you want, sister of mine, that's all you'll be able to do.

Nicole Rodrigues, Kali Brixton, and Shanna Swenson will be bringing you more spin-off stories from the characters of the Sin and Secrets series, so stay tuned!

Curious about DEA Special Agent Octavian Delgado? See how his story unfolds in Ashes to Ashes, book 1 in the new dark duet/series by Nicole Rodrigues. Keep a look out for its release this summer!

I control everything in my life.

Who lives. Who dies.

Who shares my bed. Who I let into my circle.

I wasn't always a monster, I was made into one. I started to thirst for blood at thirteen years old, when I was thrown into a life I thought I never could escape. I started to desire dominance and control six years ago, when I finally took the power back and became the head of *The Ring*: the biggest drug circuit on the East Coast.

Discipline. Patience. Order.

It's what I desire and thrive off of until Octavian Delgado steps into my office. He owes a debt and he wants to pay it on his knees for me. I let his blue eyes and wicked tongue cloud my intuition and now we're both in more danger than we can understand. He's not who he says he is but then again, neither am I.

Lust is the crossroads between human nature and animalistic instincts. Where purity and good intentions fall to barbaric urges. Or in our case? Life and death.

———

Follow Nicole for the latest updates!

ABOUT SHANNA SWENSON

Shanna Swenson is a cardiac sonographer by day and a weaver of various fictional tales by night.

She's been an avid reader all her life and began writing at the age of fourteen. She finally published her first novel, *Abundance*, after it sat patiently on her laptop for well over fifteen years and she hasn't stopped writing since.

Shanna fits her zodiac sign of Cancer with a capital C and enjoys life's simplest things—sunsets, rain, and coffee—to name a few.

When Shanna's not supporting her fellow indies with her face buried in a book or writing her next novel/novella, she enjoys action and horror movies, pro football, hiking, working out, and traveling with her own "knight in shining armor".

You can find her on the following social media platforms.

Her website is www.shannaswenson.com

facebook.com/shannaswen
twitter.com/shanna_swenson
instagram.com/shannaswen_author
goodreads.com/Shannaswen
amazon.com/author/shannaswenson
pinterest.com/shannaswen
bookbub.com/profile/shanna-swenson

Until Kingston

(Coming 2021)

~Sin and Secrets Collection~

RISE

Marked by Sin

LEARN MORE AT WWW.SHANNASWENSON.COM

www.ingramcontent.com/pod-product-compliance
Lightning Source LLC
Chambersburg PA
CBHW031247170626
46807CB00001B/19